THE
MOMENTS

Natalie Winter

ORION

An Orion paperback

First published in Great Britain in 2019 by Orion Fiction,
This paperback edition published in 2020 by Orion Fiction,
an imprint of The Orion Publishing Group Ltd
Carmelite House, 50 Victoria Embankment
London EC4Y 0DZ

An Hachette UK Company

1 3 5 7 9 10 8 6 4 2

A CIP catalogue record for this book
is available from the British Library.

ISBN 978 1 4091 8487 4

Typeset by Deltatype Ltd, Birkenhead, Merseyside

Printed in Great Britain by Clays Ltd, Elcograf S.p.A.

www.orionbooks.co.uk

For Stephanie –
my twin sister, my best friend, my everything.

There was no past, no future; merely
the moment in its ring of light.

The Waves, Virginia Woolf

Part One

Part One

I

'You're looking at me funny,' Grace accuses, her eyes narrowing.

'What? No I'm not,' Luke protests.

'Yes you are,' she insists.

'I'm just ... amazed. That a body can even ... *do* that.'

'Luke, I told you to stay near my head!'

'But I wanted to see him come out.'

'So our sex life is out the window just so you could see your son crown?'

'Shut up. I'd jump on you right now if Matthew wasn't watching.'

Grace smiles, then glances over at the crib by the side of her hospital bed. 'Do you think he is watching us? Do you think he knows who we are?'

'Of course he does. He knows our voices – we've been talking to him non-stop for the past nine months.'

'Our son,' Grace whispers, watching the faint rise and fall of his chest, thinking how something so everyday could suddenly seem so miraculous – that he was finally here, in the world, breathing all by himself.

'Our son,' Luke echoes in wonder, swallowing hard against the lump in his throat.

'I didn't know it would feel like this,' Grace says. 'I didn't think I would love him so much already.'

'I know.'

They squeeze hands, still watching Matthew, his own tiny fists unfurling like buds.

'You're going to grow up to be someone special,' Luke tells him. 'You're going to lead an extraordinary life.'

'Don't start with the parental expectations already,' Grace says.

'He will, though. I can tell. He's going to take after his old man.'

'God, I hope not.'

There's a noise outside in the corridor and they suddenly remember that the whole world hasn't stilled around them, that there are other people here in this building, whose lives have irrevocably changed just like theirs.

Matthew stirs and gives a wide yawn.

'We made him,' Grace marvels softly, running the back of her finger over his plump cheek.

'Our little miracle,' Luke says, leaning down to place a kiss on his forehead. 'We waited so long for you. You have no idea. But you were worth it.'

Grace smiles, blinking quickly. 'Yes you were.'

'We don't have a clue what we're doing,' Luke tells him. 'But we're going to do our best – I promise you.'

They fall silent for a moment, each of them caught up in their own internal vows as they gaze rapturously down at their son.

Then Grace's smile falters. 'I'm scared, Luke,' she says quietly. 'Aren't you?'

He nods, his eyes still fastened on Matthew. 'Terrified.'

2

'I don't like it,' Daphne declares.

'Why not?'

'She doesn't look like a Myrtle.'

'What does she look like then?' Elliott asks.

'I don't know, but certainly not a Myrtle.'

'We've already talked about this,' he reminds her. 'You already said yes.'

'But that was before I'd even seen her,' Daphne protests.

'Daph, it would mean a lot to me ...'

She lets out an exasperated sigh, her auburn fringe briefly lifting and then falling again. 'Why would you even want to call your baby daughter after your dead grandmother? And it's not like it can be shortened into anything. Myr? No. I'm telling you, our daughter is going to get bullied, all because you got sentimental.'

'As my mother always says, it's not the name that makes a person, it's the person that makes the name.'

'A woman called Enid *would* say that.'

'Anyway, she'll be grateful one day that she's not like everyone else.'

'You're not giving her much choice, are you?'

'Please, Daph.'

Silence.

'Daffy ...'

She sighs again. 'Fine. But you're paying for her counselling sessions when she's older.'

'Deal.' Elliott looks at her, chuckling.

'What?'

His grin widens.

'What?'

'You swore. A *lot*.'

'Did I?' Daphne frowns. 'It's all a bit of a blur now.'

'It was kind of sexy.'

She rolls her eyes. 'Can we change the subject, please?'

'Of course. Sorry, sweetheart.'

They stare down at Myrtle, swaddled tightly in a blanket. Her eyelids flutter, as if she can feel the weight of their gaze. An arm works its way free from the cocoon, a tiny fist raised in the air.

'I just hope she doesn't get my red hair or your big chin,' Daphne says. 'Or your ears, for that matter.'

Elliott shakes his head. 'She'll be just how she's meant to be. She'll be perfect.' He offers Myrtle a finger, which she grips onto tightly. 'I've never seen anyone more beautiful than you,' he whispers to her. He feels Daphne's eyes on him. 'Which is saying something, when your mother is such a knockout.'

'Nice recovery.'

He tips his head, then reaches for Daphne's hand. She inhales shakily.

'You OK?' he asks.

She shakes her head. 'I don't feel ready, Elliott.'

He squeezes her hand. 'I know. But I'm not sure you ever can.'

He glances back down at Myrtle, whose blue eyes are now open. He gently scoops her up, resting her in the crook of his arm, unsure how best to hold her. He walks carefully over to the window, the illuminated buildings below them winking in the early evening gloom. He stoops to place a

6

kiss on her downy head, breathing in the scent of her for a moment, before turning her to face the window.

'Welcome to the world, baby girl. Are you ready for it?'

3

There's something disgusting in the toilet. It's dark red, almost brown, and lumpy, like cold porridge that no one wants to eat.

Did something fall in the toilet and die? Matthew wonders.

'Dad!' he calls.

A moment later Luke pokes his head around the bathroom door. 'What's up? You want me to lift you onto the seat?'

Matthew shakes his head. 'I think something fell in the toilet and died.' He points a finger at the avocado ceramic bowl to emphasise his point.

Luke is there in one stride, flushing the handle without even glancing at it.

'What was it?' Matthew asks, but his father is already walking back down the landing.

When Matthew has done his business, he steps up onto his plastic stool so he can reach the basin and washes his hands for thirty seconds, like they taught him at nursery. Then he walks back out onto the landing and hovers outside his parents' door.

He can hear his mother crying, and his father murmuring softly to her. Only snatches come to him through the panelled wood: 'We can try again ... Don't give up just yet ... At least we have Matthew ...'

4

'I want to see him one last time.'

'Don't be absurd, Daphne,' Winnie says sharply.

'I need to be sure before we burn him.'

'Oh good grief! Why do you always have to make things about you?' Winnie exclaims, before turning away from them, her shiny court shoes echoing smartly off the stone floor.

'We can take you to see him,' the undertaker says kindly in a hushed tone once Winnie has left.

Minutes later, Daphne, Elliott and Myrtle are peering in at the casket before it is closed for the final time. Myrtle stares at his body for a long moment. Her main memory of her grandfather is him sitting in his armchair, cracking the shells of walnuts and almonds with the nutcracker he always seemed to keep in his cardigan pocket, each one sounding like a little gunshot. He'd munch down noisily on it, reach for the nutcracker once more, and then there'd come the sharp *crack!* again.

'He looks funny,' Myrtle says. She'd expected him to look like he was sleeping. But he doesn't. He looks empty, somehow.

'He's dead,' Daphne says in a strange voice, leaning in too close to him.

'Why did they put him in a short-sleeved shirt?' Myrtle asks.

'Because it's his favourite one,' her mother replies.

'But it's January. Won't he be cold? Shouldn't he be wearing his cardigan?' Myrtle says, eyeing it hanging off her mother's slender frame.

In the ten days since he died, Daphne hasn't taken it off, webby tissues stuffed in the pockets, her eyelids pink and shiny from where she's been rubbing the cuffs against them.

'It won't be cold where he's going,' Elliott remarks quietly.

Daphne turns to glare at him.

He puts his palm up. 'I meant because we're cremating him, not because he's going to hell.' Then he places his hand on her shoulder, but she shrugs it off. 'Come on, you know I loved your dad, Daph.'

While her parents are talking, Myrtle slowly reaches out and presses her fingers against her grandfather's wiry-haired forearm, half expecting his grey eyes to snap open. His skin feels cold and spongy. She snatches her hand away, rubbing her fingers against the coarse material of her pinafore dress.

Where are you? she thinks. *If your body's still here, where has the rest of you gone?*

'I'm done,' Daphne suddenly announces, turning away from the coffin before walking stiffly in front of them as they go in to join the other mourners.

Myrtle reaches for her father's hand as they take their seats in the front row.

'Happy now?' Winnie hisses to Daphne from beside them. 'And for that to be your last memory of your father ...' She tuts. 'And why on earth are you still wearing his old moth-eaten cardigan? Wouldn't a suit jacket have been more fitting for his funeral?'

Daphne ignores her, pulling the cardigan snugly around her, the nutcracker clenched tightly in her hand.

5

'I'll get it!' Matthew yells, haring down the stairs as the door-bell rings for a second time, taking the last four steps in one gallant bound.

He swings open the front door to see two tall men in dark uniform standing there. They look down at him, unsmiling, and he instantly thinks of the Yorkie bar Joseph dared him to steal from Woolies the day before. He swallows loudly, as if a lump of it is still wedged there.

'Is your mum in?' one of them asks, and Matthew can't be sure which one has spoken, both their faces grimly set like ventriloquist dummies.

He goes to shake his head, but then he hears Grace's slip-pered footsteps coming up behind him.

'Can I help you?' she asks, her voice sounding strangely muted in the too-small hall.

'Mrs Ellis?'

She nods, her dark eyebrows drawing together.

'Can we come inside for a moment?'

It feels like he has been sitting in this waiting room for days. People have come and gone, but Matthew's the only one left now. He has read every magazine and leaflet there is. His stomach gives a low grumble to remind him that he hasn't eaten since the day before. But he isn't even hungry. The knot in his stomach is twisted too tight. He kicks his heels against the metal chair legs as he continues to wait.

Finally, the door opens. He can hear the sound of his mother crying from inside the hospital room.

His uncle Xander comes over to him and puts a heavy hand on his shoulder.

'Is Dad OK?' Matthew asks. 'Can I go in and see him now?'

Xander opens his mouth to say something, and Matthew waits, bracing himself. But there is only a long, long silence.

6

'Your room is bigger than my parents' bedroom,' Myrtle says, looking around her in awe at the lacy canopy over the bed, the bookshelves filled with expensive-looking china dolls, the dressing-up box bulging with nicer clothes than Myrtle owns, and the mirrored dressing table with its own velvet cushioned seat beneath it.

'My parents made Geoffrey swap rooms with me,' Nina says. 'He still hasn't forgiven them.'

'It's amazing,' Myrtle breathes enviously, thinking of her sparse box room at home.

'It's OK, I suppose,' says Nina indifferently. 'You can stay over whenever you want,' she adds, equally offhand.

Myrtle nods, a little too enthusiastically.

'We can pretend that we're sisters,' Nina says.

'I've always wanted a sister,' Myrtle admits.

'Me too.' Nina looks at her thoughtfully for a moment and then smiles. 'I've had an idea.'

'Everyone, this is Myrtle.'

Four pairs of eyes swivel to look at her.

'Hello,' she murmurs, hovering at the threshold to the dining room like a pinned specimen.

'Myrtle, come in, come in,' says Nina's mother, beckoning her over, making no comment on the fact that Myrtle and

Nina are both wearing floor-length dresses, long lace gloves, pearls around their necks and bright red lipstick. 'Here,' she says, patting the wooden chair next to her, then places a plate heaped with spaghetti bolognaise in front of Myrtle.

'Thank you,' Myrtle says, carefully twirling a strand around her fork, trying not to splatter the satin dress.

'I'm feeling underdressed,' Nina's father remarks, smoothing down the front of his paint-spattered overalls.

'What's new?' Nina's mother responds.

'So you're the girl that kicked that lardy arse bully in the nuts?' one of Nina's brothers asks, referring to Simon, a boy two years above them, who kept picking on Nina.

'Geoffrey!' their mother scolds, as Myrtle gives a hesitant nod.

The other brother, Henry, laughs, then shoots Myrtle a quick smile, and she feels a strange fluttering in the base of her stomach.

'Ignore them, they're morons,' Nina says, beaming up at her brothers.

'Like father, like son,' Geoffrey replies.

Their father gives a deep belly laugh, smiling cheerfully.

Myrtle watches Nina and her family over dinner, seeing the easy way they have together, the way they affectionately tease each other, and she feels a tug of envy.

'Good night?' Elliott asks when he picks her up later that evening. He's playing Bruce Springsteen at full volume, the windows rolled down, a cigarette dangling from one hand. He only ever smokes in the car, and only ever when Daphne's not around.

Myrtle nods, staring dolefully down at her faded dungarees she's changed back into. As they near their street, she asks, 'Why don't I have any brothers or sisters?'

Her father hesitates, his eyes trained firmly on the road as he crushes his cigarette butt in the car ashtray. 'Your mother always said you were more than enough.'

'Oh,' Myrtle replies. Yet she can't be entirely sure whether that's a good thing or not.

7

'Fuck it!' Grace yells when the smoke alarm goes off and she pulls open the oven door to see the potatoes have charred on one side.

She never used to swear before like she does now, or fly off the handle over the smallest thing. She's become unrecognisable in her own way too, Matthew thinks.

'Mum, just leave it,' he says, wondering why she is going to all this trouble to make a Christmas dinner no one is really hungry for, especially when it's just the three of them. 'Why don't we have sandwiches or something easy instead?'

She turns to him, tears in her eyes, and Matthew hopes it's from the acrid smoke that she's batting at with a tea towel. 'Because it's Christmas,' she tells him.

Except it doesn't feel like Christmas, with the half-decorated tree no one has bothered to finish, the limp stockings hanging off the mantlepiece that Grace hasn't had time to fill, and the caved-in Christmas cake that accidentally got knocked on the floor by Luke.

Matthew shrugs. 'It's just another day.'

Grace shakes her head, now dabbing at her eyes with the tea towel. 'No, it's not. Every other day is just another day, but this is *Christmas* Day.'

He swallows a sigh. There is no reasoning with her when she gets like this. 'Then we'll just cut the burnt bits off and Jasper will eat them.'

Jasper lifts his head at the mention of his name. He sniffs the air and then lays his chin back on the floor, unimpressed.

Grace finishes dishing up their plates as they get seated. She smiles brightly at them and Matthew musters a smile in return.

There's a loud bang as Luke slaps the flat of his palm against the tabletop, making both Grace and Matthew jolt in their seats. The whole table shudders from the force of it, the plates rattling in their places.

'Don't do that,' Grace tells Luke gently.

Another thump.

'That's enough now,' she says, less gently this time.

And another.

She puts a hand out and places it on his arm. 'Please, Luke,' she urges quietly, her hand moving down to cover his. But then the banging begins again and Grace snatches her hand away. 'Why are you being like this?' she whispers, her voice thick with tears. She looks across at Matthew, imploring him to intervene.

'Dad, don't do that,' he says, reaching out with his own hand. And for some reason, this stills him.

Luke looks at him, and Matthew forces himself to look back. Even though it has been months now since they came home from the hospital, months of rehabilitation, months of comforting his mother, these moments are no less unreal. As Matthew's eyes wander over the hunched figure in the wheelchair, the pale, bloated face, the twisted hands, the unfocused eyes, a part of him still refuses to believe that it's his father in there, gazing back out at him.

Matthew picks up his fork and spears a roast potato.

'Crackers first,' Grace insists, holding out hers to pull.

Matthew grabs it and gives it a sharp yank, Luke laughing at the exploding *crack!* Then she does the same with his.

'Meh!' Luke orders, manhandling his own in excitement.

Matthew grips the other end and pulls, reaching across to

put the paper crown on Luke's head as he fingers the cheap plastic toy.

'OK, now we can eat,' Grace says, taking it in turns to feed Luke a forkful before she quickly swallows some of her own, pausing to wipe the corners of Luke's mouth with a napkin, where masticated food always seems to collect.

Matthew looks away as he concentrates on his own plate, trying not to think about how different last Christmas was, with Xander and Luke's parents there, Luke spinning a laughing Grace around the kitchen to Christmas music, everyone staying up late to play charades and board games. Trying not to think how there'll never be another Christmas like that again. He mechanically shovels in each forkful until his plate is clear, swallowing hard against the lump in his throat, the meal sitting heavy in his stomach.

An hour later, Luke is asleep, slumped in his wheelchair by the fire, Jasper curled up on his lap. Matthew glances over at Grace, who is sipping from a sherry glass that she keeps topping up.

'OK?' she asks.

He nods. He's become a master at lying without even uttering a single word.

'I'm sorry that today wasn't—'

'Mum, it was fine,' he cuts in.

She smiles at him, a wistful look on her face. 'You probably don't remember, but when you were younger, we used to leave out a mince pie for Father Christmas and a carrot for the reindeer. And your father would nibble them both, and you'd be beside yourself when you saw that half-eaten carrot the next morning.'

Matthew smiles, remembering. When Grace has finished telling him another anecdote from his childhood, he says to her: 'Tell me again about how you and Dad met,' even though he's heard it countless times before.

Grace sits up a little straighter, refolding her legs on the worn sofa. 'Well, I was running for my bus after work and I just missed it. And your dad saw me and offered to give me a lift home. I obviously said no, that I wasn't the type of girl who'd just get into a stranger's car. The next day he was there, at the bus stop, waiting for me, a bunch of flowers in his hands. He told me his name and asked for mine. And when I told him, he smiled and said, "That means we're not strangers anymore. So how about that lift?" And I replied ...'

Matthew watches his mother as she talks. Sometimes he gets her to retell these stories for her sake, to see her laugh and smile like she used to. But mainly he asks her to repeat them for his own sake, questioning her about what Luke said and did, until these vanished moments begin to feel so real, it's almost like he was there too. Because even if his father can no longer remember them, it somehow seems important that Matthew remembers them for him.

8

Myrtle presses her ear up to the closed sitting-room door, holding her breath. Nancy is sitting by her feet, blinking up at her, her tail twitching in anticipation of a walk.

'I wasn't looking for anything … It took me by surprise … It just happened,' Daphne is saying.

'It just happened,' Elliott echoes flatly.

'I'm sorry. But I'm not happy anymore.'

'You're still grieving for your dad, Daph.'

'Don't bring him into this! It has nothing to do with him. I've been unhappy for a long time.'

'Well, I'm not. You make me happy. I've tried to make you happy too, haven't I?'

'Yes. You have. But this isn't the life I pictured, Elliott. You and me, we got married because we had to. If it hadn't been for Myrtle, who knows if we'd still be together now.'

'Don't say that.'

'It's true.'

'She's the best thing that ever happened to us.'

'She was an accident. We were like horny teenagers who didn't know any better. We weren't ready to be parents.'

'Jesus Christ, Daph.'

'Look, this isn't about Myrtle. This is about us.'

'No. It's about *him*.'

Myrtle can hear her father pacing around the room, the floorboards creaking beneath his heavy footsteps.

'So, does he make you happy?' he asks.

Daphne doesn't answer.

'Do you love him?'

Still no answer.

'Forget it, I don't want to know,' Elliott says gruffly. 'But answer me this: did you ever really love me, Daffy?'

'Yes. Of course I did.'

'Just not enough.'

'Elliott, please ...'

'There's nothing I can say to change your mind, is there?'

A pause, and then, softly: 'No.'

There's the longest silence, broken only by the sound of Elliott clearing his throat. 'So what now?' he asks, in a voice that doesn't sound like his own.

When Daphne doesn't answer, he continues: 'I guess it will be me that has to find somewhere else to live, won't it? Or do you intend to move in with lover boy?'

'Elliott, please don't make this harder than it already is ...'

'Forgive me,' he says, with a bitter laugh. 'So who gets Nancy?'

Myrtle crouches down to stroke her as Nancy presses herself closer, as if she senses what is happening.

'Elliott, come on ... This is her home,' Daphne says. 'It's better for her to stay here with us.'

Us. It would be just the two of them now, Myrtle realises with a sickening jolt.

She waits breathlessly for her father to ask about who gets her. But the question remains unuttered.

9

'Your dad's a retard,' Brendan sneers as he walks past their table. 'Urghhhhh,' he groans, his face contorted in what – even Matthew has to admit – is a pretty uncanny impersonation of Luke.

The group of boys Brendan's with give an appreciative laugh. Joseph is among them, and although he doesn't laugh, he doesn't say anything either.

You're the retard, Brendan, Matthew wants to reply, but as always, he doesn't react, he just keeps his head bent low, eyes focused on unwrapping his sandwich, as if there's never been a more important task.

Tim and James don't say anything either, they just glance across at Matthew and then quickly away again. He wishes that once, just once, they would say something. That they'd stand up for him, like they always do for each other.

He watches them as he eats his lunch. They're mirror-image twins, the reflection of each other, and even though you can tell the difference between them when you know them, they are still alike enough that they can fool most of the teachers, sitting in each other's places and protesting, 'But I'm *James*, not Tim.'

'Want to play tennis with us later?' Tim asks, once Brendan and the others have moved on to find someone else to torment.

Matthew shakes his head. He always ends up being ball

boy, while the two of them, fiercely competitive, go from playing best of three, to best of five, to best of seven, until the sun goes down and they all have to race home in time for dinner.

Instead, he takes the long route back after school, via the woods, and sits down on a fallen tree for a while, not wanting to go home yet. He watches a squirrel burying acorns, wondering how it remembers where it's planted them all. When he gets up to leave, brushing the damp seat of his school trousers, he glances across and sees a male stag standing just metres from him. Matthew freezes. They both stand there, motionless, staring back at each other. Minutes go by and neither of them moves, but it feels to Matthew that a look of understanding passes between them.

Then a bird takes flight, startling them both, and the stag leaps away, instantly swallowed up by the dense greenery, while Matthew still stands there, staring at the spot it had been just a moment before, wondering if perhaps he'd imagined it.

When he gets back home, Grace and Luke are upstairs in the bathroom.

'Mum!' Matthew calls, opening the door. 'I saw a—'

'Uhhh,' Luke moans, slapping at the water with his open palms as Grace blinks against the spray.

'What is it?' his mother asks, not even glancing at him as she sponges Luke down.

But suddenly he can't find the words, hovering there uselessly in the doorway. He watches Luke, trying to remember him as he used to be: strong enough to lift Matthew onto his shoulders; knowing the answer to every question Matthew could think of; able to make Grace laugh with just a look.

Finally his mother turns to him. 'Shut the door, would you?' she says impatiently, as if Matthew's seen something he shouldn't.

10

'Are you sure this is the right one?'

Myrtle glances out of the passenger window and up at Nina's semi-detached house. She nods, her heart beating fast.

'All right, then,' Elliott says, turning the ignition off and extracting the envelope from Myrtle's damp fingers.

'Make sure no one sees you,' she tells him, sliding lower in her seat.

'I'll do my best,' he says, noiselessly shutting the driver's door and then edging slowly up the front path, his back pressed up against the hedge.

A moment later, the envelope is being pushed through the letterbox, and then Elliott stealthily rushes back down the path, pausing at the end to look both ways, before ducking into the car.

Myrtle glances up and feels sure she sees a curtain twitching in one of the upstairs windows.

Elliott starts up the engine. 'I could get into serious trouble for this,' he says, scanning the rearview mirror as they pull away. 'A forty-year-old man delivering a Valentine's card to a teenage boy ...' He shakes his head.

Myrtle looks up at him, smiling. 'Thanks, Dad.'

'So which of Nina's brothers is the lucky guy?'

She dips her head, blushing, too embarrassed to say Henry's name.

'What's so special about him then, eh?' Elliott presses.

She hesitates. 'He has a nice smile.' And laugh. And she liked his curly brown hair and green eyes, and how he never made fun of her like Geoff did.

'And does he know how special you are?'

Myrtle shrugs, playing with a strand of her red hair, thinking, *There's nothing special about me.*

When Elliott pulls up outside her house, he leaves the engine idling and leans forward to get something out of the glove box. 'Maybe you could do a favour for me in return,' he says, not quite meeting her eye as he holds out an envelope.

She nods as she takes it.

'I haven't missed one in fourteen years. It somehow seems wrong to stop now,' he says quietly, his gaze fixed straight ahead, both of them watching the winged insects dancing in the beams of the headlights.

When Myrtle walks through the front door, she can see her mother seated at the kitchen table. In front of her lies an opened envelope, but as Myrtle steps closer, Daphne quickly slips the card into the pocket of her cardigan.

'This is from Dad,' Myrtle says, holding out the envelope.

Daphne wordlessly places it on the tabletop without so much as a glance at it.

When Myrtle comes down for dinner an hour later, it is still lying there unopened, a damp tea-ring stain on the front, her father's inky handwriting bleeding into obscurity.

I I

They're waiting for the bus in the rain. It's fifteen minutes late but no one has put up their hood or an umbrella, because everyone knows only the boffs do that.

When it finally arrives, they all pile on, coats steaming in the heat from the bus and too many bodies crammed together. The windows quickly fog up, until it feels like they're travelling in their own rain cloud.

The seats on the bus are like a hierarchy in social standing: the boffs at the front, the popular kids at the back. Matthew always sits right in the middle.

'Your hair's gone like a 'fro, you gaylord,' Brendan hisses in his ear as he takes the seat behind him, even though he normally sits further back. 'Spastic,' he adds, for good measure.

Matthew ignores him, but seconds later, he can feel something being shoved into his curls. He reaches up to pull it out as the others snigger, but Brendan says, 'Don't you touch my fucking pen.' Matthew's hand falls back onto his lap.

Other bits of stationery then follow: a paperclip, a compass, even a protractor. By now, the entire bus is watching and laughing, except for Tim and James, who are staring down into their own laps.

'It's like a fucking bird's nest,' Brendan says loudly, triggering more sniggers.

Matthew ignores them, blinking hard, his throat tight, his hands curled into fists by his side.

When the bus finally pulls up at the village green, everyone disembarks, jostling each other to be the first ones out. Matthew hangs back until last, but Brendan is waiting for him when he steps off.

'You can look after that stuff until tomorrow for me. My pencil case is busted.'

Matthew walks off in the opposite direction, the laughter still ringing in his ears. As soon as he's rounded the corner, he angrily tugs the stationery out of his curls. Part of him wants to toss them on the floor and stamp on them, but he knows he'll pay for it later, so instead he shoves them in his damp pocket.

'What's wrong with using an umbrella, may I ask?' Grace says when he steps through the door, dripping wet.

Matthew doesn't bother to reply, instead heading straight upstairs and locking himself in the bathroom.

'Oh, *Matthew*,' his mother whispers when he comes down for dinner, a hand fluttering up to her open mouth. 'What have you *done*?'

He shrugs in faux nonchalance. 'Just fancied a change.'

Luke lumbers up to him, rubbing a hand over Matthew's freshly shaved head, stroking him like he does Jasper. Then he begins to laugh.

'Why?' Grace says, tears rising to her eyes. 'Are you trying to get my attention because you feel like I don't give you enough? Is that what this is?'

'No, Mum.'

'Then why would you do such a thing?'

'Just because,' he replies, sitting down as Grace begins to dish up toad in the hole and mash. He didn't feel like confiding in her about Brendan. She had enough to worry about, anyway.

Luke sits down next to him, hypnotically circling the top of Matthew's naked head with the palm of his hand, as if he's a good luck charm.

12

They'd spent the whole morning outside, watching pond skaters and stick insects and tadpoles, and then in the afternoon they made plaster of Paris moulds of different flowers they'd picked. The other girls complained about how boring it was being at Cuffley Hall for the week, but Myrtle didn't. It was a million times better than being in school. Or at home.

Now the other girls from their class are huddled at the far end of the dorm room in their pyjamas, grouped in a circle on the carpet, messing about with a homemade Ouija board.

'They shouldn't be doing that,' Nina whispers to Myrtle, from across the top of the opposite bunk. 'Geoff did it with a bunch of his friends once and one of them got possessed for a whole minute and told Geoff he was going to die while he was still a virgin. Then the glass shattered against the wall!'

Myrtle sucks in her breath.

'Geoff had to sleep in with my mum for a week after that, while Dad slept in his room. And he still goes to bed with the Bible under his mattress.'

Myrtle presses her lips together, trying not to smile as she imagines large, loud, confident Geoffrey afraid of anything.

'Do you believe in ghosts?' she asks.

'I don't know. Maybe,' Nina says. 'My mum believes my dead gran still leaves her little signs, like helping her find things that she's lost around the house.'

'Really?'

Nina nods. 'I'd only want to meet one if they were a nice ghost, though.'

'Definitely.' Myrtle lowers her voice, even though the other girls never pay any attention to them anyway. 'Maybe we should make a pact. That whoever dies first, the other one will come back to let them know what the afterlife is really like. Deal?' She reaches out her hand across the bunk.

Nina hesitates, a wary look crossing her face.

'Come on,' Myrtle says.

'OK, deal,' Nina says eventually, reluctantly shaking Myrtle's hand.

Myrtle smiles.

'I wish I was at home,' Nina says in a small voice.

'It's only four nights.'

'I miss my own bed, though. And I miss my mum's cooking. I even miss Geoff and Henry.' Nina sniffs.

Myrtle's heart gives a strange lurch at the mention of Henry's name. He's never mentioned the Valentine's card, even though she feels sure he knows it was her. But sometimes, when she's round at Nina's, she can feel the weight of his gaze across the dinner table, lingering longer than it normally would.

'Don't you miss home?' Nina asks.

Myrtle doesn't answer. She doesn't want to say that she's glad to be away. That she's sick of Daphne's constant scolding and her father's long face whenever he comes to pick her up at the weekend. She doesn't say that she wishes she could stay right here, in this moment, forever, and never have to go back home.

Nina reaches across the gap between the bunk beds to clasp Myrtle's hand in silent understanding.

'L-U-C,' the other girls are reading out breathlessly as the plastic beaker jerks across the worn carpet, 'I-F-E-R-I-S-W-A-T-C-H-I-N-G-Y-O-U—'

'Argh!' they scream, breaking the circle and clambering into their beds, tightly gripping the edges of their sun-faded duvets to their chins.

'Told you,' Nina silently mouths to Myrtle.

That night, under the blazing bedroom lights that no one is brave enough to turn off, Nina and Myrtle are the only ones to fall asleep.

13

'Jesus, you look like a cancer patient,' his grandfather Aidan says by way of greeting. He shakes his head at Matthew, his own snowy curls bouncing. 'I don't see why anyone would want to see the shape of their own skull. You better hope it grows back quickly – you'll never get a girl, looking like that. Not a nice one, anyway.'

Matthew says nothing. He sits hunched over in the armchair, doing his homework, pausing to ask the occasional question he doesn't know the answer to, except his grandfather doesn't seem to know much either, especially for someone who's lived as long as he has.

'Why does anyone need to know the speed of light?' Aidan queries. 'And who cares how many decimals Pi has? Schools today.' He tuts. 'It seems like all they're preparing you for in life is being able to answer a handful of trivia questions at a pub quiz.' He cracks open a can of Guinness. 'I need it, for my iron,' he insists, which is what he always says.

Luke is sitting beside his father on the sofa, Jasper curled up on the other side of him. Jasper always seems to sense the moments that Luke is most uneasy, and he'll instinctively press his warm body next to Luke's.

Matthew watches them from beneath lowered lashes. Luke is grasping his father's hand, tracing his palm with a finger, as if he is reading something only he can see. Aidan just sits there, not saying anything, an unreadable expression on his face.

Since the accident, his grandparents have been visiting more, making the long journey down every other month, and then looking relieved to escape until the next time.

Xander walks into the room, whistling to himself. He squats down to raid the drinks cabinet, before emerging gripping a bottle of Irish whiskey.

'Fancy a wee dram?' he asks his father, already filling two tumblers.

'Not as good as Scotch,' Aidan grumbles, but takes the glass anyway. And he gives a stiff nod of his head every time Xander offers to top him up.

Forty minutes later and three-quarters of the bottle in, Xander has a loose grin on his face, while Aidan is looking more and more morose. Luke is now sitting on the floor with Jasper on his lap, watching them.

Matthew can't help but wonder if, somewhere in that damaged brain of his, his father can dimly recall how things used to be. How he used to be. Or did he only ever live in the moment, the past forgotten as soon as it slipped by?

Aidan stares back at his son. 'Who are you?' he whispers so quietly, Matthew's unsure if he's heard him right. 'Who's in there?'

Luke chuckles as Jasper gives his face a lick.

'I remember that first day I saw you in the hospital, battered and bruised. I prayed so hard that you'd make it.' He shakes his head. 'But I didn't know what I was wishing for, did I?'

'Dad, don't ...' Xander says, an uneasy look on his face.

'We should have told them to turn you off,' Aidan continues, before emptying the rest of his glass. His eyes are red and watery, but they remain fixed on Luke.

'All right, Dad, enough of that,' Xander says more firmly. He posits the rest of the whiskey out of sight behind his chair.

'It's true. Everyone's thinking it, even if no one will say it.'

'I don't think it,' Matthew says fiercely, even though he doesn't know exactly what he thinks.

Luke's eyes travel between the three of them, and Matthew feels sure he's following everything, even though his expression is as blank and inscrutable as ever.

'Then you're a fool,' Aidan continues. 'That's not my son. And that's not your father.' He pulls a crumpled handkerchief out of his pocket and gives his nose a vicious blow.

Grace and Pru walk into the room then, and Aidan's eyes slide away, gazing out the window. Grace catches sight of the near-empty whiskey bottle behind Xander's chair. Matthew knows that she'd bought it for Luke long before the accident, and that he'd been saving it for a special occasion because he knew how expensive it was.

She glares at Xander, who won't meet her eye. 'Why don't you raid his wardrobe while you're at it?' she says. 'Or what about the tool shed?'

Pru places a hand lightly on Grace's arm. 'Come on now, love. Luke wouldn't have minded.'

Matthew hates how everyone talks about his father in the past tense, as if he isn't sat there in front of them, listening to every word.

Grace goes and sits down next to Luke on the floor, putting her arm around him, but he jerks away, burying his face into Jasper's soft fur. She hugs her knees to her chest instead, her chin resting on them, her fingers tightly interlaced, gazing fiercely down at the rug.

'Lunch will be ready in a few minutes,' Pru says into the silence.

No one says anything.

At the end of the visit, when Aidan has already wandered out to the car, belting himself into the passenger seat, and Xander is hugging Luke goodbye while Luke squirms between his arms, Matthew overhears Pru and Grace talking.

'I wish we could help out more,' his grandma is saying. 'If only we weren't so far away ...'

'I know. But I appreciate you coming down all this way. And I know Luke is always glad to see you.'

Matthew wasn't so sure that was true. Luke always looked at his parents warily during each visit, as if they were nothing more than uninvited strangers who'd outstayed their welcome.

'But you're doing OK, are you?' Pru asks, her forehead crinkling.

'We're doing just fine,' Grace replies, but Matthew can hear the lie in her voice, and wonders if his grandmother can too.

'Thank you,' Pru whispers furtively, taking hold of both Grace's hands in her own and squeezing them tightly. 'Thank you for looking after our boy.'

'You don't need to thank me,' Grace says stiffly.

'Yes. Yes I do.'

14

'I've made up the bed for you in the spare room, Mum,' Daphne says.

Winnie nods stiffly. 'I won't stay for long. Just a few days or so.'

Daphne and Myrtle eye the three bulging suitcases they've just lugged in from the car.

'I thought I could help you out for a while, now that you're ... a single parent.' Winnie purses her lips together, as though she's been left with a bad taste in her mouth.

Daphne doesn't respond, just stares coolly back at her mother.

'Plus sometimes it's nice to have a little company,' Winnie concedes. 'I know it's silly, when it's been so long since your father died, but still that house feels so big and empty with just me in it.'

Daphne opens her mouth, closes it, and then opens it again. 'You can stay as long as you want to, Mum,' she says slowly, as if she's having difficulty forming the words.

Winnie gives another tight nod and then clears her throat, her bony fingers clasping the rigid handles of her handbag. 'Well, look at this – three generations of us girls all under one roof.'

No one smiles.

★

'You look very pleased with yourself,' Winnie says suspiciously a week later.

'Do I?' Daphne replies equably, humming along with the radio as she makes Myrtle's packed lunch.

'Good evening, was it?' Winnie enquires.

Daphne nods, smiling to herself. Then she starts to laugh.

'What's so funny?' Winnie asks.

'Oh, nothing, just something Patti said. You had to be there.'

'Paddy? Is he Irish?'

'Pat-ti,' Daphne enunciates slowly.

'Oh, I thought you were out on a date. I didn't realise you were just catching up with a friend.' Winnie takes a sip of her tea. 'So you're not dating a gypsy then?'

'No, mother, I'm not dating a gypsy.'

The doorbell dings.

'I'll get it,' Myrtle says, already rushing to the door, Nancy hot at her heels, yipping madly.

She comes back into the kitchen holding a bunch of flowers. Daphne's face lights up as she takes them. She plucks the envelope out and reads the card, leaning forward to inhale deeply. Then she busies herself cutting the stems and putting them in water.

'What's the occasion?' Winnie asks.

'No occasion,' Daphne murmurs, still smiling. It's beginning to unnerve Myrtle.

Winnie saunters over to the counter and picks up the card, her eyes quickly scanning the message. Then her head jerks up in surprise. 'Another woman sent you these?'

Daphne grits her teeth. 'Yes. Another woman sent me flowers.'

Winnie waits, clearly expecting Daphne to say something more, her cheeks crimsoning with each passing second. But Daphne refuses to break the stalemate, steadily holding her mother's gaze.

'So you're a lesbian now, is that it?' Winnie whispers viciously, as if the neighbours might hear.

'No, I wouldn't call myself that. I fell in love with someone. They just happen to be a woman.'

There's a stunned moment of silence. The room feels too still. Myrtle holds her breath, unsure what is happening.

'Oh, so this is *love* now, is it?' Winnie finally splutters.

'Yes. It is.'

'What about Myrtle?' Winnie says, as if Myrtle isn't standing right there in front of them.

'What about her?'

'That girl is confused enough without you adding this to the melting pot.'

Well, *that* was a kick in the teeth.

'Leave Myrtle out of this.'

'I will not. You're a mother, young lady. You have responsibilities. A duty. What kind of example is this setting her?'

Daphne steps closer, her voice dangerously low, but Myrtle can still hear every word. 'Don't you speak to me about parenting. You were hardly Mother of the Decade.'

Winnie stares at her, taken aback. 'I did the best I could. You and Sebastian weren't the easiest of children, you know.'

Daphne stands there, visibly biting her tongue.

Winnie ploughs on. 'I'm just glad your father isn't around to witness this. He'd be so ashamed of you.'

Myrtle can see something snapping in her mother's expression and she holds her breath, waiting for it.

'No, he wouldn't, Mum. He'd want me to be happy. He wouldn't want me to make the same mistake he did.'

Winnie's face reddens even more, and then she steps forward and raises a hand, only for Daphne to reach out and grip hold of it.

'I think you're forgetting whose house you're in,' she says calmly, although her eyes are blazing. 'Perhaps it's time you went back to your own one.'

Winnie's arm drops to her side and she takes a step back, rubbing at her wrist.

Just say sorry, Myrtle thinks. *One of you, just say it.*

Except they never could. It was always just a temporary ceasefire, loaded weapons still at the ready, in preparation for the next confrontation.

'I thought ... I thought my being here would be good for us,' Winnie says in a small voice. 'That we could sort some things out. Talk about things.'

'I think you've said everything you need to say.'

'Daphne ...'

She shakes her head, refusing to hear any more. 'You know, Mum, sometimes you make it very hard to love you.' And with that she turns away, heading for her music room, the flowers still scattered across the kitchen counter.

'I'm going to pack my things,' Winnie says stiffly to Myrtle, making for the stairs.

Myrtle looks at Nancy, who gazes placidly back at her. She picks up her lunch box and then reaches for the forgotten card that's lying next to the flowers.

I love you, I love you, I love you, I love you.
Did I mention that I love you?
Patti x

Myrtle reads it two more times and then crumples it in her fist.

15

Matthew gazes around his bedroom, empty except for the tower of boxes, which are packed with all his clothes, books, posters, videos and cassette tapes. The removal men have already taken the furniture and most of the boxes this morning. These are the last few that will be taken in the car with them.

From one of the boxes he picks out his old plaster cast from when he broke his wrist climbing on the science building. It's now yellowed with age and smells faintly musty, but he can't bring himself to throw it away. He fingers the straight slit down the middle where the doctor cut it off from his arm, then he reads the messages written there, his eyes seeking out his father's message, fixing on those final two words: *Love Dad*.

Matthew puts it back in its box and then walks across the room, his footsteps echoing loudly. Everything is amplified without the furniture or curtains. The whole house looks naked. Even the light seems different – brighter, more unforgiving.

He lifts up a corner of carpet and scrawls his name on the floorboard underneath, followed by the date, wondering if the room's next inhabitant will ever find it. They'd probably never even give a single thought to him, just like he'd never given a thought to the previous occupant of the room when he moved in.

The doorbell goes, and seconds later comes the double tramp of footsteps up the stairs. The door swings open and Tim and James barrel in.

'All right, Ellis?' James says.

Matthew nods.

'Well ...' Tim says.

It's the most awkward he's ever seen the pair of them.

'Thought we should come see you off.'

'Thanks.'

'Want a hand?' James says, nodding towards the boxes.

Matthew shrugs.

They wordlessly grab a box each and the three of them troop down the stairs and load them into the boot of the car.

'Thank you, boys,' Grace says, with a too-bright smile. 'I know Matthew's going to miss you a lot, but Luke and I will miss having you around the house too.'

Tim and James nod, even though they barely came round, as Matthew always suggested going to theirs instead.

'Well, you take care of yourselves, won't you? And if you ever fancy a holiday, you always have a place to stay at ours.'

'Thanks, Mrs Ellis,' they say in unison.

Luke comes over to them, Jasper following at his heels.

'Yurr,' he tells them.

They nod in unison.

'Yurr!' he says more emphatically, and Matthew can't help but notice the pair of them take a wary step back.

'OK, sweetheart, let's go back inside so Matthew can say goodbye to his friends,' Grace says quickly, leading him back into the house.

James holds out a dog-eared comic and Tim hands over a partly eaten Easter egg. 'We ran out of pocket money,' he explains sheepishly.

'Thanks,' Matthew says, putting them on the passenger seat.

'So,' James says.

'So,' Matthew echoes.

'See you around, I guess,' Tim says.

'Yeah, see you around.'

They punch each other on the arm and then James and Tim turn and walk off down the road, pausing at the end to wave back at Matthew. He toes the kerb, watching them go, blinking quickly.

Ten minutes later, after they've wandered around the house one last time, with Grace tearfully bidding goodbye to each and every room, the three of them are buckled in the car, Jasper curled up on the back seat next to Luke.

'OK,' Grace says, as she starts up the car, inhaling deeply. 'OK. This will be just what we need. A fresh start.'

Right, Matthew thinks. As if moving house, moving town, even, could change a single thing.

'We'll be closer to Grandma and Grandpa ... There'll be lots of new places to explore and people to meet ... It will be an adventure ...'

Matthew tunes her out as they drive through the village, passing the bus stop, the primary school, the church, the village shop. He only lets his gaze linger on them a moment before he looks away again. There are so many memories tangled up with this place, so much of *him* here. But while he won't forget it, he knows the village will quickly forget him.

As they drive through the outskirts, Matthew refuses to take one last look in the mirror, to see its reflection growing smaller, closing his eyes instead as the car picks up speed.

16

'There's someone I want you to meet,' Daphne says as soon as Myrtle steps through the front door after school. Her smile looks strained, as if some invisible hand is tugging at the corners of it.

'OK,' Myrtle says with a sinking feeling. She's been waiting for this moment. She supposes they all have.

She and Daphne walk into the sitting room. Seated on the armchair by the window is a woman with bobbed dark hair tucked neatly behind her ears. She's wearing bright red lipstick, and when she smiles, Myrtle notices a slight gap between her front teeth. Her fingernails are painted the exact same shade of red and on almost every finger is a chunky ring that looks like a silver Hula Hoop. Although she's wearing turned-up denim dungarees and white sneakers, and her pale complexion is mostly unlined, there is no disguising the age difference between this woman and her mother. Myrtle guesses it must be close to a decade.

'This is Patti,' Daphne says, as if she needs an introduction.

'Hello, Myrtle,' Patti says warmly, flashing her a smile.

Myrtle doesn't return it.

'Patti is going to be staying with us for a while,' Daphne says, her own smile still fixed in place.

'Why?'

'Because ... she's decided to move out of her old place and ... she needs somewhere to stay.'

'For how long?'

Neither of them answers.

'I'm going to make us all a cup of tea,' Daphne announces, even though she and Myrtle never drink it.

Patti's eyes track her as she leaves the room and then flick back to Myrtle. She offers her a sympathetic smile. 'I know how hard your parents' separation must have been on you.'

Myrtle remains silent, staring at the gap in her teeth as she talks.

'My parents split up when I was about your age, so I understand how you're feeling.'

Still she says nothing, refusing to be enlisted.

'But I want you to know that I care about your mother very much.'

Myrtle's hands curl into fists.

'So,' Patti says, leaning back in the armchair. 'Is there anything you want to ask me or would like to talk to me about?' She looks at Myrtle expectantly.

'I don't like you,' Myrtle says, surprised by her own bluntness. She hadn't meant to say it; it just slipped out.

Patti smiles again, seemingly unperturbed. 'Well, all right then. I guess that's a start.'

17

It's happened again. Matthew wakes while it's still dark to find his pyjamas damp and sticky. He pulls them off, shoving them under the mattress to deal with later, so his mum won't find them.

He hurriedly gets changed, creeps down the hall and out into the back garden, where his bike is propped in the wood shed.

By the time he gets to the village shop, Greg is already there, divvying the newspapers out between them. They share the route together, racing each other to see who will be done first, the last one back having to fork out for a sherbet Dip Dab for them both.

'All right, Ellis?' Greg says, handing him his half.

'Cheers,' Matthew says, swinging the heavy bag across his body.

'See you later, slow coach,' Greg calls, already pedalling away.

Matthew heads in the opposite direction, going to the furthest house first and working his way back to the corner shop.

Even though it's dark and cold and more often than not raining, he loves being out this time of morning. It's strangely comforting knowing everyone else is still asleep or only just waking up, and the village is his alone for just a little while.

By the time he gets back to the shop, Greg is already

there, leaning casually against the wall, a victor's grin on his face. Matthew goes into the shop and comes out with two Dip Dabs, chucking one to Greg, who catches it mid-air. He rips into it straight away.

'Better luck tomorrow,' Greg says once he's finished it, jumping back on his bike.

'Yeah, tomorrow,' Matthew echoes.

When he gets to school, he trudges down the corridor to class. Greg is already there, sitting at the back with the other popular boys, and doesn't even glance at Matthew as he takes his chair near the front. He feels a balled-up piece of paper hit him on the back. He ignores it, but then another one lands on his desk. He unfurls it, already knowing what it's going to say: *Go back to where you came from, cumstain.*

Matthew flicks it on the floor.

At lunchtime, he avoids the canteen, where Greg and the others claim the largest table at the back. Instead he heads outside, even though it's raining, and sits out on the playing field by himself, hiding out of view behind a tree, his hands so numb he can't even feel the sandwich he's biting into.

'How was your day?' Grace asks when he steps through the door.

'It was OK,' he replies, which is what he says every day.

'That's good,' she says, which is what she says every day. She stares out of the window, at the grey buildings that seem to disappear like a magic trick against the pewter sky.

Matthew studies her profile for a moment, thinking how thin she has grown since the accident. She seems so much older than the other mothers, as if she has lived more than just one life. There is a line between her eyebrows that wasn't there before. He stares at it, and it seems like all the worry and heartache of the last three years is etched in that deep groove. Then he turns to watch Luke asleep on the sofa, Jasper curled up on his lap.

'Do you want me to take Jasper for a walk? I can take Luke too?'

Grace turns to him, the line between her eyebrows deepening. 'Luke?' she queries, blinking quickly at him, as if she doesn't recognise the name. 'He's still your father, Matthew. He'll always be your father.'

'I know that,' he says quietly, shifting his weight between feet. 'I'm going upstairs to do my homework,' he tells her, catching himself too late. He keeps forgetting there is no upstairs now.

'I've always wanted to live in a bungalow,' Grace said when they first moved in. As if the reason was nothing to do with Luke and his struggle with stairs.

In his room, Matthew goes to lift the mattress to pull out the pyjamas, so he can wash them in the bath, but he sees that there is a set of clean pyjamas folded under his pillow.

That evening at dinner, his mother doesn't mention it, and so neither does he.

When it happens again a few days later, he shoves his damp pyjamas under the mattress like before, and in the evening, there they are under his pillow, clean-smelling and freshly ironed, as if by magic. It feels like a silent conversation playing out between them, saying so much more than they ever could in person.

18

'Another *woman*?' Elliott queries. 'Are you sure?' As if Myrtle might have somehow got confused.

She nods, unclipping her seatbelt, desperate to be gone from there, to not have to watch her father's face crumple like that.

'I don't know if that makes it better or worse,' he says, almost to himself. He stares up at the house in disbelief, as if it has somehow betrayed him too. 'Maybe this is just a phase. Or a rebound. Maybe your mother's confused.'

'Maybe,' Myrtle echoes. Except Daphne didn't seem confused. She seemed more alert, more energetic than Myrtle had ever seen her.

'Does she seem happy?' he asks in a voice that sounds nothing like his own.

Myrtle hesitates and then gives a treacherous nod.

Elliott shifts in his seat, his large hands gripping the steering wheel. 'Christ!' he yells, slamming his fist against it, making Myrtle jump. Then his head droops. 'I really thought she'd come around in the end,' he whispers.

Myrtle places a hand on his shoulder, not knowing what to say. They stay like that for a while, until he says, 'You best go inside now.'

She can feel him watching her walk up the path, but when Daphne opens the door and Myrtle turns to wave at him, he doesn't wave back.

48

'Nice afternoon with Dad?' Daphne asks, shutting the door behind them.

'Yeah,' Myrtle lies.

'Good. Dinner's ready. Go wash your hands.'

When Myrtle slides into her seat between her mother and Patti, she stares at the glutinous pasta on her plate, tentatively piercing a piece with her fork, only for it to disintegrate.

Her mother has always been a terrible cook. Her idea of a healthy meal is to pour tinned tomatoes on pasta, and then garnish it with vegetables that have been boiled to a mush, so that the run-off water is greener than the vegetables are. Then she puts the water in a jug in the fridge, and Myrtle has to drink it for the rest of the week with dinner.

'It's disgusting,' Myrtle always protests.

'It's good for you,' Daphne counters.

'Then why don't you drink it?'

'Because you're a growing girl.'

When Elliott used to warily suggest improvements for the next time she made a dish, Daphne would snap at him, 'Well, maybe you should do the cooking.'

But tonight, when Patti says, 'Christ, this is really awful, Daph,' her mother just laughs and says sweetly, 'Oh god, it is, isn't it?'

'One of your worst,' Patti adds, letting the pasta fall with a wet dollop back onto her plate.

'Definitely,' Daphne agrees, loading up her fork and then shoving it into Patti's laughing mouth.

Myrtle rolls her eyes, forcing down her own forkful. She takes a gulp of green-tinged water, pausing to pick out a pea bobbing on the surface.

After she's cleared the table and done the washing-up, Myrtle goes to shut the kitchen curtains. She stands at the window, half hidden by the fabric. She can see her father's car still parked outside, his hunched-over figure silhouetted by the street lamp beyond, and her heart clenches at the sight of him. She quickly draws the curtains closed before he sees her and then joins her mother and Patti in the sitting room. She sits on the carpet, spreading out her homework on the low coffee table, Nancy's warm body pressed up beside her. Sprawled out on the sofa, Daphne puts her legs across Patti's lap, and Patti begins to massage her bare feet.

It still takes Myrtle by surprise, moments like this. Her mother has never been one for public displays of affections. Yet too often Myrtle catches Daphne and Patti holding hands, or leaning into each other, or smiling that secret smile of theirs. And the truth is, she likes watching them together. Because for some inexplicable reason, it has begun to feel normal, as if Patti has always been a part of their lives, rather than for just a few weeks. But then Myrtle feels a sharp stab of guilt, thinking of her father outside, alone in the dark.

'How about we all go away this weekend?' Patti suddenly suggests. 'My parents have a cabin by the coast they hardly ever use.'

Myrtle holds her breath, waiting for her mother to say no, like she always did when Elliott suggested something different, saying that Myrtle would have homework to do, or that she had a wedding she needed to practise for.

'Sounds lovely,' Daphne says instead, her hand seeking out Patti's.

Maybe that's what love is, Myrtle thinks, watching them beneath lowered lids. *Saying yes when you'd ordinarily say no.*

19

'Jesus, this is even smaller than your last room,' Xander complains, wedging his suitcase in the tight gap at the bottom of the camp bed.

'Tell me about it,' Matthew says.

'I thought as you were moving to the middle of arse end, you'd at least get somewhere a bit bigger.'

Matthew shrugs. He knew money was tight, with Grace only being able to do a few hours' work here and there when he was at home to keep an eye on Luke.

Xander flops out on the truckle bed. 'I'm done in.' He yawns. 'The entire flight I had a screaming baby next to me, so I haven't slept in nearly two days.'

'Where is it you've been?' Matthew asks, sprawling out on his own bed.

'Samoa. Little piece of paradise down there.'

Matthew's never even heard of it, and he's too embarrassed to ask where it is.

'So why are you back here then?'

Xander links his hands behind his head. 'For some strange reason, I got this urge to come home and see my favourite nephew.'

'Your only nephew,' Matthew corrects.

'Semantics,' Xander replies. 'So, fill me in. How's life treating you?'

Matthew shrugs.

Xander gives him a knowing look. 'Yeah, that's the same reason I got the hell out of here as soon as I turned eighteen.' He lets out another yawn. 'So are my dear parents making a nuisance of themselves?'

Matthew gives another shrug. 'We see them even less now than we did before.'

'That figures. So how's school? You fitting in OK?'

Matthew makes a movement somewhere between a nod and a shake of his head.

Xander cocks an eyebrow. 'That bad?'

Matthew nods.

'Listen, if some little dipshit is being a prick, don't take it lying down. Wallop him one. That'll teach him.'

'Yeah, right.'

'I'm serious. Trust me, I'm talking from experience.'

'Really?'

'Yes. When I was your age, I used to bully this kid, then one day he had enough and he knocked me out cold. And you know what? I never did it again.'

'Why were you even picking on him to start with?'

Xander shrugs. 'He was an annoying little dicksquirt. Anyway, my point is, after that, I respected him for standing up to me. We even became quite good friends. Until I messed his sister around. But that's another story. So that's my advice to you, for what it's worth.'

'Thanks, I guess.'

'Always a pleasure, Matty boy.'

Matthew tenses at the nickname his father always used for him. He glances across at his uncle, and for a moment, it could almost be Luke lying there. He remembers his dad telling him that when they were younger, they were always mistaken for twins, even though he was two years older than Xander.

Matthew knows their uncanny resemblance often catches his mother unaware, too. Sometimes Xander will say something in a certain tone, or make some hand gesture that is so like Luke, and Grace will bite her lip, turning away to busy herself doing something.

Xander gives another loud yawn. 'Right, land of nod is a-calling.' He stumbles back up on his feet, hastily strips down to his boxers, and then climbs under the covers.

Matthew switches the light off before he undresses and puts on his pyjamas. He lies on his side, staring out the window at the crescent moon. He can hear the rustle of covers as his uncle tosses and turns.

'Fucking jetlag,' Xander murmurs.

Matthew says nothing, lost in thought about what a country like Samoa is like and whether he'll ever get to go to all the places his uncle has.

'Knob jockey.' Shove. 'Dickwad.' Another shove.

Matthew takes a breath, steeling himself, and then spins around. 'Fuck off, Wright.'

Seamus Wright's eyeballs bulge in disbelief. 'What did you just say to me, shitwank?'

By now, some of the other boys have gathered around them, sensing a fight.

'I said: fuck off.'

Seamus laughs. 'Try and make me, fucktard.'

Do it. Just do it, a little voice in his head whispers, that sounds a lot like Xander's.

Matthew swallows, then he takes a run at Seamus, curling his hand into a fist and pulling it back, before aiming right at Seamus's nose. There is a soft snap as their body parts connect, and then a bright red ribbon unspools from Seamus's left nostril.

'Fuck!' he cries, doubling over as he cups his nose.

Matthew glances around him, his fist still raised. 'Who's next?' he asks, panting heavily.

The other boys just look at him in disbelief. And something else. Something between fear and respect.

Matthew picks up his rucksack with his uninjured hand and stalks off across the playing field. Soon after, a shadow emerges beside his own, and he glances up to see Greg falling into step beside him.

'Nice one,' he murmurs, slinging an arm around Matthew's neck and pulling him in closer. 'Didn't know you had it in you.'

'No,' Matthew says, his grin so wide it actually hurts his cheeks. 'Neither did I.'

20

'So ...' Elliott says, in between a mouthful of toast. 'How's school?'

Myrtle shrugs, shovelling in the last of the soggy corn-flakes she's eating at the small table in the corner of her dad's basement studio flat.

'And your mother and ... Patti ...' He still struggles to say her name. 'How are they?'

Myrtle's shoulders sag. She hates conversations about her mother and Patti even more than she hates conversations about school. 'Fine.'

'Everything OK between them?'

'Yeah, I guess.' She looks at her father, unsure what else to say. Did he want her to tell him her mother is happier than Myrtle's ever seen her? Is she supposed to say that when her mother talks of before, she speaks as if her entire life was set on the course of one trajectory: meeting Patti? As if her entire marriage to Elliott was nothing more than a subplot, a momentary diversion?

'A whole year,' he murmurs in disbelief, almost to himself. He stares down into his open palms. 'You know, I thought perhaps it was just ... a phase that your mother was going through. That she just needed to try something ... different. And then she'd come to her senses. That all I had to do was wait. But now ...' He swallows thickly, clenching his hands. 'Now I realise that it was me who was the phase.'

'Dad ...' Myrtle says, reaching across to cover his hand with her own.

'I thought we'd grow old together,' he says in a small voice. He has that faraway look in his eyes that Myrtle has come to know so well, as if a part of him is still back there, lost for good. He takes a shaky breath.

Please don't cry, she thinks in alarm. The only time she has ever seen her father cry is when Nancy got hit by a car a few months ago and had to be put down. He didn't even cry at his mother's funeral.

Elliott clears his throat and then slaps his thighs with his fists. 'How about we get out of this dump and do something fun?' he announces with forced cheer.

'Sure,' Myrtle says doubtfully. She stands up and heads to the front door, pulling down at the cuffs of her white denim shorts where they've ridden up.

'Umm, Myrtle,' Elliott calls from behind her.

'What?' she says, turning to face him.

'I think you might have ... hmm ... leaked ...' he says awkwardly.

'What?'

'On your shorts a little bit.' He gestures towards his own crotch.

Myrtle glances down and can see a red blot spreading beneath the zip fastening. She catches Elliott glancing at the sofa, where there is a noticeable stain on the beige upholstery.

She's been waiting so long for this day, practically the last girl in her year to get it, and of course it would choose this very moment to arrive. She hurries to the bathroom, red-faced.

When she comes back out, still feeling dirty even though she's washed and changed into a clean pair of shorts, Elliott is scrubbing at the cushion, but he quickly chucks the cloth to one side when he sees her.

'Ready?' he asks casually.

Myrtle gives a tight nod, walking slowly to the door, hindered by the bunched-up toilet roll bulking out her knickers like a nappy, thinking how strange it is that the moment she supposedly becomes a woman, she suddenly feels like a little girl again.

For the rest of the day, they don't meet each other's eye.

21

It's the first school trip of the year after the summer holidays and everything feels like it's changed. Namely: the girls. They all seem to have sprouted breasts while they've been away, which in turn has changed their posture and the way they walk, as if they're trying to hide what is happening to them.

The very girls that, before, the boys had rarely paid much attention to, have suddenly become both fascinating and disturbing, like creatures from another planet. It's like a switch has been flipped inside all of them, and now the boys are watching what they say around the girls, acting differently in their presence. Even Matthew finds he can no longer be himself around them.

'Can I borrow your rubber?' Jemima Edwards asked him the other day, flicking her hair behind one shoulder.

'Uh, yeah, yeah, sure,' Matthew stammered, passing it over to her. When she smiled at him, he just stared back at her like a simpleton. He had to pull his shirt out a little bit over his belt to hide the stiffening in his crotch. He'd sat there, his stomach pressed hard against the edge of the desk for the rest of the lesson, terrified that someone would realise and laugh at him.

It had nothing to do with Jemima, particularly. It would do this, now and again. He won't even be thinking of a girl and suddenly he has a boner. It's like his brain and body are no longer connected. And his body is changing in other ways too. Hair has begun to sprout under his arms and down below – the place that he has no word for.

'Dawn let me feel her up,' Sam Johnson is claiming now, as the boys huddle around the campfire at Cuffley Hall.

'Fuck off,' the others say.

Dawn Callow is the vicar's daughter and the only girl in their year that wears her skirt below her knees and her shirt buttoned all the way to the top.

'She did,' Sam insists.

'The only action you get is from The Stranger.'

The other boys laugh, and Matthew joins in with a weak smile. He only learnt what The Stranger was a couple of weeks ago, after Greg explained it to him.

'It's when you sit on your hand until it goes numb and then jerk off.'

'Why?' Matthew had asked, confused.

Greg had rolled his eyes. 'Cos you can't feel your own hand, so it feels like someone else is doing it.'

Matthew had tried it that night, and when he closed his eyes, it almost did feel like a stranger was doing it to him. The trouble was, the girl he tried to picture was hazy and faceless, so in the end he gave up.

He tunes back into the conversation as the rest of them brag about how far they've got with other girls. He just sits there, staring into the fire, thinking about how he has never even held hands with a girl, let alone kissed someone.

'Your mum's definitely been getting some,' one of the boys remarks, and it takes Matthew a moment to realise the comment is directed at him.

He looks up. 'What's that?'

'Your mum and Mr Young.'

'Mr Young?' Matthew says, a sick feeling churning in the base of his stomach at the mention of their headmaster's name.

Sam nods. 'Yeah, I saw the two of them parked up near

the lake the other week. The windows looked all fogged up and I'm sure it wasn't the wind that was rocking it.' He waggles his eyebrows suggestively as the other boys laugh.

'Yeah, Mr Young is definitely porking your mum,' says another.

'Fuck off,' Matthew mutters, his cheeks blazing.

He chucks another branch onto the fire and watches it burn down to nothing.

22

Daphne lets out a long sigh and turns off the engine. Myrtle's glad to have a break from Classic FM. Her mother never lets her listen to the Top 40 in the car.

'Must be an accident up ahead,' Patti says, reclining her seat a little and closing her eyes. 'I hope no one's hurt.'

Myrtle stares out of her window at the lorry in the lane next to them. There are horizontal slits running across the side of it, and it takes her a while to realise that there are animals inside. She blinks, making eye contact with one of them. It seems to hold her gaze, staring plaintively out at her.

'There are pigs in the lorry next to us,' she announces.

Patti and Daphne glance over and nod.

'Probably on their way to the slaughterhouse, poor things,' Patti says.

'They're going to kill them?' Myrtle asks. The same pig is still looking at her.

'That's the idea,' Daphne replies, reclining her seat as well and settling back.

'I'm going for a wander,' Myrtle murmurs, easing her door open.

She glances left and right at the standstill traffic, and then sidles up to the truck. The pig she'd been watching pokes its snout out and Myrtle reaches up to stroke it, its breath hot on her palm.

'Hey,' she whispers, gazing up into its blue eyes. They

remind her of Nancy's. She glances behind the pig and sees there are thirty or forty bodies pressed up against each other. She peers into the gloomy depths of the lorry and catches sight of another pig on its side, panting heavily and foaming at the mouth, its eyes wide and unblinking.

'What yer doing?' says a voice from behind her.

Myrtle spins around and sees a tall man with a baseball cap glaring down at her.

'I was just ... stroking the pig.'

'Is that right?' he says, his eyes still narrowed.

'One of them has fallen over,' she tells him.

'Mmm-hmm.'

'It looks like it can't get back up.'

He shrugs, extracting a cigarette from a packet, cupping a hand around it as he lights it.

'It won't be able to get to its food and water,' Myrtle continues.

'They ain't got no food nor water,' he tells her, his words shrouded in smoke. 'No last supper for these porkers. They'd make a right mess in the lorry otherwise.'

'But won't they get thirsty and hungry?'

'Sometimes lose a few by the time you get there. Especially on a hot day like today.' Another shrug. 'Survival of the fittest.' He lets out a smoky laugh, his teeth like yellowed piano keys. 'If you can call it that.'

Myrtle glances back at the pig she'd been stroking, who is still watching her, then beyond to the prone pig on its side. Another pig is now standing on top of it and its breathing has become even more laboured.

'Looks like the traffic's finally moving now,' the driver says, nodding to the road up ahead. 'You best get back to yer car.'

Myrtle opens the door and slides into her seat as Daphne starts up the engine.

'Homeward bound,' Patti says cheerfully.

Myrtle stares at the lorry as they slowly pull away, and the same pig stares back at her.

That evening at dinner, Myrtle gazes at her plate as Patti hands it to her.

'What is it?' she asks.

'Pork chops,' Patti responds, sitting down opposite her and pouring gravy over her meal.

'I'm not hungry,' Myrtle says.

Daphne turns to her with a sharp look. 'That's a shame because Patti's made your favourite for pudding: apple crumble.'

Myrtle looks down at her plate again and swallows against the sharp taste of bile rising in her throat. 'I can't eat it.'

Daphne's expression hardens. 'Patti has spent the last hour and a half slaving away in the kitchen to make us this delicious dinner, so the least you can do is eat it.'

'I can't!'

'It's OK,' Patti says, trying to defuse the situation.

'No, it isn't,' Daphne says. 'Is this about that truck full of pigs earlier?'

Myrtle ventures a nod.

'Oh, for Christ's sake!' Daphne huffs. 'Stop being melodramatic and just eat your dinner.'

Myrtle shakes her head. She stares at the brown- and pink-tinged meat on her plate, and all she can picture is that pig staring out at her in its last moments, as if it knew what was coming.

'I won't have a fussy child, Myrtle,' Daphne continues. 'There are children starving in Africa—'

'Oh no you don't,' Patti interjects. 'You cannot use the same lines that our own parents did on us.'

'It's true, though,' Daphne protests.

'Whether Myrtle eats that piece of pork or not makes no difference to some malnourished Ethiopian.'

'Just eat your dinner up,' Daphne orders.

'No,' Myrtle says stubbornly, too afraid to meet her mother's gaze.

'Myrtle ...' Daphne says in her warning tone.

Patti places a hand on Daphne's arm. 'You're in a battle of wills with a fourteen-year-old,' she says quietly. 'It might be an idea to remember who's the grown-up here.'

'It might be an idea to remember who's the parent here,' Daphne retorts, shaking her off.

Patti stares at her, then wordlessly returns to her meal.

'Myrtle, you're excused,' Daphne tells her.

She doesn't need to be told twice.

Later that night, when Myrtle has crept downstairs to see if she can sneak some crumble without her mother noticing, she hears the pair of them talking in low voices.

'You're too hard on her,' Patti is saying. 'Adults don't like to admit it, but sometimes children see things more clearly than we do. So don't punish her for having a conscience. You should be praising her.'

'Don't tell me what to do, Patti. She's *my* daughter.'

'Exactly. As she grows up, the world will find countless ways to undermine her. But a mother never should.'

'Don't talk to me in your therapist voice. I'm not your client anymore.'

Myrtle blinks. So *that* was how they met.

There is a low murmur as Daphne says something else Myrtle can't quite hear.

'We both have difficult relationships with our own mothers,' Patti replies. 'Don't you want something more for Myrtle?'

23

'So tell me, Matthew, what's your favourite subject at school?' Mr Young fixes Matthew with the same steely look he gives most of his pupils, as if he's just daring them to step out of line.

'Don't have one,' Matthew mumbles. Why is it that adults always ask that?

'What's your favourite sport then?' Mr Young asks.

'Don't have one.'

'Matthew!' Grace says sharply. 'Don't be rude to Peter.'

Matthew pauses, thinking how surreal it is to hear his headmaster called by his Christian name – by his mother, over dinner in their poky, cluttered sitting room. 'I'm not,' Matthew says. 'I'm being honest.'

Mr Young smiles at him. 'Well, you've still got plenty of time to figure out what it is you want to do with your life.'

Matthew doesn't smile back.

'You used to talk about being a vet, didn't you?' Grace says.

He shrugs, not willing to give anything away. 'Maybe.'

'Well, you'll need to work hard and apply yourself in the sciences if you want to do that,' Mr Young says. 'It's even longer than studying to become a doctor.' He neatly rests his cutlery at the twelve o'clock position on his plate. 'That was delicious, Grace, thank you.'

His mother beams, blushing slightly. It's the first time

Matthew's seen her smile properly in a long time. He has to look away. He glances at Luke instead, who is staring intently at Mr Young. For once, he hasn't uttered a single sound throughout the entire meal. And it hasn't gone unnoticed by Grace either, who keeps shooting worried looks at him, but Luke doesn't break his gaze from where it has fastened on Mr Young.

'Well, I'll go get pudding,' Grace announces, clearing their plates and heading into the kitchen.

An uncomfortable silence descends. Mr Young coughs politely into his fist.

'My mum is still married, do you realise that?' The words tumble from Matthew's mouth before he even knows he's going to say them.

Mr Young looks at him steadily. 'Yes, I am aware of that, Matthew.'

'Good.'

'And do you realise just how incredibly lonely your mother has been?'

Matthew's hands curl into fists under the table.

'Who wants lemon meringue pie?' Grace asks, holding the dessert aloft as she comes back into the room.

'That would be lovely,' Mr Young replies, smiling up at her.

'I'm not hungry,' Matthew says, shoving his chair back. 'And I've got homework to do.'

Mr Young stands up. 'Well, it was nice talking to you, Matthew.' He holds out his hand.

Matthew can feel Grace's eyes boring into him. He reluctantly holds out his own hand.

'I look forward to seeing a lot more of you outside of school,' Mr Young says, pumping it tightly.

24

The bottle stops spinning and lands on Myrtle. Geoff lets out a low whistle as she shimmies out of her shorts. Now she is just wearing her knickers and cami top. She can feel the boys' gaze flicker towards her and then quickly away again. She averts her own eyes from their bare chests. She shifts uncomfortably, pulling at her knickers as if she can somehow stretch the thin fabric, then leans forward to spin the bottle. It lands on Henry. He laughs and pulls off a sock, twirling it in the air before flinging it at Myrtle. She tosses it to the side in disgust, even though a secret part of her feels inexplicably glad that he threw it at her and not Eleanor Chattam, the only other girl there. Eleanor is still fully dressed, except for her shoes and cardigan, which Geoff looks disappointed about, given how he keeps staring at her T-shirt – or rather, the curves beneath it. Myrtle feels like a ten-year-old boy next to her, with her long limbs and flat chest.

Myrtle isn't even supposed to be here. She'd gone to knock for Nina earlier that afternoon and found her curled up on the sofa with a bowl of ice cream, watching a Disney video.

'Don't you want to go out for a bike ride?' Myrtle had asked impatiently, the sitting room gloomy with its curtains shut against the brilliant sunshine.

Nina had just shaken her head, her eyes fixed on the TV while her mum fussed around her, bringing her more choco-late sauce to put on top.

'She's feeling a bit under the weather today,' she told Myrtle, as if she hadn't said the exact same thing a hundred times before.

As Myrtle cycled back down the road, annoyance pumping through her with each revolution, Henry passed her on his bike.

'Follow me,' he called to her, turning off sharply to the right, and Myrtle had wordlessly done just that, pedalling to keep up with him until they reached the wooded dell, where Geoff, two other boys Myrtle didn't know and Eleanor Chattam were already waiting.

It's Henry's turn to spin the bottle now, and this time it lands back on Myrtle. He cocks an eyebrow. Myrtle swallows. Her top or her knickers?

'If you're too chicken, you can forfeit and do a dare instead,' Geoff says.

'A dare?' Myrtle asks, her voice cringingly high-pitched.

He nods. 'You've got to kiss one of us.'

'Oh.' She swallows again. 'Who?' She glances at Henry and then quickly away again.

Geoff nods towards the bottle. Myrtle leans forward and spins it. It lands on Geoff. She catches a strange look cross Henry's face as Geoff gets to his feet. She reluctantly stands too, taking a few hesitant steps towards him.

'Come 'ere,' he says, pulling her away from the rest of the group and pushing her up against a tree trunk. Then he bends his head and kisses her.

Myrtle holds her breath, unsure what to do. She can feel the rough bark through her top, digging into her back. A moment later, Geoff's tongue is probing against her lips, parting them, pushing its way in and then sliding against her own. Myrtle pulls back, shocked, wiping her mouth while Geoff begins to laugh.

'Don't tell me that's your first kiss?'

Myrtle doesn't reply, wordlessly following him back to the

group, where the others wolf whistle at them. Myrtle stares hard at the ground, wishing her pale skin didn't betray her every emotion. It's only when she's sitting back down in the same spot that she glances across and sees that Henry is no longer there.

25

They huddle in the park against the late October chill, rocking on the too-small swings like giants, spinning idly on the roundabout. They always come here, to the playground at the far end of the football field. It's as if they aren't quite ready to leave their childhoods behind, even though they sit there in over-sized hoodies, self-consciously smoking and swilling cheap cider out of plastic bottles that they then crush beneath their feet.

Matthew sits on the roundabout, kicking off with his feet now and again when its rotation begins to slow. He is trying not to watch Tammy, trying to pretend he doesn't give a shit, yet every time he looks at her, she seems to be gazing back at him.

'She likes you,' Greg says.

Matthew just shrugs, even though his heart feels like it's being squeezed too tight.

'You're an eejit,' Greg continues, sounding uncannily like his Irish father. 'She's definitely giving you the eye.'

Matthew glances at Tammy as the roundabout does another lazy revolution, and once again her eyes find his. He swallows.

'Eejit,' Greg mutters again when Matthew still doesn't move, his trainers hovering above the ground for another orbit.

Eejit, Matthew thinks to himself.

And then he's on his feet, as if someone else is propelling

him, making him walk unsteadily towards her, the ground still feeling like it's turning beneath his feet. Tammy's eyes widen as he comes closer, but she doesn't look away.

'Do you want to go for a walk?' he asks her, glancing down at his muddy trainers, waiting for her to say no, to tell him to get lost, to say she was looking at Greg, not him.

'OK,' she says.

Matthew's head jerks up.

'OK,' she says again, smiling shyly, and then steps towards him.

They skirt the edge of the field, heading towards the footpath that's shielded by tall hedgerows on either side. He's sure he can feel every pair of eyes following them, but he doesn't glance back. His heart is thundering in his ears and he cannot think of a single thing to say. He feels Tammy edge closer to him, the back of her hand grazing against the back of his. His twitches in response, then he reaches for her hand, his fingers sliding through her own. Except he's misjudged it. *Shit*. His baby finger is wedged between her middle finger, and his thumb and index finger curl uselessly around her thumb. Has she noticed too? Of course she has. She must think he's an idiot. *Fuck*. Too late to do anything about it now.

They continue walking in silence and Matthew wonders if he should stop, if he should just pull her close to him. But is he meant to lean to her left or right as he goes in for the kiss?

As all these thoughts flurry in his head, it takes him a second to realise Tammy has already stopped, that she is already stepping towards him, tilting up on tiptoes, leaning her head to the left, and so his bends automatically to the right, as if he has done this a hundred times before. And then they're kissing. They're actually kissing.

But it isn't like how he imagined. It feels too mechanical, somehow. He's too aware of her tongue in his mouth, and his tongue in hers, of their teeth sometimes biting where they shouldn't, of too much saliva being exchanged. He counts in his head, wondering how soon is too soon to pull away. But then Tammy's doing it anyway, severing the link, the moment broken.

As they wordlessly turn to retrace their steps, he has to fight the impulse to wipe his mouth. Her fingers slide free from his, but Matthew can still feel the weight of her hand in his own as they walk back.

By the time they reach the others at the playground, they still haven't exchanged a word.

Say something, he thinks, his heart hammering so hard he's sure she must be able to hear it. *Say anything.*

She glances up at him expectantly.

He nods. 'See you,' is all he manages, before turning from her to walk back to the roundabout, where Greg is still waiting for him.

Eejit, eejit, eejit.

The next day after school, before he heads out to the park, Matthew brushes his teeth, combs his hair and puts on a clean hoodie.

Go up to her right away, he tells himself, his steps quickening as he sees the silhouette of the swings ahead. *Take her by the hand and then, when you're far enough away from everyone else, tell her she's pretty. Then kiss her, and keep on kissing her.*

It takes a while for him to spot her when he gets there, because her face is turned away from him. It's only when Adam Hollander stops kissing her and Tammy leans back to smile up at him that Matthew realises.

He can feel the other boys glance at him, and some of the girls too, but he looks away, heading for the swings, even though all he wants to do is turn right back around and go home. It feels like the longest sixty-second walk of his life. He tries to affect indifference, eyes trained firmly on the worn grass, the tips of his ears burning, his throat constricting painfully. He's suddenly aware of every part of his body, as if he no longer quite fits together. When he reaches the swing, he sits there, hips wedged between the rusty chains, elbows on his knees as he rocks back and forth, staring hard at the ground. Staring anywhere but at them.

26

'So is your mum still a lesbo?' Geoff asks over dinner, chewing loudly.

Myrtle still finds it hard to look at him without thinking of his wet, muscular tongue forcing its way inside her mouth.

'Geoffrey!' his mum says sharply, fingering the gold cross hanging from her neck.

Myrtle can sense Henry, seated beside her, glance quickly at her and then away again.

'Can I stay at Myrtle's tomorrow night?' Nina asks.

Myrtle knows it's only because of Patti, who Nina always peppers with questions whenever she's over, hanging on her every word.

Her mum frowns. 'We'll see. You did have a bit of a temperature earlier today.'

Nina has had the day off school again, eating bowls of chocolate custard in front of the TV, while Myrtle, unable to face eating alone in the canteen, spent yet another lunchtime in the toilets, breathing through her mouth as she ate her sandwich, trying to chew as silently as possible whenever anyone else came in.

Myrtle is about to say that Nina can have her bed and she'll sleep on the blow-up mattress on the floor when she feels Henry grab hold of her hand underneath the table. She bites her lip, trying to keep her face a blank mask.

The last three times she's come for dinner he's done the

same thing. They clasp hands between forkfuls, and then at the end of the meal, he pushes his chair back and excuses himself, muttering something about homework, without even so much as a glance at Myrtle, and she doesn't see him again for the rest of the evening.

He is now tracing the lines of her palm with his fingertip, and Myrtle has to suppress a shiver. His fingers slide into the hollows of hers, curling around the back of her hand. Her whole hand is tingling.

How can there be so many nerve endings in one body part? she thinks. She presses her other hand against her knee, but there is nothing. Yet her right hand, enclosed in Henry's left, might as well be on fire.

She wonders if he can feel it too, or if for him it's like holding anyone else's hand – his mother's, or Nina's?

She glances at Nina, who smiles across at her as she picks at her food, having no idea what is happening beneath the table. Myrtle feels a strange lurch of guilt, as if she's somehow betraying her friend by not telling her. She has no idea how Nina would react. Or if Henry would even want Myrtle telling people.

His fingers return to their tracing. And it takes Myrtle a moment to realise it is the same shape Henry is outlining over and over on her hot palm.

A heart.

27

The autumn sunshine is hazed and golden, making the copper-leaved trees look like they're aflame. The birds are singing, the bushes twitching with their frenzied activity, and up ahead Matthew can see a hare bounding across one of the churned-up fields. He could almost be happy, if it wasn't for the fact that he is there with Peter.

'How about a trip out in the countryside tomorrow? Boys' day out,' Peter had suggested the night before over dinner. It had now been six weeks since he moved in, and Matthew still couldn't get used to the idea of sitting across the dining table from his headmaster every night.

'That's a wonderful idea,' Grace had said a little too enthusiastically, as if the whole thing hadn't been meticulously planned out by the two of them.

Matthew didn't bother to voice his opinion.

As he follows Peter's long strides, their footfalls swallowed up by the loamy floor of the woods, he thinks about the long walks he used to take with his father, and how Luke struggles to even walk to the end of the garden now.

'Fancy a sit-down for a bit?' Peter says after a while, lowering himself on a nearby fallen tree trunk.

Matthew sits down a few metres away from him. 'Do you know what that is?' he asks, pointing to a grey wagtail.

Peter squints at the bird. 'I think it's a blue tit.'

Matthew swallows a smile, thinking there was no way his father would have confused the two.

Peter opens his rucksack and gets out a sandwich for each of them. After they've finished, he pulls out his hip flask, takes a swig, smacking his lips together in appreciation, and then offers it to Matthew. He takes the flask and swallows a mouthful, coughing as it burns its way down to his stomach. Peter wordlessly takes the flask back and carefully screws the cap on. They sit there in silence for a long, awkward moment.

Then something else breaks it. There's the sound of metal grating on metal, and then an anguished yelp and frantic rustling.

Peter's head jerks towards the source of the noise and then he's on his feet, Matthew following close behind. It's not long before they find it. A fox, caught in a trap. Both her back legs are clamped in its fierce-looking jaws.

'We need to open it up,' Matthew says quickly, stepping towards her, but Peter holds an arm out to stop him.

'She won't be able to walk again either way.'

'So what do we do? We can't just leave her here.'

Peter looks around him, walks off a short distance, and then returns holding a heavy boulder.

'No!' Matthew protests.

Peter stares at him. 'It's the kindest thing to do.' He takes a breath, holds the boulder high up in the air, and then brings it crashing down on the animal's skull. She's still twitching, so he quickly repeats the action, and this time she lies there motionless. When he removes the boulder, there is just a mess of blood and brains where there'd once been her head.

Matthew looks away, bile rising up his throat.

'It was the kindest thing to do,' Peter repeats, brushing his hands down the front of his trousers.

Matthew braves another look at the creature, thinking how life could suddenly seem both fragile and insignificant once you'd bludgeoned it with a rock.

'Come on,' Peter says, striding back in the direction they'd come.

As Matthew trails behind him, staring at Peter's long, muscled back, he can't help but wonder how little he really knows this man that has so firmly inserted himself into their lives.

28

'She's almost old enough to be your ... *mother*,' Winnie hisses, stumbling on the final word.

Daphne's eyebrows shoot up. 'So what, do you think because I'm with her that I might have mother issues?'

Myrtle takes her time loading up the plate of mince pies, pretending to take no notice of them, while listening intently to every word.

Winnie purses her lips together. 'I long ago gave up trying to fathom why you do anything, Daphne. But yes, it wouldn't surprise me if you were doing this to undermine me in some way.'

Daphne snorts and rolls her eyes. 'It's always about you, isn't it, Mum?'

Winnie ignores her. 'Did she have to move in with you? It's very ... unconventional.' Her lip curls up, as if she'd really like to use another word. 'Is that why you're doing this, Daphne? Because you're trying to be different from everyone else?'

'Yes, Mum, that's exactly why I'm doing this – because I want people to judge me and pry into my private life and whisper behind my back.'

'There's no need to be sarcastic. It was a simple question.'

Daphne sighs. 'Nothing is ever simple with you.'

'I'm only honest with you because I love you,' Winnie protests.

'Love is always an excuse for bad behaviour, isn't it?' Daphne mutters.

'You would know,' Winnie retorts primly, picking up her glass of eggnog and gliding from the room while she still has the final word.

Patti opens the back door, hauling in another crate of wine from the garage.

'Whose bright idea was it to invite my mother for Christmas?' Daphne says through clenched teeth. 'It was Seb's turn to have her this year.'

'Don't be a Grinch,' Patti says, unpacking the bottles.

Daphne takes a long draught from her wine glass. 'And why on earth did you have to invite Elliott too?' she says, glancing into the next room as Elliott throws another log onto the fire. 'Wouldn't it have been easier to just buy in some fireworks? Honestly, Pats, what were you thinking?'

'I was thinking that it was time to finally meet your mother, as you were never going to get around to inviting her over. And I was thinking that Elliott doesn't have anyone else to spend Christmas with, so it would be a nice thing to do in this season of goodwill.'

'Then you're a better person than I am,' Daphne says.

'That's a given,' Patti replies, leaning in to kiss her.

Elliott chooses that precise moment to walk into the kitchen.

'Anything I can help with——?' He stops abruptly at the kitchen door, while Patti and Daphne extricate themselves from each other.

Patti gives him her most arresting smile. 'I think everyone could do with some more wine, Elliott, don't you?' she says, holding out a bottle.

He gives a stiff nod as his hand curls around it. 'Yes, I'd say so.'

*

'So, who would like to carve the nut roast?' Patti says, brandishing a large knife, which Elliott accepts.

'No turkey at Christmas?' Winnie asks, her forehead wrinkling.

'I don't eat dead bodies anymore, remember, Grandma?' Myrtle reminds her.

Elliott stares at a slice of nut roast suspiciously. He pops a crumbled-off bit in his mouth and then nods his head in approval. 'Not bad.' His words are softly slurred. Myrtle has watched him drink an entire bottle of wine to himself.

Daphne goes to take out an empty casserole dish just as Elliott walks over to the sideboard to open another bottle.

'Oh look, you're both standing under the mistletoe!' Winnie remarks.

Daphne shakes her head and begins to walk away, but Elliott grabs her by the arm and kisses her awkwardly on the lips. Daphne jerks back, her face reddening.

A moment passes and no one says anything.

After dinner, Patti and Elliott sit outside, drinking and smoking. Myrtle can tell from the smell that they're not normal cigarettes. As she stacks the dishwasher, she can hear her father softly chuckling at something Patti's said.

Daphne comes up behind her and stands there, listening to them too.

'I don't know how she does it,' she murmurs.

Winnie wanders into the kitchen, a fresh glass of eggnog in hand, dancing to a beat only she can hear. 'Dance with me, Daphne,' she says, putting her glass down and reaching for Daphne's hands, trying to spin her around. 'Come on,' Winnie urges. 'Remember us doing this in the kitchen when you were little?'

'I remember you being drunk and trying to get me to dance with you when Dad and Seb wouldn't. Yes, I remember that.'

Winnie falls still, like a wind-up toy that's run out of momentum. 'Why do you always have to do that?'

'Do what?'

'Ruin every moment.'

Daphne sighs but says nothing.

Winnie glances out the window at Patti and Elliott. 'You know, I only ever wanted you to be happy. That's all.' She presses her lips together before speaking again. 'No matter how old your child is, you never stop worrying about them, even if you find that hard to believe.'

'I *am* happy, Mum,' Daphne replies. 'It's just a different kind of happiness than everyone else's.'

Winnie gives a slow nod, her eyes still on Patti. 'Yes. I can see that now.'

When Elliott and Patti step through the back door, loose grins on their faces, Myrtle slips outside to put the empty wine bottles in the recycling bin, her footsteps crunching across the frozen crust of the lawn. Then she hears a rustle in one of the bushes.

'Hello?' she calls out, her heart lurching, and then she gasps as a tall figure emerges.

'Shh,' it says. As it nears the house, she realises who it is.

'Henry,' she says, grinning idiotically, unable to think of a single thing else to say.

'Merry Christmas,' he whispers, stepping closer until she's breathing in his own misty exhales. He holds something above their heads.

Myrtle glances up.

'Mistletoe,' he says, smiling sheepishly.

She just stands there, rooted to the spot, her heart thumping painfully in her chest. Henry bends down, his lips warm against her own. She stiffens slightly, waiting for the moment when his tongue will force its way inside her mouth, like Geoffrey's had done, but instead he just pulls her closer, kissing her repeatedly.

'Myrtle, are you all right out there?' Daphne calls.

Henry pulls away. 'This time tomorrow night,' he whispers in her ear. 'The mistletoe and I will be here, waiting for you.'

And then he's gone, dissolving into the shadows.

Myrtle stands there for a moment, not ready to go back in yet, hugging herself in the frosty cold, her lips still tingling.

29

Emily Swinton's eyes are emerald green. Matthew knows this, even though it's impossible to hold her gaze.

She is talking to him as they sit on the swings. Her little brother, Albie, is rocking on one of the springed animals while Luke is lying flat on his back at the end of the slide in front of them. Matthew normally avoids being seen in public with Luke by himself, but Grace had paid him a fiver to take him out. 'Please, I just need one afternoon to myself,' she begged.

'Do you like it here?' Emily asks, rocking back and forth on the swing.

Matthew shrugs. 'It's all right.'

'I didn't want to move,' she confides, twirling a strand of thick, dark hair around her index finger. 'But my dad left, so we couldn't afford to live where we used to anymore.'

'Where did he go?'

'No idea. He didn't even leave a note. We just came home one day and he'd packed up all his things and gone. He'd cleared out all the bank accounts and taken my mum's jewellery too.'

'That sucks.'

Emily nods. 'So what happened to your dad?' she asks, glancing across at Luke.

'How did you know ... ?' Matthew trails off, his cheeks on fire.

'Well, he looks too old to be your brother. Plus everyone seems to know everyone's business here.'

'He, umm ... He was in an accident. He was on his motorbike and he got hit. He almost died, but they managed to save him. But his brain had been starved of oxygen for a long time, so ...'

'That sucks.'

Matthew nods.

'What was he like before?'

He hesitates, thinking how no one has ever asked him this question before. 'He was great. The best. He knew everything. And he'd never get mad at me, even when I was being a little shit.'

Emily smiles at him, and something inside Matthew gives a responsive flip.

'What was your dad like?' he asks.

'He used to be a lot of fun. He was always inviting people over to our house, and he would let Albie and I stay up really late. And he was really generous too, always buying us presents when he got back from work trips. But he was away a lot. And when he was around, he was often drunk. He and my mum would fight a lot.' She shrugs. 'I miss him and I don't miss him, if you know what I mean.'

'Yeah.' Matthew rocks on his swing in time with her, then chances another glance, this time holding her gaze for one brave moment.

Emily Swinton's eyes are emerald green.

30

'How are you feeling?' Patti asks, stroking Myrtle's back.

She shrugs. How could she say she felt nothing? Only numb? Shouldn't she be crying or feeling depressed at least?

'It's OK to feel confused,' Patti continues. 'There's no right or wrong way to feel after something like this.'

'I just can't believe she's really gone.'

'I know,' Patti says, still stroking her like she's some injured animal.

Gone. Passed away. No longer with us. Dead. Every possible phrase seems nonsensical.

Nina is dead. She tries those unreal words out in her head, but it doesn't work. She keeps imagining it's all a joke and Nina is going to knock on her front door at any moment, a stupid grin on her face.

'How about I read to you?' Patti suggests, picking up a dog-eared copy of *Brothers' Grimm Fairy Tales* from the bookcase.

'I'm too old to be read to.'

'I know, but just humour me, would you?' She opens the book, the spine cracking softly. 'My mum used to read to me when I was off ill from school, even when I was a teenager, and it always made me feel better.'

She begins to read, then pauses at the end of the first story. 'Why is it that the evil characters are always stepmothers, never stepfathers?' She shakes her head. 'Even fairytales are sexist.' She looks at Myrtle, who has turned to face the wall. 'Do you want anything to eat or drink?'

She shakes her head. 'Why didn't she tell me?' she mumbles into her pillow.

Patti puts the book down. 'Because you were her closest friend. Because you were probably one of the only people who acted normal around her.'

'Because I didn't know any better! She lied to me!' Myrtle says angrily.

'I know,' Patti says. 'But she had her reasons. She spent the last five years in and out of hospital. I'm sure sometimes she just wanted to forget. She wanted to pretend that she was just like you.'

'I used to call her a hypochondriac. I used to say she was skiving. I used to get so *angry* at her.' Myrtle begins to cry now, but it's more out of guilt than sadness. 'I was an awful friend.'

'No,' Patti says firmly. 'You weren't.'

'I wish she'd told me. I didn't even get to say goodbye.'

'Maybe it was because she didn't know how to say goodbye to you.'

Henry, Myrtle suddenly thinks. She's been too scared to call or go to the house. She can't bear to see Nina's parents. Not yet.

Did you know? she wonders. *Or did they lie to you too?*

Myrtle jolts awake in the middle of the night, unsure what it is that has woken her. She listens, breath lodged in her throat, waiting.

There it is. A soft *tap tap tapping* at the window.

It can't be a tree branch, because her mum had the cherry blossom cut down earlier that year after it got canker.

Tap tap tap.

Myrtle sucks in her breath. 'Nina?' she whispers, her voice not sounding like her own.

There's only silence. And then, a moment later, as if in answer, another *tap*.

Myrtle throws back the duvet and thunders down the landing, barging into her mum and Patti's room and switching on the overhead light.

'What?' Daphne murmurs sleepily, blinking into the brightness.

'Someone's at my window,' Myrtle gasps.

Patti's already out of bed, her feet finding her slippers, before she leads the way back down the landing to Myrtle's room. She pulls back the curtains to reveal a giant moth scaling the glass, its thick body tapping at the pane.

Patti looks at her. 'Why were you so terrified?'

Myrtle gulps. 'I thought it was Nina.'

'What?'

'We made a pact that whichever one of us died first, we'd come back and communicate with the other one.'

Patti frowns and steps closer, putting an arm around her. 'You were Nina's best friend. She would never want to frighten you.'

'But we promised.'

'Come on, back to bed,' Patti urges.

Myrtle slips beneath the cold duvet, but when Patti goes to draw the curtains closed, Myrtle stops her.

'Leave them open.'

Patti nods, stoops to kiss Myrtle on the forehead, and then quietly shuts the door behind her.

Myrtle lies on her side, watching the moth as it tries to get in, before it eventually gives up and flies away.

31

Matthew glances at the clock. Only ten minutes until she gets here. He scans the piece of paper again, trying to commit it to memory. On it is written a list of things to say, in case his mind empties, which it seems to all too often when Emily is in his bedroom. At school is fine, or walking home together is fine. But when she is lying on the very place where he sleeps every night, suddenly his mind becomes a bottomless void.

He wonders if Emily has to write a list before he goes to her house. Somehow he doubts it.

When she gets there, he lets her pick out a film from his video collection.

'You have so many,' she says, running a finger along the spine of the cases.

He nods. He doesn't tell her that he spends all of his paper round money on them. He doesn't tell her that it's only when he's watching films that he can forget about everything else.

When she's selected one, they lie on their stomachs together, eating the contraband she has snaffled from her house. He glances at her, then quickly away again. Everything about her seems to shine, and it's not just from the blue glow of the TV: her eyes are sparkling, her hair glinting, her teeth gleaming, her skin glistening. It makes him think of his biology lesson the other week, the teacher saying how they are all made up of stars. When he looks at Emily, he can believe it.

She shuffles on the bed to get more comfortable. Sometimes, just her lying next to him, so close like this, he can forget how to breathe properly. Can she tell? Is his face going red?

He stares at her hand, just inches from his, and swallows. Can she hear him? He slowly edges his hand closer, but then she pulls hers away to run it through her hair. It smells of grapefruit.

At the end of the film, she yawns and stretches her pale arms above her head. 'Best be off, Matty.'

Ordinarily, he hates being called that. But when Emily says it, it makes him glow inside.

He sees her to the front door, watching her run across the road to her own house. When he shuts the door and turns around, his mother is standing in the hall.

'Emily seems like a nice girl.'

He nods.

'You two seem very close.'

Another nod.

Grace studies him for a long moment, her expression unreadable. 'I don't need to worry, do I? I don't need to tell you to be careful—'

'Mum! No!'

She holds a hand up. 'OK, OK. But I know what teenage boys can be like. And teenage girls, for that matter. I just ...' She hesitates. 'You know I'm always here if you need to talk, right?'

He gives a stiff nod. As if he would talk to her about anything like that.

'And Peter is always here to talk to as well,' she adds.

Sod that, Matthew thinks, stepping around her to go to his room.

When he lies back down on his bed, he can still feel the

warm imprint of Emily's body. He can still smell grapefruit on his duvet cover. And lying there, on his pillow, is one of her long, dark hairs. He coils it slowly around his finger.

Emily, Emily, Emily . . .

Lying in bed later, unable to sleep, his head still filled with thoughts of Emily, he hears his father's lumbering, uneven tread down the hall. Matthew sighs and flips back the covers, hurrying to the bathroom before his mother wakes up.

Luke is trying to run a bath and there is bubble bath everywhere. He has already taken his pyjamas off and Matthew inadvertently catches sight of the fleshy, thick piece of rope swinging between his legs. Luke gives the dark bush of hair around it a good scratching, while Matthew quickly averts his eyes as he turns off the taps.

'Let's get you back to bed,' he says gently, helping his father into his pyjamas and then steering him down the hall. But Luke stops short outside Grace and Peter's room, staring at the panelled wood, his hand on the doorknob.

Matthew can hear noises from within. It sounds like someone crying, but he knows it's something else.

He looks at Luke as he guides him back to his room, wondering if he knows it too.

32

Myrtle hovers in front of the door, shuffling her weight from foot to foot. It has been almost a minute since she knocked. Perhaps no one's in. Except where else would they be? She is just about to turn to go home when the door swings open. Geoffrey is standing there.

'Hi,' Myrtle says meekly, unsure what else to say.

'He's upstairs,' he says gruffly, walking back down the hall, leaving Myrtle standing there on the doorstep.

As she follows him in, shutting the door as quietly as she can, she sees the thin figure of Nina's mum hunched over the dining table, staring down at scattered photos. She doesn't glance up, even though she must hear Myrtle's footsteps, and Myrtle doesn't say anything either. Instead she heads straight for the stairs and then knocks softly on Henry's bedroom door.

When there is no answer, she says, 'It's me. Myrtle.'

When there is still no reply, she nudges the door open. Henry is lying on his bed, staring up at the ceiling. She waits to be invited in but he doesn't even look at her, so she shuts the door and goes to sit down beside him.

'My parents have split up,' he says, still glaring up at the Artex.

'What? Why?'

'Apparently they'd been thinking about separating ages ago and then Nina got ill, so they kept up appearances for her sake. But Mum says there's no point staying together now that she's gone.'

'What about you and Geoffrey?'

He lifts his shoulders. 'Exactly. What about us?'

What about us? she wants to ask him. She wants to reach for his hand and trace the question on his palm. She wants to lean down and kiss him, like they did under the mistletoe and a hundred other stolen moments. She wants to lie beside him and whisper the question in his ear. But he looks so far away from her, she's not sure he will even hear her.

How can silence be so loud? she wonders. She swallows, unsure how to fill it. Maybe she should say something normal. Act like everything is still the same between them. Maybe she should ask him why he pretended not to see her today when she passed by him in the corridor at school.

'Do you like my new jumper?' she asks, then mentally kicks herself.

Henry finally turns to look at her. His eyes no longer look like his own. They seem hollow, somehow. 'What does it matter?' he murmurs, before turning to eyeball the ceiling again.

Myrtle looks away as well, shamefaced.

'I don't think you should come around here anymore,' he tells her. 'My mum doesn't like having visitors now.'

'OK. You can come to mine instead.'

'That isn't what I meant.'

'Oh.' *Oh oh oh oh oh.*

'I'll be going off to uni in a few months anyway, so guess there's no point delaying the inevitable,' he says with a shrug.

'Right.' Myrtle gulps, her throat tight with unshed tears, her vision filming.

She blinks quickly as another deafening silence descends. When she can stand it no longer, she gets up to leave, hesitating at the threshold, willing Henry to say something more. To look at her, at least. But he doesn't.

When she walks down the landing, the door clunking shut behind her, she sees that Henry's mum is now in Nina's bedroom, her daughter's clothes heaped around her on the floor as she holds up fistfuls of fabric to her glistening cheeks, breathing in their fading scent.

33

Grace, Luke and Matthew are standing on the drive, staring at the gleaming red motorbike Xander has just pulled up on.

'Cool,' Matthew breathes, stepping closer. 'Is that yours?'

'Nope.' Xander kills the engine and then chucks Matthew the key, who deftly catches it one-handed. 'It's yours.'

Matthew stares at the key, then back at him. 'Seriously?'

Xander grins. 'Seriously.'

Grace glares between the pair of them, her nostrils flaring. 'Are you *fucking* kidding me, Xander?' For some reason, his uncle always brings out her most blasphemous side.

'Relax,' Xander replies, leaning against the bike. 'I've got him all the protective gear to go with it, and I'll pay for the lessons too.'

Grace crosses her arms against her chest, radiating fury. 'You're right. I should just relax. This is exactly what I want my only child to have – the very same thing that brain-damaged his father.'

'Come on, that was nothing to do with Luke being on a bike. That other driver was off his face. If Luke had been a pedestrian crossing the road, the same thing would have happened.'

'Oh, fuck off, Xander,' Grace says, turning on her heel and stalking back into the house.

Xander raises an eyebrow. 'Getting a warm welcome like that, it's a wonder I don't come back more often.'

Matthew watches as Luke runs his hands over the smooth bodywork, his eyes filled with child-like wonder, as if he's never seen one before.

'Why is Mum so angry at you all the time?' Matthew asks.

Xander doesn't meet his eye. 'It's a long story. But your mother can hold a grudge, that's for sure.'

'Is it because of the money you borrowed from Dad?' Matthew says hesitantly, having overheard snatches of conversation between his mum and Peter.

Xander gives him a shifty look. 'So you know about that, do you?' He sighs. 'Bad investments, that's all it was. Anyway, I'm going to pay it back eventually. Every last penny.'

'How much was it?' Matthew asks, looking again at the motorbike.

But Xander doesn't reply. He pulls out a crumpled pack of cigarettes from his pocket and offers one to Matthew, who shakes his head.

'Smart man.'

At dinner, where Grace responds to everything Xander says in clipped monosyllables, Peter is forced to steer the conversation. Matthew can see Xander studying him as he eats, taking in the bi-focals that hang on a chain around his neck, the cardigan buttoned up over his shirt, the way he chews his food oh-so-slowly and then dabs at the corners of his mouth with a napkin when he's done. He sips politely from his wine glass, filled with the expensive Rioja Xander brought with him, whereas Grace's remains pointedly untouched.

When the phone rings, Peter excuses himself. 'I'll take this in my study,' he says.

Xander looks at Grace, shaking his head in disbelief. 'This guy? Seriously?'

'Don't.' She stares at him for a silent, deadly moment. 'You can't just swan back here after two years, with your flash gifts, and judge us, OK?' Grace pushes herself up from the table to leave, but as she turns, her elbow knocks the wine glass to the floor, where it shatters loudly. She carries on to the kitchen without even turning back.

'Char,' Luke says, laughing, swiping Peter's half-empty glass to the floor in one swift motion, where it shatters too.

'Cheers,' Xander says grimly, reaching for the bottle of red wine and taking a long swig from it.

Later that night, unable to sleep because of Xander's rumbling snores emanating from the camp bed, Matthew steals down the hallway and into the sitting room to gaze out the window at the bike still parked on the driveway. It glints under the moonlight, calling to him.

He can't wait to see Emily's face when she sees it. He pictures him riding it around the winding country lanes, her sat behind him, arms wrapped around his waist, the inside of her thighs snug against the outside of his ...

Eventually he turns to head back to bed, but in the near-darkness he knocks over a box full of paperwork his mum has been going through. He crouches to stuff the scattered documents back in the box, spotting one that has skidded across the carpet by the window. He leans down to pick it up, and as he stands, he can faintly make out the words in the moonlight.

Petition for divorce, it states at the top.

Below it is his mother's printed name and signature. And beside that sits his father's name, the space beneath it still blank.

34

They stare at each other for a long, silent moment.

'Myrtle, are you coming?' the other girls ask, but she doesn't hear them.

She looks at Henry. He is standing outside the pub they've just come out of, back against the wall, smoking. That's new. He never used to smoke before.

'Myrtle, come on!' the girls call impatiently.

She glances over at them, their smuggled-out bottles of cider hanging loosely from their hands. Then she looks back at Henry, who is still watching her intently.

'I'll catch you up,' she tells them, watching as they meander drunkenly down the road in search of the next pub.

'Well, if it isn't Myrtle Brookes,' Henry finally says, breaking the silence between them.

She stands there mutely, unable to respond, too many unspoken questions heavy on her tongue. She watches as he takes one long, last drag on his cigarette before crushing it under his shoe.

'So ... results night, huh?' he says.

She nods.

'How did you do?'

She shrugs. 'OK,' she says, choosing not to mention her four As. 'I got into Bristol.'

'Congratulations.' His smile doesn't reach his eyes. He looks different, somehow. Older. She wonders if she does too.

'How's life at Leeds?' she asks.

It's his turn to shrug. 'I couldn't wait to get away from this place. But uni's not all it's cracked up to be.'

'Oh.' She bites her lip. 'So you're back for the rest of the summer then?' she says, inwardly wincing at how hopeful she sounds.

He shakes his head. 'Just a few days. Mum's finally selling up. Geoff and I are helping her move.'

Myrtle nods. She'd seen the 'For Sale' sign go up the last time she'd cycled by Nina's house, even though she normally tries to avoid going down that road.

Henry pushes himself away from the wall, shoving his hands deep in his pockets. 'I better let you get back to your friends.'

'I was thinking of heading home anyway,' she fibs.

He looks at her, as if he can see right through her lie. 'Want me to walk you back?'

She swallows, her mouth suddenly dry. 'All right,' she says quietly.

They walk side by side in silence, their footsteps echoing down the dark, deserted street. Her hand twitches between them, but his stay buried in his pockets, his shoulders hunched, his eyes trained on the tarmac in front of them.

When they walk past the turning to her road, she says nothing and neither does he. She wordlessly follows him until they're standing outside his house. She looks up at it apprehensively. She hasn't been inside since that day he told her not to come round anymore. Since she saw Nina's mum crumpled on her bedroom floor.

'I don't think I should—' she begins, but Henry cuts her off.

'It's fine,' he says in a low voice, leading her round the back of the house.

Myrtle stares at the familiar garden statues as they edge by them. They seem to stare back at her accusingly, as if they sense she's not welcome here.

Henry slides back the lock of Nina's old Wendy house and stoops a little to get through the low doorway. Myrtle's gaze falls on the miniature plastic furniture she and Nina used to perch on at their pretend dinner parties, as dozens of memories come rushing back at her. She looks at Henry, his face partly illuminated by the moonlight filtering through the dusty Perspex window, his expression unreadable, and she wonders if he's thinking of Nina too.

Myrtle stares at her feet, unsure what to do or say next. Before she can stop herself, she blurts out, 'I still miss her, you know.'

Henry says nothing, just takes a sudden step forward, yanking her towards him, then pushes aside the tiny table and chairs with one leg as he pulls them down onto the hard floor.

Oh god, this is it, Myrtle thinks, her heart thudding loudly in her chest, unsure if she's ready for it. She feels sick with nerves but tries not to let it show as she lies down next to him. She can smell the beer and tobacco on his breath as he leans into her, a cold hand sliding up underneath her jumper. His touch makes her skin hum.

Now he's kissing her neck as he undoes his jeans, then lifting her skirt up, his fingers tugging impatiently at her knickers. She shifts to the side to pull them down, unsure where to put them, so she hangs them off one of the dwarfed chairs. In that time, she has heard the sound of a wrapper tearing, then the soft rustle of plastic.

She holds her breath, trying not to look down at it as Henry positions himself above her. She looks up at him instead, but he doesn't meet her eye, his gaze fixed somewhere on the floor beside her.

A moment later, he is sliding into her. No, not sliding, *tearing.* It feels like he is stabbing her with a knife. She bites down on her lip to stop herself from crying out. He begins to move quicker and harder, panting with the effort, while Myrtle clenches her teeth with each thrust.

Finally his body stills and his full weight sinks into her as his breathing slows. She hesitates for a second, then she puts her arms around him, but he rolls away, doing up his trousers while Myrtle lies there, her skirt bunched up around her waist, goosebumps lifting the hairs on her bare legs. She hurriedly pulls her skirt down and reaches for her knickers, yanking them back on.

She looks up at Henry as she gets to her feet but he is already turning from her, stooping to get under the low doorway again. He sparks up a cigarette, gazing up at the landing light, which casts a golden square on the lawn in front of them.

Myrtle stands there, wondering if he will kiss her, or if he will ask to see her again before he leaves. Maybe he'll suggest visiting her in Bristol, or her visiting him in Leeds.

'You should go, before anyone sees you,' is all he says.

'Oh. OK,' she replies, the disappointment clear in her voice.

She hesitates a moment longer, willing him to look at her, but when he doesn't, she turns and slowly retraces her steps across the grass and through the side gate, latching it closed. As she hurries down the front path, the inside of her thighs sticky and cold, she can feel the stone statues watching her once again, as if they too know she's given away something she shouldn't have.

35

'Congratulations!'

'Thank you.' Grace looks almost giddy, her cheeks flushed, her hairdo coming loose in tendrils around her face.

'You two make such a lovely couple.'

'Thank you.' Peter shakes someone's hand. Even though there is just a hint of a smile on his lips, it's the happiest Matthew has ever seen him.

'Congratulations. Beautiful ceremony.'

Matthew swallows a sigh. He's not sure why he has to stand up here in the receiving line too, nodding at all these drunk adults when he doesn't even know who most of them are.

He glances across at Emily, who bugs her eyes out at him and pulls a finger slowly across her throat. He raises two fingers to his temple and then fires with his thumb. Emily laughs.

'I'm happy for you, Grace,' a familiar voice says softly.

Matthew turns to see his grandma standing there, blinking quickly as she looks between Grace and Peter. His grandfather stands next to her, stony-faced, not giving either of them eye contact.

'Thank you, Pru. That means a lot,' Grace says quietly.

'Alexander wanted us to pass on his apologies for not being able to come.'

Grace smiles. 'That's OK. If I was living in the Philippines,

I probably wouldn't come back for his wedding either.'

'Such a beautiful dress,' another guest cuts in, stepping forward to embrace the bride.

Matthew watches his grandparents walk over to the far corner of the room and take their seats, not talking to each other, Aidan's gaze fixed resolutely on the floor, while Pru's eyes are still fastened on Grace and Peter.

Matthew's hands clench into fists by his side. No one has mentioned Luke or asked after his whereabouts. When Matthew had asked why their next-door neighbour was coming to stay for the weekend and Luke wasn't going to the wedding, Grace had simply said, 'It would be too tiring for him,' not quite meeting his eye. Except Matthew knew what she really meant was that no one could predict how he would react.

When she had uttered her vows to Peter, Matthew couldn't help but wonder if they meant as much to her now as the first time she said them. Had she thought of his father as she spoke them, gazing into another man's eyes?

When the vicar had asked, 'If any person present knows of any reason ...' Matthew had wanted to call out: 'She doesn't love him! Not really. She's still in love with my dad.' Except he knew it was a warped, grief-stricken kind of love, at what they had lost, and what they would never have again. So he just sat there in the crushing silence, the unspoken words raging inside him.

He can't believe they've actually gone and done it. He's never doubted Peter's love for his mother. But his mother ...

He looks at Peter in the way he always does – with total bewilderment. He wonders if it is just loneliness on his mother's part. Or if it's also a kind of gratitude – for Peter staying when so many others would have left.

After the meal, when he, Emily and Greg take full advantage of the open bottles of wine on the table, he drags Emily up on the dance floor.

'How are you feeling?' she asks.

'Drunk.'

'You know that's not what I meant.' Her emerald eyes have never been more piercing than they are right now.

He shrugs. 'I don't know what I feel.' He swallows. 'But I'm glad you're here.'

She smiles up at him. 'Of course. Where else would I be?'

Tonight, Matthew vows. *Tonight I will tell her how I really feel.*

He glances across at Greg, who is dancing with one of Matthew's second cousins, letting her stand on his feet as he shuffles her around.

'Can we sit down?' Emily says. 'My head is spinning, and not in a good way.'

They collapse onto two chairs at the back of the room, gazing out at the dance floor. Matthew can't take his eyes off his mother and Peter slow-dancing. It's like staring at a car crash: it makes him feel nauseous and uncomfortable, yet he can't *not* look.

'Can I ask you something?' Emily says, pulling him out of his thoughts.

He nods, his gaze still tethered on Grace and Peter.

'If you liked someone, but you weren't sure if they liked you back, would you just go for it anyway?'

He looks at her, his attention fully hers now as his heart begins to quicken. 'Umm, well, uhhh ...' he flounders. 'That depends. Do you really like them?'

She nods, blushing, her gaze dipping to the floor.

Is she saying what he thinks she's saying?

'Chances are he likes you too,' he tells her. 'Any guy would have to be crazy not to like you back.'

She smiles, the blush spreading further across her face. He's always loved that about her: how her expressions are so transparent, her face so easy to read.

Emily looks at him; he looks back at her.

Now, he thinks. *This is your moment.*

He leans forward and kisses her.

Emily instantly recoils. 'What are you doing, Matty?'

'I thought ... I thought you were talking about me,' he stammers.

'No,' she replies, the word a whisper.

'Shit,' he whispers back.

'Yeah, shit.' She stands up, her hands clenching the thick fabric of her dress. She looks like she's close to tears. 'I'm going to get some water.'

Matthew just nods, staring hard at the floor. *Fuckfuckfuck.*

He can't just sit here and wait for her to come back, like the idiot that he is, so he escapes to the toilet, shutting the lid to sit down on it, burying his head in his hands.

Fuckfuckfuckfuckfuckfuckfuck.

When he finally works up the nerve to go back out there, he looks around for Emily but can't find her. He's thinking that she must have gone home, too embarrassed to even say goodbye to him, when he finally sees her. In the darkest corner of the room. With Greg. Kissing him. They pull apart, and then Greg leads her outside by the hand.

A memory floats back to him, of Tammy kissing Adam Hollander, history cruelly repeating itself, except a thousand times worse.

Matthew sits there alone as the room gradually empties, watching his mother and Peter dancing by themselves on the dance floor, thinking how he has never hated his life more than he does in this moment.

Part Two

Part Two

36

Matthew is standing in the corridor of his halls wearing a tutu and a Hawaiian shirt that is two sizes too big for him.

He'd shown up to the party three hours ago in a furry bear onesie, but at some point in the night they'd started playing a game where they had to switch outfits with other people, and so here he is wearing Jasmine's ballerina skirt and Ed's tropical shirt.

Every room on his floor in the halls has their door open, each one like a micro house party, spilling out into the corridor. They're having wheelbarrow races down the hall, playing Twister in the common room, squirting ketchup straight on the kitchen counter to dunk toasties into, and in another room there's a group massage going on.

Though their rooms look like prison cells with their tiled floors and bare-brick walls, this feels like a kind of freedom he's never known before.

I can be anyone I want to be here, Matthew thinks, and the realisation makes him a little dizzy.

'I love your hair,' a petite brunette tells him, before standing on tiptoe to brush her lips against his cheek, as if his curly hair could do that to a girl. He reaches for her hand but she's already drifting away, talking to someone else.

Giles, his next-door neighbour, walks by, two girls in tow, then winks at Matthew before he hangs a sock on the doorknob – the unspoken signal for 'Do Not Disturb' – and shuts his door.

'That's it, get it all out,' a red-haired girl is saying as she holds back her friend's hair with one hand and rubs her back with the other while her friend throws up in the kitchen bin.

'Jesus, Abi,' a blonde girl says, her nose wrinkled. 'You drink absinthe like it's Pimm's.'

'Urgh,' Abi moans, wiping the back of her hand across her mouth, smudging her bright red lipstick. 'I'm never drinking again.'

The redhead and the blonde exchange a knowing smile as they lead her down the stairs to their own floor.

Matthew watches them go and then leans back against the wall, listening to the other conversations going on around him, about politics, feminism, the environment, where they went on their gap year, the best bars in Bristol to go to, which lecturer they'd like to sleep with … And he just stands there, a grin on his face, taking it all in.

37

'In Plato's *Symposium*, a philosopher states that humans began life as androgynous creatures with both male and female parts,' Eric Paulson says, as Myrtle frantically scribbles in her notebook, trying to keep up with what he's saying.

Eric is her favourite lecturer. (She still hasn't got used to calling tutors by their first names, as if they're all equals.) Although he doesn't have the charisma or presence of some of the other tutors, who treat the lectern like their own personal stage, he speaks with a quiet authority that has Myrtle hanging on his every word. And it didn't hurt that he was easy on the eye, too.

'The gods split each creature in half, separating them into two beings – man and woman,' he continues. 'And ever since, humans have spent their lives looking for their other half who will make them whole again.'

Myrtle leans back in her seat, letting his words sink in as she looks around her at the other students busily writing in their notebooks. (She still hasn't got used to this either – people actually wanting to learn and not studiously trying to avoid looking studious.)

But what if your missing half is the same sex? she wonders, thinking of her mother and Patti.

'That's what I want you to focus on for this week's essay,' Eric concludes. 'If what we're all searching for in life is our lost half . . .'

As they stand as one to stuff their lecture notes in their bags, Myrtle glances across at Abi and Sophie.

'Pizza?' she suggests.

Sophie nods. 'I'm starving.'

'I fucking love Plato,' Abi enthuses, as they sit down in the student union to eat. 'That dude knew his shit.'

Myrtle nods. 'Doesn't it just blow your mind that all these great thinkers were thinking this stuff centuries ago?' she says, reaching for a slice of pizza. 'And yet we're still no closer to figuring any of it out.'

'Sure we are,' Sophie says, ever the optimist, twirling a strand of blonde hair around one finger.

'So, Eric Paulson,' Abi interrupts. 'I wouldn't mind letting him try to fill my empty places ...'

'Said like a true feminist,' Myrtle remarks.

'I don't need a guy to complete me, but I might make an exception for him,' Abi says with a grin.

'You and every other straight girl on our course,' Myrtle says, severing a string of cheese with her teeth.

'It's like Eric said: we're all just looking for our soulmate,' Sophie says.

'I'm not so sure,' Myrtle says, wiping her greasy fingertips on a napkin.

'You don't believe in soulmates?' Sophie asks, her eyes widening.

'The idea that there's only one person for each of us?' Myrtle shakes her head. 'That's such a depressing thought. I mean, who's to say you ever find them?'

'Fate, of course,' Sophie replies.

'And the idea that we're incomplete if we don't find someone?' Myrtle adds, frowning. 'What about all the monks and nuns in the world? They don't need anyone else.'

'They've found God, though,' Sophie points out.

'Or so they believe,' Abi says, picking the olives off her pizza and putting them on Myrtle's plate.

'Then what about all the hermits who aren't religious, or the people who just choose to be on their own?' Myrtle continues, chewing thoughtfully on an olive. 'You're saying all of them are incomplete?'

Sophie shrugs. 'We're not meant to be on our own. It's unnatural.'

Myrtle thinks of her father, still unable to move on after all these years, and wonders if it's true: if a life alone was only a life half-lived.

'Except sometimes a vibrator is all a gal needs ...' Abi says, as Sophie rolls her eyes and Myrtle starts laughing.

38

'You ever seen a cow give birth before?'

Matthew shakes his head.

'Well, you're about to.' The farmer – John – grins at him. 'Another half an hour, I'd say, from looking at her.'

As they stand there and wait, Matthew shuffles from foot to foot, feeling strangely nervous. This will be the first birth he's ever witnessed.

'So, how much longer until you're a qualified vet?' John asks.

'Another four years.'

The farmer shakes his head. 'Never was one for books, myself. Always preferred to be outside, learning as I went.'

Matthew nods. 'Did you always want to be a farmer?'

John laughs. 'The last seven generations of my family were farmers – I didn't get much of a say in the matter.' He shrugs. 'A job's a job at the end of the day.'

Thirty minutes later, just as predicted, two hind legs are protruding from the cow's behind, and the farmer takes hold of them to ease the calf out. It collapses to the ground, covered in blood and mucus.

'So what now?' Matthew asks, unsure if he should be rubbing it down.

'We take him away,' John says.

'To wash him?'

John shakes his head. 'The veal crates are all full right now, so this one will be shot.'

'What? Why?' Matthew asks in disbelief.

John stares at him like he's a simpleton. 'Because this is a dairy farm and males don't produce milk.'

'So you shoot him?' Matthew says, certain he must be joking.

But the farmer just nods, already stooping to pick the calf up. The mother is bending over him too, licking him, but he shoves her away. He grabs the calf's two back legs and drags him out of the stall, the mother right at his heels. Matthew shuts the gate in front of her so she can't follow them. As he begins to walk away she starts bellowing.

'I didn't realise they'd cry out for them,' he says, glancing back at her as she presses herself up against the gate.

'Just ignore her,' John says brusquely. 'They do this every time, sometimes for days. You get used to it.' He reaches for the bolt gun and offers it to Matthew. 'You want a go?'

Matthew stares at it and shakes his head, then gazes at the newborn calf, his huge brown eyes blinking up at them.

'Can't we give him to a sanctuary or—' Matthew begins, but is cut short by a muffled bang as John shoots the calf in the head. He then effortlessly scoops up the body and dumps it in the huge bin outside, where there are two other dead male calves inside, flies buzzing around their glassy eyes.

When lunch finally comes around, Matthew joins Ed and Giles, who are perched on two bales of hay and look as shell-shocked as he feels.

'Give me cats and dogs any day,' Giles murmurs.

Ed nods in agreement, his expression dazed. 'Those veal crates ... They can't even move.'

Matthew looks around him at the hundreds of cows hooked up to milking machines and the other ones in tiny metal enclosures that John and the other farmers laughingly refer to as 'the rape rack'. When they'd got assigned to help out on a dairy farm for the semester, he hadn't imagined it would be like this. He'd pictured grassy fields with calves playing in them.

He takes a bite of his cheese and pickle sandwich, washing it down with freshly pumped milk, watching the farmers doing the same. But he suddenly stops, the milk curdling in his stomach, when he hears the mother cow keening for her dead calf from inside one of the stalls. The other farmers take no notice, roaring at some joke one of them is telling. Matthew looks at them, wondering: *How can you do this, day in, day out, and feel absolutely nothing?*

At the end of the day, after they have impregnated a dozen cows by shoving their arms up their backsides, and Matthew almost loses his lunch for a second time, John turns to him and says, 'Same time next week?'

'I ... I'm not sure I'm cut out for this,' Matthew admits, not quite meeting his eye.

'I see,' the farmer replies, the disdain clear in his voice. 'Well, I guess it takes a certain kind of man to do what we do,' he says, puffing out his chest.

When Matthew joins Ed and Giles, who are waiting for him at the gate, and they trudge silently down the country lane to catch their bus home, too exhausted to even talk, Matthew can't help but think: *Maybe I don't want to be that kind of man.*

39

'Myrtle, come on, back me up here,' Abi urges. 'Isn't Liam the sexiest thing you've ever seen?'

Myrtle glances over at the well-built guy Abi arrived at the house party with. 'He's hot,' she agrees. 'But he barely speaks.'

'I know. It's kind of perfect, right?'

Myrtle frowns. 'How's that?'

'Because then I can project what I really hope he's thinking and both of us are happy.'

'So your dream guy is a mute?' Sophie says incredulously.

Abi laughs, scooping her curly brown hair into a ponytail. 'Who knew?'

'Maybe he's just shy,' Myrtle offers.

Abi shakes her head. 'No, I think he's just a little dim, bless him.'

'Then why are you even with him?' Sophie asks.

Abi holds out her hand towards him. 'I think that speaks for itself.'

'So superficial,' Sophie chides.

'And why not? It's not like I'm going to marry the guy.' Abi refills their wine glasses. 'Anyway, how did your second date with Tom go?'

Sophie dips her head, her blonde hair falling across her face, but her smile is too big to hide.

'That good?' Myrtle asks.

Sophie nods. 'We kissed.'

Abi gasps in mock horror. 'Hold the phone. Sophie Andrews kissed a guy on the *second* date?'

'I know, I know, the three-date rule went out the window. I lost my head for a moment.' She smiles again.

Myrtle and Abi exchange a look. Then Abi leans forward. 'So, tell us, how was the kiss?'

'Nice.' Sophie blushes. '*Very* nice.'

'That's good news,' Abi says.

'Why?'

'Well, you can tell a lot about a person's kiss. Good kisser usually means they're good in bed.'

'But a kiss is so much better than sex anyway, don't you think?' Sophie says.

Abi laughs, as if she's made a joke.

'I'm serious. Sex can be so disappointing. But a good kiss – you always remember that, don't you?'

Myrtle nods, thinking of Henry.

'I bet you've already been fantasising about your wedding day, haven't you?' Abi says with a knowing look.

'I've been thinking about my wedding day since I was four years old,' Sophie admits. 'I know exactly what dress I'll have, what cake, what colour the bridesmaids will wear, and where we'll go on honeymoon.'

Myrtle raises an eyebrow. 'And the lucky groom? Does he not get a say in any of it?'

Sophie purses her lips. 'Weddings are really the bride's day, don't you think? Anyway, so what about you two? What would your dream weddings be like?'

Abi shrugs. 'Nothing fancy or formal. Just a big party with an open bar, so everyone can get smashed.'

'That sounds … nice,' Sophie remarks politely. 'What about you, Myrtle?'

'I don't know. I'm not even sure I want to get married.'

Sophie looks at her, aghast. 'Why not?'

Myrtle shrugs. 'I'm not sure if I really believe in it.'

'What do you mean, *believe*?' Sophie asks. 'It's not a religion.'

'Isn't it?'

'No. It's a public declaration of two people's love for each other,' Sophie says.

'It is just patriarchal nonsense,' Abi counters. 'The man asking for the father's permission, the father giving his daughter away, like she's his property, us having to wear virginal white, and the women having to stay silent while all the men get to give a speech.'

'Exactly,' Myrtle says. 'Plus, why does a declaration of love have to be a legally binding contract? People change. People fall out of love. That's why there are so many divorces.'

'Only because they didn't find their soulmate,' Sophie protests. 'Plus, every girl wants to get married. It's what we all dream of.'

'I wouldn't go that far,' Abi says.

They glance over at the boys gathered at one end of the kitchen, shovelling crisps into their mouths, goading each other to down their pints in one before burping and tipping the empty glass on their heads, and laughing uproariously at some – most likely dirty – joke one of them is telling.

'But if you *did* get married, what would it be like?' Sophie presses. 'You must have thought about it.'

'Not really.' Myrtle thinks for a moment, trying to imagine herself standing there in a big white dress, smiling up at the man she loves and wants to spend the rest of her life with. But the image won't hold. 'Everyone would probably just get really drunk, and then my dad would insist on dancing with my mum, and then he'd try to kiss her, and then they'd argue, my dad would get emotional, and the groom's family would look at us like they'd made a terrible mistake.'

Sophie stares at her while Abi laughs. 'Your family sounds a lot like mine,' she says, topping up all their wine glasses again. 'But if I ever do get married, you two will definitely be my bridesmaids.'

Sophie's face lights up. 'Really?'

Abi nods. 'Of course.'

'When I get married, you'll both be my bridesmaids too,' Sophie says decisively.

They turn to look at Myrtle.

'Like I said, I don't think I want to get married.'

'You'll change your mind when you meet the right person,' Sophie says confidently.

Except how do you know that it's the right person? Myrtle wants to ask, thinking of her parents, and Nina's parents, and so many other friends' parents. Surely everyone whose marriage fell apart thought they were marrying the right person at the time?

'Let's make a pact,' Abi announces. 'When we get married, we'll be each other's bridesmaids, no matter what, even if we haven't spoken to each other in years.' She holds out her hands.

'Why would we not be speaking to each other?' Sophie says, her forehead wrinkling.

'I don't know. Maybe you get with some aristocrat and decide we're too common for you.'

'Never!' Sophie says, clasping Abi's left hand, before solemnly vowing, 'When I get married, you'll both be my bridesmaids.'

Abi stares at Myrtle, her eyebrows raised expectantly.

Myrtle sighs and grabs her right hand and Sophie's left. '*If* I get married, you'll both be my bridesmaids,' she reluctantly echoes.

40

'Hey,' Matthew says to Luke, but he won't even look at him. He stands close to Grace, as if for reassurance.

His mum steps over to hug him. 'It's good to have you back, sweetheart.' As she pulls away she tightens the belt of her dressing gown, her hand fluttering around her throat. Her hair is unbrushed and there are dark shadows under her eyes. 'Sorry, I forgot it was today you were coming home. I'm a bit behind this morning.'

Matthew nods, even though it's gone two o'clock in the afternoon. He looks slowly around the sitting room, taking in the partly drawn curtains, the unopened post piled up on the coffee table, the scattered plates beneath it filled with half-eaten sandwiches, the crusts spotted with mould, and the empty wine bottles standing sentry on the bricked hearth.

'Where's Peter?' he asks, an uneasy feeling rising up inside him.

His mother doesn't reply as she eases herself onto the sofa, Luke collapsing down beside her. She looks tiny, shrunken, even. She lifts a sheet of newspaper onto her lap. On it are broken pieces of a vase that she's trying to superglue back together.

'What's happened?' he presses.

'Oh, Luke knocked this over earlier,' she says, rubbing her eyes with the back of her hand, avoiding the question he's actually asking. 'I know it's only a vase, but still, it was my mother's. It just made me think of her, that's all.' Grace looks at him and smiles weakly. 'No matter how old you are, you never stop missing your mother.'

'Mum, where's Peter?' he repeats, more insistent this time.

Her gaze slides away from him. 'He's gone,' she says vaguely.

'Gone where?'

'I'm not sure.'

'When will he be back?'

'He won't,' she says quietly.

'He's left?' Matthew asks in disbelief, his heart thudding heavily against his ribcage.

Finally she looks at him. 'He said he couldn't do it anymore.' Her gaze drifts down to her lap again as she fingers the jagged edges of the vase. 'He said that sometimes, no matter how much you love someone …' She breaks off, looking down at a bright bead of blood on her index finger, raising the tip to her mouth. Luke reaches out, grabs her hand and raises it to his own lips.

She glances at Matthew again. 'How long are you back for?'

'Just a couple of nights.'

She nods.

His gaze falls again on the empty wine bottles. 'But maybe I could stay for a bit longer …'

She offers him a tired smile. 'That would be nice.'

'I'm going to unpack,' he says, already retreating from the room. The walls feel like they're pressing in on him as he walks down the narrow hallway.

Walking into his bedroom, he stares at his old desk, running his fingertips over the scarred indentations, thinking of all those moments he'd sat hunched over it doing homework, waiting for a more exciting future to begin. He looks at the narrow bed, with the same worn duvet cover from when he was little, the rows of videotapes that have gone fuzzy with age, and the sun-faded posters of bands he no longer listens to. Then he steps closer, and before he even knows what he's doing, he's ripped them down in one swift motion, as if he's tearing away a piece of his past.

41

'Say "mortarboard",' Elliott says.

'Mortarboard,' Myrtle, Abi and Sophie intone, as Elliott bends down, using his knee like a tripod, snapping away on his camera.

'Beautiful, ladies, just beautiful,' he says, switching from horizontal to portrait. 'OK, now let's get one of you throwing your caps in the air.'

'Dad, that's so cliché,' Myrtle moans.

Sophie pokes an elbow in her side. 'Come on, it's tradition. We have to.'

They count to three and then throw them above their heads, obliterating the sun for a second before gravity pulls them back down.

'Your dad ...' Abi murmurs in her ear, gazing at him rapturously.

'Don't you dare,' Myrtle warns.

'Just saying, I would ...'

'That's not saying much,' Sophie points out.

'You know, Abi, sometimes it's perfectly fine to keep your thoughts to yourself,' Myrtle says.

'Right, move over, Annie Liebowitz,' Patti says to Elliott, 'and let's get a photo of you and Myrtle together.'

'How about letting your old man play dress-up?' Elliott suggests. He dons Myrtle's cap and gown, brandishing her certificate like a baseball bat. 'How do I look?'

'Toothsome, Mr Brookes,' Abi simpers.

'Like a true scholar,' Daphne says drily.

Patti laughs as she takes their photo.

Myrtle fixes her smile in place, her cheeks aching from holding it the entire ceremony. Everything about the day feels unreal. She's been working towards this moment for so long, and now that it's finally here, she doesn't feel ready for it.

'OK, enough photos,' she insists.

'I should go,' Sophie says, glancing across at her family waiting for her.

'Me too,' Abi says.

Myrtle nods.

They stand there, arms limp by their sides.

'So ...' Myrtle says, her vision filming.

'Don't,' Sophie whispers, blinking rapidly.

'This is it then,' Abi says with a sigh. 'Us being released into the big, nasty world.'

Myrtle nods dubiously. 'I guess so.' She wonders if they feel as petrified as she does.

They stand there, hesitating. All around them are the sounds of shrieking and laughter.

'Well, all right then.'

'All right.'

They hug each other as one, Myrtle sandwiched between them.

'See you next month at my birthday barbecue,' Sophie reminds them.

Myrtle nods.

Abi and Sophie turn and head towards the car park, climbing into their families' packed estate cars.

Myrtle stands there, waving back as they drive away, not moving until they've both vanished around the corner.

She turns, watching her family from a distance for a moment, Patti and Daphne laughing at something Elliott is saying, Myrtle's gown fluttering behind him in the breeze, making him look like a caped superhero. For the first time that day, a genuine smile breaks free on her face as she hurries back to join them.

42

'This is where you'll be sitting.' Lawrence ushers Matthew towards a desk at the end of a long row of identical desks, separated by small partitions. 'Any questions?'

'What the hell am I supposed to be doing?' he wants to ask his new boss, but he just shakes his head.

'All right then. You can focus on data entry on the spreadsheet this morning.'

Matthew nods and takes a seat, switches on the computer and then stares out of the small window next to his desk. All he can see is grey clouds and grey tower blocks. When he looks around the office, everything else looks grey as well: the partitions, the desks, the chairs, the carpet. Even his colleagues seem to be dressed in various hues of monochrome, their skin pallid-looking.

'You worked in an office before?' a voice beside him says.

Matthew turns and looks at the man seated at the desk next to him. His oily hair is centre-parted and tucked behind his ears, and the grey jacket and trousers of his crumpled suit don't match.

'No,' Matthew admits. 'I'm just temping while I take a break from uni.'

'All that drinking and partying wear you out, did it?'

Matthew hesitates. 'Something like that.'

'So what are you studying?'

'Veterinary science.'

His colleague pulls a face. 'Jesus. Rather you than me. What the hell do you want to stick your arm up an animal's rectum for?'

Matthew doesn't answer.

The man holds out a damp hand. 'Ivan.'

He reluctantly shakes it. 'Matthew. So how long have you worked here?'

'Fifteen years.' Ivan gives a throaty laugh as Matthew's eyebrows shoot up in surprise, and then he shrugs. 'At least we get four weeks off a year for good behaviour.' He swivels back to face his computer and Matthew does the same.

After two hours of mindless data entry, he slips off to the toilets, just to stretch his legs more than anything else. The fluorescent strip lights are making his eyes water and the stale, regurgitated air conditioning creates a constant background hum of white noise. It's like working inside a migraine.

When he gets back to his desk after spending as long as possible in the toilet without someone thinking he has some kind of bowel problem, he finds Ivan watching porn on his computer, the sound muted.

Lawrence strides over and rests one arm on top of the partition in front of him. 'Have you got a minute, Ivan?'

Ivan holds up a finger. 'Give me a sec. I'm just finalising some numbers here ...' He lets the video run to the end, jotting down random numbers on a notepad as he stares poker-faced at his screen, while a potbellied man is whipped by two bored-looking Asian women. Then he closes down the window and leans back in his chair. 'Done. What can I do for you, Lawrence?'

'I just wanted you to clarify a few things in this report ...'

Matthew tunes them out as he begins entering more numbers on the spreadsheet, blinking rapidly as the figures begin to swim in front of him.

★

'How was it?' Grace asks when he steps through the door that evening.

'It was fine,' he lies.

'You're soaked!' his mother exclaims, reaching for his jacket.

He shrugs it off and hangs it over the radiator. 'There was a Tube strike, so I had to wait ages to get on a bus.'

'London,' Grace says, with a shake of her head. 'So, what are the people you work with like?'

'They seem ... interesting,' he says, leaning against the counter, watching her make dinner.

'Oh good. That's good.' She hands him a knife and three tomatoes. He stands next to her as he chops them. She smiles across at him. 'I could get used to this, you know.'

'Used to what?'

'Having you around.'

He smiles but says nothing, feeling the sharp edges of the folded envelope in his pocket, which had arrived for him that morning, asking a question he didn't yet know the answer to.

She holds out a strand of spaghetti for him to try. He bites into it and nods his head, watching her drain the pasta and then stir in the sauce.

'Luke!' Grace calls, handing Matthew the saucepan to take over to the table.

Luke lumbers in, sitting down next to Grace.

'It will be good for you to save up a bit of money before you go back to uni, so you're not in debt when you leave,' she tells him, pausing between mouthfuls to twizzle spaghetti around a fork to feed Luke.

Matthew nods, even though he knows they'll need the majority of his wages to pay the bills, now Peter isn't around.

Once they've finished eating, Matthew goes to clear their plates and wash up, but Grace rests a hand on his arm.

'I'll do that. You go sit down and relax, when you've been working so hard all day.'

Luke follows him into the sitting room, pressing up next to him on the sofa. He'd ignored Matthew for the first few weeks after he returned, as if he expected him to leave again at any moment, but now he doggedly follows Matthew wherever he goes around the house, like an unwavering shadow.

Matthew listens to the sound of his mum humming along to the radio as she washes up, then he glances over at Luke, who smiles sleepily at him. He pulls out the crumpled letter he'd received that morning from his university, telling him he needed to notify them of his return date as soon as possible if they were to keep his place open for him. He thinks of the countless texts Ed and Giles have sent him, asking when he'll be back, which he keeps deleting without replying to, not knowing what to tell them. He reads the letter one last time, looks across at Luke now slumped in the corner of the sofa asleep, then he balls the letter up and throws it on the fire, watching it catch and ignite.

43

What. The. Hell, Myrtle thinks, looking around the office.

She hadn't been entirely sure what to expect, but it certainly wasn't this. She'd imagined important-looking, fashionable people strutting around, taking urgent phone calls and rushing out to premieres and high-profile interviews. The reality is a bunch of mushroom-skinned, paunchy men in faded *Doctor Who* T-shirts, silently tapping away at their keyboards. None of them even glance up at her, let alone smile.

'Right, let me talk you through everyone,' her line manager Tony says, pulling out a floor plan and using a biro to scrawl people's names and phone extensions on. He has a fine layer of fur covering his arms and hands, and his breath smells like onions.

'What else do you need to know?' he ponders, tapping a biro against his coffee-stained teeth. 'We don't get overtime or time off in-lieu. They haven't given anyone a pay rise in the last five years, so don't hold your breath on that one. Oh, and we only get a staff Christmas party every other year.'

Myrtle laughs at the last part, thinking he's cracking a joke, but Tony just frowns at her.

'Oh. Right,' Myrtle murmurs, thinking, *Thirteen years of school and three years of uni – to get here?*

Tony drops a huge lever-arch file onto her desk. 'So these are the addresses for you to post out the magazine subscriptions to.' Then he dumps another one on top of it. 'We're a bit behind. Any questions?'

Myrtle wordlessly shakes her head.

The buses are heaving because of the Tube strike, so Myrtle has to wait in the pouring rain until she's able to squeeze on a 22. She people-watches as she waits, studying the throngs of resigned commuters, shoulders hunched against the wind and the rain, waiting for their cramped, over-priced transport back to their cramped, over-priced homes.

As she tries to tune out the noise of rumbling bus engines and angry car horns, and not inhale the smoggy air too deeply, she wonders if London will ever feel like home. If she'll ever feel like she belongs in a city like this.

She glances over at a man, about her age, in a crumpled business suit. When their eyes meet he actually smiles at her, unlike most Londoners, who frown at her warily or quickly look away if their gazes accidentally intersect.

When a 22 shudders to a halt in front of them, he steps back to allow Myrtle on first. She turns to smile her thanks at him but is jostled further into the already rammed bus by other impatient commuters. When the doors close, meaning everyone has to press in even tighter, and the bus pulls away, she can still see him standing there, tall and unwavering, as if he doesn't even notice the rain hammering down around him.

44

'Come in, come in,' Emily says, beckoning Matthew into the hallway. 'Do you mind taking your shoes off?'

'Sure thing,' he says, taking in the expensive rug and polished wooden floors. He slips off his shoes and realises he's got holes on both big toes of his socks.

'Wow, this is like an actual grown-up's house,' Matthew says as he wanders from room to room.

'I know,' Greg says, a little guiltily. He leads him into the guest bedroom. 'If you ever want to stay over,' he says, winking. And then he opens his and Emily's bedroom door. 'And this is where the magic happens.'

Emily whacks him in the stomach, making him groan.

Matthew nods, averting his eyes from the king-size bed with its mound of silky cushions, looking instead at the huge sash windows and tasteful artwork decorating the walls. For a moment he imagines himself living in a place like this, with a girl like Emily.

'So what do you think?' Greg says, interrupting his thoughts.

'I think you're a lucky bastard,' Matthew tells him, punching him a little too hard on the arm.

Over the next hour, the flat gradually fills up with Emily and Greg's friends, most of whom Matthew has never met before. This always seems to be the way with his friends in relationships – they tend to socialise only with other couples, as if they're all part of some exclusive club.

He stands in the corner of the sitting room, trying not to stare at a pretty blonde girl he would never have the confidence to go up to. She appears to be the only other person in the room not there with someone else.

'She's single,' Emily whispers in his ear as she passes by with a plate of something she keeps referring to as 'ordurves', which just make Matthew even hungrier.

'Who is?' he says, feigning ignorance.

Emily just gives him a knowing smile.

Later on in the evening, he sees Emily talking to her and the girl glances over at him, shrugs and then smiles.

A few seconds later, she's walking directly towards him. Matthew doesn't know where to look, so he just stares down at the holes in his socks.

'Hello,' a voice says.

He glances up. 'Hi,' he manages to force out.

'Emily was just telling me that you've known her and Greg since you were kids.'

Matthew nods dumbly.

'She also said that you're the loveliest, most genuine guy she knows, and I'd be a fool if I didn't come over here and talk to you.'

He can't help but feel a flush of pride that Emily would even use those words to describe him. He shrugs. 'She hangs out with a lot of arseholes.'

She laughs and Matthew breathes an inward sigh of relief.

'I think we're the only single people here,' she says, raising a perfectly arched eyebrow.

'Looks like it,' he agrees.

A bottle of wine later, she leans in close and whispers, 'How about getting out of here?'

He swallows. 'OK.'

Outside, she flags down a taxi in seconds.

'How do girls do that?' Matthew wonders aloud.

She grins. 'I would have got one even quicker if you weren't standing beside me.'

'Where to?' the taxi driver asks.

'Do you know any good bars around here?' Matthew says to her.

She shakes her head. 'How about we just go back to yours instead?'

Matthew hesitates. 'The thing is ... I live with other people.'

'So do I,' she says.

He steels himself. 'I live with my parents,' he says quietly.

Both of her eyebrows shoot up in surprise. 'Oh. OK.'

'You're on the meter here,' the taxi driver interrupts. 'Where are you headed?'

The girl studies Matthew for a moment, then leans forward and reels off an address to the driver. Matthew rests back against his seat, his heartbeat accelerating. So this was really happening.

'I don't even know your name,' he says to her as the taxi pulls away.

'It's Felicity,' she says, taking hold of his hand.

He's just curling his fingers around hers when she slides his hand underneath her skirt, nudging it up higher until his baby finger is grazing the smooth satin of her underwear.

Matthew swallows loudly, his hand frozen there. He's never done anything like this with another person right there, and certainly never with a girl he's just met.

She leans over and kisses him. Matthew can taste her synthetic lip gloss. He resists the temptation to wipe his mouth across his sleeve – or better yet, her mouth – and instead tries to lose himself in the moment.

Back at hers, Felicity excuses herself to go to the bathroom. He sits stiffly at the end of the bed in just his boxer shorts as he waits for her, unsure whether he should get under the covers or not. When she comes back into the room, she shuts the door with finality as she glances over at him. She's dusted something glittery across her chest, and he can smell her freshly reapplied perfume from here. It catches at the back of his throat, making him want to cough.

She takes her top off and then removes her bra, tossing it to one side.

Matthew tries to keep his eyes trained on her face.

Felicity laughs. 'Emily said you'd be shy.'

He frowns.

She steps closer. 'But that's OK. Because I'm not.'

One more step and she's astride him. 'Fuck me,' she whispers in his ear, tugging at his boxers.

'Um, OK . . .' Matthew says, shifting awkwardly back onto the bed with her still on top of him.

'Talk dirty to me,' she murmurs, her tongue darting into his ear.

He rubs at it with the heel of his hand, his mind suddenly blank.

'Come on,' she urges impatiently.

He opens his mouth, but he can't find the words. He thinks of Greg and Emily, their arms wrapped around each other most of the night, bound by their twelve years of shared history. And here he is, lying naked with a girl he's just met who probably won't even remember his name tomorrow.

'Sorry,' he murmurs as he begins to go limp.

'What's wrong with you?' Felicity says, her eyes narrowing.

'I don't know,' he replies, wondering the same thing.

45

'My daughter, the intrepid journalist,' Elliott says proudly.

'Dad, I'm a lowly assistant at an entertainment magazine no one's even heard of. Please don't start telling people I'm a journalist.'

'It's still journalism.'

Myrtle smiles at him. 'Are you hungry? Shall I make us something to eat?'

'Oh, that reminds me.' Elliott puts a cake tin on the table. 'Carrie made these.'

'Oh yeah, how is the new lodger?' Myrtle asks, biting into a biscuit.

'She's nice. She's always baking things and cooking dinner for me. She spent hours making these. She said it was all about simmering the ingredients for long enough.'

Myrtle looks at him knowingly. 'Do you fancy her?'

'She's a lesbian.'

Myrtle laughs, then catches herself. 'Sorry.'

Elliott shrugs. 'Can't seem to escape them.' He takes another biscuit. 'You'd like her. She's a hippie.'

'Why would I like her just because she's a hippie?'

'Well, she's vegan or veggie or v-something.'

'Maybe she'll convert you then, Dad.'

'If all vegan cookies taste like these, maybe she will,' he says, crunching into another one.

'I'll make us some tea to go with them.'

When she comes back, Elliott is sitting strangely in the armchair, his hands tightly gripping the arms like he's an unwilling passenger in a race car.

'Dad, are you all right?'

'I'm not sure. I feel kind of funny.' His pupils are huge.

Oh god, Myrtle thinks, rushing over and kneeling at his feet. 'Is it your heart? Can you feel me pinching you? How many fingers am I holding up? Can you stick your tongue out?'

He bats her away. 'I'll be fine in a second. It's just a funny turn. I forgot to have breakfast.'

'Maybe you need some more sugar if you feel faint,' Myrtle suggests, offering him another biscuit and stirring two teaspoons of sugar into his tea.

He bites into it. 'They're very moreish, aren't they?'

Myrtle nods, reaching for another one herself and dunking it into her tea.

'I hadn't heard of them before. Space cookies, Carrie called them.'

Myrtle freezes, the biscuit crumbling on her tongue. '*Space* cookies?'

Elliott nods. 'I think that's what she said.'

'As in *hash* cookies?'

Elliott frowns. 'Do you mean marijuana?'

'Yes, Dad, I mean marijuana.'

'Well, she did admit to smoking it now and again. But I didn't know you could cook with it.' He stares at the half-eaten biscuit in his hand. 'She did say not to eat too many at once, but I just thought she meant not to be greedy.'

'Oh shit, Dad. How many of these have you had?'

'I don't know. I've lost count.' His face has gone pale.

'Well, I've had four, so you've had at least five.'

'Except I might have had a couple on the train over here ...'

'Seven? Jesus, Dad! No wonder you feel funny. You must be as high as a kite.'

'Is that bad?'

'We'll soon find out.'

His eyes, wider than she's ever seen them, fasten on hers. 'I think I need to lie down.' He slides off the armchair and sprawls out on the rug.

'OK,' Myrtle says, putting a cushion under his head, wondering if she should move him into the recovery position.

Just then, it hits her too. 'I think I need to lie down as well,' she murmurs, stretching out beside him. Everything looks brighter, somehow, as if she's seeing things in high definition. She glances over at her dad, who's blinking up at the ceiling. He's beginning to look old now, his hair entirely grey, his jawline softening, the skin beginning to pouch under his eyes.

'Stop staring at me,' he tells her, still gazing up at the ceiling.

'I worry about you,' she says quietly.

He turns his head to look at her, his eyes not entirely focused. 'Don't. I'm tougher than I look.'

She hesitates, thinking that now is probably as good a time as any to ask the question she's wanted to for so long, but been too afraid. 'Are you lonely, Dad?'

He's silent for a while before he speaks. 'Not all the time.'

'Have you ever tried to meet anyone else?'

'Sure. I've been on dates. But none of them compare to your mother, so ...' He trails off, then shrugs. 'No one should have to settle in life.'

'It's not about settling. You've always been closed off to the idea of meeting someone new. You've spent the last however many years secretly hoping Mum would come back to you, haven't you? When it was all for nothing.'

'It wasn't for nothing.'

'Dad ...'

He blinks more rapidly, his gaze still fixed on the swirls on the ceiling above them. He suddenly doesn't look like an old man anymore; he looks like a little boy.

'Sometimes, hoping for the impossible, even when you know it's impossible – sometimes it's the only thing that keeps you going. It's the only thing that gets you out of bed each day.'

'Oh, Dad.' Myrtle leans her head on his shoulder, and he wraps his arm around her. She breathes in his familiar scent – of cut grass and creosote – thinking how one of the hardest parts about growing up is realising your parents haven't got it any more figured out than you do.

They stay like that for a while, both of them lost in their own thoughts. Then Elliott breaks the silence by saying, 'Talk to me, Myrtle. We never talk.'

'Yes we do. I call you every week.'

'You know what I mean.'

'What do you want to know?'

'Well ... is there anyone in your life?'

'Not right now,' she says, shifting uncomfortably against the carpet. She isn't going to tell him about the string of disappointing dates she's been on, no matter how high she is.

'I don't get it.' Elliott shakes his head. 'How can any guy look at you and not realise how special you are?'

'You're the only one who thinks I'm special, Dad.'

'Then the rest of them are fools.'

Myrtle smiles at him. 'Maybe the reason I'm single is because I'm subconsciously doing that thing that all daughters do: comparing every man to you, and so they're always going to fall short.'

'That's nonsense,' Elliott says, shaking his head, but Myrtle can tell he's trying not to grin. He turns his head to look at her. 'Maybe I should get stoned more often if it means having a heart-to-heart with my daughter,' he says.

'You don't need to take Class B drugs to do that.'

He laughs, a deep chuckle at first, and then it becomes louder and more drawn out, until tears are coursing down his cheeks he's laughing so hard.

'What's so funny?'

'I'm ... not ... sure,' he gasps, as Myrtle starts to join in too.

Just then the door swings open and Myrtle's housemate Ben looms in the doorway, frowning down at them sprawled out on the carpet, clutching their sides.

'What are you two on?' he says.

Myrtle points to the tin, still laughing. 'Knock yourself out.'

46

Matthew stares at the five-figure number and swallows. 'That's a lot of money.'

'Yes,' Lawrence agrees, watching him closely. 'It is. And you'd get your own office. A *corner* office.'

'A corner office,' Matthew echoes.

'And your own PA.'

Matthew's eyebrows shoot up. He'd have his own *assistant*?

'Plus you'd get an extra five days holiday a year.'

'Wow.'

'I mean, you might need to work the odd weekend here and there, take a few evening calls ... But it's a fantastic opportunity.'

'It is,' Matthew says, staring at the row of noughts again, feeling strangely panicked. He rubs his sticky palms against his knees, breathing deeply, as if he can't get enough oxygen into his lungs.

'So what do you say?' Lawrence asks.

'I say ... thank you ...'

Lawrence beams.

'... but no thank you ...'

The beam turns into a frown. 'No?'

Matthew shakes his head. His heart is beating so loud, he can barely hear his own words. 'I'm sorry ... but I can't ... I can't take the promotion.'

The frown deepens. 'Why not? Is it the money? Because

I could probably go another five grand higher. But that's my absolute limit.'

Matthew hesitates, his fingernails digging into his palms as his hands curl into fists beneath the table. 'That's ... that's really generous of you, Lawrence. But I'm sorry, I can't.'

Lawrence narrows his eyes. 'Can I ask why not?'

'Because ... because if I stay here ... then I'll never leave.'

'Excuse me?'

'I'll never figure out what it is I really want to do.'

'I see,' Lawrence says coolly. 'So am I to take it that not only are you declining my offer but you're also giving me your notice?'

Matthew clenches his fists a little tighter, his heart stuttering, knowing that he's just about to quit a job when he's got nothing else to go to.

'Well?' Lawrence prompts impatiently, his former cheery veneer well and truly locked away now.

'Yes,' Matthew forces out. 'This is me handing in my notice. I'll get a letter to you this afternoon so you have it in writing.'

'Very well.'

What have you just done? Matthew thinks as he numbly makes his way back to his desk, slumping into his chair.

Ivan's head jerks up from the panting naked woman on his screen. 'Are you all right? You look like you're going to spew.'

'I did it.'

'What?'

'I quit,' Matthew says, the reality of it making him feel dizzy and not quite there.

'What? Why?'

'Because I hate it here.'

'So? Everyone hates it here. You can't quit. You're the only thing that makes this place half fucking bearable.'

'Cheers,' Matthew replies. 'But I've already handed in my notice.'

'Why? Is it because you're not getting paid enough? Because I'll speak to Lawrence—'

'He already offered me a big pay rise to stay. And a corner office and PA.'

'What the fuck?' Ivan says.

'I know.'

'And you still said no?'

Matthew nods.

'You're a fucking idiot.'

'Maybe. But I'm tired of doing a job that's so mind-numbing that I'm just clockwatching all the time. This was only supposed to be temporary. Yet somehow four years of my life have slipped by,' he says, trying not to think about how if he hadn't had to leave uni, he'd be a fully qualified vet by now. 'I want to do something meaningful; I don't want to be putting numbers into a spreadsheet for the rest of my life.'

'What's so wrong with that? At least it's not cleaning toilets or stacking shelves or delivering junk mail.'

'So you're saying I shouldn't aim so high?'

'I'm just saying not everyone has to have a dream.'

'Maybe there aren't enough dreamers in the world.'

'So what *is* your dream job then?' Ivan says, eyes narrowed.

Matthew pauses. 'I'm still figuring that out,' he admits quietly.

Ivan shakes his head in disgust. 'Well, don't expect me to come to your leaving do.'

'That's all right, I wasn't planning on having one.'

Ivan stares at him. 'Fuck that. You're having a leaving do. I'll organise it, OK?'

Matthew smiles. 'As long as it's not in some strip club.'

'Now that I can't promise.'

Matthew looks around the office at the rest of his colleagues, thinking how he's spent more time with these people in the last four years than anyone else. It was a depressing thought, the fact you couldn't even choose the people you shared most of your waking life with.

He glances back at Ivan. 'You're the only thing that made this place half fucking bearable too, you know,' he tells him.

'I know,' Ivan says, puffing out his scrawny chest. 'I know.' He gets up and stares in the direction of Lawrence's office, rolling back his shoulders.

'Where are you going?' Matthew asks.

'To find out about this top-secret corner office.'

47

'Are you sure this is where we are on the map?' Sophie asks, turning it upside down and squinting at it.

'Give it here,' Tom says impatiently, snatching it from her hands. 'Women, eh?' he says to Liam, with a roll of his eyes.

'Don't start with that bullshit,' Abi says, 'especially when the two of you just sat there and watched as Myrtle put the spare tyre on all by herself, because you're both supposedly *sooo* hung-over.'

'Didn't see you offering to lend a hand either,' Tom points out, draining the rest of his beer can, before crumpling it up and putting it in his rucksack, along with the other two he's already drunk on the walk up.

'I twinged my back yesterday in yoga,' Abi protests, going over to stand beside Liam as he doubles over and starts dry-heaving.

'I think we need to go that way,' Myrtle says, trying to judge which direction is north from the position of the sun.

Tom acts like he hasn't heard her and continues to scrutinise the map, and then, after another five minutes, he says, 'Right, we need to go this way,' pointing in the same direction Myrtle just had.

'Funny how this is the first year the boys have joined us and the first time we've managed to get lost,' Sophie says, falling into step beside Myrtle as Tom strides ahead.

'Dead weights, the pair of them,' Abi agrees, shaking her

head as Liam stumbles over to a patch of gorse and begins retching again.

Myrtle had pretended not to mind when they suggested bringing along Liam and Tom, even though Abi had been the one to insist on the very first trip that it should be an annual event with just the three of them, no one else. 'Sisterhood is what it's all about,' she'd said emphatically.

Nothing lasts forever, Myrtle thinks, sighing inwardly, before linking arms with them as they stop for a moment at the top of the hill to gaze out at the view.

Just then, something large and white comes flying past them on a gust of wind.

'Fucking fuckety fuck!' Tom hollers from up ahead.

'I'm guessing that was the map,' Myrtle says, as they watch it sail over the edge of the gorge.

Four hours later, they have finally pitched up in a small clearing by a wooded dell. While the boys hunt for firewood, the three of them are in charge of putting up the tents, but just like previous years, Myrtle ends up doing most of it by herself, while Abi and Sophie gingerly apply fresh plasters over their blistered feet.

'You're the dead weights,' Myrtle tells them, hammering in the last peg.

'But at least we're not pretending to be anything else,' Abi says, grinning up at her.

Now they are gathered around the fire, eating Pot Noodles and drinking Liam's potent home brew.

'Mate, this is your best one yet,' Tom says, smacking his lips in appreciation.

'Yes,' Liam says vaguely, his head lolling on his neck.

'I told you to go easy after last night,' Abi says, moving the rest of the bottle out of his reach. 'So much for hair of the dog.'

'Yes,' Liam replies.

'Is anyone still hungry? I made brownies,' Sophie says, passing around a tin.

'Yes,' Liam mumbles, staring off into the distance.

'Hey, Liam, did you hear how London Zoo have successfully mated their first camel and giraffe?' Tom says. 'They're calling it a gamel.'

'Yes,' he monotones, as Tom sniggers and Abi rolls her eyes.

'Liam, is it true that you still wet the bed at night?' Sophie asks.

'Yes.'

'And when Abi isn't home, you like to wear her underwear?' Myrtle asks.

'Yes.'

'And is it true that the only way you can stay hard is for Abi to sing "Eye of the Tiger" while you're doing it?' Tom asks.

'Yes.'

'Oh, shut up, you lot,' Abi snaps, as the three of them burst into laughter.

When Tom and Liam have finally passed out, and the three of them give up trying to drag their inert bodies into the tents, they stay up, feeding the last bits of branch into the fire.

'We should do this more often than once a year,' Myrtle says, hoping the next trip will be just the three of them again.

'Definitely,' Sophie agrees.

Abi nods, smiling at them both. 'So ...' she says, nibbling at a piece of brownie. 'There was something Liam and I wanted to tell you, but given that he's such a lightweight ...' She throws a withering look at his slumbering form. Then she turns back to them and holds out her hand, and in the firelight they can see what they failed to notice in the daylight: a diamond sparkling on her ring finger.

'Wow,' Myrtle says, struggling to cover her surprise. 'Congratulations.'

'You're getting married?' Sophie says, sounding more incredulous than happy.

Abi shrugs. 'I know it's crazy. But Liam got really drunk one night – shocking, right? – and he asked me. And I said yes – I was pretty wasted too. But in the morning, we realised that neither of us regretted it.' She glances down at the ring. 'We'll probably have a long engagement. And a really small do. I don't want a big fuss.'

'Well, we'll help you any way we can,' Myrtle says, recovering herself. 'Won't we, Soph?'

'Of course,' Sophie says in a small voice, still eyeing Abi's engagement ring. 'Of course we will.'

'I know it feels like everything's about to change, but it won't, I promise,' Abi vows, as if she needs to reassure herself more than anyone. 'I won't be one of those people that turns into a boring old fart as soon as I get married. I'll still be crazy old me, just with a ring on my finger, that's all.'

Of course everything's going to change, Myrtle thinks, as Abi takes another slug of home brew and drunkenly gets to her feet. *It already has.*

'Come on!' Abi orders. She holds out her hands to both of them, humming the tune of 'Eye of the Tiger' until they're all on their feet, heads tilted back, gazing up at the spinning, star-filled sky, yelling the words at the top of their lungs.

48

'How was work?' Grace asks. She is curled up on the sofa, a half-drunk bottle of wine beside her.

'It's work,' Matthew says with a shrug, pouring himself a glass before collapsing down into the armchair across from her and Luke.

It's been almost a year now since he left his office job. In those first few months, he'd been too scared to tell Grace that not only did he turn down a promotion and pay rise, but he quit with nothing else to go to. He used to leave the house at half seven every morning as usual, walking the streets until the job centre opened, killing time in the library, responding to countless job adverts. He managed to pick up a bit of casual work, mowing public parks for the council and helping out on construction sites, but none of it lasted longer than a couple of weeks. But then Emily had put him in touch with the uncle of a friend, who got him a job building film sets. Even though he didn't love it, and it was physically exhausting, at least he wasn't stuck in an office punching numbers into a computer.

'I saw Emily's mum earlier today,' Grace says, topping up her own glass.

'Oh?' Matthew says, knowing what's coming.

'She told me Greg and Emily are getting married next summer.'

'That's right,' he replies, as casually as he can, trying to pretend that the news hadn't felled him when they told him. 'Greg's asked me to be best man.'

'That's nice,' she says, taking another sip of wine. 'And what about ... a plus one?'

'What about one?' he says, wondering if his mother is hoping he'll take her. God, he hopes not.

There's a long pause, and when he glances across at her, he sees Grace studying him closely.

'Do you like girls, Matthew?' she asks him quietly.

'What?'

'It's a simple question.'

He stares at her. 'Are you asking me what I think you're asking?'

'I just thought I should ask the question in case no one had ever asked it before, and you'd been waiting your whole life just for someone to ask it.'

'Yes, I like girls, Mum, and no, I have not been waiting my whole life for you to ask me that.'

'Then I don't understand why you haven't met anyone yet.'

He frowns. 'It's not that simple.'

'Yes it is. You go out there and you meet people. You're a good-looking boy. You're kind, you're funny in your own way—'

'Gee, thanks.'

'—you're handy. Any girl would be lucky to have a boy-friend like you.'

'Mum, no one thinks I'm special except you.'

'I find that hard to believe.' She leans forward to empty the rest of the bottle into her glass. 'It would make me so happy to see you with someone nice.'

'I'm fine as I am, Mum.'

'I know you are. I just think that once you meet the right person ...' She trails off.

'Maybe she doesn't exist,' Matthew says, feeling bone-weary tired all of a sudden. 'Or maybe the person that I'd think is perfect wouldn't even look twice at me,' he adds, thinking of Emily.

She shakes her head. 'It will happen when it's meant to.'

Matthew forces a smile. 'So everyone keeps saying.'

Grace watches him again for a moment, slowly rotating the wine glass by its stem, then smiles back at him. 'You know, sometimes I look at you and I can't believe you came out of me, that you were once that tiny baby I held in my arms.'

Matthew wrinkles his nose, shifting uncomfortably on the sofa.

'Where did my little boy go?' she asks, a wistful expression on her face.

'He grew up.'

Grace rises to her feet and pads over to the stereo, putting on some music before holding out her hands to him. 'Come on, I'll teach you how to dance properly, so you can wow all the bridesmaids. Girls appreciate a man who can dance.'

'Mum, no ...'

She looks at him, her expression serious. 'Just humour me, would you?'

Matthew sighs but gets to his feet. She shows him where to put his arms and then counts out the beat as she nudges him in the direction he should be moving in.

'You're a natural,' she says, beaming up at him. 'You'll have to be careful you don't upstage the bride and groom.'

He's starting to feel woozy, either from the wine or the tight circles they're spinning in. 'Why couldn't it have been me, Mum?' he murmurs.

She squeezes his shoulder. 'Because it was Greg, darling.'

Luke hauls himself off the sofa, tired of being an onlooker, and pushes himself between them.

'Do you remember us dancing, Lukey?' Grace says softly, as they stagger around the carpet.

Matthew has seen countless pictures of his parents dancing

at various events, which are now tucked away in the photo albums that no one looks at anymore, and he's heard the stories about how Luke was always first on the dance floor and the last one off, dancing with anyone who would let him, from toddlers to OAPs.

Matthew watches his parents as he takes Luke's still-warm spot on the sofa. The next song is a slower tempo and they're just clinging to each other now rather than dancing. Grace closes her eyes and Matthew looks away, trying to pretend that he doesn't notice the tears leaking out of them.

49

'How are you feeling?' Myrtle asks.

'I just want to get this day over and done with,' Abi mutters.

'Don't say that!' Sophie says as she fiddles with her veil. 'This is going to be the happiest day of your life.'

'This is going to be the most expensive day of my life,' Abi retorts. 'And I hate it when people say that – it makes it sound like every other day for the rest of my life is always going to fall short.' Sophie bites her tongue as Abi takes a deep, shaky breath. 'Fuck, I'm sweating so badly.'

Myrtle blots her armpits with a tissue.

'Oh god, oh god, oh god. This is it. This is really it.' She inhales deeply, as if she's about to dive underwater. 'I didn't know I'd feel this terrified.'

'I think you're supposed to be,' Myrtle says.

'No, you're supposed to be excited and ecstatic,' Sophie interjects, now fussing with the train.

'I've only ever loved one person, and now I'm marrying him,' Abi says, a panicked look on her face. 'What if Liam isn't the love of my life? How will I know?'

'Of course he is,' Sophie says soothingly. 'Do you know how lucky you are that you found him so early on, and now you get to spend the rest of your lives together?'

Abi doesn't respond.

'It's just like with Tom and me. We know we're meant to be together.'

Myrtle bites her tongue at that, thinking how Sophie has been dropping not-so-subtle hints for the past three years now and Tom still hasn't put a ring on her finger. When Myrtle had suggested that Sophie be the one to pop the question to Tom instead if she really wanted to get married that much, Sophie had just laughed at her, as if she'd made a joke, and said, 'I'm not getting down on my knee. That's Tom's job.'

Abi is staring dismally at her reflection, her forearms hidden from sight in the meringue of her dress. 'What was I thinking when I chose this? I look like a twat.'

'You look like a princess!' Sophie exclaims.

'Exactly,' Abi says. 'Jesus, how did I let myself get so carried away? I hate churches. I hate extravagance. I even let Liam persuade me into booking the honeymoon in the Maldives, which I swore I'd never go to. It's like as soon as I got that ring on my finger, I lost all my scruples.'

'You're allowed to be excessive on your wedding day,' Sophie says.

'We should have got married in a registry office, had drinks in the local pub, and then given the money we would have spent to a homeless charity. That's what we should have done.'

'But you didn't, so just enjoy it,' Sophie insists.

Myrtle uselessly pulls at the low-cut neckline of her own dress, wishing Abi hadn't chosen something so revealing.

'Don't worry, I'm not one of those bridezillas that doesn't want her bridesmaids to outshine her,' Abi had told her and Sophie when she'd first shown them the dresses she'd bought online, while Sophie gushed over them and Myrtle made vague sounds of enthusiasm, trying not to think how they were probably made in Chinese sweatshops.

'Oh god, I don't know if I'm even ready to be a wife!' Abi is saying now, collapsing onto a chair, the train bunched between her knees.

'Liam's probably feeling exactly the same way,' Myrtle tells her.

Abi stares up at her dismally. 'Is that supposed to reassure me?'

'I don't know.'

Sophie glances worriedly at her watch. 'It's almost eleven, Abs.'

Abi gives a resolute nod and then holds out both hands for them to hoist her back up. 'It's fine,' she says. 'If it doesn't work out, we'll just get divorced.'

Sophie's eyes boggle while Myrtle pats her on the back. 'That's the spirit.' She holds out Abi's bouquet. 'Ready?'

Abi just stands there, rooted to the spot, staring at their joint reflection in the mirror.

'Look, if you don't want to go through with it, just say the word and Sophie and I will sort everything, OK? It's not too late,' Myrtle says gently.

Abi lets out a bitter laugh. 'It's twenty grand too late.' She grabs the bouquet, a determined expression on her face. 'All right, let's get this over with.'

When Myrtle finds her table for dinner, she swallows a sigh as she sees it's filled with couples. There's just one empty seat next to hers. She glances at the name card: *Matthew*.

She wonders if this is Abi trying to play matchmaker, glancing across at a tall guy standing at the bar by himself. But then a girl walks over to him and he puts his arm around her.

'Ah, how lovely,' a woman at her table gasps, pointing out the marquee window.

Myrtle looks over to see another wedding party across the lawn, which has taken over the opposite wing of the manor house, the guests staring up at the sky as hundreds of silver balloons are released into the air. She bites her lip, trying not to think how close they are to the sea here, and how sea creatures will most likely swallow them and die.

Does no one even care about things like that? she wonders, as the crowd begins to clap and cheer as the balloons obliterate the evening sun for a moment, then are carried off on the wind.

'Hello, I'm Matthew,' says a voice from beside her.

Myrtle turns to the man before her. 'I'm Myrtle,' she replies, forcing a smile. She has a feeling this is going to be a long night. 'So how do you know the happy couple?' she asks, although she can already hazard a guess.

'I'm Liam's grandfather,' he says, reaching for a bottle and filling both their wine glasses. He takes a slow sip and then nods approvingly. 'He might not be the sharpest tool in the box but my grandson sure knows a good wine.'

Myrtle laughs in spite of herself.

'So, tell me, why has a lovely young lady like yourself been put next to an old codger like me?' he asks, tucking his napkin into his collar.

'Well,' Myrtle says, leaning in and lowering her voice, 'I think it's because I'm one of those awkward single people that no one knows what to do with at events like this.' She grimaces.

'You and me both,' Matthew concedes with a smile. 'My grandkids keep trying to set me up on dates, even though I keep telling them I'm perfectly happy on my own.' He gives a dry chuckle. 'It's funny how being single seems to make other people so uncomfortable.'

'Exactly,' Myrtle agrees.

'Marriage isn't for everyone, you know,' Matthew remarks, glancing over at the top table, where Abi and Liam are kissing a little too amorously, while the other diners at their table politely avert their eyes. 'Trust me, the older you get, the more you realise that no one's inseparable.'

'Except conjoined twins who share vital organs,' Myrtle says.

'Yes, maybe that's the one true exception.' He smiles.

'You want to know the best thing about being single?'

'Sure.'

'You take more risks,' he says. 'I can tell you, I've done more in the past twelve years since I got divorced than I ever did in the forty-four years I was married. Sometimes, being with someone can hold you back. You never get a chance to discover who you might have been.'

Myrtle nods, gazing at him thoughtfully.

After Abi and Liam have had their first dance, staggering drunkenly around the floor, Myrtle watches the other couples flocking to join them as another slow song comes on. She feels a tap on her bare shoulder, making her start.

'Want to dance?' asks one of Liam's rugby friends, who she'd spotted picking his nose throughout most of the ceremony.

She's about to say yes out of politeness, but then shakes her head. 'No, thank you,' she says resolutely.

He frowns, then walks on a few paces, before stopping to ask Abi's cousin the same question. Hailey smiles up at him and then stands, taking his meaty hand and letting him lead her out onto the floor.

'Not one for dancing?' Matthew asks.

'No, not really,' Myrtle lies.

'Probably just as well, as you're chatting to a man with two left feet.'

'Abi's about to throw the bouquet,' Sophie interrupts breathlessly. 'Are you coming?'

Myrtle shakes her head. She watches the single women in the room congregate behind Abi, all eyes focused intently in front of them.

'This has got to be the most demeaning, sexist wedding tradition ever,' Myrtle complains. 'Why isn't there something similar for all the bachelors?'

'Because they'd be running away from it, not trying to catch it,' Matthew points out.

She laughs, watching as Sophie rushes forward, elbowing another girl out of the way, before snatching the bouquet out of the air with a triumphant grin. Myrtle glances across the room to see Liam chuckling as he slaps a stony-faced Tom on the back.

Matthew drains the rest of his wine, smacking his lips together. 'Right, I think that might have to be my nightcap,' he says, getting unsteadily to his feet.

'Here,' Myrtle says, offering her arm for him to link, before guiding him out to the lobby.

As they wait for the lift, he holds out his hand. 'I have to say, I'm very glad I was put next to you at dinner.'

Myrtle bats his hand away and enfolds him in a hug. 'Ditto.'

He smiles at her. 'You're a wonderful young lady, Myrtle. But I'm not going to tell you that you'll meet someone soon. Because I think you're the type of person who will be just fine either way. So don't you worry about what anyone else thinks and just enjoy it.'

'What, being single?'

'No. Life.'

50

'Shit, I'm burning up,' Greg says, running a finger around the inside of his collar, flapping the lapels of his morning suit so that the coat-tails flare up behind him.

'I think the groom's supposed to be nervous,' Matthew assures him.

'I'm not nervous about marrying Emily. It's standing up in front of all these people and saying our vows. And then dancing in front of them. Fuck!' He blows a sharp puff of air out and rotates his shoulders, like a boxer readying for a fight. 'And to think we've used up all our savings for this,' he says, shaking his head.

'Stop complaining. Do you realise how lucky you are?' Matthew says, thinking he'd swap places with Greg in a heartbeat.

'I know I am, I know,' he murmurs.

'You'll be fine,' Matthew says, slapping him on the back.

'Is this your idea of a pep talk? Because you're falling short on your best man duties ...'

'Here,' Matthew says, holding out a hip flask.

'Now we're talking,' Greg says, taking a hefty swig. 'You've definitely got the rings?'

'For the hundredth time – yes.' But Matthew gives a paranoid pat on his breast pocket anyway. Then he glances at his watch. 'OK, show time.'

Greg takes another lusty glug and then follows Matthew

inside the church. Half the guests are already seated.

'Oh god,' Greg moans. 'I can't believe you're going to leave me standing up here by myself. You're the worst best man ever.'

Matthew shrugs. 'You two are getting your money's worth when I'm acting as father of the bride too,' he says, before striding up the aisle and waiting in the vestibule for Emily to arrive.

He hadn't known what to say when she asked him.

'Seeing as I no longer speak to my dad, and Albie says he doesn't want to do it, I wondered if you would ... walk me down the aisle?' she'd said nervously. 'I understand completely if you'd rather not. If you think it would be too weird ...'

'It wouldn't be weird,' Matthew had lied. 'I mean, that was a long time ago that I threw myself at you,' he'd said, forcing a laugh.

Emily had reddened. 'I meant weird because you're also Greg's best man,' she'd said, not quite meeting his eye.

'Oh. Right,' Matthew had murmured, his cheeks blazing.

He glances at his watch, hoping Emily isn't one of those brides who insist on being fashionably late. He shuffles from foot to foot, feeling strangely nervous, as if he's the one about to get married.

He hears a car pull up outside and then the bridesmaids arrive in a flurry of turquoise blue. They walk down the aisle in pairs, and then it is just him and Emily standing there.

'You look ... beautiful,' he tells her, thinking there is no word to describe what she looks like. She takes his breath away.

'Thank you,' she says quietly. She steps closer to straighten his buttonhole. 'You look very handsome yourself.'

He holds out his arm. 'You ready?'

She shakes her head. 'Not yet.'

He pulls out his hip flask.

'Thank god,' Emily breathes, taking a swig. She screws the cap back on, reapplies her lipstick, lets out a shaky breath and then links her arm through his. 'OK, let's do this.'

The rest of the ceremony passes by in a blur. Matthew stands there, hands fisted at his sides. He seems to be working on autopilot, though, because he stands where he's supposed to and gets the rings out at the right moment, yet it's like he's not quite there.

After they've finished uttering their vows and the vicar tells Greg he can kiss the bride, Greg looks at Matthew and murmurs, 'I don't feel so good.' The next moment he's keeling over, landing face-first on the flagstone floor, the loud thud echoing around the church.

The whole congregation gasps. Both Matthew and Emily drop to their knees as they turn him over, Matthew talking to him, Emily slapping his cheek. After what feels like the longest minute, Greg finally opens one eye and looks up groggily at the vicar.

'That still counts, right? Because I don't think I can do it all over again.'

The gathered wedding guests let out a collective *aahhh* and then clap as hundreds of silver balloons are released from their netting, drifting up into the sky above them. Matthew watches as they're carried on the wind, out towards the coastline just five miles away, and he can't help but think how they will most likely end up in the sea, and then eventually in the stomachs of whales and dolphins. He looks at the smiling, laughing faces around him, wondering if he's the only one who has thoughts like this.

Ten minutes later, Emily and Greg take to the floor for their first dance. The guests have formed a circle around them that is close enough for Matthew to see Greg sweating under the fairylights, as well as the mottled purple of his swollen eye.

'The poor lad looks like Quasimodo,' a man beside him says.

Matthew nods, biting back a smile.

The music starts up and he instantly recognises the song as one from their childhood. As he watches Emily and Greg spin in slow circles, grinning at each other, he smiles to himself, thinking how much the three of them have changed since then.

As the song ends, other couples swarm the dance floor as Emily beckons them over. A plump woman, who looks like she's been taking full advantage of the open bar, begins to gyrate in the middle by herself.

'I'm married to that,' the man beside him says, shaking his head.

'She looks like she's having fun,' Matthew comments politely.

'Oh aye, she's the life and soul of any party, is our Kirsty.' He gives a crooked smile. 'You can't help who you fall in love with, eh?'

'No,' Matthew says, his eyes straying towards Emily again. 'If only you could.'

He excuses himself to go to the bar, then heads outside to the terrace, where he can see another wedding party going on in the marquee across the lawn. He watches a man doubled over, throwing up on his shoes, and is just about to go over and help when a red-haired woman comes to his rescue.

'Jesus, Liam, you best not let Abi see you like this,' she says, whacking him on the back as he gives one last heave.

He wipes his mouth across his sleeve and then staggers back inside, heading straight for the bar. The woman shakes her head and then walks barefoot across the lawn, holding up the hem of her full-length dress in one hand before sitting down on the stone steps of the terrace.

Matthew watches her for a moment, deliberating whether to go over and talk to her, when a voice calls out from the darkness: 'Myrtle, get back in here! They're just about to cut the cake.'

The woman sighs and slowly gets to her feet, before scooping up the edge of her dress again and running back across the dewy lawn.

Matthew finishes his beer and then heads back inside himself. Emily catches sight of him and comes over, pulling him onto the dance floor.

'You know it's tradition for the father of the bride to dance with the bride, right?' she says, grinning up at him as he puts his arms around her, counting out the beat in his head, just like his mother taught him.

'Thank you for being so amazing today,' Emily says. 'We couldn't have done it without you.'

'I'm just sorry I wasn't quick enough to catch that lumbering husband of yours before he face-planted,' Matthew says, the word 'husband' like a hard pebble in his mouth.

'Yeah, the wedding photos are ruined,' Emily says, gazing fondly over at Greg as he dances with her mum. She turns back to Matthew, hugging him as they dance. 'I can't believe I'm finally Mrs Sanderson now, after two years of planning.'

'Me neither,' Matthew says quietly.

Emily pulls back slightly and looks up at him. 'Your moment will come too, you know, Matty. You'll make some girl very happy one day.'

'If only I could find her,' Matthew murmurs. As he breathes in the scent of Emily's perfume, he wonders if that flicker he feels every time he's near her will ever die out. Or if one day he might meet a girl who will finally snuff it out for him.

51

'What do you think?'

Abi frowns, taking in Myrtle's jeans, flowery blouse and low-heeled boots. 'You look like you're off to do your weekly food shop, not go on a hot date.'

Myrtle sighs.

'Seriously,' Abi says, 'you dress like that and you wonder why you're still single?'

'All right, enough with the tough love.'

'Good thing I have back-up,' Abi says, opening the holdall she brought with her and pulling out a handful of sparkly dresses.

Myrtle shakes her head. 'I'm not wearing anything like that,' she says, frowning at a short, skin-tight black dress Abi is holding up. 'I'll look like a twelve-year-old girl playing dress-up.'

'No you won't.'

'Plus I don't want to give Caleb the wrong idea. It's only our second date.'

'You won't. You just want to get him a bit hot under the collar. Keep him coming back for more.'

Myrtle eyes the dress dubiously.

'Come on, live a little,' Abi tells her.

A few minutes later, Myrtle emerges from the bathroom, tugging self-consciously at the short hemline of the dress. 'How do I look?'

'Like a woman who's about to get lucky,' Abi says, grinning wickedly.

Four hours and three glasses of wine later, Myrtle is shrugging on her coat and tugging Abi's dress down where it's ridden up once again. She wishes she hadn't listened to her and just worn jeans.

Caleb holds the door open for her as they step out into the chilly October night. Myrtle smiles up at him nervously, wondering if he'll ask to see her again, or if he'll try to kiss her when they say goodnight.

As they walk down the street, he takes hold of her hand. She bites back a smile.

'I had fun tonight,' he says, their clasped hands swinging casually between them.

'Me too.'

'It felt like it was over too soon, though.'

She nods, glad it's dark so he can't see her blushing.

'If you wanted, you could come back to mine for another drink?'

Myrtle hesitates.

'I don't live far from here, then I can call you a cab from there, if you want,' he says. Then he squeezes her hand. 'But it's fine if you'd rather not.'

She hears Abi's words from earlier: *Live a little, Myrtle ... This is why you're still single.*

'OK,' she says eventually. 'Just one drink then.'

When they get to his, they climb three flights of stairs before they reach his flat. 'It's worth the climb every day. I've got the best views of the whole building.'

She follows him in as he opens the door, leading her to the huge sash window in his sitting room.

'Wow,' she breathes, staring out at the glittering London skyline.

'It's pretty breathtaking, right?' he says, looking straight at

Myrtle. He steps towards her, his arms sliding up underneath her coat and easing it off her shoulders. He kisses her neck, his hands straying down to her waist, and then to her bum.

She laughs nervously, taking a small step back until his hands fall away. 'So how long have you lived here?' she asks, trying to sound more nonchalant than she feels.

'Do you really care?' he says, closing the gap between them again, kissing her hard, his hand around the back of her head, his other hand dropping to her bare thigh, his fingers grazing up the inside of it.

'OK, easy there, tiger,' Myrtle says with another nervous laugh. 'What's the rush?'

'I've been wanting to do this all night,' he murmurs, his fingers now tracing the lace of her knickers.

Myrtle steps back again, her heart thudding. *Too fast,* she thinks. 'So how about that drink you promised?'

He regards her for a long moment, his expression unreadable. Something seems to shift between them.

Get out, she thinks. *Get out now.*

Finally he nods. 'All right,' he says, retreating to the kitchen.

As soon as he's gone, Myrtle picks up her coat and heads towards the front door. Just as she reaches the end of the hall, a hand grabs hold of her wrist and yanks it, her coat falling to the floor.

'Where do you think you're going?' Caleb says. He's smiling, but there's a harshness to his words.

'I was looking for your bathroom,' Myrtle lies.

'This way,' he says, spinning her around and leading her down the other end of the hall.

'Thanks,' Myrtle says, quickly locking the door behind her. She stares at her reflection as she runs cold water over her sweaty palms. *What now?*

She looks around the room but realises there's no window. She thinks of her phone in her coat pocket, lying in a heap in the hallway. *Idiot.*

She eases the door back open, wondering if she should just make a run for it, but Caleb is leaning against the doorway of the sitting room, waiting for her.

'Here's your drink,' he says, holding out a glass to her.

'Actually, I'm feeling pretty tired, so I think I'm going to head home now. Plus my housemate will be waiting up for me,' she lies, knowing if Ben is still awake, it's because he's brought someone home with him. 'I don't want him to worry.'

'Ah, you're a big girl. What would he have to worry about?'

Myrtle forces a smile. 'Like I said, I'm feeling tired. But maybe we could meet up again later in the week?'

He smiles back at her. 'I don't think so.'

Myrtle swallows. 'Well, that's up to you. But I'm going home now,' she tries to say firmly, but there's a quaver to her words.

'Come on, don't be like that,' Caleb says, stepping between her and the door. 'We were having a nice evening together, weren't we?'

'Yes. We were. And now I want to go home.'

'So why did you come back to mine then?'

'Excuse me?'

'Why did you come back to mine if you didn't want something to happen?'

'I came back to yours to talk more and have another drink. That's all.'

'I think you're just playing hard to get,' he replies, stepping closer towards her, then pressing himself against her until her back is against the wall.

'Caleb, don't.'

He ignores her, grinding his groin into hers.

Myrtle tries to push him away but he's stronger than she is. 'Caleb, stop it.'

'Come on, you can't dress like that and not expect

something to happen,' he says. 'I've been sat in that bar with a hard-on all night.' He grabs hold of her hand and presses it against his crotch, as if to prove his point.

Myrtle snatches her hand back and tries to shove him away again. 'Get off of me!' she yells loudly, hoping one of his neighbours will hear and come up to investigate.

'Shut the fuck up!' he snarls, slamming her head so hard against the wall that her vision momentarily blurs. Before she knows what's happening, he has both her wrists pinned behind her back, and with his free hand he is fumbling with his zipper.

No no no no no, Myrtle thinks. She's just about to yell out again when he forces his mouth on hers, his tongue darting into her own. She struggles in his vice-like grip, but it's no use, he's twice the size of her.

Please, god, no, she thinks wildly as he begins to tug at the hem of the dress. She hears the sound of fabric ripping as his fingers take hold of the lace of her underwear.

No!

She bites down hard on his tongue, making him rear back, but he doesn't loosen his hold on her.

'You like to play rough, do you?' he says, grabbing a fistful of her hair and yanking it, making her whimper.

'Let go of me,' she pleads.

'Don't pretend like you don't want it,' he says, dragging her into the sitting room and forcing her down on the floor.

'Stop it, please,' she begs, crying now. 'Just let me go.'

But it's like he can't hear her now, lost to the moment. A memory rushes back at her – of Henry lying on top of her in Nina's Wendy house, thrusting painfully inside her, unable to even look at her.

Myrtle turns away, staring fixedly out of the window at the illuminated skyline as tears slip down her cheeks, watching the slow-moving hands of Big Ben, waiting for it to be over.

52

'Cut!' Ethan yells. He glares at one of the actresses. 'What was that?'

'I ... I'm sorry,' she stammers.

'That was fucking *abysmal*, that's what that was. Now let's go again, and this time, don't fuck it up.'

Matthew bites his tongue as they re-set the lighting, trading a loaded look with his boss Ralph. He's so sick of working with egotistical directors and conceited lead actors throwing their weight around, while everyone else just takes it. It is days like this where he almost wishes he was back in an office, mindlessly punching numbers into a computer, Ivan sitting beside him watching porn.

We're not saving lives here, he wants to tell the others, even though everyone acts that way, as if there is nothing more important in the world than what is unfolding on set.

Just as they are about to do another take, Ethan grabs a runner by the front of his T-shirt. 'What the fuck do you think you're doing?'

The boy stares at him, a panicked look on his face. 'What? What did I do?'

'Take that piece of shit off.'

'Sorry?'

'I said take that piece of shit off! You wear red on my fucking set, when everyone knows that I fucking hate red!' he hollers, shoving the runner hard against the wall.

The boy gazes around him in bewilderment, trying to gauge from the rest of the crew if this is all some elaborate prank.

Matthew is just about to offer the boy his jumper when Ralph holds out an arm to restrain him. 'Leave it,' he hisses under his breath.

'I don't have fucking time for this!' Ethan bellows, grabbing another fistful of the red shirt and hauling the boy towards the door. 'Now get the fuck off my set!' He storms back to his position behind the camera, his eyes blazing. 'OK, let's try this one more time and see if the *talent* can finally do what it's being paid to fucking do.'

The actress – Rosie – walks back to her marker, her cheeks aflame.

'Why does he have to be such a prick to everyone?' Matthew mutters.

Ralph shoots him a warning look as the cameras start rolling.

Thirty seconds into the take, Ethan hurls his chair across the room, which narrowly misses one of the cameramen. But he doesn't let out a single expletive. He walks over to Rosie, his steps exaggeratedly slow, until he's standing right in front of her.

'I'm wondering why exactly you're here?' he says, his voice disturbingly calm. 'Do you not care that you're wasting every single person's time?'

Rosie says nothing, staring just above Ethan's left shoulder.

'Do you realise that my five-year-old daughter is a more convincing actress than you are?'

Rosie presses her lips together, blinking quickly.

Matthew's hands curl into fists by his side. Everyone on set is watching, bracing themselves for the next eruption.

'You're a fucking amateur,' he spits.

Rosie's bottom lip trembles as tears begin to fall.

'The only reason you're standing here right now is because

you must have parted your legs for some dickhead casting director. But you can't fuck your way out of this mess now.'

Before he even knows what he's doing, Matthew is striding towards Ethan and then spinning him around to face him, his curled fist catching the director square in the face. Ethan's head snaps back, he staggers and then collapses to the floor, unconscious.

Matthew glances at Rosie, who is staring at him in wide-eyed horror, as are the rest of the cast and crew. He turns to Ralph, whose normally ruddy complexion is now ashen.

'I guess I don't need to tell you this is my last day,' Matthew says quietly, before walking off set.

53

There's a knock at the front door and Myrtle pads down the hall in her onesie pyjamas, having slept in late. She peers through the spyhole, wishing she had a chain on the door, but at least she can see the street beyond is busy. She carefully inches the door open.

'Hello?' she says to the man standing on her doorstep.

'Are your parents around?' he asks her.

Myrtle frowns. 'Do you mean are they alive?'

'No, I mean are they at home?'

'I don't live with my parents. I'm the homeowner.' She stands a little straighter, the fabric of her onesie puckering at the crotch.

'Oh.' He doesn't even look embarrassed, just disbelieving. 'I'm here about double-glazing,' he says, holding out a leaflet.

Myrtle nods and takes it, then shuts the door, bolting it shut behind her. She walks slowly down the hallway and into the sitting room, which is filled with boxes she hasn't yet finished unpacking.

'Home,' she murmurs to herself, trying it out, the word echoing off the bare walls and floor. 'Home.'

'OK, pass me the rawl plugs,' Elliott says later that afternoon, after he and Patti have come over to help.

Myrtle digs around in the toolbox and then hands them

to him. He knocks them into the wall and then fixes in the screws for her to hang the mirror on.

'Bit to the left,' Patti says as Myrtle readjusts it. 'Perfect.'

'What next?' Elliott asks.

'The flat-pack needs putting together,' she says, grimacing.

He nods, unfazed, getting off the ladder and heading into her bedroom, while Patti carries on unpacking boxes.

Myrtle watches her dad as they build the wardrobe together, her reading the manual and handing him the right bits. She feels a strange pang, thinking how she'd always imagined she'd be doing this with a boyfriend, excited that they'd just bought their first home together, painting walls, trying out furniture in different positions, then giddily christening every room.

'Penny for them,' Elliott says, glancing up at her.

'I was just thinking that I'm glad you're here.'

'Where else would I be?'

Myrtle smiles. 'Do you remember me helping you with DIY when I was little? Or trying to help, anyway.'

'You always were like the son I never had,' he jokes.

'The son you always wanted, you mean.'

He shakes his head. 'Not true. You're more than I ever could have hoped for.'

Myrtle dips her head to hide her smile. 'But you did want more, though, didn't you?' she presses.

He shrugs. 'Sure. I would have kept going. But your mother ...' He gives another shrug.

After they've righted the wardrobe on its end, Elliott says, 'Anything else?'

'Maybe another lock for the front door?' Myrtle says.

They go out to the hall and Elliott examines the two locks already on there. 'It looks pretty secure.'

'Three's good luck,' Myrtle says, forcing a smile. Patti catches her eye, holding her gaze for a moment until Myrtle looks away.

Patti is the only person she told about that night. Myrtle had called her on the night bus home, unable to form a sentence she was crying so hard, and by the time she got back to her old flat, Patti was already there waiting for her, saying nothing as she enfolded her in a hug, rubbing her back in warm circles as Myrtle sobbed into her shoulder. She'd stayed with her for a week when Myrtle called in sick to work, and she promised she'd never breathe a word to anyone, not even Daphne.

When Elliott's done fitting a chain to the door, Myrtle holds out her palm and he high-fives it. 'Thanks, Dad.'

'Always a pleasure, never a chore.'

They go into the sitting room, where Patti has finished hanging all of the pictures and alphabetised Myrtle's books on the shelves.

'How about getting a takeaway and watching a crappy film on TV?' Myrtle suggests.

Elliott and Patti glance at each other and both nod. Myrtle smiles to herself, secretly glad her mother is away performing at a concert this weekend.

Half an hour later, the three of them squeeze onto the threadbare second-hand sofa Myrtle needs to re-cover, eating curry straight out of the containers. She can't find which box she's packed the cutlery in so they're having to use spatulas instead.

Myrtle gazes around the room as the film begins, dizzy at the thought that this is all hers and no one else's (never mind the hefty mortgage that she'll probably be paying back for the next twenty years).

She settles back against the sofa, wedged in tight between Patti and Elliott, who have both dozed off, snoring softly beside her. She scrapes out the last of the masala with her spatula, then shoves it into her grinning mouth.

54

'Are you sure you still want to go?' Matthew asks, as he steps into his boxer shorts.

The forecast had been sunshine and twenty degrees, but it's now overcast and a chilly twelve.

'Of course,' Rosie says, hooking up her bra. 'If you still want to?'

He nods. He doesn't care where they go. He'll happily sit in a car park for hours if it means spending time with her. Ever since they got together, he spends every waking hour they are apart thinking about Rosie, and when they are together, all he wants to do is kiss her and hold her, wondering if enough time has passed before he can reach out for her again. Because it feels physically impossible to be next to her and not touch her.

They go on his motorbike, which is still going strong all these years after Xander bought it for him. Rosie's arms are wrapped tightly around his chest, the inside of her legs tracing the outline of his. Every time they slow for traffic lights, he reaches back to squeeze her knee. Then he holds out his hand with his thumb up, and she mirrors him to let him know she's OK.

When he brakes sharply for a parking spot, she jerks forward, her helmet crashing into the back of his.

'I'm so sorry,' she says, laughing as she pulls off her helmet once they're there. 'I've probably given you concussion.'

He answers her with a kiss. 'I don't care.'

'There you are,' Ed says when they walk across the deserted beach to join them.

'We thought you were going to be a no-show cos of the weather,' Giles says.

'Sorry, it's my fault we're late. I got held up at rehearsals,' Rosie lies.

Matthew nods, trying not to grin at the thought of her greeting him at her front door in just her underwear when he came to pick her up, before yanking him into her bedroom and whispering in his ear: 'I want you now.'

'Sorry, we've eaten most of the picnic stuff. We were starving,' Hazel, Ed's fiancée, says apologetically.

'You mean Giles ate most of the picnic,' Ella, Giles's girlfriend, corrects.

'What can I say, I'm a growing boy,' Giles replies, patting his rotund stomach.

'That's all right, I'm not really hungry anyway,' Matthew says. 'No one ventured in the water yet?'

'I've already got goosebumps underneath my jumper just from being sat on the beach, so no, I won't be jumping in the sea,' Hazel says, reaching for another strawberry.

'Me neither,' Ella echoes.

Matthew looks at Ed and Giles but they shake their heads.

'It's dangerous to swim so soon after eating,' Giles says, patting his stomach again.

Matthew glances at Rosie, eyebrows raised. 'I'm game if you are?'

'You're on,' she says, already stepping out of her skirt and pulling her sweater off, until she's standing there in just her bikini.

Matthew catches Ed and Giles gazing at her appreciatively, while Hazel and Ella pretend not to notice.

Rosie is already running towards the water, so Matthew has to race to catch her up as she rushes straight into the waves, not squealing or tiptoeing in like most girls.

He dives in after her, swimming up to her, not even bothering to tread water as he starts kissing her, so that they begin to sink, still kissing as their heads disappear beneath the surface.

When they re-emerge, she cups her hand around the back of his head, pulling him in closer to kiss him again. God, it kills him when she kisses him first. Even though there is no space left between them, he puts his arms tight around her, like she's a life ring he's afraid to let go of.

'Get a room!' Giles hollers from the shore, as Ed lets out a wolf whistle.

But Matthew can barely hear them. Everything else around them fades. All there is is Rosie.

They reluctantly pull apart from another lingering kiss, gasping for air, grinning at each other. As they tread water, he stares deep into her eyes, and she looks right back at him, holding his gaze. It feels like the most incredible thing, he thinks, to look so intently at another person, without awkwardness or shyness; to look at them in a way that feels like they actually understand each other – that they see everything that everyone else before them missed.

'What are you thinking?' Rosie asks, her fingertips tracing the muscles in his shoulders as they continue to tread water.

'I'm thinking that it's impossible to look at you without wanting to kiss you,' he murmurs.

Rosie smiles, her cheeks dimpling. God, he loves those dimples.

'So kiss me every time you look at me then,' she tells him.

He closes the space between them for another long, salty kiss, thinking: *This is it. This is what everyone's always chasing after.*

They stay in the water until they can bear it no longer. Back on shore, they hurriedly get changed, their clothes sticking to their damp skin, the cool air making them shiver.

I love you, he thinks as he watches her run her fingers through her long hair. He wants to tell her how much, but he thinks it might terrify her. It terrifies him.

'Who's up for chips from the café?' Giles asks.

'Sorry, we have to go,' Rosie says to the others. 'We're having dinner with my parents tonight, remember?' she lies, smiling up at Matthew suggestively.

'Oh yeah, that's right,' he says, nodding eagerly.

'Have fun with the in-laws,' Ed says, giving him a knowing look.

When they get back to where they parked, Matthew holds out the helmet to Rosie and sits on the bike. But rather than putting it on and sitting behind him, she climbs onto his lap, straddling him, her hand around the back of his head, pulling him down for one more kiss until she's resting against the handle bars.

'Do you have any idea what you do to me?' he murmurs before he kisses her back, sensing that this, right here, is the moment – the one that every other will be measured against.

55

Myrtle fiddles nervously with her necklace while her date, Josh, continues his monologue about how important his job in finance is.

The waiter appears beside them, his eyebrows raised in question.

'Ladies first,' Josh says gallantly.

'Is the risotto your only vegan option?' Myrtle asks.

The waiter nods.

'I guess I'll be having that then,' she says with a thin smile, even though she doesn't much like risotto. It tastes like savoury rice pudding.

'I'll have the steak – rare,' Josh says.

'Good choice, sir,' the waiter replies, before taking their menus with a flourish and turning on his heel.

'Your profile didn't mention you were vegan,' Josh says, his tone almost accusing.

'I did say I was an animal lover,' Myrtle points out.

'So am I,' Josh says with a frown, refilling his empty wine-glass. 'You not drinking?' he asks, nodding towards Myrtle's glass, which she's barely touched.

'I've got a bit of a headache,' she lies, taking a sip from her water glass instead.

As the evening wears on, Josh finishes the bottle of wine and orders another, steadily emptying it as he continues to talk about himself. He'd come across as witty and self-assured in their online messages, but in person, he just seems witless and arrogant.

Aren't you curious about me at all? Myrtle thinks, stifling a yawn. *Or are we all just the same to you – a pair of ears to listen to you re-tell the same stories over and over again?*

She slowly spins her still-full wine glass by its stem, thinking how futile it all seems, trying to make a connection with a stranger when it only leaves you feeling even more disconnected.

'So, Myrtle,' Josh finally says, his gaze lingering a little too long on her neckline, even though she'd been sure to choose something that wasn't remotely revealing. 'What is it you're after in a guy?' And then he leans back in his chair, a confident smile on his face, as if the answer is sitting right there in front of her.

'Umm, I don't know,' she says, nonplussed by the question. 'It's not like I have a list or anything.'

'Everyone has a list,' he declares.

'What's on yours then?'

He thinks for a moment. 'Great body, takes pride in her appearance, good cook ...'

Myrtle shifts uncomfortably in her chair as he reels off everything she isn't.

'Oh, and gets on well with my parents,' Josh finishes.

'What about kindness or sense of humour?' she asks.

He shrugs. 'Sure, those too.'

'I guess it would be nice to meet someone who cares about the same things I care about,' Myrtle finally offers, trying not to look at the half-eaten bloody steak on Josh's plate.

He drains the rest of his wine, refills it again and holds out the bottle to Myrtle, who shakes her head. He puts it back on the table, then his hand vanishes underneath the tablecloth, and a second later, Myrtle can feel his fingers grazing against her thighs. She instinctively jerks back, kneeing the table in the process and knocking over Josh's full glass of red wine, most of the contents pooling onto her pale jeans rather than the snowy white tablecloth.

'Shit,' Myrtle breathes, getting to her feet and uselessly dabbing at her lap with a napkin. 'I'll be right back,' she says, rushing towards the ladies.

Once there, she locks the door, staring at herself in the mirror, her eyes wide, her breathing ragged.

Calm down, she tells herself. *It's OK. You're OK.*

But her breathing is becoming more laboured, her vision beginning to curl in at the edges. She bends over, inhaling deeply, scared she's going to pass out.

When her ears finally stop buzzing and her heart is no longer racing, she shakily pulls her mobile out of her bag, calling the only person who will understand.

'Hello?' Daphne answers.

'Is Patti there?'

'No, she's out. Why?'

Myrtle's heart sinks. 'I just needed to talk to her about something. But it doesn't matter.'

'OK,' Daphne says. There's a long pause. 'Did you want to talk to me—?'

'It can wait,' Myrtle says quickly. 'I'd better go.'

'All right then,' Daphne says, before Myrtle hangs up.

'You're fine,' she tells her reflection again, avoiding looking at her ruined jeans. 'You're going to be just fine.'

She takes a deep breath, unlocks the bathroom door and heads back out to the restaurant. She can see the side of Josh's head, his fingers drumming on the table impatiently as he waits for her. She imagines them inching up her leg again, tugging at her flies, then her knickers …

She turns on her heel and rushes out of the restaurant, hailing the first black cab that drives by.

56

Matthew whistles cheerfully as he hangs the washing out on the line. He looks at Rosie's pastel-coloured satin underwear interspersed with his grey and black boxers, her lacy camisole tops next to his cotton T-shirts, and he grins to himself. He doesn't know why the sight of their clothes pegged up together like this makes him so happy – but it does.

He goes inside and re-makes the bed, which is still rumpled from where they'd had early morning sex and then breakfast in bed before Rosie rushed off to rehearsal. A part of him still can't quite believe that every night he gets to fall asleep next to her, and every morning wake up next to her again.

He walks around the flat they've rented together. If he ignores the signs that Rosie likes to hang off every doorknob, saying things like: 'Home is where the heart is' and 'Friends are like stars', and the fairylights she insists on stringing up even though it's the middle of summer, it's actually a pretty nice place.

He sifts through the post, unable to stop himself grinning at the letters addressed to both of them, even though they're just bills. Then he calls his mum, like he does every day.

'How's Luke?' he asks.

'The same as always.'

'And how are you?'

'The same as always.' He can hear the sound of a glass being topped up and he wonders how many she's had already today. 'We're fine, Matthew,' she tells him. 'You don't need to keep checking in on us all the time. You've got your own life to live.'

'I know. But you know I'm always here, right? I can come round whenever you want, even if it's just to change a light bulb or put out the bins.'

'I'm perfectly capable of doing those things by myself,' she says, and he can hear the glug of more wine being poured.

When Rosie comes back that evening, he has dinner waiting for her, flowers from the garden stuffed in a jam jar in the middle of the table.

'You are too good to be true,' she tells him, sitting on his lap rather than across from him, pausing between each mouthful to kiss him.

'How was rehearsal?' he asks.

'Good,' she says. 'It's coming together but I'm still bricking it that opening night is only a week away.'

'You'll be amazing,' he says, meaning it.

She kisses him again. 'And how was your day?'

He shrugs. 'Pretty quiet. That house removal turned out to be moving a couple of pieces of furniture, so I was done by midday.'

'Things will pick up,' she says, running her fingers through his curly hair. 'And at least you get some time to think about what it is that you really want to do.'

He nods, not quite meeting her gaze. He hates that Rosie is the one that pays the majority of the rent and that he can't always treat her to things as much as he'd like.

'Hey. It doesn't matter who earns more,' she says quietly, reading his thoughts. 'As long as you're happy, that's all that matters.'

'I am happy,' he tells her, thinking, *Happier than I've ever been.*

'Then I am too,' she replies, kissing him.

When they're doing the dishes after dinner – him washing,

her drying – Rosie begins to laugh when he starts drumming on a saucepan with a pair of wooden spoons in time to a song on the radio.

There is no greater feeling in the world than making the girl you love laugh, Matthew thinks, as she grabs his sudsy hands and starts spinning him around.

'This is our song now,' she tells him as they sway in the middle of the kitchen.

We have a song, Matthew thinks, stooping to lift her up, kissing her hard as she wraps her legs around his waist.

He backs out of the kitchen towards the bedroom, the rest of the dishes forgotten. He lowers her gently down on the bed and then slowly lowers himself on top of her, Rosie panting softly beneath him, her fingertips digging into his back.

After he rolls off her, she curls into him, her head on his chest, and within seconds she is asleep.

He's never told her that she snores or that she always pulls the duvet off him in the middle of the night, so he wakes up cold. He doesn't say that he sleeps better when she's not in the bed with him. Because when he watches her dreaming, like he is now, he knows there are more important things than sleep.

57

'Bloody children, bloody breastfeeding,' Abi grumbles, hoisting up her bra after Lila's finished feeding. 'They sag so much now that I can hold a beer bottle underneath them. Can you believe that? Liam has started to ask me to keep my bra on when we're having sex.'

'What? That's disgusting,' Myrtle says.

'That's pretty much what his expression says when he sees me naked.' Abi shrugs. 'I don't blame him. I avoid looking at them in the mirror, so why subject him to them?' She glances at Myrtle's chest. 'You're lucky yours are so small they'll never sag.'

'Small mercies,' Myrtle replies drily.

'Here, you have her,' Abi says, passing Lila to Myrtle as she reaches for a cupcake.

Myrtle holds Lila awkwardly, trying to rest her in the crook of her arm, but she keeps squirming, as if she senses she's not in safe hands.

'Shh,' Myrtle whispers ineffectually, rubbing her tummy like she used to do to Nancy, but instead of stretching out blissfully like Nancy would, Lila just wriggles even more. Just as Myrtle is debating whether to hand her back to Abi, Lila finally stills, blinking slowly up at Myrtle as Myrtle stares back down at her, both of them trying to get the measure of each other. For a moment, Myrtle tries to imagine Lila is her baby, that it's her not Abi who is having the sleepless nights, that she is the one who has to take care of this tiny person for the next eighteen plus years of her life. Myrtle swallows, wondering if her parents felt this terrified when she came kicking and screaming into their lives.

As if reading her thoughts, Lila begins to cry.

'For god's sake,' Abi moans, unhooking her bra again as Lila opens her mouth in anticipation, attaching herself like a leech.

'It's not just the sagging boobs,' Hannah, one of Sophie's work friends, is saying. 'It's down below that's the worst. I tore so much giving birth to Benji, I wasn't able to sit down on anything hard for six months. I had to carry a piles cushion with me everywhere I went.'

'And why does no one warn you beforehand that you'll shit during labour?' Abi says. 'Some strange man has his head near your vagina while you're actually *shitting*.'

'And the first time you have sex after?' Tandy, Sophie's cousin, says with a shudder. 'Agony. I swear, it was worse than when I lost my virginity.'

The others grimly nod in assent.

'The very next day Liam asked when we could have sex again,' Abi scoffs. 'And I was like: "Are you kidding me? I just ejected a nine-pound person out of my uterus."'

'You lot are like a contraception advert,' Myrtle remarks.

'What? No! It's the best thing ever,' Hannah insists, and the others murmur their agreement.

Myrtle glances around at the other baby shower guests as they wait for Sophie's arrival. Apart from Myrtle, every single one of them is either pregnant or already has at least one child. They seem to fall into two camps: either fiercely maternal, where all they do is talk about babies, sleep cycles and feeding routines; or they seem slightly vacant, incapable of even holding a conversation, an emptiness behind their eyes that seems more than just sleep deprivation.

The doorbell goes.

'OK, no more horror stories in front of Sophie,' Tandy says.

'Isn't it better to warn her?' Myrtle asks, standing up to answer the door.

'No!' they all chorus, as Abi replies, 'It's too late for that now.'

When Myrtle opens the door, Sophie steps into the hallway and immediately bursts into tears.

'What's wrong?' Myrtle says, putting an arm around her.

'Nothing. It's the hormones,' Sophie says, dabbing at the corners of her eyes with a tissue. 'I cry when I'm happy. And I cry when I'm sad. Also when I'm angry or tired. Or hungry. Basically I cry all the time.'

'Bummer,' Myrtle says, patting her on the back as she leads her into the sitting room, wondering how Sophie will cope with the arrival of a tiny person who does the exact same thing.

After Sophie has unwrapped and cooed over the mound of presents, all the while rubbing her bump with the palm of her hand – *Why do pregnant women always do that?* Myrtle wonders – there are the compulsory baby shower games the others insisted on, which sees Sophie eating chocolate mousse, Thai green curry and custard out of nappies, before guessing what they are.

When the others have had their fill of sandwiches and scones, it's just Myrtle, Abi and Sophie left. Myrtle watches her two friends, feeling an unexpected pang of sadness at the fact that they are no longer constants in each other's lives now. Because the truth is – the thing she finds hard to admit even to herself – is that these additions in everyone else's lives just feel like losses in her own.

You both went from young to old so quickly, she thinks. *What was the rush?*

'All right, enough baby talk,' Abi says, as if reading her

mind, lifting Lila to her chest so she can latch on again. 'What's new with you, Myrtle?'

She shrugs. 'Same old. Still doing crazy hours at work for hardly any money. Still questioning on a daily basis what it is I'm doing with my life.'

'What about guys?' Abi asks.

'What about them?'

'I know someone I could set you up with,' she says.

Myrtle shakes her head. 'No more blind dates. Not after last time,' she says, remembering the guy Sophie had set her up with, who spent the whole date flexing his biceps and checking out his reflection in every mirrored surface.

'Liam insists he's one of the "good ones",' Abi says. 'Whatever that means, coming from another guy.'

'Exactly,' Myrtle replies. 'Just tell him thanks but no thanks.'

Abi looks at her. 'Come on, Myrtle—'

'Don't say it!' she cuts her off. 'I don't care if you think I've got nothing to lose, or I need to live a little, or tonight could be the night, or whatever other cliché gets thrown at single people. I don't want to hear it.'

'I wasn't going to say any of that,' Abi protests, as she begins to burp Lila. 'All I was going to say is that he's got a nice smile, he works out, he's never been married, he's got no kids, *and* he owns his own place,' she says, as if those are the only attributes someone like Myrtle could hope for.

'What about sense of humour or kindness or intelligence?'

Abi shrugs. 'That I can't tell you. He's a guy, after all. So what's your answer?'

'Remind me again why I'm friends with you?'

'So I'll tell him that's a yes then, shall I?' Abi says, waggling her eyebrows until Myrtle finally nods in defeat, just to shut her up.

'It would make me so happy if you found someone and

finally settled down,' Sophie says, hypnotically rubbing her bump again.

'Maybe I'm not ready to settle yet,' Myrtle retorts.

'Settle *down*, not *settle*.'

What's the difference? Myrtle thinks as the doorbell goes.

'That will be Tom,' Sophie says, struggling to stand. 'Want a ride home?' she asks Abi.

She shakes her head. 'Liam's coming to pick me up soon.'

Sophie nods, her hand still rhythmically circling her stomach. 'Well, I guess the next time I see you, I'll have bags under my eyes and baby sick down my clothes.' Her eyes sparkle.

'Enjoy the last few days of freedom,' Abi says. 'Seriously.'

Sophie nods, even though it's clear she's just on count-down now.

'And then there were two,' Abi says as the front door closes.

'Three,' Myrtle says, nodding towards Lila, her eyelids fluttering as she dreams.

'Oh, right, how could I forget?'

Myrtle collapses against the arm of the sofa. 'That's the last one of these I'm hosting, so you better not be popping any more out.'

'God, no.' She glances down at Lila and then presses her lips together, her shoulders beginning to shake.

'Hey,' Myrtle says, sitting up and wrapping an arm around her. 'Abs, what's wrong?'

'I don't know,' she murmurs tearfully. 'Liam's worried I'm suffering from post-natal depression. But I don't think it's that. I think it's just facing up to the fact that I'm failing as a parent.'

'What are you talking about? You're a great mum.'

'Am I? Because I feel like I don't even recognise myself anymore. I always vowed I'd never be one of those mums who doesn't care about anything beyond their own children, who doesn't give a shit about anything going on in the rest of the world.' She takes a shuddering breath. 'I always said I'd never use disposable nappies, that I'd make all my own organic baby food, that I'd be one of those mothers that takes their kids on protests and travels around third-world countries with them so they realise how privileged they are. But I'm just so tired all the time. And then I feel guilty, picturing the mountains of nappies that are going into landfill and all the junk food I give Rufus just to keep him quiet. But I guess I don't feel guilty *enough*.'

'At least you're aware,' Myrtle says. 'I'm sure most people don't even think about these things.'

Abi stares down at Lila, as if she doesn't recognise her as her own. 'I never imagined it would be like this. It's the hardest, loneliest thing, being a mother. It makes you question everything you ever thought about yourself. No one ever tells you that. It's like this big secret that no one's talking about.'

'It won't always be this hard,' Myrtle says, not sure what else to say. In her opinion, teenagers were even worse than toddlers and babies.

'I know. Everyone keeps telling me that. It's just that sometimes it feels like I've sleepwalked through the last three years of my life and I've finally woken up, and I honestly don't know how I got here. I used to be fun. I used to be interesting, didn't I?'

'You still are.'

Abi grips her hand, squeezing it a little too hard. 'Don't do it, OK? Whatever anyone else says, don't do it.' She looks again at Lila. 'I love her, I do. And I'd do anything to protect her and Rufus. But if I could turn back time ...' Abi bites her lip, but the words spill out anyway: 'my life would be completely different second time around.'

58

The stranger takes off her bra and throws it across the room, where it lands on Matthew's lap, who hastily puts it on the table in front of him. The woman begins to slowly gyrate around the tiny dance floor. Matthew eyeballs his empty glass, not knowing where to look. He feels bad for her. She has a painted-on smile, and although she gazes out into the crowd as she moves, it's as if she's looking right through them.

Matthew glances across at the other stags, and apart from a few who are leering at the dancer, trying to persuade her to remove her sparkly G-string, most of them look decidedly uncomfortable.

'You having fun?' he says to Ed.

He grimaces. 'I told Giles no strip clubs.'

Matthew smiles. 'This is Giles we're talking about.'

'Hazel will kill me if she finds out we ended up at one of these. She says they're sexist and anti-feminist, and only perverts go there.'

Matthew looks at the middle-aged man on the table next to them with his hand down his trousers. 'She's got a point.'

A topless waitress bends down to refill their glasses. Both of them stare into their laps until she sashays on to the next table.

'So, Hazel's pregnant,' Ed says.

'Wow. Congratulations.'

He nods, still staring at his lap.

'Marriage *and* fatherhood – you feeling ready?'

Ed swallows a long draught of his beer before he answers. 'How do you know if you're in love with someone?'

Matthew shrugs, thinking of Rosie. 'I guess when you can't stop thinking about them. When you want to be with them all the time. And when you're not, you're just counting down until you are again.'

Ed shakes his head. 'That's lust, not love. Five years with a person, and trust me, there are plenty of times when you're counting down until the next time they're away for the weekend and you've got the house to yourself. When you can lie in until you want, with no one shouting at you that you've left toast crumbs in the bed or that you're squeezing from the wrong end of the toothpaste.'

Matthew looks at him. 'Are you having second thoughts?'

Ed rotates his glass between his palms. 'Like I said, she's pregnant.'

'Ed, you can't marry her if you don't think you love her.'

He drains his beer and wipes his top lip. 'I'm not going to be one of those dads that only gets to see his kid every other weekend. That's how it was with my dad, and we still don't know how to be around each other.'

'Would you rather he stayed with your mum and they were both unhappy?'

'They were both unhappy anyway. And it's not like Hazel and I are unhappy all the time. I mean, don't get me wrong, when it's bad, it's fucking awful. But when it's good ...' Ed shrugs. 'I guess we're both holding on for those moments.'

Giles stumbles over to them, his shirt rumpled and bunched around his waist. 'Right, you two: private lap dance in five. On me. You can thank me later,' he says, before weaving his way to the bar to order another round of shots.

Matthew and Ed trade an apprehensive look.

'I noticed the toilets had windows opening out onto the street,' Matthew says.

Ed grins for the first time that night. 'You read my mind.'

59

'Happy birthday,' Myrtle tells her reflection as she washes her face with a flannel.

She swallows a sigh, thinking of the day stretching out before her, with nothing to do and no one to see. Maybe she'd go out for a walk, then go eat lunch by herself in that new vegan café she's been wanting to try. Just because she had no one to spend it with didn't mean she had to spend it cooped up indoors all day.

'You're thirty now,' she says to her reflection. 'And thirty-year-olds don't think anything of going out and eating alone.'

But the thought of sitting there all by herself, with no one to talk to or share dessert with, only made her feel more lonely.

Just then the doorbell goes. Myrtle looks down at her crumpled onesie, thinking she should quickly change, but figures it's probably only a courier for her upstairs neighbour, who is always ordering things online but is never in.

She pulls open the door and sees a bald-headed man about her age, standing there with a huge bunch of flowers.

'Happy birthday, Myrtle!' he says, grinning at her.

'Umm, thank you,' she replies, frowning slightly as she takes the flowers from him, bewildered how he knows her – and why he's buying her flowers.

'Oh, sorry, I'm just the florist,' he says, sensing her

confusion. 'I wrote out the card that your friends ordered. I'm having to do deliveries today too as we're a man down,' he chatters on, still smiling.

'Oh right,' Myrtle says, plucking out the card to read it.

Happy dirty thirty to our bestie! Sorry we can't be
there to stuff your face full of cake and shots. We'll
make it up to you.
Love you loads,
Abs and Soph xx

Myrtle smiles to herself. 'Thanks,' she tells the florist, who is still standing there, looking at her expectantly. Is she supposed to tip him?

'I'm Oli,' he says. 'Only seems right you know my name when I know yours. Maybe I should give you my address and phone number too, so we're even!' he adds with a chuckle.

Myrtle tenses, her smile faltering.

'Sorry, bad joke,' he says quickly. 'I'm not a weirdo, I promise.' He turns to head down her front path and then stops at the gate. 'Nice onesie, by the way,' he calls back, his eyes crinkling. 'Enjoy the rest of your birthday, Myrtle.'

She shakes her head, smiling in spite of herself as she shuts the door. She heads into the kitchen to put the flowers in a vase, and then calls Abi and Sophie to thank them, but as usual neither of them pick up. She's about to finally get changed out of her onesie when the doorbell goes again.

'What are you lot doing here?' Myrtle asks when she opens the door to see Patti, Daphne and Elliott standing on her front step, holding a homemade 'Happy Birthday' banner between them.

'We've come to tell you that it's never too late to find God,' Elliott quips.

'It's definitely too late for that,' Myrtle says, opening the door wider to let them in.

'Still in your PJs at noon – I like your style,' Patti remarks.

Myrtle shrugs. 'Start the next decade as I mean to go on, right?'

Patti laughs.

'You really didn't need to come all this way,' Myrtle tells them, as she boils the kettle to make tea. 'It's just another day.'

'It's your thirtieth,' Daphne says. 'As if we would miss it.'

Although Myrtle has a strong suspicion that this is all Patti's doing.

'We brought picnic food with us, but it looks like we might be having it indoors,' Patti says, gazing out at the ominous grey clouds. She shakes out two blankets and begins to unpack the bulging hamper.

'So no wild parties planned then?' her dad asks, sprawling out on one of the blankets.

Myrtle shakes her head as she reaches for a veggie sausage roll. 'This is what happens when all your closest friends have kids – you become a hermit.' She shrugs. 'It's fine, though. I was more than happy to have a lazy day in watching feel-good films with a takeaway.'

'Sorry we gate-crashed your plans then,' Patti says with a wink, loading up a cracker with olive tapenade and shoving it into her mouth whole.

'Thirty years old,' Daphne marvels, shaking her head. 'It seems like no time at all since that day in the hospital, does it?' she says to Elliott.

'Our baby girl's all grown up,' he says, blinking quickly.

'Hardly,' Myrtle replies. 'I still feel like a kid most days,' she says, shifting in her onesie.

'Don't we all?' her dad says.

'So how do you feel about turning the big three-oh?' Patti asks.

Myrtle shrugs in faux nonchalance. 'It's just another year, isn't it?'

'It's still a milestone, though,' Patti comments.

Myrtle nods, not wanting to admit how anxious she's been feeling at the thought of leaving her twenties behind. Thirty sounded so *old*. Like she was actually, finally an adult. An adult who should have achieved significant things by now. Most of her friends were married with kids, living in three-bedroom houses, with important jobs, and here she was, still single, barely able to keep her pot plants alive, living in a poky one-bed flat, in a low-paid job that constantly had her questioning what she was doing with her life.

Patti pops the cork on a bottle of bubbly to make Buck's Fizz, then hands the drinks around and the four of them clink glasses.

'Here's to your best decade yet,' Elliott declares.

Myrtle gives a derisive laugh. 'I think that one's already behind me.'

'Pfft,' Patti says. 'Twenties are great, don't get me wrong, but you're still figuring out who you are and what you want in life. Thirties are when things start to get a whole lot clearer.'

'Really?' Myrtle asks, feeling relieved.

'Forties are even better,' Daphne remarks.

'Nah, fifties are where it's at,' Elliott adds sagely.

'So you're saying the best is yet to come?' Myrtle asks them.

'Most definitely,' Patti says with a wide smile, sinking the rest of her Buck's Fizz in one.

60

'She was the most kind-hearted person.'

'She would do anything for anyone.'

'She was such a good woman.'

Faces float in front of Matthew but he can't focus on any of them. All he can manage is a stiff nod at each platitude.

'She had such a big heart,' a man is saying now, with a shake of his head, as if that is what killed her. Except, of course, it is. Her big, generous, kind heart had failed Grace one evening when she was getting an apple crumble out of the oven.

'It would have been quick,' the doctor had told Matthew when he arrived too late at the hospital. 'And probably pain-less.'

He didn't want to think about the 'probably' part. He preferred to imagine that it was like a light switch turning off: one moment his mother was there, the next she was gone.

'Time to go in,' Matthew murmurs in Luke's ear, leading the way into the crematorium. They take the front row, Luke rocking gently back and forth, his mouth open but no sound coming out.

A stranger stands at the front and addresses the gathered mourners, telling second-hand stories about a woman she's never even met. Matthew sits there numbly listening to them. Most of them he knows, but some he's never heard before.

He realises then that there are things that he'll never know about his mother. And now it's too late: he'll never be able to ask her anything again. He'll never be able to find out if she'd been in love with anyone before she met Luke; how many children she would have wanted if she hadn't had to stop at Matthew; whether she'd ever dreamt of living anywhere else.

You should have asked her more when you had the chance, he tells himself. Except sometimes it was hard to know the right questions to ask. And you never really thought about how one day it would be too late and there'd be nobody to ask.

There were things I didn't tell you too, Matthew thinks, staring at the enlarged smiling photo of his mother next to her coffin. Because he'd never once thought to thank her for everything she did for him: changing his wet bed sheets, staying up with him when he was sick, comforting him when he and Rosie argued, which they seemed to be doing all too frequently lately. He'd always felt Luke took all Grace's attention and energy. But she'd done so much for him too, and now he'd never get to thank her.

It only hits him then: the person who loved him most in the world was no longer here. No one would ever care about him as much as she did. Not even Rosie, he realises with a jolt.

The celebrant continues her speech, using euphemisms like 'passed on' and 'slipped away', as if Grace had merely lost her grip on the world.

She died. She fucking died, Matthew thinks. *Why can't you just say it?*

After the celebrant finishes and the final song has played, everyone politely waits for the curtains to close around the coffin, and then they slowly file back out into the weak October sunshine. But Matthew and Luke remain behind, staring at the closed curtains, as if expecting some kind of miraculous encore.

★

Matthew is standing in the corner of the pub they're holding the wake in, his untouched pint growing warm in his hand. He studies the photo collage that he'd put together for the day. He hadn't looked at these early photos of his parents in years. Maybe because they only tell half the story, as after Luke's accident, the camera rarely came out. Luke had a way of gurning or grimacing at it that always looked like he was in pain. In fact, all of them look like they're in pain, standing there stiffly, forced smiles on their faces, trying to pretend they're like any other normal family.

He turns away, glancing around the room, but he can't face making small talk with distant relatives and family friends he hasn't seen in years. Where were all these people after his dad's accident? Why did they only show up when someone died?

He checks his phone to see if Rosie has tried to call, or at least messaged, but there's nothing. He'd pretended he was fine about it when she told him she wouldn't be able to get the time off for the funeral.

'It's the last week of shooting,' she'd explained. 'I'd hate to hold the whole film up.'

He's just about to try calling her when he sees a familiar figure walking towards him from across the other side of the pub. Emily stops in front of him, then wraps her arms around him, not saying anything. They hold onto each other for the longest moment.

'I'm here for you, Matty,' she breathes in his ear. 'I'll always be here for you. You know that, right?'

All he can do is nod as she squeezes him tighter, the hard lump that has been permanently lodged in his throat since Grace died finally easing. He wishes he could stay like this for the rest of the day and not have to speak to anyone else.

Emily is the first to pull apart, her green eyes shining with unshed tears as she cups his stubbled cheek in her hand. Greg comes over, laying his arm around Matthew's shoulder.

'I'm so sorry, mate. You know I loved your mum.'

Matthew nods.

'Fuck,' Xander murmurs, for what must be the fiftieth time that day, as he joins them, handing Matthew a fresh pint of beer that will grow just as warm and flat as the last one.

Matthew nods again. It seems that is all he is capable of today.

'I always thought I'd be the first one to go.' Xander shakes his head. 'Your mother – she was the good one. She never did drugs. She never smoked. She rarely drank ...'

Matthew doesn't say anything to that.

'She had people who *needed* her. It should have been me.'

'Except it wasn't,' Matthew says, resenting the way Xander always managed to make any situation about himself.

'Except it wasn't,' he sombrely agrees. He gazes around the room as he sinks the rest of his beer, then he lowers the glass as his bottom jaw falls. 'Fuck. Me,' he says slowly.

Matthew turns to look in the direction Xander is staring in and sees Peter standing awkwardly by the door, looking like he's debating whether to stay or leave. Just then Luke lumbers over and throws his arms around him. Peter stiffly pats him on the back. He glances up and meets Matthew's eye, then quickly looks away. Once he manages to extricate himself from Luke's grip, he murmurs a few words to him, pats him on the shoulder again, then turns and strides back through the door.

'Fucking coward,' Xander mutters as the door bangs shut.

Matthew stares after him, thinking: *You couldn't even stick around for her funeral, could you?*

61

'Do you have to wear those pyjamas?'

'They're comfy.'

'They look like something my mum would wear.'

'Your mother's a sensible woman,' Myrtle says, sliding under the bed covers.

Oli looks at her.

'What, you expect me to float around in a lacy negligee every night you stay over?'

'I just didn't think that six months in you'd be wearing tartan flannel already. Why do you never wear that pink lacy thong I love anymore?' he asks.

'Because it's like cheese wire and every time I sit down, I'm afraid I'm going to circumcise myself.'

'But it's so sexy ...' Oli murmurs, pulling her closer.

'Some men think erotic asphyxiation is sexy. That doesn't mean I'm going to do it.'

He laughs. 'You always know how to win an argument, don't you?'

Myrtle straddles him in her tartan pyjamas. 'Yes,' she says. 'I do.'

Afterwards, when Oli has loudly come, and Myrtle pretends that she has, because Oli always seems unmanned otherwise, they lie there in the darkness. Oli reaches for her hand, turning over to face her. She can feel his warm breath on her cheek.

'I love you, Myrtle,' he says quietly.

She freezes, too shocked to even react for a moment, thinking how this is the first time someone's ever told her that. She opens her mouth to say it back but the words won't come. She likes him. So much. He's kind and funny and patient. And he makes her feel safe. But did she actually *love* him? How could you know for sure?

Oli senses her hesitation. 'It's OK if you're not there yet,' he tells her, kissing her forehead. 'I'm not going anywhere.'

62

Matthew opens the wardrobe door and a pile of shoes tumble out at his feet.

Rosie glances over. 'There isn't enough wardrobe space here,' she complains, even though Matthew had taken all of Grace's belongings to the local charity shop when they first moved in. The problem is Rosie is always buying things, then shoving them to the back of wardrobes and cupboards when she's tired of them.

Why do you need all this stuff? he wonders, stepping over the shoes.

Rosie shimmies into a skin-tight black lacy dress, then turns her back to him so he can do up the zip.

'How about doing something this weekend, just the two of us?' he asks. 'I've barely seen you in the last few weeks.'

'Like what?' she says as she curls her eyelashes with something that looks like what they use to pin rabbits' eyelids back for cosmetic testing. 'Because I'll probably be pretty tired.'

'We don't have to do much. How about a bike ride and a picnic in Richmond Park?'

'We've got a back garden, Matthew. Why would I want to sit in a park with bird shit everywhere and screaming children? Plus I'm always worried the deer are going to stampede.'

'OK. Never mind.'

He watches her as she applies the final touches of make-up and runs her fingers through her curled hair. His heart clenches at the sight of her. She doesn't look like his Rosie; she looks like every other movie star.

'You've got to fake it until you make it,' she likes to say. And it seems to have worked because now she is landing supporting actress parts in films and leads in plays. And when she goes out, there is normally a photographer lurking somewhere nearby. He only knows this from glancing at the magazines Rosie is always buying and scouring, smiling triumphantly when she sees her picture inside, or throwing it in the bin in disappointment if she hasn't made it into that issue. But not before she's pored over the stories of the other actors and actresses, sucked into their personal dramas.

You're more invested in their stories than you are in ours, Matthew often thinks.

Lately it has begun to feel like they exist in two different worlds, the overlapping common space between them slowly shrinking.

You've changed, Matthew thinks, still watching her as she regards her reflection from various angles, wondering how it's possible you can be with someone for so long, share so much with them, and then suddenly feel like they were never the person you thought they were.

Or maybe I just wasn't looking hard enough.

'Is that what you're wearing?' Rosie asks as she slips on a pair of heels she's pulled out of the pile.

'Yeah, why?' he says, looking down at the suit he bought last week in Oxfam.

'It's just it ... well, it looks like you're wearing someone else's clothes.'

'But it's the smartest thing I've got.'

'That's because you made me take back the designer suit I got for your birthday.'

'Because—'

'Yes, I know, because you think they use sweatshops.'

'They *do* use sweatshops. You watched the documentary with me.'

Rosie glances at the alarm clock. 'Whatever. We don't have time for this. If you really insist on wearing that, we better go and grab a cab.'

'Have fun,' Noah, Luke's carer, says as they walk down the hall towards the front door.

'I'll leave my phone on, so call me if you need me, OK?' Matthew says, glancing worriedly over at Luke, who is staring blankly at the TV.

'Relax,' Noah says, grinning. 'We're going to have a great night, aren't we, Luke?'

Luke doesn't react. At first Matthew had thought it was just the shock of losing Grace, but it's been more than four months since the funeral and still Luke hasn't so much as looked at him. It's like no one exists for him now, the rest of the world falling away.

'Come on, Matthew,' Rosie urges. 'I don't want to be late.'

Once the taxi has dropped them off by Leicester Square, Rosie strides confidently down the red carpet in her stiletto shoes, which Matthew is always worried she's going to break an ankle wearing. She stops to pivot, glancing coquettishly over one shoulder as the photographers and fans take her picture, a hundred flashlights going off at once. Matthew hovers to one side, like an unwanted minder, while a female journalist asks Rosie who she's wearing. She names the same designer they'd been talking about earlier and Matthew can't help but glare at her.

'And are the rumours true that you and your co-star Adam George might have continued your on-screen romance off-screen?' the journalist presses.

Rosie gives a coy smile. 'No, Adam and I are just good friends.'

Matthew waits for her to add that she has a boyfriend, but she's already being ushered by her entourage on to the next journalist. He's read Rosie's comments before in interviews on the rare occasions that she does mention him, and when she's questioned about what he does for a living, she'll use phrases like 'entrepreneur' or 'runs his own successful company'.

I'm a man with a van, Matthew thinks. *Why can't you just say that?*

He waits for her at the end of the red carpet in the cinema foyer, shifting his weight between feet.

'Jesus Christ, I was standing just three feet from Rosie Bletchley!' a bald-headed guy is saying as he walks by Matthew. 'Wait until I tell everyone at work.'

'Do you realise you're still drooling, Oli?' his auburn-haired companion says, one eyebrow arched, as he starts to laugh. 'Just remember to keep your mouth closed during the film, all right? That suit is dry-clean only,' she says, taking hold of his hand as they disappear through the cinema doors.

Matthew watches the last of the suited and gowned guests go in to take their seats as he waits for Rosie. The cast finally take their leave from the hordes of fans and journalists still crowding around the red carpet and drift through to their VIP room. But when Rosie glides by, she doesn't even look for him.

63

Fuck. Fuckfuckfuckfuckfuck. This can't be happening.

Myrtle flicks through the pages of her diary once again, just to be sure. She reaches for her phone, dreading the conversation she'll have to have with Oli later. But first she needs to speak to someone else. Someone who will understand.

As she waits for Abi to pick up, she cracks into a bar of dark chocolate, wondering if her hormones are already kicking in.

'Speak,' Abi answers bluntly.

'I'm late.'

'What? Lila, stop doing that!' Abi barks. 'Sorry, she's being such a little bitch at the moment. What were you saying?'

'I'm two weeks late. And I'm craving foods I never normally eat.' Myrtle reaches for another square of chocolate.

'Don't you dare put that in your mouth!'

'What?' Myrtle's hand freezes mid-air, but then she defiantly shoves it in her mouth anyway.

'Spit it out now! I mean it!'

Myrtle obediently spits it out in the palm of her hand. 'But how did you know?'

'What is that? Oh my god, it's a slug!'

'What?'

'Myrtle, I'll have to call you back. Lila's just bitten a slug in half.'

And then the phone goes dead.

★

That evening, Myrtle hurries from the Tube to the pub where Oli is already waiting, impatiently checking his watch.

'Sorry, I got held up at work,' she lies, feeling the bulky box of the pregnancy test in her bag.

'You work too hard,' Oli says, leaning across the table to kiss her.

Once they've ordered, Myrtle stares into her glass of wine, only half listening as Oli tells her about his day. She presses her calf against her bag and can feel the sharp corner of the box.

'Are you OK?' he eventually asks.

She nods. 'I'm just going to the loo,' she says, knowing she won't be able to focus until she knows either way.

Locked inside a cubicle, Myrtle opens the box and stares at the plastic wand.

Please be negative, please be negative …

She pulls down her knickers and squats to wee on it when there is a loud bang on the door.

'Can you hurry up in there? I'm bursting!'

'Sorry,' Myrtle calls. As she fumbles with her knickers, she loses her grip on the wand and it falls into the toilet. 'Shit.' She reaches down to get it but triggers the sensored flush and watches in despair as it's sucked away.

When she gets back to the table, their meals have already arrived.

'Are you OK?' Oli asks again. 'You don't look so good.'

'I'm fine,' Myrtle says, reaching for her wine and taking a large gulp. 'So …' She trails off.

'So?' Oli prompts.

Myrtle's heart is beating so fast she can't hear anything else. 'So the new girl at work thinks she's pregnant and can't decide whether to tell her boyfriend she's going to have an abortion or just go ahead with it and not tell him.'

Oli frowns. 'She's got to tell him.'

'But it's her body, so ultimately it's her decision.'

'But it's his baby too.'

'But what if he says he wants her to keep it and she doesn't want to?'

'I don't know, but he has a right to know at least, don't you think?'

Myrtle swallows the rest of her wine. 'I guess so,' she murmurs.

'Maybe they both need a lesson in contraception,' Oli says, grinning.

'They were using it, but the pill's, like, only ninety-nine per cent effective or something.'

'What?' Oli's face turns white. 'How did I not know this? Jeez. Maybe we should start using condoms as well as you being on the pill.'

'Yeah. We wouldn't want to end up in their situation, would we?'

Oli shakes his head. 'But the difference with us is we'd always be honest with each other.'

Myrtle nods stiffly, thinking how she'd always been so careful with the pill, taking it the exact same time every morning. Plus, they rarely had sex these days anyway. They were both either too tired or just not interested. She'd even questioned Oli about it the other week.

'Do you think we don't have sex enough?' she'd asked.

He shrugged. 'Sex isn't everything. Anyway, everyone pretends that they're doing it all the time when they're actually not. Life gets in the way, doesn't it?'

She nodded, but couldn't help thinking: *Maybe it wouldn't get in the way with someone else. Maybe we wouldn't be able to keep our hands off each other.* And then she immediately felt guilty for having such a thought when she was lying in bed with Oli. She'd moved over to kiss him, but when her hand had strayed down to his boxers, he'd murmured, 'Do you mind if we don't tonight? I'm pretty beat.'

And she'd nodded, feeling secretly relieved.

'So ... What would your reaction be if I did find out I was pregnant?' she asks Oli now.

He ponders the question for a while. 'Scared shitless at first,' he admits. 'But then ... I don't know ... Maybe I could get used to the idea.'

Myrtle stares at him. 'You wouldn't want me to have an abortion?'

'I don't know. Would you want to have one?'

'I think so.'

'Oh.'

'I've never imagined myself as a mum.'

'Not even if I was the dad?'

She doesn't answer.

'Maybe it's just because you don't have a great relationship with your own mum that you feel like this right now,' he says.

'Maybe. Or maybe not everyone is supposed to be a parent. Plus, the planet's over populated enough without us adding to the gene pool and bringing more consumers into the world.'

'I guess.' He regards her for a moment. 'But what happens if we leave it too late and then regret not having them?'

'Oli, I've probably spent more time really thinking about whether I want kids than most parents ever will.' She thinks of Abi. 'I'd rather regret not having them than regret having them.'

He nods. 'Me too.' But his words seem to have less conviction than hers.

The next morning, Myrtle wakes to a dull throb in her abdomen. She rushes to the toilet and pulls down her knickers, weak with relief at the sight of the dark red stain in them.

'What are you grinning about?' Oli asks as she practically skips back into bed.

'Life,' she says, leaning over to kiss him.

'Life?'

She nods. 'That it's all ours to do exactly what we want with.'

64

Matthew starts awake and sees a shadowy figure at the bottom of his bed.

'How was the last night?' he asks sleepily.

'Good,' Rosie murmurs. 'We got a standing ovation.'

He hears a rustle of fabric as her dress slides over her thighs, and then a soft thud as it crumples onto the carpet. She climbs in next to him, scrolling through emails on her phone, her back to him.

Matthew shuffles closer to her, his finger tracing out letters on her naked back. When they first started dating, they always used to do this, criss-crossing each vertebra, spelling out the words they were too afraid to speak out loud.

I-L-O-V, he begins, until Rosie twitches her back.

'Don't, that tickles,' she says, shifting away from him.

Matthew rolls away from her, turning to face the wall.

When his alarm goes off at seven the next morning, Rosie is already up and showered.

'Coffee?' he asks as he wanders out to the kitchen to start making Luke's breakfast. But he stops short when he sees three suitcases standing in the hallway.

'I thought you didn't have any more work lined up until next month?' he says.

Rosie nods. 'I don't. I thought I'd go and stay with my mum for a while.'

Matthew frowns. Rosie found her mum insufferable and always got Matthew to field her calls, saying that she was in the shower or out at dinner or caught up late in rehearsals.

'What's going on?' he asks, suddenly feeling uneasy.

She looks at the floor, not saying anything.

'Rosie, talk to me ...'

'I'm not happy anymore,' she says quietly, her eyes still avoiding his own.

He stares at her, his heart thudding painfully in his chest. 'Since when?'

She doesn't answer.

'Since my mum died and we had to move in with Luke?' he asks bluntly. His throat feels like someone is squeezing it. 'Or before then?'

'I'm sorry,' is all she says, finally looking up at him. 'This hasn't been an easy decision.' She lowers her gaze again, and he realises then there's no talking her round.

Outside there comes the sound of a horn beeping. Rosie picks up her coat and steps towards him. 'I really am sorry,' she repeats, hugging him briefly, like she might hug a stranger. 'I just ... I didn't sign up for this, Matthew.'

No, he thinks as he watches her taxi pull away, Luke standing close beside him. *Neither did I.*

65

As soon as it's one o'clock, Myrtle grabs her lunch and heads up the fire escape to the roof terrace. It's windy and overcast, so she knows no one will be up here. But even on a sunny day, she's normally the only one, everyone else mindlessly eating their sandwiches in front of their computers, crumbs drifting down onto their grubby keyboards.

Just as she's about to sit down at her usual bench, something catches her eye. Scrawled on the paving slabs in chalk are the words: *YOU PUSHED ME*.

Myrtle frowns, stepping forward, and that's when she sees the hunched figure sitting on the terrace wall, legs dangling over the side. Her heart lurches.

'Tony,' she calls softly, not wanting to startle her boss.

He slowly turns around, his bloodshot eyes not quite focusing on her.

'What are you doing up here?' she asks, taking another step closer.

'Just taking in the view,' he says, before swigging from a can of beer.

Myrtle's standing just a few feet from him now. 'Maybe you should come sit with me over there,' she suggests, gesturing to the bench behind her.

'I'm fine exactly where I am, thanks,' he replies, turning back to gaze out at the high-rise buildings surrounding them. 'London, eh? Eight million people out there, living their lives, eating, sleeping, shitting, fucking, arguing, stuck in traffic jams, sweating on treadmills, staring at computer screens. Eight million people. Yet this city feels so fucking lonely sometimes, doesn't it?'

Myrtle takes another step closer. 'What's going on, Tony?'

He drains the rest of his beer and then opens another can from beside him. 'What's going on, Myrtle, is that I woke up this morning and realised just how much I loathe my life.'

'Why?'

He gives a bitter laugh. 'Do you even need to ask that question when you work for the same bunch of morons I do?'

'Then quit your job. Find something better.'

'You don't think I've been trying? Six interviews I've been on in the last nine months. And over a hundred job applications that I never even heard back from.' He takes another swig of beer. 'Almost twenty years I've worked here, and not once have I ever got a bonus or a proper pay rise, not even a *thank you*, despite all the overtime I've done, despite it ruining my marriage because I was always fucking here, making sure we never missed a deadline. And every time I broach the subject with those fuckers, they always palm me off with the same excuse about reviewing it next year, that money's too tight right now. Then they swan home at five o'clock in their fancy sports cars to their six-bedroomed homes, while I stay here till gone midnight, then have to get a night bus back to my shitty little studio, which is all I can afford because I'm forking out most of my wages on maintenance for two teenagers that won't even give me the time of day anymore.'

Myrtle stares at him, thinking how even though they've sat across from each other for the past eleven years, this is the most he's ever told her about himself.

'I know this place can suck at times,' she agrees, 'but the rest of us are all in the same boat. You're not alone in this.'

Tony shakes his head. 'It's different. You're young. You've

got your whole life ahead of you. It's too late for me to start over now.'

'It's never too late,' Myrtle protests.

He raises the can to his lips again, but it slips out of his grasp, plummeting six storeys to the pavement below, where it bursts open in a fountain of foam. Both of them stare at it for a moment.

'Tony, please come away from the edge. Let's get out of here and go somewhere and talk properly.'

He shakes his head. 'I'm done talking. I'm done pretending that things are going to get better. I'm done pretending like I don't regret the last twenty years of my life. That I didn't fuck up my marriage and my relationship with my kids, all because of a job where I don't even matter.'

'Of course you matter.'

'There's got to be more to life than this, Myrtle.' He turns to look at her. 'Get out while you still can, OK? You're too good for this place. You'll never go anywhere here. And before you know it, it's too late and you're trapped, because no one else will have you.' His eyes narrow. 'Promise me?'

She nods.

'Say it.'

'OK. I promise. Now please come sit over there with me. You're scaring me, Tony.'

'Sometimes it's good to be scared.' He drums the back of his heels against the brickwork, leaning forward a little to gaze at the busy road below. 'Sometimes it's the only time you really feel alive.'

'Then do something else that scares you. Go down there now and quit. Tell them all where to stick it. Then rent out your flat. Go off travelling somewhere you've never been to before. Sit by the sea and watch the sunset every night.' She takes a step closer, trying not to look down. 'Just don't do anything stupid. Don't think this is the only way out.' She holds out her hand. 'Please, Tony.'

He doesn't reach for it, still gazing out over the rooftops. 'You make it sound so easy.'

'It is. There's nothing to stop you walking out of here right now and starting over again.' She takes a steadying breath as she edges closer to him. 'Things are never as bad as they seem.'

'Aren't they?' He turns to look at her, his bloodshot eyes searching hers. 'Are you happy, Myrtle? I mean *really* happy?'

She hesitates for a moment, the question taking her by surprise.

Just then a pigeon swoops towards them, and as Tony ducks, he loses his balance, his arms grappling at nothing but air.

'*No!*' Myrtle yells, reaching for him, but he's already hurtling towards the pavement below.

She hears a sickening thud and forces herself to peer over the edge. Tony has landed on the roof of a van that has reversed into a loading bay, his limbs spread-eagled around him.

Myrtle races across the terrace, flying down the stairwell, until she reaches the ground floor, flinging open the fire exit door. A crowd has already gathered around the van, and someone is on their phone, ringing for an ambulance.

'Tony, can you hear me?' she calls, reaching for his hand.

He lets out a low moan but squeezes her hand in response. 'I didn't mean to …' he murmurs so quietly Myrtle has to stand on tiptoe to hear him.

'I know you didn't,' she says.

'I don't want my kids thinking that …'

'It's OK. You just got too close to the edge, that's all. It was an accident.'

'The words I wrote …'

'I'll sort it. Don't worry,' she reassures him.

The ambulance is already here, and two paramedics are wheeling over a stretcher. Myrtle gives Tony's hand a final squeeze and then steps back, watching as they ease him off the roof of the van and then strap him onto the stretcher. He locks eyes with her as he's wheeled away and she nods at him in silent understanding.

She turns and retraces her steps back up the stairwell and out onto the terrace. She stares at the words one last time: *YOU PUSHED ME.* Then she rubs at them with the sole of her shoe until they're smudged into obscurity.

She takes a hesitant step towards where Tony had been sitting, watching as the ambulance pulls away, its flashing lights revolving. And as the wailing siren fills her ears, she thinks again of his unanswered question.

Are you happy, Myrtle?

When she gets home that evening, Oli is sprawled out on the sofa watching Formula One.

'Good day?' he asks, not even taking his eyes off the TV.

'I've had better,' Myrtle replies wearily.

Oli just nods distractedly, his gaze locked on the cars as they do another lap. The noise of it sets Myrtle's teeth on edge, so she walks into the kitchen to make dinner.

She stops short at the scene before her. The kitchen looks like a group of toddlers have been unleashed on it: dirty saucepans piled on the counters, food spilt down the cupboard doors. Myrtle inhales slowly and then rolls up her sleeves to start cleaning up.

Even though it's been over a year since Oli moved into her flat, Myrtle still feels like she hasn't got used to living with someone. Especially someone as messy as Oli.

How does everyone do it? she thinks. When two lives collided together, how could it be anything other than chaotic?

Lying in bed later that night, unable to sleep, her mind still filled with thoughts of Tony, Myrtle whispers in the darkness, 'Are you happy, Oli?'

'Hmmmm,' he moans, rolling over.

She pokes him in the side, her fingertip disappearing in his spare tyre. 'Oli, I need to talk to you.'

'What?' he murmurs, reluctantly turning over to face her. She can still smell the curry they'd had for dinner on his breath.

'Are you happy?' she asks again.

'It's two o'clock in the morning,' he says sleepily, 'and you've woken me up when I have to be up in three hours. What do you think?'

'I'm serious, Oli. This is important.'

He sighs. 'Can't it wait until the morning?'

'No,' she says stubbornly, reaching for his hand and squeezing it. 'I need to know: are you happy?'

He yawns. 'Yeah. I guess.'

Myrtle frowns in the darkness. 'You *guess*?'

'I mean, sure. I'm happy enough.'

'What does that even mean: "happy enough"?'

He lets out another weary sigh. 'It means that generally the happy moments outweigh the unhappy moments.'

'And that's enough for you?'

'Yeah, I guess it is. Why? Are you trying to tell me you're unhappy?' he asks, pulling his hand away.

'No. Of course not,' she says, a little too quickly, reaching for his hand again. 'I just think that we don't ask ourselves that enough. That maybe we just plod along like we always do and never really question anything.' *Or perhaps we've become trapped and we don't even realise it,* is what she really wants to say.

'OK,' he says with another yawn, rolling back onto his side. 'Well, I'm glad we cleared that up then.'

'Yeah,' Myrtle says quietly, as Oli begins to softly snore. 'Me too.'

66

The alarm clock goes off and all Matthew wants to do is roll over and go back to sleep. But today is Noah's day off and already he can hear Luke banging around in the bathroom. He goes down the hall and turns off the tap just before the water begins to overflow. Then he goes into Luke's bedroom and lays out his clothes for the day on the bed, just like his mother used to do.

Today is Friday, which means that after he has bathed Luke, he'll have to shave his face. Then he'll clip his finger-nails and toenails, which are so long now they've started to curl, because Noah always leaves it for Matthew to do. And if Luke hasn't completely lost the plot by then, Matthew will brave trimming his shaggy hair. (The last time he'd taken Luke to the barbers, he'd lashed out, and both Matthew and the hairdresser had needed bandages.)

As he shaves Luke, he remembers how he used to watch his mother doing this, her lathering up the soap with the brush, applying it to his father's cheeks in cloudy swirls, the razor skimming it off in slow, methodical strokes, careful over the lump of his Adam's apple, before she swished it in the basinful of water and began on the other side. Luke would sit there for ages as she did it, almost in a hypnotic trance as she chattered away to him. But when Matthew does it, Luke gets restless, jerking and twitching, so that by the end, his jawline and neck are covered in nicks.

Matthew gets out the nail clippers and Luke shakes his head.

'Yes,' Matthew insists. 'You're beginning to look like Nosferatu.' He reaches for Luke's hand but he snatches it away and stands up. Matthew blocks the door, locking it and slipping the key in his pocket.

'Nuuuh!' Luke wails.

'It will only take a couple of minutes,' Matthew reasons, still guarding the door like a bouncer, arms crossed, legs set apart, a determined expression on his face.

'Nuuh!' Luke repeats, shoving Matthew aside and rattling the doorknob.

'Just let me do your fingernails,' Matthew tells him, reaching for his hand again, but Luke angrily swats it away, now pounding on the door. 'Stop it, you'll break the wood,' he says, pushing Luke aside to stand in front of it again. Luke starts hammering the tiled wall instead, still wailing.

'There's no one else here,' Matthew points out. 'It's just you and me.'

Luke glances at him, and Matthew thinks he's going to sit back down and let him finish what he's started. But then he's flying at Matthew, and they both crash against the wall, knocking the wind out of him. He shoves back and Luke falls to the ground, but he kicks out with his legs and swipes Matthew's own legs out from under him. The next instant Matthew has Luke on his back, his legs straddling Luke's chest, his hands pinning down Luke's wrists.

'Why do you have to make this so fucking difficult all the time?' Matthew hollers at him. 'I'm the only one you've got now. Don't you get that? I'm the only one who's left!'

Luke is breathing loudly through his nostrils, his chest heaving.

'This is it now,' Matthew tells him, the fight draining out of him. 'It's just the two of us.'

Luke won't look him in the eye but he stops struggling.

Matthew gets off him, pulls the key out from his pocket and unlocks the door, before walking down the hall. It's a long time before Luke follows him. He sits down beside Matthew on the sofa, holding out a DVD he wants to watch. Matthew stands to put it on for him.

He studies his father's profile as he watches the film, Luke absentmindedly fingering the tassels of a cushion while he laughs in all the wrong places.

'I'm sorry,' Matthew murmurs. 'It wasn't meant to turn out this way, was it?' he says, thinking how most days it feels like he's living someone else's life, just going through the motions. He takes a shaky breath. 'I miss them too, you know.'

It's been three months since Rosie left and still he wakes up every morning, half expecting to see her lying beside him. And the realisation that she'll never lie next to him again feels just as unbearable as that first morning she walked out. He's never felt this raw and hollowed out before.

If this is always how painful it is when relationships end, I don't ever want to fall in love again, he thinks.

'How can someone be the best thing that ever happened to you and the worst thing that ever happened to you?' he asks his father.

Luke laughs again at something on the TV, their earlier argument entirely forgotten now, and Matthew wishes he could be more like him, not agonising about the past or worrying about the future, but just being in the moment.

'We're going to be all right,' Matthew tells him. He reaches for his father's hand and squeezes it. 'We're going to be all right,' he repeats, perhaps because he's the one who needs to hear it the most. 'I promise.'

67

'So what do you think of the hotel?' Oli asks.

'It's nice,' Myrtle lies. It's horrific: one of those monstrous eyesores that looms above everything else, its name gaudily lit up at night, with a huge outdoor swimming pool and overpriced Western restaurant. She's never stayed in a place like this in her life – out of principle more than anything – always picking local, family-run places for their faded charm.

'I thought it would be nice to go somewhere fancy for a change.'

Myrtle nods, forcing a smile. She'd been excited when Oli said he was taking her away on a surprise trip in Europe. She'd imagined somewhere romantic like the Italian Lakes or a dusty historic city with narrow, maze-like streets they could get lost in. She hadn't imagined an all-inclusive beach resort in Ibiza. The fact that Oli would even think she'd like a place like this unnerved her.

'It's pretty spectacular here, isn't it?' he continues, as they gaze out to sea.

'Mmm-hmm,' Myrtle agrees, thinking how they'd had to trek an hour from their hotel just to find a quiet cove away from the endless stretch of plastic sunbeds filled with sunburnt tourists. There is only one other couple on this stretch of the beach with them. The man is standing waist-deep in the water, while the woman's legs are wrapped tightly around him as they kiss each other deeply.

You won't be doing that after four years together, she tells them silently. And then she catches herself, thinking: *But we were never like that, not even in the beginning.*

She turns away from the amorous couple to look at Oli, studying his profile as he gazes out to sea. His face is so familiar to her – even more than her own. She knows every freckle, every scar. She knows that his eyebrows pull together when something's upset him and that the tips of his ears redden when he's embarrassed.

She loves him. She does. And yet ... Yet her heart doesn't race when she looks at him. Her breath doesn't catch in her throat when he leans in to kiss her. Her hand doesn't tingle when he holds it in his own.

She loves him but she isn't in love with him. She never has been.

Maybe the in-love stage is just temporary, she reasons, glancing back at the couple, who are now sprawled out on the wet sand and look like they're doing more than just kissing. *Maybe we've just skipped a step and still landed up where everyone else does anyway.*

'We came here on a family holiday when I was teenager,' Oli is chattering away. 'It was the best holiday. Although it's a bit different from how I remember.'

'Places change,' Myrtle says, watching as the sun sinks behind the watery horizon, leaving trails of red, gold and pink in its wake.

'Sam and I went snorkelling every day. I'm pretty sure we came to this beach, actually ...'

After another five minutes of Oli's meandering monologue, Myrtle finally snaps. 'Oli!'

'What?'

'Can't we just enjoy the sunset without your endless commentary?'

He looks at her, his eyebrows knitted together, the tips of his ears reddening, and Myrtle instantly feels bad.

'Sorry,' he says. 'I'm just feeling a bit anxious, that's all.'

'What? Why are you anxious?'

'I want to ask if you'll do something.'

Myrtle lets out a sigh. 'Look, if you're really worried about that mole on your back, you should get it checked by the doctor, rather than keep asking me to—' She stops mid-flow as Oli stands up, pulls Myrtle to her feet, then gets down on one knee, his eyeline level with her crotch.

'What are you doing?' Myrtle asks, her heart drumming in her chest at the realisation of what is happening.

'Myrtle ...' Oli stutters, still addressing her crotch. Then he finally looks up at her, a mixture of fear and hope in his wide blue eyes as he holds out a small velvet box, his hand visibly shaking. 'Will you marry me?'

Part Three

Part Three

68

Myrtle stretches out in her swag, her breath escaping in misty swirls above her cold cheeks, the last of the stars beginning to disappear as the sun starts to inch its way above the horizon. In a couple of hours the heat will be close to unbearable, but still they'll hike in it, climbing the rocky outcrops of the national park to take in the panoramic views at the top, where it feels like they're so high they only have to reach up their hands to touch the clouds.

Myrtle's never been to a place like this before, with its dramatic coastlines, tropical rainforests, rocky canyons and sun-parched outback. And all of it teeming with poisonous plants, venomous reptiles and bizarre-looking animals.

She's so far away from everything she knows here – literally the furthest place she could be. And even though she doesn't know a soul, it isn't loneliness she feels, it's freedom.

She thinks back to her life in London. That place has always felt like the centre of the universe to her, but sitting here, she realises she's been living in a bubble, unaware how big the world really is.

Maybe that's what travelling is all about, Myrtle thinks, staring up at the endless sky. *Bursting the bubble.*

She stands up, stretches again, and then carefully picks her way around the other slumbering bodies to use the tin shack toilet. She wees, trying to avoid the frogs that lurk in there.

Back at camp, once everyone in the group has eaten and

packed up, they set out for the day. As she walks, Myrtle's thoughts stray to Oli again, like they have done countless times on this trip, as much as she tries not to. She sighs, wondering if she's blown her one chance at love. If she'll ever meet anyone again who saw something in her the way Oli did. Who made her feel safe like he did.

But feeling safe isn't really living, she tells herself, thinking of Tony saying the same thing on the roof terrace, right before he'd fallen. *You deserve more than that. Both of us do.*

'Hey, I'm Courtney.' An American girl about her age, who she hasn't yet spoken to, falls into step next to her.

'Myrtle,' she replies.

'How long are you in Oz for?' She speaks with a soft southern accent.

'Just two weeks.'

'Where are you flying next?'

'Home,' Myrtle says with a grimace, thinking how in five days, she'd be back in her little flat, getting ready for work, where she'd sit at her desk, staring out the window at the grey tower blocks and grey London sky, her time in Australia feeling like nothing more than a fading dream. She realises how much she's going to miss this place.

'How about you?' she asks.

'Indonesia next. I'm only halfway through my trip – still got another six months to go.'

'You're doing this for a whole year?' Myrtle says enviously.

Courtney nods. 'I quit my job at a law firm, sold everything I owned, rented out my flat and bought an open-ended ticket.' She grins. 'My parents think I'm having an early midlife crisis.'

'And you're travelling all by yourself?' Myrtle asks, looking at this slight girl whose backpack is almost as big as her.

Courtney nods again. 'It's the best way. Then you can go wherever you want to go. I travelled with my boyfriend a few years ago – well, ex-boyfriend – and all we did was row over the best route to travel. Now I get to trust my gut, and if I get lost or something doesn't quite go to plan, then at least I don't have to deal with someone else's meltdown, just my own.' She laughs.

'But don't you get lonely?'

She shrugs. 'Sometimes whole days will pass and I won't have spoken a word to anyone. But sometimes that's nice, in a weird way. I feel like I've figured out a whole lot of personal shit on this trip that I've been avoiding for a long time. Being alone – I think that's only when you really, truly get to know yourself.'

'And don't you ever get scared?' Myrtle questions.

Courtney gives another shrug. 'I did at first. But not any-more. I love it now, not knowing what's going to happen one day to the next. What scares me more is the thought of not doing things like this. Of settling down and knowing what my life is going to be like for the next however many years.'

Myrtle nods thoughtfully. 'I wasn't supposed to be here on my own. This was going to be my honeymoon,' she admits.

'Wow,' Courtney breathes, her eyes wide. 'What hap-pened?' she asks bluntly.

Myrtle hesitates. 'I loved him but …' She trails off.

'But you weren't in love with him?' Courtney finishes.

Myrtle gives a guilty nod. 'It took me a long while to realise you can love someone and still know they're not right for you.'

She thinks back to her and Oli breaking up a month before the wedding. Her telling him that she wanted something more.

'No one's perfect, Myrtle,' he'd said. 'Not even you.'

'I know that. But it feels like … like something is missing between us. Something important.'

He'd stared at her, and something seemed to crumple in his expression. 'Maybe you expect too much.'

'Maybe I do,' she'd agreed quietly.

His expression had hardened then. 'You're going to end up old and alone, do you realise that?' he'd said, right before he slammed the bedroom door in her face and started hurling all his clothes into suitcases.

'Well, good on you for still coming out here,' Courtney says.

Myrtle smiles. 'Most people, when I tell them, just look at me pityingly and tell me how tragic it is.'

'I don't think it's tragic,' Courtney declares. 'I think it's fucking awesome. Who wants to settle in life?'

'Yeah, who wants to settle,' Myrtle echoes.

She thinks again of returning to London, how everything will be exactly the same, except for the huge Oli-shaped hole now in her life, and she feels a wave of dread.

'So where exactly are you going to in Indonesia?' she asks Courtney.

69

'We did it,' Ed says.

Matthew nods slowly. 'We really did it.'

He looks at the name emblazoned across the side of the two matching vans – *Ellis & Maguire Gardening Services* – and then he glances over at Ed again. They grin at each other like excited schoolboys.

Ed pops the cork on the bottle of bubbly they'd splurged on, even though they haven't received their first pay cheque yet, and pours it into their two chipped enamel mugs.

'Here's to not being a removal man anymore,' Matthew says, raising his mug.

'Here's to not having to put down animals anymore,' Ed says, raising his too.

'Here's to being our own boss and not having to answer to anyone else.'

'Here's to having a job that is no longer soul-destroying.'

'Here's to being outdoors every day and not stuck in an office or on a motorway.'

'Here's to getting divorced,' Ed says.

'Here's to ...' Matthew stops, lowering his mug, and stares at him. 'Wait, what?'

Ed shrugs, not quite meeting his eye. 'Hazel and I have decided to call it a day.'

'Shit. Really? Why?'

'She's been cheating on me with her personal trainer.' He

shakes his head. 'I knew something was up when she started going to the gym every day.'

'Fuck,' Matthew breathes. 'I'm so sorry, mate.'

Ed gives another shrug. 'I'm feeling OK about it now. I mean, I was fucking raging at the time. But I realise now she did us both a favour. We both felt trapped and neither of us knew what to do. So she did her fitness instructor instead.' He forces a grin and then nods thoughtfully to himself. 'Sometimes, being with someone, you become a better version of yourself. But sometimes you become a worse version, and you don't even see it at the time.' He looks at Matthew and raises his mug again. 'So here's to being single again at thirty-five and trying to be a better man.'

'Here's to being scared shitless this is all going to go tits up, but to finally having a job I care about,' Matthew says.

'Here's to living the dream.'

They look at each other, grinning.

'Here's to the future,' Ed adds.

Matthew bangs his mug against Ed's. 'Here's to us,' he says, before they sink their champagne in one.

70

Myrtle looks around her at the throng of people crammed into her mother's house – most of whom she either hasn't seen in years or has never met before – the tables piled high with expensive food and wine, a violin quartet playing in the garden, thinking that Patti would have hated something so over the top.

'I just can't believe she's gone,' she overhears a woman saying, a tissue pressed to the corner of her eye.

There it is again – *gone* – the word that keeps being whispered from every corner of the room. Myrtle wants to be gone. Away from there. Away from everything. Because the thought of carrying on without Patti seems impossible.

'Douglas, did you really have to wear that god-awful tie?' she can hear one of the neighbours saying. Myrtle remembers her from childhood, always yelling at children playing rounders on the green or puncturing footballs that landed in her garden. 'And you didn't even comb your hair!' She clucks in exasperation, turning back to the buffet table to reload her plate, while Douglas smoothes his balding hair into place.

Why did she get to live? Myrtle thinks, staring at the woman. *And you had to die?*

Because she didn't have terminal cancer, Patti's voice answers back.

'How are you holding up?' Abi asks quietly, as she and Sophie walk over to join her.

'OK,' Myrtle lies.

'I'm so sorry, Myrtle,' Sophie says.

Myrtle just nods. The three of them stand there awkwardly, unsure what else to say.

Just be normal with me, Myrtle thinks. *Please. Just for a moment let's pretend everything is fine.*

'I have a really great self-help book on grief, if you want?' Sophie says. 'I can drop it around to you this weekend?'

'That's OK, Patti's got a ton of those kind of books in her study,' Myrtle says. *And I've no intention of reading any of them,* she thinks. As if a book could change anything.

'I say we go out for a girls' night soon, just the three of us,' Abi says. 'Eat and drink whatever the hell we want. What do you say?'

Myrtle smiles gratefully at her. 'Sounds good.'

'Let me get out my diary,' Sophie says, flipping through her Filofax.

As she and Abi go back and forth on their scant free dates, they eventually pick one seven weeks from now.

'Sorry, life's just so crazy at the moment,' Sophie says.

'It's fine. I'll put it in my diary later,' Myrtle replies, knowing that chances are either one or both of them will end up cancelling nearer the time anyway, like they usually did, citing some child-related emergency.

'You'll have to tell us all about your travels,' says Abi. 'Make us sick with envy.'

Myrtle nods, giving a wan smile. Her year abroad feels like a dream now. Like it all happened to some other person, selfishly struggling to find meaning and purpose in her life, not even realising how lucky she had it until it was too late.

Myrtle catches sight of her mother weaving her way across the room, a half-empty bottle of wine dangling from her fingertips. She feels another jolt of disbelief that Daphne had kept Patti's illness hidden from her while she was travelling.

'It was what Patti wanted,' her mother told her when she

flew home the day after Patti died. 'She didn't want you to see her that way.'

'You should have told me!' Myrtle had said, needing to direct her shock and anger at someone. 'I had a right to know. I had a right to get to say goodbye to her too.'

'I told her you'd blame me for it,' Daphne had said flatly, as if she'd already made her peace with it.

Myrtle doesn't understand how people who supposedly loved her could do this. First Nina, then Patti. Why wouldn't they want to say goodbye to her?

'How are you doing, dearie?' Myrtle's great aunt asks Daphne, eyeing the bottle of wine that she is now swigging from.

'Do you really want me to answer that? Or are you just making small talk because you don't know what else to say?' Daphne says, swaying slightly.

The aunt looks taken aback. 'I ... uh ... I just wanted to check that you were OK, dear.'

'Of course I'm not OK!' Daphne cries, so loud that one of the violinist's head jerks up at the noise. Other heads swivel to look over at them.

'Daph ...' Elliott murmurs, suddenly at her side.

Daphne ignores him, taking another gulp from the bottle. 'You know, Aunt Cordelia, I'm not sure why you're acting concerned now that Patti's dead, because you were never happy for us when she was alive.'

Cordelia reddens, her mouth flapping open like a dying fish.

'Funny that the Christmas and birthday cards stopped coming after Patti moved in, isn't it?'

'That's enough now,' Elliott says, trying to steer her away.

'No, Elliott, it really isn't,' Daphne says, brushing his hand off her shoulder. She turns to the rest of the guests brave enough to meet her gaze. 'Patti was the love of my life ... and none of you ...' She lets out a shuddering breath. 'None of you could ever see that in the twenty-four years we were together. So don't any of you pretend, don't you *fucking* pretend, that you see it now!'

Myrtle steps beside her mother and reaches for her hand. Daphne doesn't even glance at her but she squeezes back tightly.

'You should all go home,' Daphne says, her eyes blazing. 'I don't know why I invited most of you anyway.'

Everyone stands there, unmoving, for an awkward moment, then they begin to stir, reaching for their bags and jackets, murmuring quietly to each other.

'Sorry,' Myrtle mouths to Abi and Sophie as they head for the door.

'This will give you all something to gossip about,' Daphne calls out as a parting shot to the guests as Myrtle and Elliott usher her upstairs.

'I'm sorry, I'm so sorry,' he tells people as they pass.

'I'm not!' Daphne calls down as they reach the landing. 'You can all go to hell!'

Myrtle presses her lips together, trying not to smile. She has a feeling Patti would have enjoyed the spectacle.

Elliott guides Daphne towards her bed but she collapses in the middle of the carpet, folding in on herself, her palms braced against the floor as she begins to sob.

'What do I do now?' she whispers, her breathing ragged, as if she's used up all the oxygen in the room. 'What am I supposed to do now?'

Neither Elliott nor Myrtle answer.

'Hold me, Elliott,' Daphne says, tearfully gazing up at him. He kneels down beside her, wrapping his arms around her. 'Tighter,' she insists. *'Tighter.'*

Myrtle knows how she feels. She wants someone to wrap their arms around her, tight like a tourniquet, as if that might somehow stem the pain.

'I don't want to be here without her,' Daphne moans.

'Shh,' Elliott says. 'Enough of that.'

'This is my punishment, isn't it?' she whispers.

'What are you talking about?'

'Karma. This is because I treated you so badly. I'm being punished for it.'

'Shut up, Daffy.'

'It's true.'

'I'm not going to talk to you when you're being like this.'

'OK, then let's not talk.' Daphne leans in and kisses him, but Elliott jerks away.

'What are you doing, Daph?'

She answers by unsteadily getting to her feet and unzipping her dress, until she's standing there in just her underwear. Then she begins to unhook her bra.

'Daphne, don't ...' Elliott says, his eyes trained firmly on the rug.

'I'm going to bed,' Myrtle says, wondering if her mother even realises she's standing right there. She backs quickly out the door, but leaves it open, hovering in the corner of the unlit landing where she can still partly see inside the room, waiting in case her dad needs assistance.

'Stop it, Daph,' she hears Elliott say as Daphne pulls down her knickers.

'What? Don't you want me anymore?'

'Daffy ...'

'Elliott, I need this,' she says, stepping closer and kissing him again. 'I need *you*.'

He returns the kiss momentarily, but then pulls away, shaking his head. 'I'm not who you need, Daph. We both know that.'

She stares at him and then begins to cry again. 'Just fuck me, Elliott!' He tries to restrain her as she starts hitting his chest. 'Why won't you just fuck me?' she whispers hoarsely, sliding back to her knees.

'Let's get you into bed,' he says.

'No. I don't want to sleep in that bed anymore.'

'OK.' He pulls the duvet off the bed and wordlessly drapes it around Daphne's naked body. When she curls up on her side, he puts a pillow under her cheek, then stretches out next to her on the floor.

'She's gone. She's really gone,' Myrtle can hear her mother say dully, as Elliott rolls over and hugs her body still cocooned in the duvet.

Myrtle swallows against the hard lump in her throat, blinking back tears. She can't imagine a world without Patti in it. It's like trying to imagine a world without trees or sunshine or oxygen.

'It wasn't supposed to end up like this, Elliott,' Daphne murmurs.

'No,' he says. 'I know it wasn't.'

Myrtle retreats to her own room, lying on her bed fully clothed, curling herself into a tight ball. Down the hall, her mother is still crying like she's never going to stop.

71

Matthew stares into her chocolate brown eyes, already knowing he's a goner.

'What's her background?' he asks.

The woman – whose name badge says Michelle – consults the folder. 'She was a yard dog in Romania, so she would have lived outside, probably chained up most of her life. That's why her claws are so long – she hasn't been exercised in a long time. Probably ever.'

'Jesus,' Matthew whispers, bending down to hold out his hand to her. Rather than tentatively sniffing it like he'd expected her to, she flings herself against the bars, groaning as he rubs her chest.

'Dora's fully vaccinated and has been neutered,' Michelle adds. 'If you're interested, you can foster her for a couple of weeks to see how you both get on, then if everything's OK, we can arrange a home visit ...'

'I'm definitely interested,' Matthew murmurs, still staring deeply into Dora's eyes while she continues to groan as he massages her ears. He looks up at Michelle. 'So that means ...?'

Michelle nods.

Matthew glances at Dora, whose eyes are rolled back in bliss. 'Looks like you're coming home with me, Dora,' he tells her.

When they walk out to the car park after he's filled out

all the necessary paperwork, Dora trots happily by his side, and when he opens the boot of his work van, she needs just one word of encouragement before she leaps in. By the time Matthew has walked around and seated himself in the driver's seat, Dora has curled up in the passenger seat beside him, letting out a sigh as she shuts her eyes.

'I see you know your place,' he says, smiling as he pulls away. 'Got to say, I'm not sure about the name Dora, though ...'

Her eyes flick open at the sound of her name.

'But I guess you've already had enough change in your life, haven't you?' He glances over at her as they wait at traffic lights and she stares right back at him, blinking, as if she's listening to every word.

When they get home, she jumps out, squatting on the tiny patch of grass in the front garden to relieve herself. Matthew opens the front door but when he gives her lead a gentle tug to coax her in, she digs her heels in.

'It's OK,' he tells her. 'You're allowed inside.' He gives the lead another shake but she won't budge. 'Don't make me carry you in like a newlywed,' he says.

She cocks her head, her ears alert.

He shuts the front gate and then unclips Dora's lead, praying she won't try to jump it. 'Wait here,' he tells her, rushing inside to the kitchen and taking out a leftover veggie sausage from the fridge. When he goes back outside, she is still sat in exactly the same spot. He breaks off a bit of sausage and holds it out to her, close enough so she can smell it but far enough away that she'll have to come forward to take it. Her nose twitches and she looks up at him, sensing a trap.

'It's OK,' he says again.

She inches forward and then gently takes the bit of sausage, before reversing back to her original position. Matthew takes a few steps back down the path, breaking off another bit of sausage and holding it out to her. He can see her nostrils flaring, but still she doesn't budge.

'I'm going inside now and I'm going to leave the door open, so you can come in and get it whenever you want, OK?' He rests the chunk of sausage on the doormat, then takes a few steps back, breaking off another bit, repeating the action until he's reached the sitting room. He sits down on the sofa, turning to look out the window, watching to see she doesn't make a bid for freedom.

After almost an hour, he hears the scrape of claws on wood, then a scurrying sound as she retreats again. Thirty minutes later, he hears the telltale tapping again, then a snuffle, but this time no scurrying back. When he leans forward to look out into the hall, he sees Dora standing there, watching him.

'You still hungry?' he asks.

She cocks her head to the other side. When he stands to go back into the kitchen, she bolts, glancing over her shoulder at him. But she hovers just inside the door when she sees he isn't right behind her.

He puts the rest of the leftovers from last night's dinner in a casserole dish and puts it on the floor next to a bowl of water, then opens the back door, so she doesn't feel trapped. Then he heads back to the sofa and waits.

A little while later, Matthew jerks awake at the sound of Luke and Noah coming through the door. They stop short in the doorway, Luke's face lighting up in a way Matthew hasn't seen in a long time. Matthew glances at the floor to see Dora curled up into a tight comma by his feet, regarding him thoughtfully as a slow grin spreads across his face.

72

'How's she doing?'

Elliott shrugs. 'Today's a bad day. She hasn't left her room yet.'

Every day's a bad day, Myrtle thinks. She looks around the house, still feeling the injustice of it every time she walks through the door. Patti is supposed to be here. She is supposed to be waiting here, just like she always was.

'Shall I go up and see her?' Myrtle asks reluctantly.

'I'm hoping she'll come down if you're here.' The timer on the oven goes. 'Daffy, dinner's ready!' Elliott calls up. This announcement is met only with silence. 'Myrtle's here!' he tries again.

Myrtle listens out for a response or the creak of floorboards above, but there is nothing.

'Let's eat,' Elliott says, the hinge of his jaw twitching. 'I'm sure she'll come down eventually.'

He dishes them up pasta, which neither of them really have the stomach for. Myrtle watches her father as she picks at her food, thinking how tired he looks.

'Dad, you don't have to be here all the time. I can check in on Mum more.'

'I know that.' He wipes a hand down his face, his stubble sounding like sandpaper against his palm. 'But I need to do something. I need to ...' He lets his head hang, his shoulders slumping.

Myrtle reaches across the table to squeeze his hand.

'I miss her too, you know,' he says thickly.

'I know,' Myrtle whispers, her throat tight. 'We all do.'

He gives a gruff cough. 'Anyway, I'm sure you'll be wanting to get back to your travels soon.'

'I can stay for a bit longer,' she says.

Elliott gives her a grateful smile.

For some reason she doesn't tell him that she's already decided she won't be finishing her trip. She knows it won't be the same. *She* isn't the same anymore. The problem is, she doesn't know what to do or where to go now.

Tell me what to do, Patti. Tell me how we're supposed to carry on without you, she thinks. And then: *God, I need help. I'm talking to a dead person.*

Everyone needs help, Patti's voice replies.

'Right,' Elliott says, getting to his feet and picking up Daphne's plate. 'Let's go see if we can force-feed your mother something.'

Upstairs, he raps loudly on the door. 'Daph? Myrtle's here.'

'I don't want to see her!'

Elliott shoots a look at Myrtle, who rolls her eyes. 'Tough shit,' she says, swinging open the door. She stops short, not only at the sight – her mother, hair like a bird's nest, naked in the tangled bed sheets – but at the smell that is coming off her. 'Jesus, Mum,' she says, holding a hand up to her nose.

'She refuses to take a shower,' Elliott mutters, stooping to pick up the broken pieces of a plate Daphne must have chucked across the room.

Myrtle goes to open the curtains.

'Don't!' Daphne barks. 'I don't want to see outside.'

Myrtle hesitates, and then pulls them apart anyway. 'Get up and shut them if you want,' she tells her.

Her mother regards her for a moment, then flings back the duvet and strides naked to the window, where she yanks them closed again before stalking back to bed.

'Here's your dinner,' Elliott says, putting the plate of pasta beside her.

Daphne rolls onto her side so her back is to both of them. Myrtle can see every vertebrae of her spine. Her skin is so pale it is almost translucent.

'Come on, Daph, you've got to eat.'

'Fuck off, Elliott,' she tells the wall.

'Don't you want to spend some time with Myrtle while she's here?'

'She's here to see you, not me,' Daphne replies coldly.

'I wanted to see you too,' Myrtle lies.

'Well, I'm not really in the mood for company, so perhaps you can call ahead next time.'

'Daph, don't be like that—'

'I don't want you here either, Elliott.'

He ignores her as he begins to tidy up the room.

'I don't *want* you, Elliott,' she says emphatically to the wall. 'Why is that so hard for you to understand?'

'Don't speak to him like that!' Myrtle finally snaps. 'He's doing everything for you right now.'

Daphne rolls over, pulling the duvet up to her chest to keep herself covered this time, then narrows her eyes at Myrtle. 'Your father just keeps on coming back, like an unwanted boomerang. Like some puppy that I can't kick hard enough.'

'Shut up, Mum.'

'Why don't you just give up?' Daphne hollers, hurling the plate of pasta at him. It bounces off his chest and falls with a thud to the floor, still intact. He stoops to pick it up, scooping the spaghetti back onto it with his bare hands.

'Why, Elliott? Why won't you just leave me alone?' Daphne says, beginning to cry.

'Because that's the one thing I can't do,' he says quietly, before carrying the ruined meal back downstairs.

73

'Oh shit,' Emily whispers.

'Holy fuck,' Matthew agrees, as they both stare down at the puddle that has pooled between her legs.

'No, no, no, no, no,' Emily cries, clutching her distended stomach. 'You're not supposed to show up for another month!' Then she sinks to the floor, letting out a low, guttural moan as the first contraction hits her. Once it's passed, she glances up at Matthew, her green eyes panicked. 'Greg's going to miss it!'

'No he won't,' Matthew says firmly, already pulling out his phone to call him. Then he looks back at Emily as she lets out another wail. 'Or should we get you to the hospital first?'

'Call Greg!' she cries, bracing her hands against the floor. 'If this one is anything like Lois, it could take hours to make an appearance.'

'OK,' Matthew says, walking into the other room as he dials.

'Man, am I glad you called,' Greg answers. 'I hate eating room service by myself,' he says, chewing noisily.

Matthew opens his mouth but nothing comes out.

'What's up?' Greg asks.

'Emily ... she's having the baby.'

'What? But she's not due for another month! Are you sure?'

Matthew looks over at Emily, who is now biting down on the corner of the sofa, still on all fours. 'Yep, pretty sure ...'

'Fuck! Of all the weeks to be in Scotland for work.' Matthew can hear the sounds of him throwing things in a suitcase. 'I'll be there as soon as I can. Take care of her, won't you?'

'Course I will. And don't drive like a maniac on the roads, OK?'

'Yeah, yeah,' Greg mutters, already hanging up.

'How you doing?' Matthew asks Emily as he re-joins her in the sitting room.

She glares up at him.

'Sorry, stupid question,' he says sheepishly. He stands there, shuffling his feet. 'So ...'

'Call ... the midwife,' Emily pants, nodding towards her phone. 'The plan was ... a home birth. I'm only going ... to the hospital ... if I have to.'

Matthew nods, scrolling through her phone until he finds the number, waiting impatiently for the midwife to pick up as he paces up and down the hallway. It eventually rings through to voicemail.

'Umm, hello ...' Matthew stammers. 'I'm calling on behalf of Emily Sanderson. She's gone into labour. So if you could give me a call back as soon as you're able to, I'd be grateful,' he says stiffly, before quickly hanging up. He walks back into the sitting room, unsure what to do next.

'Well?' Emily asks, her face shiny with sweat.

'She's a bit tied up right now but she'll be here as soon as she can,' he lies, not wanting to stress her out more. 'Can I get you something to eat or drink? Maybe a cup of tea? Or a sandwich?'

'Gas and air!' Emily groans. 'I need gas and air.'

'Right,' Matthew says, swiftly exiting into the hallway to try the midwife again, but there is still no answer.

'Call my mum,' Emily says when he comes back. 'Tell her ... I won't be picking Lois up. That she'll need to ... stay at hers tonight.'

Matthew does as he's told, reassuring Emily's mum that all is in hand and the midwife is on her way. After he's hung up he tries the midwife once more, to no avail.

'Can you run me a bath?' Emily says after another contraction has passed. 'I think it might help with the back pain for a while. Just until the midwife comes with the good stuff.'

'Sure thing,' Matthew says, rushing upstairs to the bathroom. Once he's filled it with bubbles and scented salts, he goes back downstairs and helps Emily to her feet, leading her towards the stairs. But when they reach the bottom step, she doubles over, panting heavily. She crawls up the first step, moaning softly, then pauses before she attempts the next one.

'Here,' Matthew says, lifting her up and carrying her up the stairs, trying not to stagger under her weight. He sits her carefully on the lid of the toilet as she breathes noisily through her nose.

'Can you take my socks off?' she asks.

He nods, pulling them off. She heaves herself to her feet and begins to pull her leggings down as Matthew quickly averts his eyes.

'You're going to need to help me with the rest too,' she says, steadying herself against the towel rail.

Matthew swallows, easing her leggings down over her knees and ankles, then pulling off her knickers as he looks the other way. Emily lifts her arms for him to pull her jumper over her head, crying out as he gets the neck stuck around her mouth, until finally working it free.

'Sorry,' he says, as she turns around for him to unhook her bra.

It falls to the floor and she reaches for his hand to walk over to the bath, putting one arm around his shoulder as she lowers herself into the water, so that her left breast ends up pressed against his cheek.

'My turn to say sorry,' she says, managing a weak smile.

'Highlight of my week,' Matthew jests, then inwardly

kicks himself, but Emily isn't even listening, her eyes closed, breathing deeply.

'Maybe I should leave you in peace for a bit?' he says, taking a step towards the door.

'Don't go,' Emily says, her eyes flying open. 'Please, I don't want to be on my own for this.'

'OK. I'll be right here,' he says, sitting down on the bath mat, clutching her sudsy hand as she squeezes his back tightly.

'Ooohhhhhhh,' she moans, bracing herself for another contraction, her fingernails digging into his palm. When it passes, she looks at Matthew, her eyes not quite focused. 'I don't think it's going to be that long. They're pretty close together now.' She closes her eyes as another contraction hits her, her face screwed up in pain.

'I'm going to call the midwife again,' Matthew says, his heart hammering.

It rings and rings, but just as he's about to hang up, a voice answers.

'Thank god!' Matthew breathes, quickly filling her in on what stage Emily is at.

'Right, here's what's going to happen,' she says authoritatively. 'I'm across town attending another birth, but I'll be on my way shortly and should be with you within the next half an hour, OK?'

'OK,' Matthew says, relaxing slightly at the thought of someone else taking charge.

When he goes back into the bathroom, Emily has pulled the plug, her knees raised in the air.

'Do you need a hand out?' Matthew asks, staring hard at the plant on the windowsill.

'It's already crowning!' she says, close to tears, her hand between her legs. 'How long is the midwife going to be?'

'Shit,' Matthew says, looking down to see that the top of the baby's head is, in fact, emerging. And it looks like it's splitting Emily open in the process. He crouches down and puts his head between his knees, suddenly feeling light-headed.

'Matthew, talk to me,' Emily says.

He looks up into her green eyes. 'She said she'll be here in under thirty minutes.'

'Oh god, I don't think we can wait that long!'

'Shall I call an ambulance?'

The only answer she gives is an almighty bellow so loud, Matthew's sure his eardrums just popped.

'Or I can drive you in the van if that's quicker?'

'What's happening?' she says. 'How far out is it now?'

Matthew reluctantly looks down between her legs again. 'Oh fuck,' he moans softly, seeing half the head has now forced its way out.

'What?' Emily cries.

'No, it's OK, it's still coming,' he says, kneeling down beside the bath, almost breathing as heavily as Emily is.

She gives another push, groaning from the exertion.

'I can see its nose and mouth now!' Matthew cries.

'You'll need to ... wipe them ... in case they're ... blocked,' Emily pants.

'All right,' Matthew says, grabbing a sheet of toilet roll and carefully rubbing at the tiny nostrils.

'Aarrrghhhh!' Emily hollers as she pushes again.

'I can see a shoulder!' Matthew tells her. 'Keep going!'

'Get your ... hands ... underneath ... ready,' Emily says through gritted teeth.

Matthew cups his hands beneath the baby as the other shoulder begins to emerge. Emily gives one last push and then the baby slithers out into Matthew's waiting hands. He carefully turns it over as the baby blinks up at him, before it screws up his eyes and lets out an ear-piercing bleat.

'That's a good sign, right?' Matthew says, staring at the tiny person he's holding, thinking how much it looks like an alien. His gaze travels down. 'It's a boy!' he says excitedly.

He stares deeply into the baby's blue eyes for a long moment, feeling something indescribable pass between them. He looks at Emily, who smiles tiredly back at him.

'You were amazing,' he says quietly, as he lies her son on her chest.

'Thank god you were here.' She blinks quickly at him. 'I couldn't have done it without you.'

Just then the doorbell sounds and Matthew rushes to answer it.

'How are we doing?' the midwife says, not even waiting for an answer as she pushes past him into the hallway and takes the stairs two at a time.

Matthew follows close on her heels, but the midwife turns to him at the top and says, 'It's fine, I'll take over from here.'

Matthew nods, peering in to check on Emily, but her eyes are fastened on her son. He reluctantly goes back downstairs to wait on the sofa but can't stay seated for long, feeling too keyed up and restless. After the midwife has left, telling him mother and baby are fast asleep, he wanders uselessly around the house until Greg finally arrives home.

'Did I miss it?' he asks as soon as he walks through the door.

'Just go see them,' Matthew says, ushering him upstairs.

He can hear the sound of Greg laughing, then crying. 'A boy,' he says in amazement. 'Our son.' He leans down to kiss Emily, murmuring how much he loves her.

Matthew retreats back down the stairs, feeling uncomfortably like a voyeur. He quietly lets himself out the front door and sits in his van. But he's unable to even turn the ignition. He just sits there, shell-shocked, thinking how this was the most horrific yet most beautiful moment of his life.

74

Myrtle hovers at the entrance to the restaurant, watching her parents making small talk as they devour the bread basket. To an onlooker, they might think they are just like any other retired couple. But only Myrtle knows there is something wrong with the picture. That something is missing.

'Sorry I'm late,' she says as she takes her seat between them.

It had been her father's idea to organise the meal, as today would have been Patti's seventy-fifth birthday. Myrtle had expected her mother to say no. Or to agree and then not show up. She wonders what exactly her father said to persuade her. She looks across at Daphne, who is even thinner than the last time Myrtle saw her, and wonders if perhaps her mother hadn't needed any persuasion at all.

The conversation is stilted, despite Elliott's valiant efforts. Whenever they slip back into silence, their gazes stray to the empty chair across from them.

You're the reason we fell apart in the first place, Myrtle tells Patti in her head, thinking back to her angry eleven-year-old self, and how she'd wished so furiously that Patti would just disappear from their lives and for it to just be the three of them again. *Yet now that you're gone, it's like we don't know how to be a family again without you.*

Talk to each other, Patti's voice urges her. *It's as simple as that – just talk.*

'So how's the job going?' Elliott asks.

Myrtle shrugs. 'It's a temp job. Nobody's even bothered to learn my name.'

'I don't know why you're working there when Patti's money is just sitting in the bank, doing nothing,' Daphne remarks.

'Because ... Because I want to do something with it that matters,' Myrtle says quietly. 'Something that makes a difference.'

Something that Patti would have been proud of.

'Like what?' Daphne asks.

Myrtle hesitates. 'I don't know yet. I'm still working on that. All I know is that I don't want to be stuck in an office for the rest of my life.'

You'll figure it out, Patti's voice assures her.

Daphne shakes her head. 'You always were trying to change the world, even when you were little.' She turns to Elliott. 'Do you remember her bringing home shell-shocked mice the neighbourhood cats had been playing with? And then you had to bury the poor little mites when they died during the night, and we had to tell Myrtle they'd escaped into the fields.'

Elliott nods, smiling. 'Or how when we took her to the beach, all the other children would be making sandcastles, but she'd be scurrying along the sand, picking up all the discarded carrier bags and plastic bottles, so they didn't get washed into the sea. Or if we saw a fisherman by a river and he'd caught a fish, she'd cry until he put it back in the water.'

Daphne laughs. 'God knows where you got it from.'

After they've ordered, Myrtle excuses herself to go to the toilet, and slams into someone coming out of the men's.

'Sorry,' she says, sidestepping around them.

'Myrtle?'

She turns, and the sight of him renders her speechless. A tense moment unfurls.

'How are you?' Oli finally asks.

'Fine,' Myrtle manages to force out. 'You?'

'Fine.' His eyes search hers briefly, then he looks away as he says quietly, 'I'm sorry about Patti. I heard, and I thought about getting in touch, but then I thought perhaps it was best not to ...'

Myrtle shrugs. 'It would have been nice to hear from you.'

'Well, I was thinking of you.'

'Thank you.'

'I should get back,' he says, indicating a table across the restaurant.

Myrtle glances over and sees a dark-haired woman watching them. Sitting opposite her is a dark-haired little girl in a yellow dress.

'It's Amy's second birthday today,' Oli says.

'Wow.'

'I know.'

'Congratulations,' Myrtle says, catching herself. 'She looks gorgeous.'

'Thanks. I think so,' he says, beaming proudly.

'So where are you living now?'

'Back near my parents. Great for babysitting,' he says with a smile. 'Plus there are lots of decent schools nearby. Got to think of boring things like school catchment areas now,' he says, rolling his eyes but still grinning. Then he hesitates. 'Do you ... want to come over and say hello? Or would that ...?'

'Yeah, that might be ...'

'A little weird?' he finishes.

Myrtle nods.

'OK.'

'OK.'

'Well ...'

'It was good seeing you,' Myrtle lies, thinking how impossible it seems that the person she was once closest to is now little more than a stranger.

257

He smiles. 'Likewise.' He pulls her into a hug, and she can't help but breathe in his familiar scent, trying not to think how long it's been since someone last held her like this.

You were mine once, she thinks, hugging him tightly. *And now you're someone else's.*

'You take care of yourself,' he whispers in her ear, and then he's gone.

Heart hammering, Myrtle rushes into the ladies, flips the lid down and sits on it, bunching a wad of toilet paper in her hands before pressing it into the corners of her eyes.

She used to picture this moment – seeing Oli, what she'd say to him, what he'd say to her. She'd imagined it over and over, in countless different ways. She'd just never imagined it like this.

You didn't want that life. You would have hated it, she tells herself. *But he's happy. So be happy for him.*

She blows her nose and then slides her phone out of her pocket, calling the only person she can think of. She listens as it goes straight to voicemail.

'Hello, this is Patti. Sorry I can't take your call right now. Leave me a message and I'll call you back.'

75

'You were expecting a guy, weren't you?'

'Ummm, well, the name threw me a bit,' Matthew admits. He's getting neck ache from looking down at her she's so short. He can't imagine her being able to lift Luke out of the bath.

'I'm stronger than I look,' Harri tells him, as if she's read his mind.

Matthew nods, unconvinced. 'Well, come and meet him,' he says, leading her out to the garden, where Luke is sprawled on a blanket next to Dora.

'Luke, this is Harri,' Matthew tells him.

Luke regards her warily. 'No,' he says.

'Noah's moved to Germany, remember? So Harri's going to be spending time with you for a while.'

'No,' Luke repeats, rolling on his side and pressing his face into Dora's fur.

Harri looks at him. 'Maybe you could give us some time alone?' she suggests.

'Good idea. I need to go food shopping anyway.'

'Great,' Harri says, sitting down on the grass a few feet from Luke. 'Take your time.'

When Matthew arrives home two hours later, the two of them are curled up on the sofa with Dora between them, watching a David Attenborough programme. As he stands there in the doorway, for just the briefest of moments, he almost thinks it's his mother sitting there with Luke.

76

'I want one that's house-trained already, and is good on the lead. And it mustn't moult. I don't want to be hoovering up after it every day. And it needs to be small enough for me to pick it up. Oh, and it must like cats,' a woman is telling one of the staff, who is nodding wearily.

Myrtle carries on walking by the kennels, her heart clenching at the hopeful faces staring out at her. 'Which are the dogs who have been here the longest?' she asks the woman showing her around.

'There's one in this section who has been here over a year. This,' she says, stopping in front of a pen, 'is Worzel.'

'Worzel,' Myrtle repeats, gazing at the scruffy ginger terrier, who is curled up in the far corner. He slowly lifts his head at the sound of his name, regarding them warily.

That's him, Myrtle thinks as they lock eyes.

That's him, Patti's voice echoes back.

Myrtle bends down and offers her hand. Worzel approaches her slowly, sniffs it, and then gives it a tentative lick.

'He likes you,' the woman says. 'He usually ignores most people. That's why he's been here so long. Everyone always wants the ones that can do all the tricks and that instantly flip on their backs for tummy rubs. But Worzel, you have to work a bit harder with him.'

'That's OK,' Myrtle says. 'We've got all the time in the world, haven't we, little man?'

He retreats to his bed, turning his back to both of them.

'How old is he?' Myrtle asks.

The woman checks his notes. 'Two.'

'So he's been here half his life,' Myrtle says. 'Poor boy.' She gazes around the concrete pen, thinking how it looks like a prison cell. Then she looks at the woman, her mind already made up. 'I want to take him home with me.'

'We'd have to do a home check in a couple of weeks' time.'

Myrtle nods.

'It's a big responsibility,' the lady insists. 'And Worzel has his problems.'

'We all do,' Myrtle says, looking at him again. 'And I know it's a big responsibility. But I'm ready for it.'

When she's filled out the paperwork, she takes Worzel outside to her car. He slinks low to the ground, as if he's ducking under an invisible fence, the wispy fur of his underbelly grazing the ground. And when she opens the boot, he refuses to get in. She tries one of the back doors instead, but still he won't budge, so Myrtle lifts him up and he gives a low growl.

'I know. I'm sorry. But it's the only way.'

On the journey home, Myrtle talks to him as he curls up tightly on the back seat, his eyes on her the whole time.

'I know this is scary for you. I know you have no idea who I am or where I'm taking you. But I'm going to look after you, OK? I'm not going to give up on you, no matter what. Your new home, it's for keeps, I promise.'

When she pulls into the drive, he refuses to get out, so Myrtle has to lift him out, which provokes another growl. Once inside the house, his eyes bulge, as if on sensory overload; his body tenses, as if waiting for a blow. He watches her every move closely, startling at every sound she makes as she begins to make his dinner.

'What did we do to you?' Myrtle asks softly.

When she puts the bowl down, he won't even come over to it. He just sniffs the air suspiciously, as if it's a trick that he knows better than to fall for. So Myrtle leaves the kitchen, because no one likes to be watched while they're eating.

When she comes back ten minutes later, the bowl is empty, licked clean, and though Worzel's eyes still track her as she crosses the room, he has lain down on his makeshift bed of blankets by the radiator.

'It will get easier, I promise,' Myrtle tells him.

The next morning, she walks into the kitchen, bracing herself for destruction, or at least wee on the floor. But there is nothing. Just Worzel, on his bed, looking up at her apprehensively.

'Hello, Worzel.'

He gives a half-hearted thump of his tail.

Myrtle's heart skips a beat. She bends down to stroke him and his tail gives another thump.

'You know what today is, Worzel?' she asks him, and he cocks his head slightly, as if he's following every word. 'Today's my birthday. Aren't I lucky, getting to spend it with you?' He licks her hand. 'But more importantly, today is the first day of the rest of your life. Of *our* life together. And that's definitely worth celebrating,' she says, standing up to cut them both a thin slice of the cake she'd made the day before.

'Cake for breakfast today only, so don't get used to this,' she warns, putting a slice in his bowl. Worzel goes across to it, sniffs it, then devours it in two bites.

'That good, huh?' Myrtle says, taking a big bite of hers.

When she stands up to take the plate over to the sink, the cake knife clatters to the floor, skittering across the tiles. Worzel bolts, pressing himself into the corner of the room, his eyes wide and fearful, his body shaking.

'It's OK,' Myrtle whispers to him, crouching down. 'It's

OK. Nothing's going to hurt you. You're safe now.'

When they go out for a walk an hour later, Myrtle lets Worzel off in a fenced-in park so he can't run away. As they walk laps of the grass, he keeps looking back at her to check she's still there.

'I'm not going anywhere,' she tells him.

As soon as they get home, Worzel flops out on his bed, and within seconds he's fast asleep, snoring softly.

Myrtle watches him, smiling. 'I love you already,' she whispers to him. 'I really do.'

77

Matthew rolls out of bed and sleepily heads to the bathroom. He's brushing his teeth before he remembers.

Fuck, he thinks, studying himself in the mirror, noticing the grey hairs now sprouting from his curly head and the lines deepening around his eyes and mouth. He spits and then looks at himself once more.

'Happy birthday,' he says to his unsmiling reflection.

After he's got ready, he gets Luke washed and dressed, then rushes towards the door with a slice of toast still in his mouth when Harri arrives late.

'Sorry, I had to pick up some food shopping on the way here,' she tells him.

'No worries,' he says between mouthfuls of toast, already heading out to his van. 'Come on, Dora,' he says, opening the passenger door for her to jump in.

'I told you to take the day off,' Ed tells him when Matthew turns up.

'Why? So I can sit at home counting my grey hairs?'

Ed laughs, whacking him on the back. 'Happy birthday, old man.'

'Yeah,' Matthew says dully. 'I'm officially middle-aged now.'

'Welcome to the club.'

Forty years old, he thinks, as he starts trimming the laurel hedges, Dora curling up on the grass beside him. He realises with a start that this was the age Luke had his accident. The year that life changed for all of them, and Matthew's childhood effectively ended overnight.

He thinks back to his nine-year-old self, sitting in the hospital waiting room alone, not knowing what was to come.

Would you be disappointed in who I've become? Matthew wonders, thinking how little he's achieved in his life. And he can't help but think the answer would be yes.

When he gets home from work, he jumps straight in the shower, scrubbing at the dirt encrusted on his hands. When he emerges for dinner, hair still damp, Harri is sitting at the kitchen table with Luke, a birthday cake between them, aglow with burning candles.

'It was hard trying to cram forty of them on there,' she says, grinning at him.

'I bet,' he says, sitting down opposite them, feeling the heat coming off the lit candles.

'Remember to make a wish,' she tells him.

He nods and then closes his eyes, thinking: *Let this be the year that changes everything.* But just as he's about to blow them out, Luke beats him to it, laughing uproariously as Matthew shakes his head.

'I did make veggie lasagne,' Harri says, watching as Luke sinks his fork into the cake and scoops off a big chunk of icing. 'But we could have cake for starters instead,' she says, laughing.

'Sounds like a plan,' Matthew says, digging his own fork in and taking a bite. 'Mmmm,' he says appreciatively. 'You know, no one's made me a cake in years. Not since I was a teenager.'

'I figured you weren't planning to celebrate it, so I had to do something.'

'How did you even know about it?'

'Emily dropped this around for you yesterday,' she says, placing a gaudily wrapped present on the table in front of him.

He tears open the paper to see a framed picture of one of Matt's nursery drawings, showing two stick figures, one much taller than the other. Under that one is written *Big Matthew*, and under the shorter one is written *Small Matt*.

Matthew smiles to himself, standing up to put it on the bookcase.

After they've had their fill of cake, Luke passing out on the sofa with Dora, chocolate still smeared around his mouth, Harri loads the dishwasher and picks up her bag.

'I'd love to stay but I've got a date tonight.'

'Go, go, don't let us make you late,' Matthew says. 'And thank you for the cake. Seriously. It means a lot.'

She smiles at him. 'Everyone should celebrate their birthday, no matter how old they are. Birthdays aren't just for kids.'

He nods. 'You're right.'

Harri stands in front of the hall mirror, deftly applying a coat of dark red lipstick. 'Third date,' she says, holding up crossed fingers, her nails bitten down to the quick.

He smiles. 'He'd be a fool not to ask you out for a fourth.'

'How about you?' Harri asks, spritzing her short, spiky hair with hairspray to give it more volume. 'You know I'd be happy to stay with Luke if you wanted to go out on a date.'

'It's not just the dates, though, is it? It's what comes afterwards.' He shakes his head. 'It's too complicated with Luke.'

Harri frowns at him in the mirror. 'It's as complicated as you want to make it.'

'I guess ... I just don't feel ready yet.'

'Why not? Haven't you been single for ages?'

He nods. 'But you get your heart broken badly enough and ... well, you wonder if relationships are worth all the heartache.'

'I think so,' Harri says lightly, squirting perfume onto her neck and wrists.

'Sometimes I think it's just easier being on your own. Then there's no one to disappoint you.' He smiles. 'Except yourself, of course.'

Harri turns to look at him as she shrugs on her jacket. 'But who wants the easy option in life?'

78

Myrtle looks around her at the towering piles of boxes her mother has filled, the house looking exposed and vulnerable now it's been stripped bare.

'It's crazy,' Daphne says as she tapes another box closed. 'We spend so much of our lives saving up and acquiring all this *stuff*, and then you get to an age when it feels like it's weighing you down, so you spend the remainder of your life trying to get rid of it all again.'

Daphne stacks the box on top of another, accidentally knocking over a lamp in the process. Myrtle tenses, her eyes fixed on Worzel curled up in the middle of the carpet, waiting for him to bolt to the corner of the room, but he doesn't even blink. She grins to herself, thinking how much he's changed in the two years he's been with her.

'Here,' Daphne says, handing Myrtle a flat-pack box and roll of sellotape.

'I can't believe you're actually moving,' Myrtle says as she tapes shut the box flaps. Memories of her childhood years and visits home to see Patti and Daphne echo back at her from the corners of every room. So much of her – of all of them – is tied up in this place. And now some other family would be here, living out their own dramas, creating their own memories.

'I thought I'd see out my days here,' Daphne agrees quietly, glancing around the bare sitting room. 'But I'm tired of living in a house full of empty rooms. I don't know how my mother did it for all those years after my dad died. Anyway, you should be pleased – you'll be getting a large chunk of your inheritance early.'

Myrtle just stares at her mother, as if money could in any way compensate for what they've lost.

'And you've still got Patti's money as well.' Daphne looks at her. 'You really should do something with it.'

'I intend to,' Myrtle says, more hotly than she meant to. 'I'm actually thinking about opening up my own rescue centre, so I can save more dogs like Worzel.'

He looks up at them at the sound of his name, his tail twitching madly.

'Good for you,' Daphne says, as she picks up a paintbrush and begins to paint over Elliott's pencil lines on the kitchen doorframe, marking Myrtle's height each year of her birthday, until she left for uni at eighteen. 'Patti would have liked that.'

'So what have you done with all Patti's stuff?' Myrtle asks, watching as Worzel brushes against the doorframe as he rushes over to the French windows to look outside, a stripe of white now smeared across his wiry fur.

'I've taken most of her clothes to charity, but I've kept some of her personal things.'

Myrtle glares at her mother. 'You didn't think to ask me if I wanted anything before you gave it all away?'

'She was a foot taller than you, Myrtle. Nothing would have fitted you.'

'That's not the point!'

'Don't shout at me!'

'This is just what you do, though! You shut me out. Just like how you didn't tell me when Patti was dying.'

'I'm not going over this again, Myrtle,' Daphne says, clenching her teeth.

'You should have told me!'

'What does it matter? She's dead. Whether you watched her die or not, she still died.'

'But there were things I would have wanted to say if I'd got the chance.'

'Like what?'

That I loved her. That no one will ever understand me like she did. That she was more of a mother to me than you ever were, Myrtle thinks. But instead she says, 'Wasn't there anything Patti wanted to say to me?'

Daphne shrugs. 'It's impossible to put some things into words.'

'Not the important things.'

Her mother sighs. 'She wasn't in a good way, Myrtle. She was bloated from the drugs and she was so confused. It was hard for her to even form a sentence she'd lost so much of her vocabulary.'

Myrtle can't imagine it – eloquent, opinionated Patti reduced to that.

'Then she lost control of her bladder. She was in so much pain, even though she tried to hide how bad it was. And there wasn't a single thing I could do to help her.' Daphne blinks quickly, gazing out the window into the garden that she and Patti had landscaped together. 'She didn't want you to see her like that. And you wouldn't have wanted to see her like that. Trust me.'

Myrtle looks out at the garden too. There are two gardeners out there, cutting the lawn and trimming the hedges that Daphne has allowed to grow out of control in Patti's absence. They are wearing polo shirts emblazoned with the words *Ellis & Maguire Gardening Services* on the back, and a dog is lying by the shed, observing them impassively as they go about their work. Worzel starts whining as he spots the dog out the window, desperate to go outside and play.

'Can I at least see Patti's things that you've kept?' Myrtle asks her mother.

Daphne shakes her head. 'Maybe some other time. It's all packed away in boxes now.'

Myrtle's fingernails dig into her palms. 'It's like you want to keep even the memory of her all to yourself.'

'Don't be a child, Myrtle.'

'I'm not, I'm forty-three years old!' she snaps. But it is the voice of her teenage self that slips out.

It's just stuff, Patti's voice tells her. *Let it be, Myrtle. Let her be.*

Daphne exhales heavily as she sits down on the box she's just taped up, pressing her thumbs into the corners of her eyes. 'You know what the hardest part about someone dying is?' she asks. 'Knowing that you have to go on without them.'

Myrtle sinks down onto another box.

'You know those stories of people dying of a broken heart?' Daphne continues, still rubbing her eyes. 'How they couldn't go on without them and their heart just gave up?'

Myrtle gives a stiff nod.

'Every morning I wake up feels like a betrayal,' Daphne whispers, tears leaking down her cheeks.

Myrtle doesn't know how to respond to that. She doesn't know how to comfort her mother. Without Patti, it's like something has become lost between the two of them, their grief tearing them further apart. Or perhaps it had never been there in the first place. Perhaps it was only Patti that had held them together, when otherwise they would have fallen apart.

79

Luke grabs the box of salted popcorn off Matthew, shoving a huge fistful into his grinning mouth as the trailers begin.

Usually Matthew is on high alert when taking Luke out in public, but going to the cinema is the only time he doesn't have to worry as Luke stays completely quiet throughout, enraptured by the whole experience. They go every week, Matthew not even caring what film they see, just picking whatever is showing next.

'Ever heard of ladies first?' Harri says to the pair of them as she grabs a handful of popcorn, throwing a piece at Matthew's head, which he manages to catch in his mouth.

Five minutes into the film, he feels like he's been punched. Filling the screen, completely naked, is Rosie.

'Ruh,' Luke says, grabbing his wrist excitedly. 'Ruh.'

'Yes. Shh,' Matthew says, holding out the box of popcorn until Luke fills his mouth with another handful.

For the next hour and a half, Rosie is in almost every shot, the camera seemingly in love with her, lingering on her lips, the hollow below her neck, her bare stomach – the secret parts of her that once only Matthew knew about.

He can barely follow the film, staring up at her enlarged image, feeling dwarfed in the darkness. He watches her writhing naked on a bed with her brawny co-star and something tightens painfully inside him. If he wasn't here with Luke and Harri, he would walk out right now.

He thinks back to the two of them at the beach all those years ago, how they had rushed into the waves like little kids, then kissed each other like horny teenagers. He struggles to remember that person he was when he was with her. It feels like a lifetime ago, like it all happened to someone else.

But that moment . . . Matthew thinks. *That Rosie, in that moment, she's still mine.*

As they stroll home afterwards, Luke mumbles to himself like he always does when they come out of the cinema, as if there is too much going on in his brain to process. Matthew walks silently beside him, still thinking of Rosie. Thinking how differently his life might have turned out.

'You OK?' Harri asks, sensing he's quieter than usual.

'She's my ex,' he says after a pause.

'Who?'

'The actress in that film – Rosie Bletchley.'

'*You* used to date Rosie Bletchley?' Harri asks incredulously.

'A long time ago. Before she was famous.'

'Wow. Were you in love with each other?' Harri asks bluntly.

Matthew hesitates, then nods. 'Until we weren't.'

Harri smiles in understanding. 'Relationships, huh?'

Matthew gives a half-hearted smile in return, knowing Harri is still struggling after her recent break-up.

As they turn down their road, Harri suddenly reaches for his hand, swinging it gently between them. Matthew is too surprised to say anything – he had no idea that Harri even saw him that way – yet he doesn't take his hand away.

He studies her out of the corner of his eye as they walk, thinking how different she is from any other woman he's ever fancied, with her short, spiky hair, her tattooed arms, her ripped jeans and that ring through her nose. Holding her hand, he doesn't get the same jolt he did when he was with Rosie. But maybe that was OK. Maybe a warm palm curled around his own was enough.

80

'You can stroke him. He's friendly,' Myrtle says to the little boy standing in front of Worzel.

He sinks his chubby fingers into Worzel's wiry ginger fur. 'Can I have him?' he asks.

'No,' Myrtle says, laughing. 'Worzel lives with me. But all the other dogs here are looking for loving homes.'

'I'll show you around,' Annabel says to the family, leading them away to give them a tour of the centre.

Sandra walks through the reception door, a duffel bag in hand. 'Litter of five found dumped by the canal.'

'Poor babies,' Myrtle says, peering in to look at them. 'Get the vet to give them the once-over and I'll sort out a kennel for them.'

After she's done that, she stops in at Gertie's pen, who has just come in after her elderly owner died and none of the relatives wanted her. Myrtle sits with her awhile as she climbs onto her lap, rolling onto her back for tummy rubs.

'You won't be here long,' she promises her.

Back in the office, the phone is ringing non-stop, and Myrtle spends the next hour answering calls. Then she tackles her to-do list, which is never-ending. Top of the list: *Book gardener*.

Myrtle flips through the Yellow Pages, running her finger down the ads, picking the first one that catches her eye: *Ellis & Maguire Gardening Services*. Something about it sounds familiar.

She calls the number, but it just rings and rings. Rather than leave a voicemail, she dials the number of the next ad – *Frank Herbert Garden Designs* – and books him to come the following week to mow all the grounds.

She manages to tick off three more tasks before five o'clock rolls around.

'Ready for the fundraiser?' Annabel asks with a knowing grin.

Myrtle grimaces. 'I hate these things.'

'I know, but they bring in a lot of money,' Annabel points out.

Myrtle nods. 'As long as I don't have to give a speech.'

'Thank you everyone for coming here tonight,' Myrtle begins nervously, her untouched glass of cheap white wine clamped in her hand. 'Second Chance has only been open six weeks, but already our humble little shelter has rehomed one hundred and twenty-two dogs.' She pauses as everyone claps. 'We wouldn't be able to do what we do if it wasn't for the generous support of people like you. So while tonight is about having fun and socialising, for the eighty dogs we currently have in our kennels, and the thousands more just waiting for our help, tonight is about digging deep so we can give them all the second chance at life they deserve. Thank you.'

There's another smattering of applause as Myrtle hurriedly slips back into the crowd, gulping half of her wine in one go.

'Good job,' Annabel whispers, giving her a quick thumbs up.

Callum, their resident vet, smiles as she passes by, his gaze lingering on her, and Myrtle feels her cheeks reddening under his scrutiny and her heart beating just a little bit faster.

Stop it, she tells herself. *You're acting like a teenage girl, when he's at least ten years younger than you.*

After two hours of circling the room, performing the

obligatory small talk with the most important patrons, Myrtle escapes out of a side door and walks down the corridor towards the kennels. She takes off her heels, which have been pinching her toes since she first put them on, and pads barefoot around the kennel block, the concrete cold beneath her feet. It's quiet back here, most of the dogs slumbering, but she can still catch strains of music and laughter from the fundraiser.

'The things we have to do,' Myrtle murmurs to Gertie, bending down to rub her head through the bars, the hem of her satin dress grazing the floor.

She reaches for the nearest tub of dog biscuits and offers one to Gertie, who devours it in one bite. Then she moves on to the next kennel, bidding each of the dogs goodnight and slipping them a treat through the bars.

Sometimes Myrtle feels like a prison warden, keeping them all locked away like this, even though they've never committed any crime. But she reminds herself that every day a dog is rescued by someone, she can then take in and save another dog.

She heads back to reception to collect Worzel, who rests his paws against her knees, sniffing her dress for the other dogs' scents and letting out a low grumble.

'No need to get jealous,' Myrtle tells him. 'You'll always be my first love, Worzel. Always,' she says, kissing the top of his scruffy head.

As she walks around switching off the office lights, she glances at the smiling photo of Patti that sits on her desk.

This is all because of you, she silently tells her. *I might not be changing the world. But maybe I'm changing my tiny corner of it.*

81

'Got to say, I never thought I'd see this day.'

'You and me both,' Xander replies, loosening his tie.

Matthew shakes his head in disbelief. 'What happened to you?'

'I guess I finally grew up,' Xander says with a grin.

They both look over at Mai-Lin in her ivory dress as she dances with Xander's best man.

'But I thought you were against marriage? That you were all for being anti-establishment?' Matthew presses, feeling strangely unnerved that Xander – unreliable, unpredictable, free-spirited Xander – has, in the end, become just like everyone else.

He shrugs. 'What can I say? I've grown soft with age.' His gaze slides over to Mai-Lin again, as if he can't bear to take his eyes off her. 'And I guess a secret part of me always wanted what your mum and dad used to have. It just took me this long to figure it out. Too long, really.'

'Yeah,' Matthew says quietly. 'Well, I'm glad you finally found each other.'

Xander nods. 'Better late than never, eh?'

Mai-Lin catches sight of them and rushes over as the next song starts up.

'Time to dance,' she tells Xander, grabbing both of his hands and pulling him to the centre of the dance floor.

Matthew watches them together for a moment, their grey

heads glinting under the fairylights, thinking how sad his mother would have been to miss this day. Then he looks over at Luke, who is sitting next to Harri as she feeds him forkfuls of wedding cake. Once the plate's empty, Luke gets to his feet and staggers over to the buffet for more food.

Matthew walks over to Harri and she glances up at him, smiling. Her whole face lights up when she smiles, and it's impossible not to smile back.

'Want to dance?' he asks.

Her smile widens as she gets to her feet and takes his hand.

'Thanks for coming today,' he says as they begin to spin in slow circles, just like his mother taught him.

'You don't need to thank me.'

She'd looked so pleased when he first invited her, but her expression turned reproachful when he offered to pay her extra because it was her day off.

'This is more than just a job to me, you know,' she'd replied curtly.

He looks again at Xander and Mai-Lin as they do another rotation, his hand resting in the small of Harri's back. He shuts his eyes. They're dancing so close he can feel her heart beating fast against his chest, and he tries not to think about why his own heart never quickens when they're together.

'Oh fuck!' Harri hisses, and his eyes flick open again.

Luke is bent over the chocolate fountain, his arms elbow-deep in the molten run-off. He turns to look at Matthew and Harri, who stand unmoving, rooted in mutual horror, as he raises one dripping arm to his mouth, a puddle of chocolate pooling down his white shirt.

'Fuck,' Matthew echoes.

Xander catches sight of his brother and strides over, putting his arms around Luke, and Matthew thinks he's going to drag him away. But the next moment Xander is shoving his own hand into the fountain, then scooping the chocolate into his grinning mouth. Luke starts to laugh, wiping his hands down Xander's shirt, and Xander retaliates by dragging his hand down Luke's face, until they're both covered in chocolate.

Mai-Lin steps closer to Matthew and Harri. 'What happened to growing old gracefully?' she asks, shaking her head but smiling. 'Still acting like a pair of toddlers in their seventies.'

Matthew nods. 'Welcome to the family.'

82

'Does he always do this when you bring a guy home?'

There's another loud thump at the bedroom door.

'No,' Myrtle says, not wanting to reveal to Callum that he's the first guy she's brought home in a very long time. 'But he normally sleeps in the bed with me, so he's probably a bit confused what's going on.'

'Territorial,' Callum murmurs. 'Males often are.' He begins to kiss her again, one hand travelling down her side, his skin on her skin making her shiver. It is the most strange, intimate thing getting naked with someone, she thinks as he fumbles with the clasp of her bra. She's never understood why people do it so unthinkingly.

This is only the third date they've been on, after Callum kept asking her out and Myrtle kept refusing.

'Why not?' he'd asked, as he stitched up an unconscious dog he'd just neutered. 'Is it the age thing?'

'No,' Myrtle had lied, even though the fact that she was almost ten years older than him did make her feel more than a little uneasy. 'I just don't think it's a good idea for colleagues to date, because if it all goes wrong, then we still have to see each other every day at work.'

'Well, if the sex is that bad, you can just fire me and get in another vet,' he'd said, grinning, while Myrtle blushed furiously, which only made him grin more. 'I'm not going to stop asking until you say yes,' he'd added, his cheeks dimpling.

God, he was cute. Too cute. She didn't even know what he saw in her. It wouldn't last. She knew she would come to regret it. And yet, that voice in her head, which sounds so much like Patti's, was whispering: *Stop saying no and start saying yes.*

So Myrtle said yes, and here they are, at the end of their third date, naked in her bed.

After they'd finished their meal, and were standing outside the restaurant waiting for a taxi, Callum had suggested going back to his for a drink. Myrtle had instantly tensed up at the idea, and for a long moment she said nothing, her heart racing as Callum looked at her expectantly.

Stop saying no, she told herself.

'How about we go back to mine instead?' she suggested.

Now that he's here, in her bed, she suddenly feels like a teenager again; she's so nervous she almost feels nauseous. It's been so long since she's dated anyone, let alone slept with anyone, she's forgotten what it's like, constantly dancing around that unspoken question: did they really like each other? When she was younger, it didn't seem to matter so much, as if she had all the time in the world and it was fine to kiss a few frogs along the way. But now ...

There's a third thump at the door, and then Worzel begins to howl.

'I can't perform with this going on,' Callum mutters.

Perform? Myrtle thinks, suppressing a laugh. *You're not a West End actor.*

The door shakes in the frame as Worzel hurls himself at it again.

'All right, you win, you little swine,' Callum declares, throwing back the covers and stalking naked across the room, before yanking the door open. Worzel dashes in, leaping up on the bed before laying his head proprietarily on the pillow next to Myrtle's.

Callum shakes his head. 'Looks like I'll be sleeping on the sofa then.'

'Sometimes he gets lonely at night,' Myrtle says apologetically.

'Don't we all?' Callum grumbles, grabbing his pile of clothes off the floor and padding downstairs.

Myrtle turns on her side and stares at Worzel as he stretches out beside her, letting out a sigh of contentment. 'You're still top dog,' she whispers, pulling him closer and rubbing his stomach. 'You'll always be top dog,' she says, before planting a kiss on his head.

83

'Thank god it's the weekend, eh?' Matthew says to Dora as he pulls into the driveway after an exhausting day at work spent erecting a customer's elaborate two-storey summerhouse. He leaves his muddy gardening boots by the back door and is just about to scrub his equally muddy hands in the kitchen sink when he stops short at the sight in front of him. Luke is lying spread-eagled in the middle of the sitting-room carpet, one hand resting on his bloated stomach, surrounded by the remains of what looks suspiciously like the cake Harri had been baking that morning for Matt's tenth birthday party tomorrow.

'Where's Harri?' Matthew asks, frowning.

Luke slowly turns his head to look at him, icing smeared around his mouth. He points towards the bathroom as Dora rushes over to him, frantically licking his face as he tries to push her away, laughing.

Matthew strides down the hall and knocks on the bathroom door, but there is no answer, even though he can hear the steady rush of running water coming from within.

'Harri,' he calls.

Still no response. He tries the handle but it's locked. He can't help imagining the worst, picturing her collapsed unconscious in the shower, her cheek pressed against the plughole, the rising water level slowly inching its way up towards her mouth and nostrils.

'Harri, open up!' he hollers, banging on the door.

When he still hears nothing, he takes a few steps back and then runs at the door, ramming it with his shoulder. It takes another attempt before it finally swings open.

Matthew takes in the scene before him: Harri is sitting on the floor of the shower, knees hugged to her chest, her tattooed arms wrapped tightly around her calves, the spray bouncing off her naked back. Next to her is something small and bloody, turning the water a faint pink.

Matthew reaches in and switches off the water, which is now cold.

Harri gazes up at him, eyes unfocused, and Matthew thinks he has never seen her look so small and vulnerable.

'What's going on?' he asks softly, and when he looks down again at the bloody mess by her feet, he realises what it is. He grabs a handful of loo roll and then scoops it up, flushing it down the toilet, and gets a sudden flashback of his dad doing the same thing after Grace had miscarried.

Matthew grabs a towel to wrap around Harri and tries to help her to her feet, but when she doesn't budge, he sits down next to her in the shower and puts his arm around her instead, the water seeping into the seat of his muddy jeans.

'I only found out the other day after I did a test,' Harri says, still clasping her knees to her chest, her teeth beginning to chatter.

'Why didn't you tell me?' Matthew asks, rubbing her back through the towel.

'I didn't know whether you'd be happy or not.'

Matthew doesn't know how to respond to that.

'Maybe it's for the best then,' Harri says dully. 'No point bringing someone else into the world unless both of us want that.'

'Harri, I ...' He hesitates, wanting to say: *Isn't the world overpopulated enough without us adding to it?* But instead he says, 'Don't you think we've got our hands full already, just looking after Luke?'

Harri doesn't answer, but he can see the tears leaking down her already-wet cheeks. She lies her head on Matthew's shoulder as he holds her shaking body.

84

Myrtle hauls herself out of the pool and wanders back to her sun lounger, joining Abi and Sophie, who are sprawled out on theirs, both of them watching her intently.

'What?' she asks, suddenly self-conscious.

'We were just saying you look different,' Sophie says, still studying her.

'Do I?'

'Yes. You look ... happy,' Abi accuses.

'Don't I usually?' Myrtle says with a laugh.

'Yeah, but you look like that kind of smug, content happy that young people in love look like.' Abi's eyes narrow. 'You're not in love, are you?'

'God, no,' Myrtle says. 'But there might be someone I meet up with now and again ...' she admits coyly.

'I knew it!' Abi crows. 'I can read you like a book, Myrtle Brookes.'

'It's nothing,' she says offhandedly.

'It's definitely something,' Sophie says knowingly.

'It's just a ...' Myrtle struggles to think of a word for what it is. '... a *thing* with a guy at work. It's nothing serious.'

'Not that hot young vet we saw at your fundraiser?' Abi asks in disbelief.

Myrtle nods and then blushes. 'It's just sex, though.'

'You lucky bitch,' Abi says enviously.

'Just be careful that you don't wind up getting hurt,' Sophie warns, her forehead creasing in concern.

'Neither of us have any expectations, so no one's going to get hurt,' Myrtle insists. 'That's the beauty of it.'

Sophie looks unconvinced.

'Soph, it's fine. We're both adults. We're just having some fun, that's all. And he makes me feel young again.' She lowers her voice and leans in closer. 'Plus, the sex is ... well, let's just say I thought multiple orgasms were an urban myth until now,' she adds, trying not to grin.

'Good for you,' Abi says.

Sophie just presses her lips together.

'You know what, I've finally come to the conclusion that maybe I'm not cut out for relationships,' Myrtle tells them. 'People just end up disappointing you. Or you end up disappointing them,' she says, thinking of Oli.

'The right person wouldn't disappoint you,' Sophie interjects.

'Look, not everyone is like you two, meeting the loves of their lives when they're still teenagers,' Myrtle points out. 'And maybe not everyone is destined to have this one big, lifelong relationship anyway. Maybe some people aren't meant to stick around that long. Maybe they just come into your life in the moments you need them to.'

'Well, I don't think you should close yourself off to meeting the right person just yet,' Sophie declares. 'You can't spend the rest of your life alone.'

'I'm not alone. I've got Worzel. And Callum on speed dial.'

'Dogs and bed buddies don't count. Myrtle, come on. Everyone should be with someone they love. And everyone needs to feel loved. That's what matters most in life. I mean, if you don't have that, what do you have, really?'

'Your friends,' Myrtle counters. 'Your family. Your passions in life. Feeling like you're making a difference in the world ...' She trails off as Sophie reaches for her hand, looking at her earnestly.

'One day you'll meet someone, and all the other shitty relationships, all the heartbreak, all of it will feel worth it. Someone is going to be worth the wait. They will.'

Abi scoffs. 'Oh, please. This is why people get married, because they buy into the fairytale that everyone keeps peddling. It's frigging hard work, no matter how much you love someone and how "right" for you you think they are. Are you going to sit there and pretend it's all sweetness and light with you and Tom?'

Sophie hesitates, a troubled look crossing her face. 'Well ... no ... It's not perfect. But I feel like we know each other better than anyone else. And I can't imagine spending my life with anyone but him.'

Abi turns to Myrtle. 'I say just do whatever makes you happy and don't worry about anything else.'

Myrtle shoots her a grateful smile.

Abi lets out a low whistle. 'Check you out, snagging yourself a hot, young fuck buddy at nearly fifty years of age.' She holds up her palm until Myrtle reluctantly high-fives it, rolling her eyes.

'God, it's times like this that I wish Liam and I had met later in life,' Abi says.

'Why?' Sophie asks.

'Because I never got a chance to do all that fun, crazy stuff that you're supposed to do when you're young, like sowing my wild oats with loads of different men. Christ, I've only slept with three men in my life, and the first two were both virgins so they had no idea what they were doing. Not that Liam was much better in the beginning. Luckily I trained him up well.' She smiles and then lets out a weary sigh. 'Oh, to be single again,' she says wistfully.

'You don't mean that,' Sophie says.

'Course I don't. I love that twonk. But sometimes, just sometimes, you can't help but wonder, can you?'

When they're out at dinner later that night, Myrtle watches Abi and Sophie as they bicker over what wine to get and smiles to herself.

'What?' Abi says, catching her grinning.

Myrtle shakes her head, still smiling. 'I was just thinking how crazy it is that it's been three decades since you two nutters came into my life.'

'You're a lucky lady,' Abi says with a smirk.

'I am,' Myrtle agrees. 'But we shouldn't wait until every big anniversary to go away together. We should make this an annual thing,' she says, remembering herself saying the exact same thing on one of their camping trips all those years ago.

'I'm in,' Abi says.

'Me too,' Sophie says.

'I'd say let's make a pact, but we know Myrtle isn't very good at keeping those, whereas we always keep our end of the bargain, don't we, Soph?' Abi says with a wink.

'I did say *if* I ever get married you two would be my bridesmaids,' Myrtle protests.

'I think that was the moment you cursed yourself,' Sophie says, making Myrtle laugh.

Abi's phone buzzes with the arrival of a text message. She glances at the screen, her expression darkening. 'For fuck's sake,' she mutters.

'What's up?' Myrtle asks.

'Children,' she says with a sigh. 'Rufus has just been fired again for falling asleep on the clock. That's the third security job he's lost in six months. That boy has less sense than his father does, which is saying something. And don't even get me started on Lila. She's barely at home anymore, sleeping over at her boyfriend's most nights – who already has two kids by two different girls, I should add – and she only comes back when she needs to borrow money. I say "borrow" except she never pays us back. And god knows if she's even going to finish her exams to make it to uni.'

'Kids, eh?' Sophie says.

'Except yours are little angels in comparison,' Abi says.

'Only because Tom insisted on shipping them both off to boarding school. The teachers did all the hard work, not us,' Sophie admits.

Abi lets out another heavy sigh. 'I remember when they were little, when it was really tough, and the only thing that kept me going was the thought of them when they were older. Imagining how I'd be the cool mum and I'd be best friends with them. But it's like they don't even want to know me now.'

'They're all so self-involved at this age,' Sophie reassures her. 'Once they're out in the real world, properly fending for themselves, then they'll realise how good they've got it with you.'

'God, I hope so.'

They lapse into silence for a while, watching three teenage girls at the bar, who are acting like they haven't noticed the group of young men eyeing them up as they play with their hair and laugh loudly among themselves.

'So Tom's going to be a father again,' Sophie says, breaking the silence.

Myrtle and Abi's jaws drop open.

'I'm not the mother, don't worry,' Sophie hastens to add.

'What the fuck?' Abi and Myrtle say in unison.

'It seems he's been sowing his wild oats,' Sophie says drily.

'Who is she?' Abi asks furiously.

'I don't know the details. I've never wanted to know the details,' Sophie replies quietly.

Myrtle and Abi stare at her.

'This isn't the first time?' Myrtle asks.

Sophie is motionless for a moment, then gives a tight shake of her head.

'Jesus. How can you stay with him, Soph?' Myrtle asks in disbelief.

'You can't help who you fall in love with,' Sophie says, with a small shrug of her shoulders.

'You'd seriously rather stay with him, knowing he's sleeping with other women, than leave him?' Abi asks.

'He loves me. I don't doubt that. And he's a great father. I have the kids to think of too.'

'And you have to think of yourself as well,' Myrtle says.

'I *am*,' Sophie says hotly. 'I'm not like you, Myrtle. I don't want to do this alone. Plus we made a promise to each other. And I'm not just going to give up on that.'

'As long as giving up isn't staying with a person,' Myrtle says.

Sophie doesn't respond to that.

'How could you not have told us?' Abi says.

'What was I supposed to say? That my husband can't control himself around other women? And I choose to look the other way because I love him and don't want to lose him?'

'Jesus, Soph,' Myrtle says. 'Don't you think you deserve more than that?'

'Don't judge me, OK?' Sophie snaps. 'I still love him, in spite of everything. And sometimes ... sometimes you have to do whatever it takes to save a marriage. And you don't talk about it to other people because they won't understand.'

'Is this what you imagined when you said "I do"?' Myrtle asks her.

'Of course not. But when you have children with someone, you have to think of what's best for them too.'

'And what about this child he's having with someone else?' Abi asks.

Sophie fiddles with the corner of the tablecloth. 'They've

agreed he won't have any involvement. He'll just support them financially.'

'So you're really OK with this?' Myrtle asks.

'I've made my peace with it.' Sophie hesitates, then says more quietly, 'I don't want to be a divorcee. I don't want to have failed at my marriage, like my parents did.'

'Ending your marriage because your husband is knocking up other women doesn't make you a failure,' Abi says.

Sophie just shakes her head.

'So does this ... agreement of yours swing both ways? Can you go out and shag whoever you like?' Abi asks.

'I wouldn't want to,' Sophie says, her cheeks colouring.

'Well, I think you should,' Abi declares. 'See how the fucker is in *agreement* with that, knowing some other guy is climaxing his wife.'

Sophie pulls a face. 'It's probably happening in more marriages than you realise.'

'That doesn't make it OK,' Myrtle points out.

They fall into silence once more, Sophie gazing at the three young women seated at the bar as she picks at the remainder of her meal.

Who are you? Myrtle wonders, watching her, thinking there was once a time when they told each other everything. *I don't even recognise the person you've become. The Sophie I knew never would have put up with this.*

'Soph—' Myrtle begins, about to tell her as much, but Sophie cuts her off with a sharp look.

'OK,' Myrtle says in defeat. 'It's your life.'

'Yes,' Sophie says firmly. 'It is.'

'Just don't expect us to be nice as pie with Tom, though,' Abi warns.

Sophie looks at them with a small smile. 'I'm counting on you two not to be.'

85

'Are you sure?' Matthew asks for the third time, staring at the document.

The solicitor smiles patiently and nods. 'It's all in his will.'

'But I haven't seen or heard from him in over twenty years,' Matthew says. 'Apart from him showing up to my mother's funeral, then leaving five minutes later without even speaking to me,' he adds, more bitterly than he intended to.

The solicitor doesn't respond to that, just glances pointedly at his watch.

'So there was no one else in his life? He's left everything to me?' Matthew queries again.

'Yes,' the solicitor says, his patience wearing thinner now.

'And all I need to do is sign here, then all that money is mine?' Matthew says, still feeling stunned by it all.

The solicitor nods and holds out a gold-tipped fountain pen.

Matthew scratches out his signature at the bottom of the document, gripping the pen tightly.

'Oh, and before I forget, Peter instructed for this letter to be passed to you,' the solicitor says, handing over a sealed envelope.

Matthew nods his thanks and then leaves the office, walking down the street in a daze. He wonders if this is how people feel when they first find out they've won the lottery.

He sits down on a bench in a nearby square, trying to take

it all in. Over three hundred thousand pounds. All of it his.

He pulls the envelope out of his jacket pocket and tears it open, his heart clenching a little at the sight of the familiar handwriting he hasn't seen in so many years.

Dear Matthew

I won't tell you how many times I have re-written this letter, trying to find the right words to say to you after so long, when in fact there are no words to convey just how sorry I am. The simple truth is that I wasn't the man the three of you needed me to be, however much I wish I could have been. I'm sure this makes little difference to you now, but please know that I've spent the rest of my life regretting how badly I let your mother down. How I let all of you down. Even though I probably didn't express it very well at the time, the years we spent together as a family – well, they're the only time in my life where I felt I was a part of a family.

Matthew stops reading for a moment, blinking quickly, remembering Peter telling him once how he had grown up in foster care for most of his childhood and couldn't even remember his birth parents.

'You're an incredibly lucky boy,' Peter had told him.

Matthew remembers looking across at Luke as he had yet another meltdown and thinking: *You don't even know what you're talking about.*

But you were right, Matthew thinks now, hit by a sudden, sharp longing to feel Grace's warm arms around him. He glances back down at the letter and continues reading.

I know it's been a long time since we last saw each other, but I'm sure you've grown into a man your mother would have been proud of. I hope Luke is doing OK. And I hope this money will help in some way with the remainder of his care. But most importantly, I hope you see fit to use it in

*whichever way you think best. And that you are able to live
the rest of your life doing what you've always wanted to,
with no regrets.*

    Yours,
    Peter

Matthew sits back against the bench, the letter quivering in his hands.

I wish you could have stuck around for her sake, he thinks. *But I don't blame you. Even after everything, I can't blame you for that.*

He carefully folds the letter up and puts it back in his jacket pocket. Then he gets to his feet and heads for home, where Harri, Luke and Dora will be waiting for him.

86

They lie naked in bed together, watching the fireworks out of Callum's bedroom window, Myrtle still thinking about the awful date she'd been on just hours before and how she'd spent the whole night comparing him to Callum.

'I know what you're thinking,' Callum says.

'What?' Myrtle says, blushing in spite of herself.

'You're thinking about how the noise will be scaring pets and wildlife, and how bad the chemicals are for the environment, and how child slave labour was probably used to produce them ...'

Myrtle doesn't say anything.

'I know you too well, don't I?' he says, nudging her with his shoulder.

'Doesn't it bother you?' she asks. 'You see how traumatised some of the dogs at the home get.'

'It's just one night.' He shrugs. 'You can't get upset about everything.'

So you care about nothing instead? Myrtle thinks to herself, as Callum's fingertips begin to graze up her body, until his hand is cupping her left breast.

'I'm actually pretty tired,' she says, the night finally catching up with her. 'Can we just spoon instead?'

He raises an eyebrow. 'You know this isn't how it's supposed to work, right? You booty-called *me*, remember?'

'I know,' Myrtle says, smiling at him. 'But I sleep so much better with you next to me. Sometimes I just ... I just miss someone being there, that's all,' she says softly. 'Don't you?'

He shrugs again but doesn't answer.

'I went on a date tonight,' Myrtle tells him.

'Oh yeah? Any good?' he asks, and she can't help but feel a little annoyed that he's not even remotely jealous.

'Not really. Although better than the woman's at the table next to mine, whose boyfriend ended up collapsing on the floor.'

'Jeez. Heart attack?'

'I don't think so. He was sat up talking to the paramedics by the time we left.' She hesitates, the little voice in her head, that sounds so much like Patti, saying: *Tell him. Just tell him. Better to know than to keep on wondering.*

'The problem with going on dates is that ... well, I always seem to compare them to you.' She pauses, her fingernails digging into her palm. 'And they always seem to fall short.' She waits, holding her breath.

Callum exhales slowly. 'Myrtle, come on – we said no expectations, remember? Don't make this into something it isn't.'

She looks at him, stunned. 'Callum, we've been sleeping together for two years. We see each other every week. I tell you things I don't tell anyone else. Are you trying to tell me this doesn't mean anything to you?'

'Yes, it means something, but I'm not after a relationship. I've always been honest with you about that. I'm happy with how things are. No expectations, no disappointments, right? I thought that's what you wanted too?'

'I do. I did.' She falls silent for a moment, and then asks, 'So that's it? You never want to be in a committed relationship again? Ever?'

He shrugs. 'Never say never. Maybe one day I'll meet someone who will make me change my mind.'

'Oh,' Myrtle says. *Oh,* she thinks again, blinking quickly. She sits up, putting her bra back on.

'Where are you going?'

'Home. I need to get back for Worzel.'

'Myrtle, come on, don't be like that.' His fingers trace the ridge of her shoulder blade, making her shiver. 'We both agreed that monogamy isn't realistic.'

Maybe with the right person it is, Myrtle thinks, standing up to wriggle into her jeans. She doesn't trust herself to look at Callum before she lets herself out of his flat, and he doesn't try to stop her either.

You idiot, she thinks, swallowing against the hard lump in her throat. *You didn't stick to the rules. You've only got yourself to blame.*

She waits at the bus stop, watching an older couple walking down the street, their wrinkled hands clasped between them. The man says something and the woman looks up at him, laughing, then leans her head on his shoulder, still smiling, as he puts his arm around her.

I want that, Myrtle thinks with a start. *I don't care about the sex or the thrill of the chase or the spontaneous, romantic trips away. I just want that.*

She quickly rubs at the corners of her eyes as her bus finally pulls in.

Back at home, lying in bed, Oli's words from all those years ago float back to her: *You're going to end up old and alone, Myrtle.*

It is moments like this, her back pressed against the cold, hard wall, the rest of the bed lying empty beside her, when she wonders if perhaps he was right.

'Worzel,' she calls, and a moment later there is the drum of feet on the stairs, then a thud as he launches himself onto her bed. She buries her hands and face into his fur, breathing in his earthy scent.

'If I didn't have you …' she whispers, pulling him closer. 'Thank god I have you, Worzel.'

87

Harri smiles at him. Expectantly, Matthew feels. As if she senses what's coming. He has brought her to her favourite restaurant, after all. The place is covered in fake cherry blossom branches and coloured lanterns, and all the waiting staff are wearing embroidered silk kimonos.

'So ...' he says, his mouth suddenly cotton-dry. He gulps from his water glass.

'So ... ?' Harri prompts.

'Here are your menus,' the waitress says, then leans across to refill Matthew's empty water glass.

'Thank you,' Harri says, smiling up at her.

Matthew just sits there, panic-stricken, trying to think of something to say. Maybe he should tell her about the money Peter left him. Because for some reason, he still hasn't, even though it was months ago that he met with the solicitor. Lately, there's a lot he hasn't been telling her.

'What's wrong?' Harri asks, frowning up at him in concern.

'I'm just gonna go to the loo,' he says, on his feet before Harri even has time to respond.

In the toilet he splashes cold water on his face. He dries his hands and then pulls the box out of his pocket. He stares at Grace's engagement ring, holding it between his fingers, remembering how it had looked on his mother's hand. She had put it away in a drawer after she and Peter got married, yet he still used to catch her looking at it sometimes when Peter wasn't around.

He imagines himself asking Harri the question, then slipping the ring on her finger, and he begins to break out in a sweat.

He loves her. But was he in love with her? Would he even need to ask himself that question if he was?

He stares at his reflection. He's starting to look his age, more than half his hair grey now, his face more deeply lined.

If you don't do it now, maybe you'll miss your moment, he tells himself. *She's good for you. You're good together. You might never meet anyone else who's as good as her.*

Except maybe that was the problem – good somehow didn't seem good enough. He's never had the exhilarating highs with Harri that he'd had when he was with Rosie. But then there aren't the crushing lows, either. He knows where he stands with Harri – she's never distant with him, or closed off, or moody. She's just Harri – easy-going and straightforward.

Matthew looks at his reflection once more, making a decision, then snaps the box shut again and walks back out to the table. Harri smiles up at him as he takes his seat. He forces a smile in return.

While they eat, he watches her, trying to imagine sitting across from her every mealtime for the rest of his life. Then he thinks of the children that Harri so desperately wants, and another wave of panic rears up.

Harri reaches across the table and squeezes his hand. 'Are you sure you're OK?'

He nods, undoing another button on his shirt. The lanterns are beginning to wink in his periphery and the background noise of the restaurant suddenly feels too loud.

He takes a breath. He knows there isn't a more perfect moment to do it than right now. Except ... He can't. He just can't ...

'Matthew? Are you all right? Oh my god, Matthew!'

The next thing he knows, he's lying slumped on the restaurant floor, his mother's engagement ring box still clenched in his clammy fist.

'Someone call an ambulance!' he hears another diner shout.

Harri's face hovers over him, the lanterns still winking behind her.

'Matthew! What are you saying? I can't hear you.'

'I'm sorry,' he murmurs to her. 'I'm so sorry ...'

Part Four

Part Four

88

'You've got my number. I'll keep my phone on me at all times, so call me for any reason.'

Jacob smiles at him. 'Don't worry. We're going to be just fine, aren't we, Luke?' he says.

Luke ignores both of them, staring fixedly at the TV. He barely looks at Matthew anymore, and the only time he does, it's with a reproachful stare. Matthew knows Luke still blames him for Harri leaving. And even though it's been almost two months since Jacob started looking after him, Luke still refuses to engage with him either.

'He'll come round eventually,' Jacob keeps saying, and Matthew just nods, hoping he's right.

When he arrives at the venue, Emily and Greg insist he takes a seat right at the front as they stand in front of everyone to renew their vows. He watches them as they tearfully read out their handwritten troths, thinking back to that day forty years ago when he walked Emily down the aisle and stood beside Greg as his best man. He was single then and forty years on he's still single now, and in all that time, Emily and Greg always had each other.

'Your parents are the luckiest people I know,' Matthew tells Matt afterwards, as they stand at the bar.

'Yeah, they sure are, ending up with a son like me.' He grins as Matthew laughs.

'Seriously, though,' Matthew says, watching Emily and

Greg glide around the room, smiling as broadly as they did on their wedding day. 'Do you know how rare that is? Finding the person you want to spend the rest of your life with right at the beginning?'

Matt nods, watching his parents for a moment too. 'Maybe it is just luck. While the rest of us unlucky ones have to spend our whole lives searching.'

'So how about you?' Matthew asks.

'How about you?' Matt retorts.

'Touché,' he says with a dip of his head.

'Actually, there is someone I like,' Matt admits quietly. 'A woman at work. Isobel. She's got two kids, though.'

'Does that bother you?'

He shrugs. 'I guess not. But anyway, I'm not even sure she's interested.'

'Then you should find out. There's nothing worse in life than what ifs.'

'Yeah, apart from every day at work having to face the woman who turned you down,' he replies, making Matthew laugh.

'But then at least you know.'

Matt nods. 'But then at least I know,' he echoes.

Later on in the evening, Matthew finally manages to corner Emily.

'Sorry, I've been wanting to talk to you all night,' she says, standing on tiptoes to hug him. 'It's like our wedding all over again.'

He smiles. 'And you look just as beautiful now as you did then.'

'Oh, shush, you,' she says, smiling back as she whacks him lightly on the shoulder. Then she reaches for his hand, squeezing it. 'I'm so sorry about you and Harri.'

He nods, not knowing what to say.

'Don't give up,' she tells him. 'She's still out there. I know she is.'

'So everyone keeps on telling me,' Matthew says with a tight smile.

He thinks of all the years he's known Emily, and how she knows him better than anyone else.

Will I ever love anyone like I love you? he thinks, watching her walk across the room towards Greg, who is turning towards her with a big smile on his face, as if it's been days, not minutes, since he last saw her.

89

Myrtle dries off Worzel's feet after their walk and watches as he hobbles across to his bed.

'This is what happens when you tear around, acting like you're still a puppy,' she tells him.

'Sometimes it's easy to forget you're not young anymore,' Daphne comments, switching the kettle on to make them both a cup of tea.

'Not when you look in the mirror and see how much your chin sags and how every single hair is now grey.'

'Except what's the alternative?'

'Plastic surgery,' Myrtle deadpans.

Daphne shakes her head. 'Growing old is a privilege. Not everyone is so lucky.'

Myrtle thinks of Patti and Nina. 'You're right,' she says.

Her mother smiles. 'I'm always right.' She turns on the radio, raising an eyebrow at Myrtle when the sound of Classic FM fills the kitchen.

'I even enjoy gardening now, too,' Myrtle admits, as Daphne's smile widens. She gives a defeated shrug. 'Maybe we all eventually turn into versions of our parents.'

Her mother nods. 'No matter how hard we try not to.'

As they sit across the kitchen table from each other, sipping from their steaming mugs, Myrtle thinks how much has changed between the two of them over the years. Lately, Daphne keeps finding excuses to come visit, and before, when Myrtle would have come up with her own excuse why not, now she finds she looks forward to her mother's company. Even more so since Elliott died.

She blinks quickly, remembering how she'd let herself into his garden flat one morning, over six months ago now, her arms laden with his weekly food shop. The jars of pickled onions and jam had smashed loudly on the tiled kitchen floor when she saw him slumped in his armchair. She'd rushed over to him, screaming, 'Dad!' even though she already knew it was too late.

Beside him was a cold cup of tea and a half-finished crossword in that day's paper. Myrtle took some comfort thinking that it must have been quick.

'I hear Abi's become a grandmother,' Daphne says now.

Myrtle nods. 'Twins. She says they'll be the death of her.' She watches her mother for a moment. 'Does it bother you that you never got to experience being a grandma?'

Daphne shrugs. 'Not really. I find that as I get older, I have less and less patience with children. Well, with people in general, really.'

Myrtle hides a smile as she drains the rest of her tea.

'But your father – he would have made a good granddad.'

Myrtle nods, remembering how Elliott used to patiently shuffle back and forth across the floor on all fours when she was little, while she rode on his back, kicking her heels into his ribcage, shouting 'Giddy-up!' to get him to go faster.

'And Patti would have made a good grandma,' Daphne adds.

Myrtle smiles. 'She would.'

'Do you ever regret not having children?' her mother asks carefully, not quite meeting her gaze.

'No,' Myrtle answers truthfully. 'I've never felt like that was something that was missing from my life.'

Daphne nods. 'And have you ... tried to meet anyone since Dan?' she asks, equally as carefully.

Myrtle knows her mother had a soft spot for Dan. The trouble was, Dan had more of a soft spot for his job than he did for Myrtle, always firing off work emails when they were together and 'quickly popping' into the office most weekends.

Myrtle shakes her head, forcing a smile. 'The only guy I need in my life is Worzel.' He lifts his head, his tail thumping against his bed at the mention of his name.

'Myrtle ...' Daphne gives her a searching look.

She shrugs. 'There are some days when I wonder if maybe I missed my moment,' she admits quietly. 'If I got on the wrong bus, or didn't speak to the right person at a party, or I stayed in the wrong guest house on holiday.' She stares down into her empty mug. 'Or perhaps I just missed out on a whole lot of heartache.'

They fall into silence, then Daphne breaks it by saying, 'I was going through your childhood photos the other day.'

'Urgh,' Myrtle groans. 'There's a reason why I don't have any of those pictures up.'

Daphne shakes her head, smiling. 'You were beautiful. Even from the first day you were born.'

Myrtle says nothing, refilling both their mugs.

'You know, even though you weren't planned, even though I was scared senseless, those early years were the happiest of my life,' Daphne remarks.

Myrtle looks at her, surprised. 'Really?'

'Really. I'd never felt love like it. I felt like I didn't deserve you.' She gazes out the kitchen window, a faraway look in her eyes. 'It's funny, the best years of my life we spent together, and you can't even remember them. You can't know what they meant to me.'

Myrtle stays silent. Partly because she doesn't know what to say. But mostly because she doesn't want her mum to stop talking. It's been so long since they've talked like this. Or perhaps they never have.

'I know I could have been a better mother to you,' Daphne admits, her gaze still fastened on the view outside. 'I always promised myself I wouldn't end up like mine. Yet still I made a lot of the same mistakes she did.' She rotates her mug slowly between her wrinkled palms. 'It's hard, being a parent. It's the hardest thing in the world.' Her gaze flicks back to Myrtle. 'But I know how hard it is to be someone's child, too.'

'Families ...' Myrtle says with a smile.

Daphne nods, smiling back at her. 'You were my biggest achievement, do you know that? I often think that I did the world a great service by having you.'

Myrtle shakes her head. 'That's not true.'

'It is. You care about others. You always have. And you make other people care.'

Myrtle looks down at the table, blinking rapidly, not trusting herself to speak. Just then the buzzer on the oven goes.

'Oh good. I set that so I wouldn't miss *Coronation Street*,' Daphne says, easing herself up slowly from her chair.

'*Corrie*?' Myrtle looks at her incredulously. 'You always used to tease Grandma for watching that.'

Her mother smiles. 'Like I said, I ended up making a lot of the same mistakes that she did.' She leans heavily on her walking stick as she edges towards the sitting room, but then stops at the door and turns back. 'Are you coming?' she asks.

Myrtle nods, getting up to follow her.

90

Matthew stares out at his mother's favourite view. The wind picks up a notch and the empty urn rattles on the wooden slats beside him.

He knows he failed his father; that in the end, he wasn't enough for him. He knows Luke felt abandoned after Harri left. And then when Dora died, it was like it was all too much, he couldn't cope anymore, and so he finally gave up.

The one thing Matthew's grateful for is that it must have been painless. He'd walked into Luke's room the morning after they'd buried Dora and his father was just lying there in bed, his eyes closed, his face relaxed, his body stiff and cold.

Matthew didn't cry then and he hasn't cried since. It isn't so much relief he feels – just emptiness. Because the thing he'd secretly been waiting for – the thing that he couldn't even admit to himself – hasn't set him free like he thought it would; it's just made him feel even more lost and alone than ever.

It only hits him now, on this bench at the edge of a deserted lake, the cold wind making his eyes water: he's an orphan. He'd been a son all his life, and now he isn't even that. He's just the final link in a broken chain.

The only thing worse than having a family is not having one, Matthew thinks as he puts the urn back in his rucksack. He takes one last, lingering look at the view, and then he turns and heads for home.

When he opens the front door, the silence that greets him feels deafening. His footsteps echo noisily on the dusty floorboards and even his breathing sounds too loud.

He sits down at the kitchen table, the palms of his liver-spotted hands flat against its scarred surface. He realises he hasn't eaten for hours. He thinks about cooking something, but the thought of laying the table with one solitary plate and knife and fork stops him.

What now? he wonders. *What the hell am I supposed to do now?* He takes a shuddering breath. *I don't want to be alone,* he thinks, the walls of the kitchen feeling like they are closing in on him.

He gets his phone out of his pocket and taps out the only number he can think of.

'I didn't know who else to call,' he says apologetically when they answer.

Half an hour later, there's a knock at the front door. He lets her in. They stand there wordlessly in the hallway, and then Harri takes him by the hand and leads him into the bedroom.

They still don't speak as they undress and get under the covers. They don't need to say anything. Matthew knows what this is: Harri is giving in to the moment, but not to him.

He thinks of the last time they saw each other: Harri's face crumpling when he told her that he wasn't going to change his mind about having kids; telling her that she deserved more than he was able to give her; her throwing things; them hitting him. He hadn't known what to do other than to stand there and take it.

'You've broken my heart, do you realise that?' she'd screamed at him.

'I'm sorry—' he starts to say to her now.

'Don't.' She stops him. 'Just don't, OK?'

Afterwards, he lies there in her arms, her familiar, warm body wrapped around his, holding him until he finally drifts off to sleep.

In the morning, when he wakes, she's already gone.

91

Myrtle pants as she begins the steep incline up the hill that she forces herself to cycle every morning, pushing down hard on the pedals, wondering if today will be the day that she has to get off and walk. Worzel peers out from the front basket, giving a languid yawn as she turns the last bend of the hill. She smiles to herself as she overtakes a young couple on a tandem.

When she pulls up outside her house, still breathing heavily, she opens the gate to find Sophie sat on her doorstep, arms wrapped around her knees, a suitcase by her feet.

'What's happened?' Myrtle asks in alarm, more at the fact that this is the first time she's seen Sophie without a full face of make-up in years.

'Tom ... He's ... he's left me. He's moved in with his ... therapist.' Her voice breaks on the last word.

'That *bastard*,' Myrtle fumes, putting an arm around her as she leads her inside.

'I didn't know where else to go,' Sophie says tearfully, collapsing onto the sofa. 'I haven't told the children yet. And I can't bear to be in the house by myself.'

'You know you're always welcome here,' Myrtle says, sitting down next to her.

Sophie stares at her lap, a shell-shocked expression on her face. 'I can't believe he's left me. That's he's actually walked out and left me, as if the past forty-one years together mean absolutely nothing to him.'

'I know right now it feels like you're all alone,' Myrtle says gently, reaching for her hand, 'but you're not. I'm here, no matter what, OK? You're going to get through this, Soph. I promise.'

'I'm so scared, Myrtle,' she whispers tearfully. 'I don't know who I am without him.'

'You're one of the kindest, most generous people I know – that's who you are. And Tom has always taken you for granted.'

'But I don't want to be on my own. I don't know how to be.'

'You're not on your own,' Myrtle reminds her, squeezing her hand. 'You've got me.'

Sophie doesn't respond, blinking furiously at her lap.

'Maybe you'll come to look back at this moment and be glad,' Myrtle says, as confidently as she can. 'Maybe this will be the beginning of an exciting new chapter for you.'

Stop talking in clichés, she inwardly chides, catching herself.

'What's there to get excited about?' Sophie says in a small voice. 'Our best years are already behind us.'

'That's not true,' Myrtle protests.

Sophie fixes her with red-rimmed eyes. 'It is and you know it.'

'We're only sixty,' Myrtle says. 'We might still meet someone yet.' But the words sound hollow, like a line from a prayer that she no longer quite believes in.

Sophie shakes her head. 'No man's going to look at me now. I'm too old.' She takes a shuddering breath, dabbing at her eyes with a crumpled tissue.

'Then who says you even need to find someone else?' Myrtle counters. 'Who says you can't be perfectly happy by yourself?'

'Oh god, I don't want to be a spinster!' Sophie moans.

Myrtle bristles at the word. 'Surely being happily single is better than being unhappily married?' she says, wondering how Sophie has endured Tom's wandering eye for as long as she has.

'But we're not meant to be on our own,' she insists. 'I honestly don't know how you've done it for so long.'

'Look, let's not talk about that bastard anymore,' Myrtle says. 'I say we order takeaway, get drunk and watch some trashy films. It'll be like our uni days all over again. What do you say?'

Sophie offers up a ghost of a smile, pulling a credit card out of her handbag. 'I say this one's on Tom.'

Myrtle grins. 'Atta-girl.'

The next morning, Myrtle grips the banister as she slowly navigates the stairs, her head throbbing and her stomach roiling. Yet despite the worst hangover she can remember in decades, she can't help smiling to herself at the thought of the day ahead with Sophie, thinking perhaps they could go for a picnic by the river and maybe even rent one of those long rowboats she's always been meaning to.

'What were we thinking?' she groans as she steps into the kitchen, heading straight for the kettle and studiously avoiding looking at the empty wine bottles and congealed curry containers littering the kitchen counter. She glances across at Sophie to offer her a cup of tea and sees she is already showered, dressed and has a full face of make-up on. 'How do you look like you've had eight hours of beauty sleep?'

'Tom's coming over,' Sophie says quietly, not quite meeting her eye.

'What? Why?'

'He called me up first thing this morning, absolutely beside himself, saying he's made a terrible mistake. He wants to come back home.'

Myrtle's eyes narrow. 'I hope you told him to fuck off.' Then she notices Sophie's suitcase standing by the door. '*Soph!*'

She gives a defeated shrug. 'Don't judge me, OK? I don't want to spend the rest of my life alone.'

'What's so wrong with being on your own?' Myrtle asks. 'Surely it's better than being with someone you can't even trust?'

Sophie stares at her. 'We can't all be like you, you know.'

'What's that supposed to mean?' Myrtle asks.

But just then the doorbell goes.

Sophie eagerly gets to her feet. 'Thanks for last night,' she says, embracing Myrtle for a brief moment before she hurries out to the hall, trailing her suitcase behind her. 'I'll ring you later,' she calls back.

Myrtle doesn't even get a chance to respond before the front door slams shut. She looks over at Worzel, whose tail thumps in anticipation of breakfast. Then she slowly sits down at the kitchen table, feeling strangely bereft, as if she's just lost something she hadn't even realised she wanted.

92

'Want one?'

'Sure.' Matthew takes a chilled beer from the ice chest they've brought with them to the beach. 'Cheers.'

'Tune!' someone shouts, turning the speakers up to full volume as a few of them jump to their feet, grinding to the music.

'You probably prefer listening to classical, don't you, granddad?' one of the guys says.

'Ignore Dale, he's just acting like a dick because Leanne told everyone he's shit in the sack.'

'Fuck off,' the boy mutters, rounding his thin shoulders and loping off down to the sea edge.

Matthew watches them as he swigs from his beer can, their youthful faces lit up by the campfire.

'So are you all friends from school?' he asks.

'Uni,' the girl tells him. 'We've just finished our final year.' She grimaces.

'Real life now, huh?' Matthew says.

She nods. 'But some of us are going to travel for a few months first. Until the money runs out.'

'Good idea. Travel as long as you can. You've got the rest of your lives to work.'

'So why are you here all by yourself?' she asks. 'Don't you have a wife?'

'Shut up, Stacey,' another girl says. 'He's probably widowed.'

Stacey looks at him in alarm.

Matthew smiles. 'It's OK. There's no wife, dead or alive.'

'Is that why you're here? Are you trying to pick up a young Latino wife or something?'

'Jesus, Stacey.'

Matthew smiles again. 'No, I'm just taking a break from work and doing some long overdue travelling.'

'Oh.' She looks disappointed. 'Don't you mind being out here all by yourself, though?'

He shrugs. 'You've got to do the things you want to do in life, even if you've got no one else to do them with, right?'

'I guess,' she says dubiously.

'Who's up for a late-night dip?' one of the boys yells, already stripping down to nothing and staggering across the beach.

The others follow suit, running and whooping as they sprint to the water's edge.

'You coming?' one of the guys asks him.

'Why not?' Matthew says, standing to take off his T-shirt, but deciding to leave his shorts on, suddenly conscious of the fact that he's a good four decades older than the rest of them. He jogs down to the shoreline, diving straight into the water and paddling out.

God, it's been years since he swam in the dark. He'd forgotten how good it feels. He keeps on swimming, the reflected moonlight lighting his way.

'Don't go out too far, granddad,' Dale calls. 'We don't want to have to haul your geriatric ass back into shore.'

Matthew sticks a thumb in the air, swimming out a bit further, then rolling onto his back, spreading out his limbs until he's bobbing on the surface. He stays like that for a while, staring at the sky, mesmerised, thinking how different it looks from night skies at home – bigger, somehow, and the stars burning so much brighter. Eventually he rolls onto his front and slowly makes his way back to shore. By the time he reaches the shallows, all of the others are already on the beach, sprawled out on the sand, either asleep or gazing drunkenly up at the full moon.

Matthew quickly gets dressed and thinks about heading back to his guesthouse, but it's at least a thirty-minute walk and mostly uphill.

'Maybe I'll join you,' he says to Dale, stretching out on the sand beside him.

'Sure thing, granddad,' Dale says. 'You're one of us now.'

Matthew smiles to himself as he shoves his rolled-up jumper under his head, staring once more at the star-filled sky.

Just as the sun is inching above the horizon, Matthew stirs, feeling its warmth on his skin. He slowly sits up, his joints stiff, his head pounding, gazing around him at the others, who are still fast asleep.

He thinks of all the people he's yet to meet on his travels and all the things he's yet to experience. He's only just started out on his planned six-month around-the-world trip, funded by Peter's money, now there are no carers to pay for anymore.

He watches the others as they sleep, their young, golden bodies untouched by time, and then he looks down at his own legs, covered with grey hairs, and his hands, freckled with liver spots, and he wonders if he's really up for this trip, or whether the moment has already passed for him. And besides, isn't it a selfish way to spend the money, when he could be doing something meaningful with it, helping out others who actually need it, rather than chasing unfulfilled dreams from his youth?

He stretches out, then gingerly gets to his feet and bends over to write a message in the sand:

Thanks for making an old man feel young again.

Then he begins the slow walk back to his guesthouse. When he gets there, he sits down in the breakfast room, pouring himself a coffee.

'Sleep well?' the waiter asks when he brings over the menu.

Matthew smiles. 'Like a teenager.'

93

There's a loud bark from downstairs and Myrtle is instantly awake. She rushes down the stairs to find Worzel collapsed on the kitchen floor, whimpering because he can't get up. Myrtle eyes the large puddle that is spreading out from beneath him and Worzel's shame-faced expression as he gazes up at her.

'It's OK,' she tells him, thinking how this is the third time this week.

She rolls up a towel and slips it under his stomach, gripping each end to hoist him up and guide him back to bed. She rubs his ear in the special spot that makes him groan.

'How do I know when it's the right time?' she says to him. 'Will you let me know?'

He licks her hand.

'I don't want you to suffer,' she whispers. 'But I'm not ready to say goodbye to you yet.' She kisses his head, breathing in his familiar scent.

Eventually she stands up to go back to bed, but when she gets upstairs, she hesitates in front of her bed, then grabs the pillow and duvet and heads back down to the kitchen, where she curls up in the old armchair she has in one corner.

Worzel gazes up at her, his tail giving a single thump.

'Just for tonight,' Myrtle tells him, wondering how many more nights she'll have with him.

★

The next day, when Worzel still can't haul himself out of bed and then turns his head away from the bowl of food Myrtle offers him, she makes the call, her hand shaking as she dials the number.

'Can you come here?' she says down the phone, her voice not sounding like her own. 'I want him to be in his own surroundings.'

When the vet arrives, he smiles sympathetically at her, and Myrtle wonders how many times he's had to do this and if it ever gets any easier.

'I feel like an executioner, decreeing his death,' she says, her eyes fixed on Worzel, whose breathing is becoming more and more laboured.

The vet gives a slow nod. 'It's the hardest decision many of us will ever have to make.' He places a warm hand on Myrtle's shoulder. 'There's nothing more you can do. It really is the kindest thing.'

Then why doesn't it feel like that? she thinks. She rubs at her salty cheeks with the back of her hand. 'Can you give us a moment?'

He nods and discreetly steps out of the room.

Myrtle kneels down beside Worzel. He briefly opens his eyes, but they flicker shut again, as if the effort is too much.

'Seventeen years,' she whispers to him, thinking that's longer than any relationship she's ever had. She takes a shuddering breath. 'Do you remember the day I brought you home? Do you remember how scared you were?' She strokes his wiry fur. 'I was scared too. I'd never had to look after anyone else before.' She swallows. 'I thought I was saving you, Worzel. But who rescued who, huh?' She lets out a shaky sob, pressing her face into the back of his neck, unable to comprehend this will be the last time. 'Who rescued who?'

94

'Here you go, then,' Ed says, handing the keys for both vans over to the two young men.

'All the tools are in the back,' Matthew tells them. 'We've cleaned them all and oiled them, so they're as good as new.'

'Cheers,' one of them says. The other one is already inspecting the van, seeing if he can tease up the edge of the stickering that says *Ellis & Maguire Gardening Services*.

'What are you calling yourselves?' Matthew asks.

'Lawns R Us,' the one with the keys replies.

'Catchy,' Ed says politely. 'Right then, lads, we'll leave you to it.'

'Enjoy it,' Matthew tells them.

'Enjoy what?'

Being young, he almost says.

'Being your own boss,' he says instead.

As Matthew and Ed walk away, they can hear the pair of them bickering.

'Don't scratch the paint doing that!'

'I'm not driving around in a van with someone else's name on it.'

'For fuck's sake, just wait until it's in the garage, will you?'

Ed smiles at him. 'We did all right, didn't we? Almost thirty years working together, and I don't think we ever had a cross word to say to each other, did we?'

Matthew nods, slinging an arm around Ed's shoulder. 'No

one I would have rather done this with.'

'Ditto, mate,' Ed replies, rubbing at his eyes with the cuff of his jumper. 'Damned hay fever,' he mutters.

Matthew smiles. 'So I guess that's that, then,' he says with a sigh. 'Time to hang up the old gardening gloves.'

He hadn't wanted to retire. He would have kept going if he could, but customers had started to complain that they weren't as efficient as they used to be, and so their client list began to dwindle. And it was true. Even simple tasks like cutting lawns and trimming hedges seemed more arduous, the tools feeling more unwieldy, their joints less forgiving.

'I guess we've become old boys in a young man's game,' Matthew had said sadly.

'So what now then, eh?' Ed says, as they stop off at their favourite pub for one last pint on the way home.

But Matthew doesn't have an answer to that.

95

'What are *you* doing here? Where's Patti?'

'She's just gone out for the newspaper,' Myrtle lies.

'Oh.' Daphne looks uneasy. 'When will she be back?'

'Soon,' she reassures her, reaching over to squeeze her mother's hand, but Daphne just looks back at her warily, as if Myrtle is the one who's losing her mind.

Myrtle loads up a spoon with the breakfast she's pureed and holds it up to her mother's lips, but she refuses to open them. Myrtle tries two more times but Daphne eyes it suspiciously, as if it might be poisoned, turning her head away like a stubborn child.

'Mum, please eat something,' Myrtle cajoles, holding the laden spoon in front of her again.

Daphne finally opens her mouth, but then turns at the last moment, so that it ends up smeared across her cheek.

'For fuck's sake, Mum!' Myrtle rubs fiercely at Daphne's cheek with a tissue, her temper fraying. 'Come on, you've got to eat.'

'Why?' Daphne asks. There's a faint red mark rising on her cheek, like she's been slapped.

'You need to eat to stay alive,' Myrtle says more gently.

'I don't want to,' Daphne says, and the double meaning of her words is not lost on Myrtle.

She sighs, letting the spoon fall to the bowl with a clatter.

'What's taking Patti so long?' Daphne asks, craning her neck as if she might be hiding behind the furniture.

Myrtle dreads these questions, having to repeat the same lies over and over. Yet a part of her dreads more the day when Daphne finally stops asking altogether.

'She's had to go to the shops but she'll be back soon,' Myrtle tells her. 'As you're not hungry, how about a bath? I've brought that nice bubble bath that you like.'

Daphne doesn't respond but she lets Myrtle help her out of the armchair and down the hall to the bathroom, where Myrtle begins to undress her while the bath is running.

She tries to avoid looking at her mother's naked body as much as possible during moments like this, pretending it's a stranger's body instead. That's the only way she's able to do what she needs to do – to bath her, change her incontinence pads and clip her hardened, yellowed toenails. She thinks how her mum had done all this for her when she was little, so it only seems right that she looks after her now, rather than some stranger doing it.

As Daphne slips beneath the warm water, Myrtle rolls up her sleeves to sponge her down. She looks at her mother's thin frame, her vertebrae sticking out sharply beneath her blue-white skin, and she can't help but think of all the years the two of them spent in silent battle, never being the person the other one needed.

But you need me now, don't you? she thinks, rinsing off the soap suds. *We both need each other now.*

Once Myrtle has towelled her mother off and helped her into bed for her morning nap, she goes into Daphne's study and begins to pull out files and boxes to sort through. Since her mother's rapid deterioration over the last few months, Myrtle has decided to go through Daphne's possessions room by room until everything is in order, so she can check things while her mother's still here if needed.

In the second box she goes through, she finds a folder with her name scrawled on it. She opens it up to find her old school reports and school photos. She shuffles through them like a flipbook, seeing her younger self growing up before her eyes, remembering how unsure and self-doubting she'd been at that age.

'You were beautiful, you silly girl,' she says out loud, shaking her head.

She casts the photos aside and sees that beneath them is an envelope, also with her name on. Her heart skips a beat seeing the familiar handwriting. She carefully opens it and begins to read.

My darling Myrtle,

It's a strange thought to know that by the time you read this, I'll already be gone. I know you'll be angry at my decision not to tell you. But I figure you can't remain angry with a dead person forever, can you? So I'm writing you this letter, not to say goodbye – because we both know that's impossible – but to explain why, in the hope that you'll forgive me.

You see, I thought I'd be good at dying. I thought I'd be brave and wise and strong. That people would be in awe of how gracefully I've come to terms with it. But I am none of these things. All I am is scared and angry and weak. Because I don't want to die. Not yet. Not like this.

That's why I've asked your mum not to tell you. I don't want you to cut your trip short. And most of all, I don't want you to have to be a part of this painful, shitty ending to an otherwise pretty wonderful life.

Although it might not have been the life I envisaged for myself when I was your age, it's more than I ever could have hoped for. I never wanted children, as you know. Yet you made a mother out of me anyway, Myrtle.

My daughter. My darling, beautiful daughter. I know you're going to be hurting. I know you're going to feel all alone. And I wish more than anything that I wasn't the one causing that.

I've thought long and hard over this letter, but in the end, I don't have anything profound to tell you. Because the secret of life is – there is no secret. None of us have got it figured out. All I know is life is as good as you make it. So make it count, Myrtle. As many moments as you can – make them count.

All my love,

Your Patti x

Myrtle lets the letter drift to the floor, tears slipping down her cheeks, the pain of thirty-one years ago rushing back at her.

She can't believe her mother kept it hidden away all this time. She thinks of all those unhappy, lonely moments she could have read it, the comfort it would have brought.

How could you? she thinks.

She picks the letter up again. The paper is thin and shiny, as if it has been handled a lot. As if Daphne has taken it out and read and re-read Patti's words, because they were a comfort to her too.

She can hear her mother stirring in the room next door. Fury courses in Myrtle's veins, making her want to holler at Daphne, hit her, even. She goes to stand in the doorway, watching her mother gaze around the room in bewilderment, as if she's unsure where she is. She looks so tiny lying there, dwarfed by the double bed.

At least you kept it, Myrtle thinks, the fight draining out of her. *At least you did that.*

Daphne turns and her gaze fastens on Myrtle. 'What are *you* doing here?' she asks. 'Where's Patti?'

'She'll be back any moment now,' Myrtle says quietly, stepping closer to help her mother out of bed.

96

'We don't normally insist on rehoming dogs together, as not many people want to take on two,' the rehomer – Annabel – is explaining to him. 'But when Olive got adopted, Popeye pined for her so much, he wouldn't eat, and we almost lost him. The same with Olive. So the owners brought her back as they didn't want to rehome two.'

'That's true love, isn't it?' Matthew says, gazing at the pair of them curled up together in their concrete pen.

'It really is,' Annabel says, smiling.

'So would you need to do a home-check beforehand?' Matthew asks, his eyes still fastened on them.

Annabel hesitates. 'Ordinarily, yes, but we're so understaffed and we have so many dogs right now ...'

As if to prove her point, a woman rushes by them with a box full of puppies in her arms.

'Myrtle, I thought you said we weren't taking in any more?' Annabel calls out, exasperated.

'Puppies will go in no time,' she calls back, before disappearing into a kennel at the far end.

Annabel shakes her head, muttering, 'More heart than sense, that one.'

'Sounds like you'll be needing a spare kennel, then?' Matthew says, smiling hopefully.

After he's filled out all the paperwork and is just about to leave, Matthew stops in his tracks, then turns and walks back to the reception desk. Olive and Popeye sit obediently by his feet.

'I'd like to make an additional donation,' he says. 'Do you accept cheques?'

Annabel nods. 'Absolutely. We're always grateful for donations, as that's the only thing that keeps our doors open.'

Matthew takes out his cheque book, thinking of the rest of the money from Peter still sitting in his bank. He didn't need it. But this place did. He writes out a figure, then scratches his signature in the corner, before tearing the cheque off and handing it over to Annabel. Her eyes widen at the amount, and she looks up at him, as if it's a prank.

'It won't bounce,' he promises.

'This is ... very generous,' Annabel says carefully, her eyes still wide.

'I'm just glad it will be put to good use,' Matthew says. 'Right, then, I guess I should be heading back to introduce these two to their new home.'

'Before you go,' Annabel says, rising quickly to her feet, 'would you mind holding on for a moment so I can tell the manager about your kind donation? As I know she'll want to thank you personally.'

Matthew wafts his hand in the air. 'That's not necessary, honestly,' he says, already heading towards the door again, Olive and Popeye trotting beside him. 'You can just put it down as an anonymous donation,' he calls back.

Just before the door swings shut behind him, he can hear Annabel saying, 'Myrtle, you'll never believe what's just happened ...'

When Matthew gets them home, Olive and Popeye curiously sniff around every room, never letting each other out of sight.

Even though it's been years since Dora died, Matthew only realises now just how much he's missed having a dog around: the scratch of claws on the floor, the tinkle of the metal tag on the collar, the knowledge that someone will always be excited to see you as soon as you step through the door ...

When they're finished with their reconnoitre of the sitting room, Olive and Popeye jump up on the sofa, claiming their spot at one end, curling up together, as if they've always been there.

'So this is how it's going to be, is it?' Matthew says, smiling to himself as he settles into the armchair opposite them. He snaps open the newspaper, holding it out before him, but he doesn't read a single word, unable to tear his gaze away from the pair of them snoring contentedly in front of him.

97

'I remember the morning of our wedding, being absolutely petrified, and thinking: It's OK, if it doesn't work out, we'll just get divorced,' Liam says to the packed room, raising a few titters.

Myrtle glances across at Sophie and they share a secret smile, remembering a panicked Abi saying those exact same words.

'It was hard, as a twenty-five-year-old, trying to imagine spending the rest of my life with someone,' Liam continues. 'And I know a lot of you didn't think we'd last, that it's a miracle we're still together.' He looks down at Abi, blinking quickly. 'But maybe the reason is because you changed me. You made me a better person.'

Would I have been a different person if I'd married Oli? Myrtle wonders. Or perhaps not being with someone changed you more, she thinks. Maybe she wouldn't have done half the things she has if they'd stayed together. Maybe she wouldn't have quit her job and gone travelling. Maybe she wouldn't have got Worzel. Maybe she wouldn't have put all her savings into opening the dog shelter.

'I almost lost you a few years ago,' Liam continues, referring to Abi's battle with bowel cancer. 'But you always were a fighter, Abs. You've never been one to give up. Not even on me. Not even when you probably should have.'

Here Abi shakes her head, gazing up at Liam tearfully, and Myrtle thinks of those dark few years when it seemed Liam's dependency on alcohol would finally get the better of him.

'After everything we've been through together, it's made me realise how lucky I am. Because some people have to deal with all the shit that life throws at them alone, without anyone in their corner.'

Myrtle shifts in her seat as Liam stops to take a sip of water. When he speaks next, his voice breaks. 'But I've had fifty years with you by my side. And my life ... it wouldn't have been half of what it is without you.'

There's a chorus of *ahhhs*, and Myrtle smiles tearfully, then raises her drink in the air to toast them, swallowing hard against the lump in her throat.

After the speeches, Abi and Liam circle the room together, stopping to talk to people. Myrtle watches them, how they lean into each other, touch each other on the arm, how Liam's eyes always follow Abi and how he smiles at her in a way that's reserved just for her. Fifty years and they are still in love. It is like witnessing a miracle.

When they reach Myrtle, she bursts into tears.

'Jesus, Myrtle, it's supposed to be a celebration,' Abi says, pulling her in close.

'I'm sorry,' she murmurs, rubbing at the corner of her eyes, trying not to smudge her make-up. 'I'm just so happy for you, that's all.' She smiles at them, shaking her head. 'Fifty years ...'

Abi smiles back, leaning into Liam again. 'I know, right? Some call it marriage, others call it a life sentence ...'

Liam laughs, kissing her forehead.

Just then the music starts up, and the song that played for their first dance all those years ago comes on.

'Oh Jesus, not again,' Liam says, as Abi pulls him out onto the dance floor as people clap and whistle.

Sophie comes to stand next to Myrtle, their shoulders touching as they watch them dance. 'I thought they'd last two years tops,' she says.

'Ditto,' Myrtle agrees. 'But they proved us all wrong, didn't they?'

'They sure did.'

When the next song starts up, Abi strides over, pulling her and Sophie onto the dance floor.

'I requested this one especially for you two,' Abi says, spinning them in circles as their favourite song from their university days leaks out of the dusty speakers. 'You know, as much as this is a celebration of Liam and I somehow managing not to kill each other after all these years, it's also made me think about how my longest ever relationship is with you two. Fifty-six years we've been friends.'

'Fifty-six years,' Myrtle echoes in wonder.

'I didn't even get that long with my mum and dad,' Sophie says.

They all blink at each other.

'I guess what I'm trying to say is … that … I couldn't have done it without you either. You two …' Abi swallows. 'You've always been there, no matter what.'

The three of them hug each other tightly, Abi sandwiched between them.

'What's happening to me tonight? I can't stop crying,' Myrtle says as the other two laugh.

When the next song starts up, she excuses herself to go to the bathroom, swaying a little on her heels from the wine. She looks in the mirror at her greying hair and wrinkled face as she reapplies her make-up, wondering just who she's doing it for.

So no man loves me, Myrtle thinks, applying another coat of lipstick. *Maybe no man will ever love me again. But maybe that's OK. Maybe I'm enough.* She fluffs up her hair. *Maybe I've always been enough.*

She smiles at herself and then leans over the sink to kiss her reflection, before heading back out to join the party.

98

Matthew carefully laces up his shoes and then regards himself in the mirror. He rarely looks at his reflection these days – what was the point? – but when he does catch sight of himself in a bus stop or shop window, it is always with shock. Each year just seems to add another wrinkled layer to the outside, like papier mâché. He finds he can no longer wear T-shirts, as they expose too much of his neck and the material is too thin and clingy. So instead he wears shirts and knitted jumpers. He remembers as a boy wondering why old men always seemed so well dressed. He had thought it was just the fashion of their time but realises now that it's necessity.

He studies his reflection, feeling like he should properly take note of his appearance for once, because today he is meeting someone. Today he is going on a *date*.

He almost laughs at how ludicrous that word sounds. A seventy-five-year-old man *dating*.

His first response when Matt had told him that he'd put his profile online and a lady had messaged saying she'd like to meet ('There may have been a few messages from your end too,' Matt admitted, adding quickly, 'Don't worry, you came across funny.') was to say no.

'My dating days are long over. I'm too old for all that now.'

'Says who?'

'Says me.'

'No one's too old to fall in love,' Matt had said.

Matthew didn't respond to that.

'She looks all right, for an old person,' Matt had continued.

When Matthew still didn't reply, he pressed, 'Go on. Take a chance. What have you got to lose?'

Matthew had shaken his head. 'If you knew how many people have said that to me over the years ...'

'So are you going or not? Because you'll have to let her down when she's really looking forward to it. It sounds like she doesn't get out much. So you already have that in common.'

'Smart arse,' Matthew had muttered, knowing he was well and truly backed into a corner.

He regards himself in the mirror one final time and feels that long-forgotten flicker that he used to get when he was younger – the nervous yet excited anticipation, the secret hope that someone would look at him and think: *I see you. I see what everyone else has missed.*

He gets to the country pub they've arranged to meet at five minutes early, but sits there waiting on his own for almost half an hour, worried that he's been stood up, before Collette finally arrives, sweeping through in a cloud of perfume that catches at the back of his throat. She is smartly dressed, wearing a patterned scarf around her neck and an expensive-looking blouse.

'I hope you haven't been waiting long?' she says breezily, by way of apology. Her steel-grey, bobbed hair sits unmoving, like a helmet on her head.

'It's fine,' Matthew says, not knowing what else to say.

'Why didn't you order a drink?' she queries.

'I thought I'd wait for you.'

'I'll have a pinot grigio, then. Large.'

'Coming right up,' he says, getting to his feet.

As he waits at the bar for their drinks, he can't help but

feel disappointed that there was no immediate spark there. But perhaps that no longer happens at their age, he reasons.

When he sits back down at the table, Collette sizes him up as she sips from her wine glass, but he gets the sense that he somehow falls short.

'So ...' Matthew says, struggling to think of what to say to this total stranger.

'You look older than in your photographs,' Collette says.

'Sorry,' he replies, wondering which photos Matt put up of him. 'It's been a while since I've been on a date,' he admits, deciding that honesty is the best policy.

'Are you recently widowed?' she asks, her eyes narrowing. 'Because you didn't mention that in your messages.'

'No, not widowed. I've never been married.'

'Oh,' she says, looking slightly nonplussed. 'Eternal bachelor, are you?'

'Something like that,' Matthew says. 'And how about you?'

'Married and divorced three times. They never quite lived up to their early promise,' she replies.

Matthew just nods, unsure how best to respond to that.

'So how long *has* it been since you last went on a date?' Collette asks, her manicured fingernails tapping against her glass.

Matthew thinks back, mentally counting. 'About five years,' he admits sheepishly, thinking of Janine, a neighbour he had dated for a few months, which never went anywhere because she refused to venture more than a couple of miles' radius from her home. 'We've got everything we need right here. Why do you want to go off exploring new places all the time?' she'd said to him when he suggested a weekend away by the coast.

'How about you?' he asks.

'About a week ago,' she says blithely.

'Oh,' Matthew remarks, wondering if everyone their age is more like Collette than him, out on dates most nights.

'Five years,' Collette repeats incredulously. 'Don't you mind being on your own all the time?'

'Sometimes,' he admits. 'Probably more so now than when I was younger. I always liked the idea of growing old and grey with someone. But it doesn't happen for everyone, does it?'

'I still believe there's someone out there for everyone,' Collette declares, 'even after three divorces.'

'But what if you never find them?' he says.

'How do you expect to if you stop looking?' she counters.

'You make a good point,' he concedes.

'So what are your hobbies?' she questions, as if there's a mental checklist she's working her way through.

'Well, I like walking with the dogs, being out in nature, wild swimming, gardening ...' He can see her gaze sliding over his shoulder towards the bar. 'How about you?'

'Oh, the usual: eating out, shopping, the theatre ... Definitely not wild swimming,' she says with a shudder.

He nods, wondering if there's anything they have in common.

'Do you fancy another drink?' he asks, looking at her empty wine glass.

'I'll get these,' she says, quickly getting to her feet, her gaze still fixed on the other side of the pub.

'OK, thanks, I'll have a pint of—' Matthew begins, but she is already halfway to the bar.

Fifteen minutes later, wondering what's taking so long, Matthew turns in his chair to see Collette sitting at the bar, laughing at something the barman is saying as he pours her a glass of wine. He gives it another five minutes, but when she still hasn't returned, he realises that she has no intention of carrying on with their date.

What did I do? Matthew thinks.

He stands and slowly puts his jacket on, glancing at Collette one last time, before he heads out the door.

On the walk home, more disappointed than he cares to admit, he thinks of Matt persuading him to take a chance.

'At your age, you can't afford to be fussy,' he'd said, grinning.

Matthew had shaken his head at the time, grinning back in spite of himself. Except now it feels like he hasn't just taken a chance – it feels like the last chance, and he's blown it.

99

Myrtle only knows the doctor is still talking because his lips are moving, even though she can't hear what he's saying. The same few words he'd uttered earlier are still circling around her head: *cancer, malignant, aggressive.*

'I know this is a lot to take in,' he tells her gently. 'I'm happy to go into more detail about our treatment plans, so we can decide on a plan of action going forward.'

'What's the prognosis if I don't get treatment?' she asks.

He raises his eyebrows.

'I mean, I know I'm going to die. But how long will I have? In your professional opinion?'

'Well, it's hard to estimate these things, but given how far it has already spread, I would say between six and nine months.'

Not even a year, Myrtle thinks, her hands gripping the armrests of the chair so tightly her knuckles have turned white.

'But with treatment and surgery, you could make a full recovery,' he says.

'But I might not, right? I might go through all that, spend what time I have left being pumped full of radiation and chemicals, have my body cut open, and still die within a year.'

He nods slowly. 'You might, yes.'

Myrtle presses her lips together, a wave of nausea already hitting her. 'You see, the thing is, doctor, I don't have a

344

partner or any family. If I get treatment ... well, it's just prolonging the inevitable, isn't it?'

'Have a think on it for a few days,' he says kindly. 'We don't need to decide anything right now.'

Myrtle nods and slowly walks out of the hospital, blinking in the brightness of the spring afternoon. As soon as she sees a bench by a green, she lowers herself onto it, not trusting her legs beneath her.

Not everyone gets to reach old age, she tells herself, looking unseeingly at the clumps of daffodils and crocuses before her. She thinks of Nina, so much of her life still ahead of her when she died. *You're lucky,* she reminds herself. *Seventy-six is a pretty good innings.*

She tries to imagine what the rest of her life would be like if she did get the treatment. She pictures herself getting older and more feeble, eventually winding up incapacitated and alone, with no one to look after her.

Maybe this is just how it's meant to be, she thinks, her racing heart finally slowing to its normal beat. *We don't always get to choose our moment. Sometimes the moment chooses us.*

100

'So what do you think?' Greg asks.

They've just finished their grand tour of Silver Birches, and the manager, Ellie, has left them seated in the sunroom with a pot of tea, overlooking the expansive landscaped gardens.

'I don't know ...' Matthew looks around at the other residents, but none of them meet his eye. They either seem to be gazing off into the middle distance or staring into their laps. 'It kind of feels like a waiting room – no one's talking, and everyone's wishing they didn't have to be here.'

Greg grins. 'Then we'll have to liven things up, won't we? Get some poker nights going, some weekends away, some pub quiz outings ...'

'It's a *care* home, Greg.'

'It's a *residential* home,' he corrects. 'And a pretty damn nice one at that. Home-cooked meals, always someone here looking out for us ... What's not to like?'

'I just never imagined I'd end up in a place like this, though.'

'I know,' Greg says, his smile slipping. 'But neither of us are getting any younger. And now that Emily's gone ... I don't want to be a burden to the kids ...'

It's only been four months since Emily died and Matthew knows Greg can't stand being in the house anymore without her in it. He's grown thin in those few months and seems to have aged more.

'We'll still be fully independent,' Greg continues.

'Until we get to the point when a stranger has to wipe our arses,' Matthew replies. He gazes around again at the other residents. Everyone looks so fragile; he can see the shape of their skulls beneath their mottled skin. It makes him feel vulnerable. 'I don't know. We move into a place like this and we're signing away the rest of our lives. It's the beginning of the end.'

Greg pointedly ignores that. 'It will be fun,' he insists. 'Plus we'll have each other. It's better than being shut up at home alone, counting down the days and hours until the next visitor.'

Matthew says nothing to that, thinking how he has no one who would come visit him anyway now that Ed and Giles are gone, both of them dying last year of heart attacks.

'Plus they have lifts, so we don't have to slog our way up the stairs anymore,' Greg says with a wink.

'Jesus, it feels like we're giving in already,' Matthew replies, his thoughts wandering to Luke, and how he was no longer able to use the stairs after his accident, and what a huge defeat that had felt like to both him and his mum.

Greg shrugs. 'There's no escaping the inevitable, is there?'

They lapse into silence, gazing back out to the gardens as they drain the rest of their tea. Greg stares into his empty teacup, as if he's reading his leaves.

The front door opens and a teenage boy dumps a stack of newspapers on the hall table, casts a wary look at the residents, and then scuttles back out. Matthew chuckles to himself.

'What's so funny?' Greg asks.

'I was just remembering us as boys, delivering the papers every morning, then bunking off school, paying strangers to buy us cheap cider from the corner shop ...'

'Those were the days,' Greg says wistfully.

'They were,' Matthew echoes.

'We got old.'

'We did,' Matthew agrees, looking down at his wrinkled hands. 'We really did.'

Ellie wanders back over to them. 'So, gentlemen, what are your thoughts?' she says brightly.

Greg glances at Matthew, who shrugs his shoulders in defeat.

Greg looks up at Ellie, a grin on his face. 'Where do we sign?'

IOI

'They're lovely, aren't they?' Myrtle says with a smile, as she and Sophie sit on a bench people-watching, unable to take their eyes off a group of young Italian girls lounging on the grass in the middle of a square. She remembers so clearly being that age, the vulnerability she'd felt.

'Nothing lasts forever,' Sophie replies, a trace of bitterness in her voice. 'They'll be sat here one day, just like we are.'

'And when we were young, there were probably a pair of old biddies sat on a bench, watching us with envy too, and we didn't even notice them,' Myrtle says.

'We had our moment,' Sophie agrees.

'It isn't over yet,' Myrtle points out.

Sophie looks at her. 'Sometimes it feels a little like that, though, doesn't it?'

Myrtle gives a reluctant nod. This is the whole reason they're on this trip, after Sophie persuaded Myrtle to keep her company.

'We need to celebrate you being two years in remission,' Sophie had insisted. 'Plus everything's organised. We won't have to worry about a single thing.'

'But that's half the fun about a holiday,' Myrtle had protested, 'not knowing what's going to happen.'

Sophie had frowned. 'Not at our age, Myrtle.'

So against her better judgement, she'd let herself be cajoled. But just as she suspected, the coach was full of gossiping old women and haunted widowers, rather than fun-loving pensioners hellbent on a good time, no matter their aching joints or cataracts.

Sitting on the coach this morning, she had stared out of the rain-lashed windows, wondering why she'd even come as she tuned in and out of people's conversations. All the women seemed to be busybodies, talking with self-importance about the cake stalls and church events they organised back home, or complaining irately about cars parking half on the pavement, or that the postman now delivers an hour later than usual.

Small things, Myrtle had thought to herself, as she listlessly eavesdropped. Yet none of them seemed to care about the bigger stuff. When they read their newspapers, they'd flick impatiently over the stories about the refugee crisis, or global warming, or factory farming, homing in instead on stories about train fares going up or which washing machine was the best value for money. She'd looked at their pinched faces and beady eyes, and she couldn't help but think: *You've lived your entire lives and you've never truly woken up. You never stepped back for a moment and saw the bigger picture, did you?*

And the men were no better. On her first day, she'd made the mistake of sitting next to Richard, who had a friendly, open face, yet all he did was talk about his dead wife and how he missed having a warm body to curl up to at night. He'd looked at her, a hopeful expression on his face, until Myrtle had quickly pointed out the window and said, 'Oh look, is that a kestrel?'

After that, she'd made sure to sit by Sophie.

Myrtle's gaze is drawn towards an old Italian man across the park, leaning heavily on his stick, walking so sedately it looks like he's going in slow-motion – either that or the whole world has speeded up around him.

'You know that phrase: "life is passing you by"?' Sophie asks, watching the man too.

Myrtle nods.

'I didn't really know what that meant until I got old. But I understand it now. It's like you get to a certain age and you can't be a player any longer, only a spectator.'

'That's not true. We're here in Italy, aren't we?'

'But we're just sat on benches people-watching or staring out of a coach window. We're not really *here*, are we? Not like everyone else,' Sophie says, waving a hand towards the group of young girls, who are now doing handstands and cartwheels in the middle of the grass. She sighs. 'Growing up seemed so painful when we were young, but growing old is even more so. It scares me sometimes,' she says quietly. 'When you're young, you know you're going to get old some day, but it seems so far away, you can almost pretend it's never going to happen. And then all of a sudden, you realise you *are* old, and there's no pretending anymore.'

Myrtle nods. 'I know. But maybe this holiday we should pretend – that we're still in our twenties, that we have our whole lives stretching out before us ...'

'And then what? We try to flirt with the good-looking barmen and they look right through us? So then we think: *Screw them*, get drunk, only to wet our beds?'

'Ah, come on, it's not all bad,' Myrtle replies, laughing.

'You like being old?' Sophie asks her pointedly.

'I like being alive,' Myrtle qualifies.

They fall into silence, both of them thinking of the people they've lost in the past few years: Abi, Liam and Tom. And Myrtle thinks how close she came to the end too.

'I wish Abi was here,' Sophie says quietly. 'It doesn't feel right, somehow.'

'I know,' Myrtle agrees, thinking it would have felt like more of a holiday if Abi had been with them. 'So how are the grandkids?' she asks, trying to lift the mood.

Sophie's face instantly brightens. 'Good. Charlotte is off to university soon, and Kieron has just got a big promotion.' She hesitates. 'And Molly is pregnant,' she says lightly, referring to Tom's daughter by another woman, who she only met for the first time at Tom's funeral two years ago. 'She's already found out it's a boy. She's going to call him Kai.' She smoothes her skirt over her knees. 'It's funny, but I probably see more of Molly than I do my two now. Which is fine, as I know Tom was very fond of her.' She smiles as Myrtle reaches for her hand. 'I've become fond of her too, in my own way.'

'That's good,' Myrtle says, squeezing her hand. 'Right, I think I might go for a wander, stretch these old legs,' she announces, easing herself up from the bench.

'Don't forget we have to be back at the coach in an hour,' Sophie says worriedly, glancing at her watch, ever the time-keeper.

'I won't,' Myrtle replies with a smile as she walks away.

Although she's enjoying visiting all these new places, Myrtle resents the rigidness of the trip, how they always have to be checking the time and thinking about where they had to be next, rather than just losing themselves in the moment. It makes her wistful for solo travelling.

In the space of ten minutes walking, Myrtle has got herself well and truly lost down the labyrinthine back alleys. But rather than panicking, she wanders further into the maze, admiring the colours and smells of the market stalls, listening to the chattering and hollering of the vendors. She stops to sample the different produce, then fingers a beautiful cotton scarf that Patti would have loved. It's not something Myrtle would ever wear, but she finds herself buying it anyway.

It takes her another forty minutes to find her way back to the designated meeting point, by which point everyone is already on the coach, waiting impatiently for her.

'Sorry, sorry, I got lost,' Myrtle apologises as she makes her way to her seat.

'We thought something had happened to you,' Sophie says, her forehead creased with worry.

'No, nothing happened,' Myrtle replies, fingering the scarf. She wraps it around her neck, tucking the ends into the open collar of her shirt, her fingertips brushing against the raised ridge of her scar where her breasts used to be. She leans her head against the window as the coach pulls out of the car park and they head towards their next destination, thinking how, in spite of everything, she's glad she's stuck around.

102

They sit around the table at breakfast, eating in sombre silence, or quietly murmuring for someone to pass the marmalade or sugar.

Matthew hates days like this, when there is one less among them, an unwelcome reminder that any one of them could be next.

Sally, who had been the one to find Madeline, looks shell-shocked, her brittle toast remaining untouched in front of her. Matthew knows how she feels. He'd been the one to find Greg six months ago, and the image of him lying prone in bed, an anguished look on his face, still haunts Matthew. Greg had only been in Silver Birches a few weeks before he had the heart attack.

You duped me, Matthew thinks, looking around at the other solemn faces at the table, slowly buttering toast that none of them really have the appetite for. *I only came here because of you and now you've left me on my own.*

'When's our next outing?' he asks the new manager, Christina, as she brings over a fresh pot of tea to them. She's only been here eight months, and the manager before her only a year; not even the staff seemed to stick around for long.

Christina is Matthew's favourite member of staff. She's one of the few that doesn't talk to them slowly or loudly or in short syllables, and doesn't tell them off when they spill something down themselves, like they're little children who don't know any better.

'Next week. We thought we could take you all on a boat ride and then have a picnic, if it's a nice day.'

'Sounds great. Count me in,' Matthew says, glad to have something different to look forward to.

Christina's smile begins to slip when there are no other murmurs of enthusiasm from around the table.

'I thought you might like to try something new. But we can go for tea and cake at the museum café like we normally do, if you'd rather ... ?' she says hesitantly.

Everyone except Matthew says they'd rather.

Christina nods in defeat and Matthew swallows a sigh, wondering why everyone is so set in their ways, so sure of their likes and dislikes, so unwilling to try anything new. They are like a bunch of dusty, hardened fossils, content to stay shut away from the rest of a world they no longer feel a part of.

If he didn't have to eat, Matthew would avoid mealtimes altogether. All the other residents do is talk about the past, starting sentences with: 'In our day ...' and with a shake of their head at the current state of the world, as if they'd known all along that the next generation hadn't been up to the job. It's like they've already given up, and Matthew can't bear to see the grim acceptance on their faces. He remembers his grandparents being the same when he was younger, as if the present was nothing more than a bitter disappointment to them and something to be endured.

The only time the other residents seem to get animated is when they talk about their children and grandchildren, trying to outdo each other with stories of graduations and marriages and births, while Matthew just sits there mutely between them. And if they aren't talking about their progeny, they're talking incessantly about their favourite TV programmes, as if the far-fetched storylines had actually happened to them or concerned people they knew.

After they're done with breakfast, most of them go back to their rooms to have a 'lie down', even though they've only been awake a couple of hours. Sometimes Matthew does the same. Sleep is no longer just a necessity, he's found – it's a way to hasten time, to swallow great chunks of the day. But he finds that often when he falls asleep in the day, he dreams that he's returned to his younger self again, and when he wakes, the disappointment he feels when he looks down at his worn slippers and wrinkled hands is almost crushing.

He sits alone at the breakfast table, watching the others' stooped-over backs as they retire to their rooms, feeling that familiar sense of panic rising up in him again that he's made a terrible mistake coming here. It feels like he's just one step away from oblivion. Yet there seems to be no way to scramble back off the cliff edge now.

103

Myrtle sits down on the sofa, letting out a little exhale. She's noticed that when she sits down or gets up now, she does this, as if from the sheer exertion of it.

It's happening, she thinks sadly. Next she'd be wearing her clothes inside out and her slippers on the wrong feet.

She pulls her cardigan tighter around her, even though the central heating is on. She's taken to wearing Daphne's old cardigan lately, which had also been her grandfather's. The cuffs are now frayed and tattered, loose holes in places where the knitting has come undone. But there's something comforting about wearing it.

Her stomach grumbles, reminding her that she hasn't eaten anything yet today. She gets to her feet, expelling another little sigh, and makes her way to the kitchen, hands held out to graze the top of the furniture as she passes, because the dizziness can take her unaware at any moment.

She's fallen three times in the past year. But that is her secret. She doesn't tell her next-door neighbour, Helena, a kindly woman in her forties who pops in every week to ask if she needs anything from town. And she doesn't tell her doctor either.

After each fall, Myrtle waits on the floor, breathless, and then struggles back up, which only bruises her more.

That's another thing: bruises take so long to fade now, she finds. They are like one of those ink experiments she used to do in school, turning green, then yellow, then violet. So even in summer, it's tights and cardigans. She's become one of *those* old ladies.

She slowly chews her sandwich at the kitchen table, breaking off her crusts to give to Rufus, who is waiting in anticipation by her feet.

'How about I make us your favourite for dinner, as it's New Year's Eve?' Myrtle says, hoping lasagne will be enough distraction for Rufus to not get too stressed out by the fireworks. 'I doubt we'll last until midnight, though,' she says, handing him another crust, thinking how there is nothing lonelier than seeing the new year in all by yourself. 'It's just another day, after all, right, Rufus?'

He blinks up at her, the disappointment clear in his face when he realises there are no more crusts coming.

After she's washed up, Myrtle shuffles towards the hall to get Rufus's lead to take him out for a walk, but halfway there, she stumbles, her slippers catching on the rug. It happens so quickly, she isn't even able to put her hands out in time to break her fall.

She lies there, winded, blinking from the shock of it. Eventually she manages to turn on her side, feeling the place where another bruise will bloom to the surface, but she's too weak to lift herself back up just yet.

'Just give me a moment, then we'll go out,' she promises Rufus, who is sitting by her, licking her hand. She stretches her arm to stroke his head. 'If I didn't have you to talk to, Rufus, I might forget the sound of my own voice,' she whispers.

She thinks of how Worzel was at the end, how he felt the indignity of it too: collapsing in the kitchen, wetting himself, then needing a towel to support him underneath because he was so unsteady. Except she has no one to help her up.

Again Myrtle tries to get to her feet but is still too weak. She swallows, trying not to panic.

'Today isn't the day,' she says out loud. 'I'm not ready for you yet.'

She often thinks about where it will happen, when the moment finally comes. Keeled over in a supermarket, strangers gathered around her? Out on a walk with Rufus, alone in the countryside somewhere? In her own bed, like her mother was lucky enough to be? Or sprawled out on the floor, like she is now?

She thinks of her neighbour, Gemma, who was dead for three days before anyone found her. And even though she knows it doesn't matter, because when you're gone, you're gone, Myrtle doesn't want the same fate, or for poor Helena to find her like that.

Two hours later, she is still lying there, unable to move. She can't reach the phone; the neighbours are too far away to hear her cries, not that they'd be able to hear her anyway over the sounds of their noisy New Year celebrations; and the only person who used to regularly visit her was Sophie, and she's been gone almost nine months now.

This is it, Myrtle thinks, feeling strangely calm rather than panicked. *This is how I'm going to die.*

She watches Rufus in the corner of the room, whining, and then eventually weeing on the rug, his ears pinned back in shame.

'I'm sorry, Ruf. I thought you'd go before I did,' she says tearfully, wondering whether a neighbour will take him in, or whether he'll end up back in the rescue shelter that she got him from – the very one she set up all those years ago, which has been renamed and renovated so many times that it no longer looks like the same place anymore. 'When I'm gone, I give you permission to eat my remains,' she tells Rufus.

He cocks his head and then lets out another whine.

Myrtle can feel her own full bladder pressing against her insides, and when she tries to get up again, the exertion causes it to empty itself.

'No,' she whispers, feeling the warm dampness spread down her legs. 'No,' she says, with more determination. She tries to push herself up once again, and this time her limbs finally obey, until she's kneeling on the floor, shaking. She takes a breath and then clambers to her feet, pressing the palms of her hands flat against the wall as she edges towards the bathroom to clean herself up.

She stares at her pale reflection as she reaches for a flannel. 'Enough now, Myrtle,' she tells herself. 'Enough.'

104

Matthew stoops to pick up the newspaper from the coffee table and then walks over to the settee to sit down to read it. He has to think about it, though. There is a whole thought process involved for something that had once been automatic. It has crept up on him, old age, slowly taking away the things he'd always taken for granted, so that he can't even trust himself anymore.

He positions himself over the sofa, his joints cracking in protest as they bend, his trousers catching on his bony knees, and then he lets himself go for a split-second of free-falling before he lands awkwardly and has to right himself against the cushions. He opens the newspaper and sighs at the depressing headlines, scouring the pages for something remotely uplifting but finding nothing except political scandals, corporate corruption and celebrity divorces. He carefully refolds the paper and puts it beside him. He looks down at his hands, which are now dappled with liver spots, his thumbs starting to curve inwards.

Feeling restless, he decides to go out. He bends over to put his shoes on and has to sit down again because he feels so unsteady. This has been happening more and more lately, but he struggles to remember when it started. When was the last day that he stood unaided, slipping on his shoes, taking for granted just what a tiny yet significant thing it was?

He packs a bag with his towel and swimmers, clips Olive

and Popeye on their leads, then marks himself as 'out' on the resident register.

When they get there, Matthew slowly undresses and walks down to the lake edge, while the dogs potter around, sniffing at scents half-heartedly before collapsing on the pebbles. Matthew tenses as the cold water licks at his calves, but he forces himself to wade further in, until the water wraps itself around his ribcage. He takes a breath and then dunks his whole head under, breaking the surface when he can stand it no longer.

He floats on his back, arms and legs stretched out, drifting on the skin of the water. He watches the slow-moving clouds, the birds swooping above him, the willow trees trailing their branches into the lake, and his heart swells at the sight of them. Another moment rushes back at him – swimming at night-time with a group of twenty-somethings he'd only just met while he was travelling. He smiles at the memory, remembering how young they'd made him feel.

If this was his last day on earth, he realises he'd be OK with that. Because actually, the thought of not having to wake up in a bed that countless others have died in, of not having to make stilted conversation with others who have all but given up, seems rather welcoming.

More and more lately he has been pondering his own death, wondering whether, when the moment finally comes, it will be a sudden, violent thing – alive one moment, gone the next – or if it will be a slow ebbing away, like an old clock winding down, so that when the end finally comes, he won't even be aware.

He thinks of everyone that has gone before him – Grace, Peter, Luke, Xander, Giles, Ed, Emily, Greg – thinking how when you're the last one left at the party, it no longer feels like much of a party anymore.

He glances again at the scudding clouds, listening to the bird song. *This would be a nice place to die,* he thinks.

He remembers reading once that drowning is one of the most peaceful ways to go, although he isn't sure how anyone can actually know that for certain. But out here, the chill water lapping against his skin, his breath misting out in plumes in front of him, it's easy to believe it might be.

He exhales slowly, his body slipping beneath the water, his eyes blinking in the murky gloom. The strange internal workings of his body sound amplified down here. He can hear the steady beat of his heart, hear the thrum of his blood, hear the bubbled pressure in his lungs and ears ... He wonders if this is what it felt like when he was in the womb.

It would be so easy, he thinks, drifting further down. *Surely it would be better to go now, on my own terms, rather than leave it too late, when I'm bed-bound and at the mercy of others.*

His lungs start to burn as he sinks even further towards the bottom.

No one needs you ... No one will miss you ... Just let go ...

But then some atavistic instinct kicks in, and he thinks of Olive and Popeye, and how he is all they have.

No, he tells himself. *You're not done yet.*

He fights his way back to the surface, sucking in great lungfuls of air. He can hear Olive and Popeye barking at him from the water's edge, as if they could sense his morbid thoughts, and he thinks how they are all he has too. He turns and slowly makes his way back to them on shore.

105

'Jenna, would you like to introduce Myrtle to the other residents now that I've shown her around?' Maria suggests. She looks at Myrtle. 'There's not much going on around here that Jenna doesn't know about. We call her the eyes and the ears of the home.'

'And if I don't know about it, then it's not worth knowing,' Jenna adds self-importantly.

Myrtle gives a wan smile. This is the third place she's looked around in the last week, and none of them have felt like a place she'd want to call home. Nor has she felt like she's had much of an affinity with any of the residents. They all seem so serious and sombre, as if they're guests at their own funeral.

'Follow me,' Jenna says, shunting her Zimmer frame in the direction of the bedroom suites.

She moves surprisingly quickly for someone so unsteady on her feet. Myrtle wonders how long it will be before she has to get a frame.

'So why aren't your children here looking around with you?' Jenna asks. 'Too busy, are they?'

'I don't have any children.'

'Oh,' Jenna says, looking nonplussed. 'Well, at least you haven't got to worry about frittering away anyone's inheritance money then.'

'That's true.'

'So why do you want to come somewhere like this, if you don't mind me asking? Because you still seem pretty active and independent.'

'I guess I want to be able to choose while the choice is still mine to make,' Myrtle admits, not adding that she doesn't want to die in some hospital where the only people who know her name are the ones reading it off a clipboard at the foot of her bed.

'Wise decision,' Jenna says, nodding sagely. She stops outside one of the bedrooms and knocks loudly on the door, then turns back to Myrtle. 'Craig's a bit hard of hearing – and a little bit slow, if you ask me – so you need to speak loudly and clearly when you talk to him.'

After Myrtle has met Craig, who seems to be having an entirely different conversation to the one Myrtle and Jenna are holding, she then meets each of the other guests, accompanied by Jenna's running commentary on all of them.

There's: Annie ('She's losing her marbles, poor dear.'); Michael ('He loves to play the piano, and he's very good, but once he starts, he'll play for *hours*.'); Frankie ('The less said about her, the better.'); Zara ('She's just lost her husband, so she prefers to keep herself to herself.'); Rachel ('She's a love but she never stops talking. We're thinking about banning her at film nights, but you didn't hear it from me.'); Lisa ('All she wants to do is play cards all day long, which can get rather tiring when sometimes you just fancy a game of Scrabble, you know?'); Felix ('He's a sweetheart but you have to watch him at mealtimes, otherwise he scoffs the lot before the rest of us get a chance to have seconds.'); and John ('He's a bit of a letch when he's drunk. He kissed Rachel once, and then kissed Annie the very next day. So don't say you haven't been warned.').

'And that's everyone,' Jenna finishes, coming to the end of the corridor. She points to the door in the corner. 'And this would be your room, if you decide to move here.'

Myrtle thinks about asking whether the previous inhabitant died in the room, but then decides she'd rather not know.

'Is there no one who would be next door to me?' Myrtle asks, looking at the adjacent door.

'Oh yes, but he's not here right now. He's gone off on a weekend trip by himself, which he does a lot, even though we're not supposed to go off solo,' Jenna says with a disapproving shake of her head.

Myrtle likes the sound of him already.

'What's his name?' she asks.

'Matthew.'

Part Five

Part Five

106

Myrtle watches the other residents in wheelchairs being pushed around, like overgrown, wrinkled babies. They tightly clutch the blankets on their laps, their bony fingers translucent at the knuckles, as if this is the only way they can hold onto the world, by not letting go.

God, this place ... Myrtle thinks, unable to tear her eyes away from them.

Matthew turns to her and says, 'Let's get out of here. Let's go for a walk.'

Myrtle smiles at him, at the uncanny way their thoughts always seem to collide. She goes back to her room to get her coat and fetch Rufus's lead. When she goes outside, she sees Matthew waiting for her. He stands, hands clasped behind his back like a footman, rocking backwards and forward on his feet so that the heels and toes of his shoes lift slightly. Myrtle watches him for a moment, smiling, her heart giving a little kick inside her chest.

She likes everything about him: his quiet laugh that comes so easily (she doesn't think she's ever heard a nicer laugh than his); how he's a man of few words but everything that comes out of his mouth seems carefully considered; his strong-looking hands, the fingernails short and shiny; his bright hazel eyes, and the way they crinkle when he smiles; and his smile – it makes everything better. He smiles freely at everyone and everything, whereas with the other residents when they smile, it's as if it's somehow costing them.

And Myrtle notices other things about him too. Like how he steps around pigeons and magpies. Most people just walk right through them, expecting them to fly out of the way. But Matthew always skirts them, and always stops to pick up worms and bees that are in the middle of paths, so they won't be trodden on. Small things like that say a lot about a person, Myrtle thinks.

Just then Matthew glances up and catches sight of her, his face breaking into a smile, and she smiles back as she hurries forward to meet him.

When they get to the park, they watch Rufus leaping into the stream, dragging out branches three times his size, then writhing on his back in the long grass in ecstasy.

'Foolish mutts,' another owner says in passing, shaking his head at his own dog as he bounds in circles around Rufus, both of them yapping in unbridled glee.

'Or maybe we're the foolish ones,' Matthew muses, 'for forgetting how to play.'

'Exactly,' Myrtle agrees.

'I still miss my two,' he says quietly, 'even though it's been almost two years now.'

'We never stop missing them,' Myrtle says, thinking of Worzel.

Matthew nods as they begin another loop of the park.

Myrtle can't help watching the young couples picnicking on the grass, kissing and holding hands, lying next to each other in a tangle of toned limbs. She smiles to herself, then catches Matthew looking at them and smiling too.

'You know, you have lovely posture,' Myrtle remarks.

'Thank you,' he says, walking a little taller.

'It's the first thing I noticed about you,' she says. 'Most people our age, they look like they've been slowly crushed by life. But you don't.'

He smiles at her, then gazes around the park again. 'You know, I used to come here a lot when I was younger.'

'Me too,' Myrtle says.

'I used to get the number twenty-two out of London and spend the whole day here.'

'That was the bus I used to get!' Myrtle exclaims.

'Who knows, maybe we even sat next to each other on it one day,' he says, smiling.

'Imagine that,' Myrtle replies, watching as Matthew steps around a mallard duck.

107

Matthew walks into the sitting room and scans it, looking for her. Because out of everyone there, he only wants to talk to her.

Myrtle looks up and catches his eye, patting the empty seat on the sofa next to her that she's been saving for him. His eighty-year-old heart skips a beat just at the sight of her. She stands out from everyone else in the room. All the other residents are sat there in their faded pastel outfits, but not Myrtle. Today she is wearing a bright teal jumper and rust-coloured trousers.

'Youth is wasted on the young,' Felix is saying in disgust as Matthew sits down.

'It sure is,' Jenna agrees.

Everyone has gathered around the TV after dinner, watching a reality programme about a group of twenty-somethings living in an eco commune. But rather than focusing on growing organic produce and becoming more sustainable, they seem to be crying about who's slept with who when they were supposed to be sleeping with someone else.

'The world's buggered when their generation comes into power,' John announces grimly.

The others grumble their agreement while Myrtle and Matthew exchange a secret smile.

After the programme has finished, everyone else bids each other goodnight and shuffles off to bed, but they stay where they are, flicking over to the film channel.

'Oh look,' Myrtle says. 'I've always loved this film.'

'Me too,' Matthew says. But he finds he can't stay focused on it, his gaze constantly straying back to her, watching her profile as she reacts to each scene.

She catches him looking at her. 'What?' she says.

'I was just thinking … Well … I …' He dips his head, suddenly feeling bashful. Too often he feels like a teenage boy again around Myrtle, unable to get his words out properly.

'You were just thinking … ?' she prompts, nudging his shoulder with her own.

'I was just thinking that … I'm glad you moved here, Myrtle,' he says quietly. 'Before you came … well, you can imagine what it was like.'

She smiles at him. 'People our age love to say youth's wasted on the young, but maybe old age is wasted on us too. Children know how to be children, but we don't know how to be old, do we?'

Matthew nods thoughtfully. 'It's like people reach a certain age and suddenly they no longer want to be a part of the world anymore. They aren't even interested in how it's changing.'

'That's the way you grow old quickly, I say.'

Matthew nods again, thinking how long it's been since he's had a meaningful conversation like this with someone.

They turn back to face the TV, but once again Matthew's gaze keeps straying towards Myrtle.

'You're doing it again,' she says, turning to him with a smile that almost fells him.

'Sorry. I was just thinking …' He hesitates again. But something in her expression, something in those bright blue eyes of hers, makes him answer truthfully. 'I was thinking how you and I might have been great friends if we'd met earlier in life,' he says, no longer looking at her but at his liver-spotted hands folded in his lap.

'We might still be great friends,' she says, nudging her shoulder against his.

'We might,' he echoes with a smile, their shoulders still touching as the film starts up again.

108

'Where do you want to sit?' Matthew asks.

'At the back, of course,' Myrtle replies.

They get to the end of the bus and take their seats, falling into each other as the bus driver pulls sharply away.

'Want one?' Myrtle says, holding out a bag of sweets to Matthew.

'I never sat at the back of the bus at school,' he says, taking one. 'I was always stuck somewhere in the middle.'

'Me too.' Myrtle smiles. 'Looks like we've gone up in the world.'

'That's one way of looking at it.'

They spend the rest of the half-hour journey sucking on pear drops and pointing out things to each other through the window. When they get to their stop, they follow the signs to the footpath and start the steep incline to the top of the hill. Matthew takes out his pair of secateurs that he always carries with him on walks and prunes back the overhanging brambles.

'Sometimes you remind me of my dad,' Myrtle tells him, remembering Elliott doing the same thing on walks.

'Is that a good thing?'

She nods. 'Definitely.'

When they finally reach the summit, they are both breathless and lightheaded, their backs damp from the exertion.

'Now there's the issue of sitting down,' Myrtle says, eyeing the uneven ground.

'If I could sweep you off your feet right now, I would,' Matthew replies.

'Who says you can't?'

Matthew looks at her, then in two strides is in front of her, his arms scooping her up. Except he's misjudged it and the next instant he's toppling backwards, landing heavily on the grass, and a moment later comes the second blow of Myrtle landing on top of him. Both of them are too winded to move.

Myrtle can feel Matthew shaking beneath her, and at first she thinks he's crying, that he must be injured. But then she hears his laugh and it is like music to her ears.

'You daft old fool,' she says, peering down at him, their faces almost touching.

When they've both righted themselves, they spread out their picnic on the blanket.

'This would be a pretty nice spot for a bench,' Matthew remarks.

'It would,' Myrtle agrees, gazing out at the view. It almost takes her breath away. 'Aren't we lucky?'

'Very,' Matthew says, looking at her.

Myrtle leans back against the tree trunk and catches sight of two pairs of initials: *DJ ♥ LK*. Next to that is another one: *HR + TW 4EVA*. She tuts.

'Why do people feel the need to deface something beautiful?'

Matthew shakes his head. 'I guess some people just want to leave their mark, to show that they were really here.'

'Kids,' Myrtle says, smiling.

'Kids,' Matthew says with a chuckle.

After they are full with sandwiches and cake, they lie down next to each other, their clasped hands resting on the mounds of their stomachs. It isn't long before they drift off, lulled by the sound of the birds and insects.

When they wake, the sun is already slipping below the horizon and the stars are beginning to come out.

'We should probably go soon, so we're not trekking back in the dark,' Matthew murmurs sleepily.

Myrtle nods, but neither of them makes a move to leave.

I'm not ready for today to be over yet, she thinks.

She can sense Matthew's hand lying on the grass close to hers. She thinks about reaching for it, yet something holds her back, making her feel like a shy teenager again.

What are you waiting for? Patti's voice urges.

Myrtle takes a breath and then nudges her hand closer, only to find Matthew's is already reaching out for her own.

109

Matthew knocks on Myrtle's door, holding the newspaper in his hand. He is always finding excuses to go to her room – dropping off a crossword for her to do, or taking her some flowers in a jam jar that he's sneakily picked from the garden, or bringing her a bar of vegan chocolate because he knows she has a sweet tooth.

The door swings open and Myrtle stands there, beaming up at him, as if she might, just might, be as happy to see him as he is her.

'I brought us the crossword to do,' he says, handing it to her as she beckons him in. 'But it's such a nice day out, I wondered if you wanted to go somewhere?'

'Always.'

That's what he loves about her. Not where, or when, or why. But simply: yes.

'OK,' he says, trying not to grin like a little boy. 'I'm going to take you to one of my favourite places.'

When they get there, he stands for a moment, watching Myrtle taking it all in.

'It's beautiful,' she breathes, gazing at the lake, the sunlight glinting off its surface, the weeping willows lazily sweeping their tendrils in the water, the water lilies clustered together in the centre. He feels like he is seeing it anew through her eyes, as if she is somehow repainting everything just by being there.

'It's going to be cold, isn't it?' Myrtle says, already sliding off her shoes and dress, standing there in just her swimsuit.

Matthew looks carefully away as they walk to the lake edge. She gasps a little, but doesn't hesitate as she wades in further, and when the water gets to her waist, she dives in. She resurfaces, grinning as he paddles over to her. They move slowly in circles, their thin, pale bodies buoyant in the water, their white hair glistening.

He thinks of the last time he came here and what he'd contemplated doing, how ready he'd been for it to be the end. His throat tightens at the thought of if he'd gone through with it. If he'd never even met Myrtle. And how it is only because of her that he no longer wants to leave.

'Are you OK?' Myrtle asks, instantly sensing the change in his mood in that uncanny way of hers.

He smiles at her. 'Better than OK.'

'Good.'

They roll on their backs, bobbing on the surface next to each other in silence, staring up at the sky as they stretch out their limbs.

When they finally get out of the water and wrap their towels around themselves, they sit on a sun-warmed rock, letting the breeze air-dry their skin.

'We should come here every morning,' Myrtle says. 'Before everyone else is even up. We could even bring breakfast with us.'

She uses that word a lot, Matthew's noticed. 'We'll have to check this place out ...' 'We should go here soon ...' 'When we next go out for the day ...'

We, Matthew thinks giddily. *We're a we*.

Myrtle glances across at him and places a finger over the scar on his knee. 'How did you get that?'

'I fell out of a tree.'

'And this?' she asks, her finger moving to above his right eyebrow.

'I fell off the school roof after I climbed up for a dare.'

Myrtle laughs, almost girlishly, and he can picture her as she would have once been.

'And what about this?' she says, her finger trailing up to his hairline.

'Chicken pox,' he replies softly, trying not to shiver under her touch.

'And here?' Her finger moves down to his forearm.

'Rusty nail in a fence.'

They gaze at his scars, at all those moments of life etched upon his skin.

'Life has a way of leaving its mark on you, doesn't it?' she remarks, idly fingering her own scar on her chest.

He nods, shifting closer to her. 'It sure does.'

110

It's Saturday morning and the residents are more garrulous than usual, excited at the prospect of their families coming to visit. It's like this every week: come Thursday, they start talking loudly about who is coming that weekend, and by Monday morning, they've all slipped into a deep funk at the thought of another five days with no visits from the outside world.

Myrtle watches as Zara's family arrives. Zara's eyes are shining at the sight of them, while her grandchildren's already look weary, as if they've been cajoled into coming.

'Mum, your jumper's inside out and you've got odd shoes on.' While the grandchildren laugh, the son rolls his eyes, as if Zara is nothing more than an embarrassment to him.

Zara's granddaughter sidles over to Myrtle and Matthew. 'I'm four and three-quarters,' she announces, with a toss of her ponytail.

'Is that right?' Matthew says.

Myrtle smiles, thinking how she'd been the same when she was little, counting off the months of her age, so desperate to grow up already. Yet now she struggles to remember how old she is in years, let alone months. Now she wants to dig in her heels and slow it all down.

'Off to big school next month, aren't you, Amber?' Zara says proudly.

Amber nods and then drifts over to the other side of the room, already losing interest in the conversation.

Jenna, who is sitting at the same table as Myrtle and Matthew, is flicking through one of her many photo albums. Myrtle watches her blotched hands turning the album pages reverentially, as if she's handling a rare artefact.

'Did I ever show you the photos of me and Andrew on honeymoon?' she asks, already pushing the album towards them, even though they've seen it countless times before.

'It looks like it was a lovely holiday,' Matthew says politely.

All the other residents are the same – always talking, talking, talking about the past, as if that could somehow bring it back. They are so eager to show people their photos, brandishing them proudly, a faraway look in their eyes, as if they're trying to say: 'Look! Look at the life I lived. Wasn't it something? Look at the person I used to be. Wasn't I something?'

People keep telling the same old stories, over and over again, because they're not making any new ones, Myrtle thinks.

As Matthew dutifully finishes flicking through the album pages, Jenna looks at them both and says, 'Don't you two get lonely, with no children or grandchildren?'

We've all ended up in the same place, though, haven't we? Myrtle wants to say. But she just shrugs. 'I'm happy enough in my own company.'

'Me too,' Matthew agrees, his hand brushing against hers as he passes the album back to Jenna, making the hairs on her arm stand on end.

After Jenna excuses herself for her siesta, clutching her albums to her chest, Myrtle says, 'I wonder who will take all of Jenna's photos after she's gone?'

Matthew nods thoughtfully. 'All those photos, all those albums of other people's lives that must end up in landfill ...'

They are quiet for a moment. Myrtle watches Lisa sitting at a table with her bored-looking grandson, showing off her faded stamp collection to him, and Felix with his children on the sofa, as they all stare passively at an old film on TV.

'So do you have any photo albums?' she asks Matthew, thinking how she's never even seen so much as a picture frame up in his room.

'Just a handful. Not much point in keeping more, is there?'

Myrtle nods. 'How about we bore each other with them?' she suggests.

Matthew smiles, a twinkle in his eye. 'You're on.'

In his room, Matthew pulls out the shoebox of photos from his side cabinet. 'It's been a while since I've looked at these,' he admits, gazing at them first before passing them on to Myrtle.

'You were very handsome,' she says, looking at a photo of him in a suit at a wedding. 'Not so much here,' she adds, laughing as she looks at a photo of him as a teenager with a shaved head, frowning at the camera.

'I hated my curly hair and thought it would be a good idea at the time.'

'I hated my red hair too.' Myrtle hands him a photo from her box, of her teenage self with bleached hair. 'This will make you feel better.'

Matthew gives a dry chuckle as he looks at it. 'You look like a scarecrow.'

'Yeah, I got that a lot.' Myrtle smiles, looking at another photo of her as a teenager, sunburnt and scowling. 'I didn't stand a chance, did I?' she says, laughing.

'You were beautiful,' Matthew says, studying it. 'You still are,' he says quietly.

Myrtle shakes her head, her cheeks aflame, glad she's sat beside him so he can't see her expression. She looks at a photo of her, Abi and Sophie at Abi's wedding, her eyes misty with memories, her mind dizzy at the thought of what time could do to a person. And then she pulls out a photo of her and Nina at eleven years old, dressed in floor-length gowns with pearls around their necks, their arms slung around each other's shoulders, beaming up at the camera. Myrtle wonders what Nina's life would have turned out like if she'd lived. Whether they would have stayed friends.

Matthew hands her another photo, pulling her out of her reverie. 'This is me and my uncle Xander. He'd just bought me a motorbike, and my mum was furious at him.'

Myrtle smiles down at a youthful Matthew, wide-eyed and curly-haired, leaning proudly against the bike with a helmet in one hand. *All these moments,* she thinks, flicking through the rest of his photos. *All these things you lived through that I'll never even know about. All these different versions of yourself I never got to meet.*

'What are you thinking?' he asks, watching her.

She looks up at him. 'I'm thinking I want to know everything about you.'

He smiles sadly. 'I don't think either of us have time for that.'

She nods. 'I know.'

When they've looked at the last of the photos, they store them back in their boxes, putting them at their feet. Myrtle glances across at Matthew, with his ready smile and his thoughtful words and his kind eyes, and she thinks: *No, I didn't get to meet all those other versions of you. But maybe I got to meet the best one.*

III

This is it, Matthew thinks, his stomach knotted in dread as he sits in the waiting room of the doctor's surgery. *This is really the end.*

He's been feeling sick for months now, and it isn't getting any better. He hasn't told Myrtle because he doesn't want to worry her, so he lied to her this morning, saying he was just going for a routine check-up.

In the doctor's office, he explains his symptoms and has his blood pressure taken, iron levels checked and heart rate monitored.

'Hmmm,' the doctor murmurs. 'Well, your heart rate is a little faster than usual. And you do seem to have lost some weight.'

'I don't have as much of an appetite as I used to,' Matthew admits.

'That does happen with old age,' the doctor replies, and Matthew tries not to bristle at that. 'Has anything changed in your circumstances lately?'

Matthew thinks for a moment. 'I guess I have been more active in the last nine months or so. A new lady has moved into the home and we often go out on day trips together. And I guess we do stay up late talking, so I'm probably not getting as much sleep as I used to. And there have been a few instances where she's made me laugh so hard I've become short of breath, which I've never had before.'

'And is this lady friend of yours quite attractive?' the doctor asks.

'Well, yes, but ...' Matthew says, frowning, unsure if he's misheard the question.

'Ah. I see,' the doctor says, a serious expression settling on his face. 'I think I know what's causing this.'

'You do?' Matthew says, bracing himself.

The doctor smiles at him. 'I suspect you might have butterflies, which is making you feel nauseous, and so you're eating less and not sleeping as well.'

'Butterflies?' Matthew repeats, sure he must have heard wrong.

The doctor nods, his smile widening. 'This is a common case of, what we call in the medical profession, lovesickness.'

'Oh,' Matthew says, startled. 'So I'm not dying?'

'No. You're not dying.'

Lovesick, Matthew thinks as he walks out of the doctor's office. He smiles to himself, thinking that this is one illness he hopes he doesn't recover from.

'Everything OK?' Myrtle asks when he gets back, standing on her tiptoes to kiss him, making his heart flip.

'Yes,' he says, still grinning so broadly his cheeks are beginning to ache. 'Everything's just fine.'

112

'Neither of us have been married before. And we both thought we never would. Yet here we are today ...'

The seated guests begin to laugh and cheer from their tables, as all heads turn to face the top table.

'A lot of you were surprised we decided to get married so late in our lives. I know my wife was certainly surprised when I asked her.'

The words 'my wife' are met with more cheers and whistles.

'But sometimes you meet someone,' Matt continues, looking at Greta. 'Someone you'd given up hope of ever finding. And you realise that they're your second chance at the life you'd always wanted.' He pauses, visibly overcome with emotion for a moment, before he continues. 'And it just hit me one day – the thought of not having this amazing woman as my wife suddenly seemed unbearable.'

Greta gets to her feet and kisses him passionately on the lips as everyone begins to clap.

Matthew reaches for Myrtle's hand under the table and squeezes it. They smile at each other, blinking quickly.

'You OK?' she asks softly.

He nods. 'I'm happy for them. But I'm sad, too, that Greg and Emily didn't get to see this day.'

Myrtle nods. 'I know.'

'And I'm sad you never got to meet them either,' Matthew

says. 'They would have loved you. And you would have loved them too.'

'I'm sure I would,' Myrtle says, thinking of her own friends and family that she wishes Matthew could have met.

He leans over to kiss her, and Myrtle notices a teenage couple on their table quickly look away, mortified, as if old love is somehow offensive to them. As if they cannot believe that she and Matthew had once been young and smooth-skinned too, and full of passion. *All you see is two doddery, white-haired, out-of-touch eighty-year-olds, don't you?* she thinks with a smile.

After the meal, they watch as the huge tiered cake is cut, laughing as Matt and Greta messily shove chunks of cake in each other's mouths.

'Did you ever come close to getting married?' Myrtle asks, picking all the glacé cherries from her slice of cake and putting them on Matthew's plate, because she knows how much he likes them.

Matthew hesitates, chewing on a cherry, and then gives a slow nod. 'Once. I even had my mother's ring ready to give her. But I couldn't ask the question. I guess I knew deep down that we weren't right for each other. That we wanted different things.' He reaches for another cherry. 'How about you?'

'Someone asked me once,' she reveals. 'And I did say yes, even though my heart was screaming no. But as soon as we started to plan the wedding, and talk about things like favours and seating plans and where to go on honeymoon, I panicked and realised I couldn't go through with it.'

'Funny to think how differently our lives could have turned out,' Matthew muses.

'Or maybe we would have still ended up here anyway,' Myrtle says, feeding him the last cherry from her plate.

Just then the music starts up and they turn in their seats to watch Matt and Greta dancing to a Bruce Springsteen song as everyone else claps and cheers around them.

'This song reminds me of my dad,' Myrtle says, remembering Elliott playing it on repeat on his car stereo.

'Mine too,' Matthew says, a faraway look in his eyes. 'The oldies are the best.'

'Aren't they just?' Myrtle says with a smile.

When the next song comes on, other couples move onto the dance floor to join them. Matthew takes Myrtle by the hand, leading her out to the centre, where they spin in slow, unsteady circles, leaning on each other for support. Her heart stutters when he pulls her in closer, and she breathes in his familiar scent, leaning her head on his chest. She feels the steady thump of his heart against her cheek, and she can't help but think how one day soon it would stop, just like hers would too.

But not today, she thinks. *Not yet.*

The next song isn't one they recognise, and the beat is too fast for them to keep up, so they drift back to the edges of the room, sinking gratefully into chairs as they watch the younger couples dance.

'How do you know Matt and Greta?' a middle-aged woman seated next to them asks.

'I'm Matt's godfather,' Matthew says. 'How about you?'

'I'm Greta's maid of honour.' She rolls her eyes. 'Always the bridesmaid, never the bride,' she says with a brittle laugh, then takes a long sip of her champagne.

'There's no rush,' Myrtle tells her kindly. 'Better to wait for the right person than end up with the wrong one.'

The woman looks at her, nodding thoughtfully. 'So how long have you two been together?'

'Six years,' Matthew says, smiling at Myrtle as he rests his arm around her shoulder.

'Is that all?' the woman asks, her eyebrows shooting up in surprise. 'You look like you've been together your whole lives.'

Myrtle shakes her head. 'We only met when I moved into

the same residential home Matthew was living in.'

'Oh, how sweet!' the woman exclaims. 'Aren't you lucky, finding love so late in life?'

Myrtle thinks of the few friends of hers who are still alive, all of them single, either widowed or divorced.

'Yes, we are lucky,' she echoes, before the woman excuses herself to rush onto the dance floor, standing behind Greta as she prepares to throw her bouquet.

'Some things never change,' Myrtle remarks with a smile, watching the single women jostle each other as they fiercely eyeball the wilting bunch of flowers.

The crowd around them whoop and whistle, and Myrtle and Matthew choose that moment to quietly slip out of the room unnoticed, making their way out to the car park, the day finally catching up with them.

As Matthew navigates the car through the tree-lined country lanes, he briefly takes one hand off the wheel and places it on top of Myrtle's, squeezing it.

'Watching the two of them tonight ... it made me think ...' He hesitates, and Myrtle can see the faint outline of his Adam's apple bobbing in his throat. 'It made me think that you've been my second chance, Myrtle.'

'And you mine,' she whispers back.

113

Matthew edges along the outside of the railing, trying not to look down, his hands gripping the metal banister. He gets to the end and takes a deep breath.

Just do it, he tells himself. *Just jump.*

His heart racing in his chest, he lets go of the railing and launches himself. A moment later, he is gripping the railing of Myrtle's balcony, swinging one leg up and over, then the other. He goes up to the sliding glass door and peers in to her sitting area, where he can see her, reading a book. He watches her for a while. Then, as if she senses his gaze, her head jerks up, a startled expression on her face. She gets to her feet and slides open the door.

'Get in here, you daft old fool,' she says, lifting up on her toes to kiss him.

'I've always wanted to do that,' he says, grinning.

She shakes her head, but she's grinning too. 'You forget that you're not young anymore.'

You make it easy to forget, Matthew thinks.

'I've made your favourite cake,' she says, cutting him a slice.

He lets out a moan as he bites into it. 'Where have you been all my life, Myrtle?'

She dips her head as she sits down next to him, but he still catches the smile that breaks free on her face.

He swallows the last bite of cake, then goes to put his

empty plate on the coffee table, but something twinges in his back. He winces out loud.

'I think I twisted something when I jumped.'

'Maybe you should lie down on the floor for a bit,' Myrtle suggests.

He stretches out on the carpet, and a moment later Myrtle comes over, putting a cushion beneath his head, then lies down next to him, her head resting on the pillow of his stomach. He feels like he can't breathe normally with her lying like that, but he doesn't want to disturb her, even though he is beginning to feel lightheaded now, like he isn't getting enough oxygen. Except Myrtle often has this effect on him anyway.

He thinks about the first time they met just eight years ago, yet how it feels like he has known her his whole life. How strange it is to think he'd spent seventy-nine years of his life without her, without even knowing she existed. And now, he doesn't know how he could exist without her.

How can a person go from being nothing to everything? he wonders, idly tracing the lines of her palm with his fingertip. He shifts slightly and then groans as his back gives another painful twinge. 'I think I might have to sleep on the floor tonight,' he murmurs.

'Then I am too,' she replies. 'We can camp out here, like we're little kids again.'

'Little kids with sciatica.'

She laughs. She is even more beautiful when she laughs.

'I don't want to get old, Myrtle,' he murmurs.

'We are old,' she points out.

'I know. But I don't want to feel old.'

She squeezes his hand, her palm warm and soft against his own. 'Me neither.'

114

Myrtle walks out of her bathroom, but it's like her feet aren't obeying her properly, and before she knows what's happening, before she can even put her hands out to break her fall, the carpet is rushing up to meet her and she catches her temple on the edge of the bedside table.

'Oomph,' she says, the wind knocked out of her. She tries to turn on her side and lift herself up, but no part of her body will obey.

'Help,' Myrtle says, but it comes out as nothing more than a whisper.

Just lie there for a bit and get your strength back, Patti's voice tells her.

But even her vision is funny, flickering like a faulty TV screen, and her ears are buzzing, which has never happened before. She can feel something wet creeping down from her hairline but can't move to wipe it away.

'Help,' she tries again, but it's even weaker. And now her vision keeps coming and going.

This is it, she thinks, her heart stuttering. She wouldn't have chosen this moment, if she'd had a choice. But it seems the moment had chosen her.

An image comes to her then: of her and Nina holding hands across the bunk beds at Cuffley Hall ... Then there's Patti, sitting nonchalantly in their lounge that first time Myrtle had met her ... Then she and Henry are holding hands under

the table, writing secret messages on each other's palms ...
Then she, Abi and Sophie are throwing their mortarboards
in the air at graduation ... Then she's on a beach and Oli is
getting down on one knee ... Now she's bringing Worzel
home, and he's slinking across her kitchen floor ... Then
she's opening the rescue centre ... Then she's reading Patti's
letter that Daphne had hidden from her all those years ...

Now she's sitting at the back of the bus with Matthew ...
Holding hands with Matthew ... Dancing with Matthew ...
Kissing Matthew ...

Matthew ...

Matthew ...

'Matthew ...' she whispers, before everything goes black.

115

'Myrtle? Are you awake?' Matthew knocks loudly on the door again, sensing something's wrong. She never misses breakfast. 'Myrtle, I'm coming in,' he calls.

He opens the door and gazes around her room but she's nowhere to be seen. He walks around the bed and that's when he sees her – collapsed on the floor, like an abandoned rag doll.

No. No. No.

He rushes over. 'Myrtle! Can you hear me?' He gently lifts up her head but her eyes don't open.

Oh Jesus. No.

'Myrtle,' he moans, still cradling her head in his hands. 'Please don't leave me.'

Just then her eyelids flutter open and her eyes meet his. 'Am I dead?' she croaks.

Matthew laughs, weak with relief. 'If you are then I am too.' He gently pushes her hair back from her face, which is crusted with blood at the roots. 'What happened?'

'I fell, and then I couldn't get back up.'

'Let's get you up now, then,' he says, getting to his feet, before gently scooping Myrtle up on hers.

'I really thought I was a goner,' she murmurs, encircling her arms around him, her whole body trembling.

'So did I,' he says, his voice breaking.

They hold onto each other for the longest moment, their hearts beating in time together.

'Thank goodness you found me,' Myrtle whispers.

'Yes,' Matthew says quietly, holding her tighter as a lump forms in his throat, thinking how the past nine years with Myrtle have been the best years of his life. 'Thank goodness I found you.'

116

Myrtle cracks open her eyes and looks straight into Matthew's. 'What are you doing?' she murmurs sleepily, pulling back slightly, worried she has morning breath.

'Looking at you,' he says, propping himself up on one elbow and staring down at her.

'Oh god, do you have to?'

'Yes, Myrtle, I have to.'

She turns her head, burying her smile in the pillow.

'Myrtle,' he says. He whispers it, as if it's something precious. His fingers trace a pattern on her bare shoulder, then he leans down and kisses her. Even after ten years together, his kisses still make her stomach feel like it's being turned inside out.

This is happiness. This moment, right here, Myrtle thinks, wishing she could pause it and live in it forever.

'Imagine if I hadn't chosen Silver Birches,' she wonders out loud. 'Imagine if I'd moved somewhere else.'

Matthew shakes his head. His hair is standing up at the back, like curled stalks of grass reaching for the sun. 'You and I, we were always going to meet.'

Myrtle pulls back to look at him. 'Do you really believe that? That the future has already been mapped out? That it's just there the whole time, waiting for us to catch up with it?'

He looks back at her. 'Perhaps. Do you?'

'I don't know.' Except being with Matthew made her believe in things she never had before.

His finger trails the length of her scar on her chest, making her shiver, then he leans down and kisses it.

All those years without you, she thinks. *Why did we have to wait so long?*

She rests her head on Matthew's chest and can feel his ninety-year-old heart beating beneath her. She thinks of all those lonely nights by herself, and all those lonely nights lying next to the wrong person, and an indescribable sadness washes over her.

'What's up?' he says, sensing a change in her mood.

'It's silly, but ... do you ever wonder, if perhaps we'd met when we were younger, what might have happened?' she asks.

'Yes,' he says quietly. 'I think about that a lot.' He puts his arms around her, his chin resting on her head, so that when he next speaks, his words vibrate down the whole length of her body. 'Then sometimes I think: maybe we met each other exactly when we needed to the most.'

117

It is a warm and sunny spring day, with just the gentlest of breezes. The sky is a brilliant, cloudless blue, and the rolling green hills are studded with sheep. Birdsong fills the trees and hedgerows.

A lone wooden bench sits at the crest of a hill, overlooking the valley below. It is new, not yet weathered. On it is screwed a shiny brass plaque, just waiting to be tarnished.

In the distance come two figures: a man and a woman. Together they slowly climb the hill, the man waiting at the top for the woman to catch up with him, and then they gratefully sit down on the bench, their damp backs leaning against the sun-warmed plaque, gazing in silent wonder at the view. It stretches unbroken for mile upon mile, as if there is no one else around except the two of them.

'This is nice,' she says. 'I can see why they liked coming here so much.'

Matt nods, pulling out the two urns from his backpack.

'Hey,' Greta says softly, reaching out to put her hand on his arm. 'Are you sure you're up to doing this today?'

He nods, blinking quickly, feeling more emotional than he thought he would. 'Today's as good a day as any,' he says thickly. He picks up one of the urns, pulling off the lid and peering inside at the ashy remains. 'At least they died peacefully in their sleep.'

'It's kind of romantic, isn't it?' Greta says. 'Both of them dying on the same day. As if they couldn't go on existing without each other.'

'I guess so, when you put it like that,' he says, thinking of his own parents, Greg dying just months after Emily, as if he had given up on the world once she was no longer in it.

Matt stands up and takes a step forward, emptying the contents of the urn in the gathering breeze. Then he reaches for the second urn and gently empties that one too, watching as the ashes drift to the ground, joining the rest. When he sits back down, putting the empty urns in his bag, Greta curls her hand around his.

'Maybe one day, when our time is up, we'll have our own bench looking out over a view like this.'

Matt smiles. 'And another couple can come sit on it and wonder about our story.'

She leans her head on his shoulder as they watch the sun disappear behind the hills, shafts of pink and gold trailing in its wake. Finally, reluctantly, they get to their feet, hands still clasped together, ready to walk back down the hill. But before they do, they pause for a moment to read the inscription engraved on the bench:

In memory of Myrtle & Matthew
We were here.

Acknowledgements

Writing a novel was a secret, long-held dream of mine – one that I never told anyone about until I seriously tried to start writing after I quit my job in publishing. After two failed attempts (which I learnt *a lot* from), I began to write *The Moments*. Unlike the previous two books, I knew the ending of this book before I knew anything else. I wanted to write a story about two people who only meet each other right at the end of their lives. I wanted to write a love story, but not a love story in the traditional sense. I wanted to write about the (often complicated) love we have for our family and friends, and how that shapes us and our lives, as well as write about the romantic kind of love that so many of us search for throughout our lives.

Writing can feel like a very solitary experience and this book has been a huge part of my life for the past two years. Luckily I have had the best group of people cheering me on from the sidelines.

Firstly, I'd like to thank Nicola, my amazing, wonderful agent. (There really aren't enough adjectives to describe how great she is.) I was lucky enough to know you before you became my agent, and there is no one I would rather have in my corner than you. I am so glad I get to share this experience with you, and so grateful for everything you have done for me and the book. *The Moments* wouldn't be what it is without you. Thank you, thank you, thank you.

And to Clare, my lovely editor. From our very first meeting, I knew you were someone I would love working with. Again, your insight and input have been invaluable. I feel incredibly lucky.

Thanks also to Olivia, Alainna, and Cait at Orion.

To all my friends who have supported me along the way and read various drafts of various books – I am so grateful. Special mention to Jess, for all your encouragement and feedback, and for being the best travel buddy! And special shout out to Anna and Bhurut, who have always had faith in me.

To Bill – I'm so glad I get to hold your hand as I cross the finish line.

To my parents, Gillian and Colin, who have always supported me in everything I do, even when I quit a job I loved to go and live abroad for a year – which ended up turning into five. There are a lot of family anecdotes that have worked their way into my writing, so thank you for all that material! And special thanks to my mum, not only for all the endless reading and critiquing of drafts that you've done, but for instilling a love of books into me from a young age, and for raising me to care about the important things in life.

To my darling girl, Hattie. (Yes, I'm one of those authors that puts her dog in the acknowledgements ...) Like Myrtle and Worzel, you have rescued me as much as I have rescued you. Even though I was terrified at the thought that my long-term travel days were over now you were in my life, every day is an adventure with you. You are my constant companion, always by my side when I'm writing, reminding me to take much-needed breaks for walks, and you make me laugh constantly. It breaks my heart to think about how badly you were treated by people for the first eighteen months of your life, yet you are still so loving and forgiving. You have taught me the true meaning of living in the moment.

To my twin sister and better half, Stephanie. You've been

my sounding board from the very first day. It is no exaggeration to say that I could not have written this without your input and encouragement. For someone who doesn't even read that much, you have given me some of the best advice! You are the greatest friend a sister could hope for. No one knows me better than you do, no one makes me laugh like you do, and no one knows how to push my buttons like you do either! I'm so lucky I've got to share so many of my best 'moments' with you.

And finally, thanks to you, the reader. I hope you enjoyed reading this as much as I enjoyed writing it.

Credits

Natalie Winter and Orion Fiction would like to thank everyone at Orion who worked on the publication of *The Moments* in the UK.

Editorial
Clare Hey
Olivia Barber
Victoria Oundjian

Copy editor
Francine Brody

Proof reader
Laetitia Grant

Audio
Paul Stark
Amber Bates

Contracts
Anne Goddard
Paul Bulos
Jake Alderson

Design
Debbie Holmes

Joanna Ridley
Nick May
Helen Ewing

Editorial Management
Charlie Panayiotou
Jane Hughes
Alice Davis

Finance
Jasdip Nandra
Afeera Ahmed
Elizabeth Beaumont
Sue Baker

Marketing
Cait Davies

Production
Ruth Sharvell

Publicity
Alainna Hadjigeorgiou

Rights
Susan Howe
Krystyna Kujawinska
Jessica Purdue
Richard King
Louise Henderson

Sales
Jen Wilson

Esther Waters
Victoria Laws
Rachael Hum
Ellie Kyrke-Smith
Frances Doyle
Georgina Cutler

Operations
Jo Jacobs
Sharon Willis
Lisa Pryde
Lucy Brem